THE LAST

TO

DISAPPEAR

JO SPAIN

QUERCUS

First published in Great Britain in 2022 by Quercus
This paperback edition published in 2023 by

QUERCUS

Quercus Editions Ltd
Carmelite House
50 Victoria Embankment
London EC4Y 0DZ

An Hachette UK company

A CIP catalogue record for this book is available
from the British Library

PB ISBN 978 1 52940 735 8
EB ISBN 978 1 52940 733 4

10 9 8 7 6 5 4 3 2 1

Typeset by CC Book Production
Printed and bound in Great Britain by Clays Ltd, Elcograf S.p.A.

Papers used by Quercus Editions Ltd are from well-managed forests and other responsible sources.

Praise for *The Last to Disappear*

'A dark and terrifying mystery that kept me constantly guessing'
Sarah Pearse

'So vivid, atmospheric and chilling. A triumph!'
Claire Douglas

'Thrilling and twisty. Jo Spain never disappoints'
Chris Whitaker

'Tense and atmospheric, beautifully written'
Catherine Cooper

'I absolutely loved it'
Liz Nugent

'A tense, breathless thriller with such an evocatively drawn setting'
B. P. Walter

'A superb crime thriller, brilliantly written . . . Unforgettable!'
Allie Reynolds

'Spain's best mystery yet'
Irish Independent

'Ideal poolside reading'
STELLAR magazine

'Gripping, expertly crafted, with unexpected twists'
Sunday Independent

'Compelling, immensely satisfying'
Belfast Telegraph

'A fast-paced thriller with captivating characters'
Candis

Jo Spain is a full-time writer and screenwriter. Her first novel, *With Our Blessing*, was one of seven books shortlisted in the Richard and Judy Search for a Bestseller competition and she's become a regular Top Ten Irish bestseller with her subsequent novels. Jo co-writes the internationally acclaimed Harry Wild TV series and is currently working on several TV productions, including the adaptation of her own Detective Tom Reynolds series. Jo lives in Dublin with her husband and their four children.

Also by Jo Spain

INSPECTOR TOM REYNOLDS MYSTERIES

With Our Blessing
Beneath the Surface
Sleeping Beauties
The Darkest Place
The Boy Who Fell
After the Fire

STANDALONE NOVELS

The Confession
Dirty Little Secrets
Six Wicked Reasons
The Perfect Lie

For Tommy, never forgotten

Prologue

Koppe, Finland
1 November 2019

At first, white-hot agony.

She can't think. Can't react.

The ice-cold water paralyses every muscle.

Her entire body becomes one desperate plea: *let it end*.

Nobody can bear this and live.

Just when it feels as though she might die from the pain, the stinging needles recede, replaced with a deep ache as her cells attempt to adjust to the shockingly low temperature.

The surface. She needs to get to the surface. The thought crowds everything else out.

Survival instinct kicks in, over the fear, the denial, the incomprehension.

Her legs kick, her arms flail, seeking the hole through which she fell, the break in the ice.

Up, up, and her head is clear and she's gasping for air.

The sudden intake of oxygen brings an explosion of adrenaline and now she knows what she has to do.

One. Fight the debilitating throbbing that could force her back under.

Two. Get out of the water and on to the ice.

Three. Find safe ground.

She's lucky; this registers somewhere in the back of her brain. Some people go in and never find their way out. The last thing they see is a sheet of impenetrable ice, the promise of light on the other side. She has been trained for this. She, at least, has a chance.

Her hand throws itself on to the frozen surface, the section that hasn't cracked, and splays there like a safety anchor.

She sees a figure; remembers who it is. She calls for help. At least, she thinks she does. Her mouth opens, but she's not sure any sound is coming out. There's so much to say.

You're wrong. It doesn't matter. I won't tell anybody.

The figure just watches. There's no offer of help. And now, the person is walking away.

The woman in the lake sees crimson splashed on the white snow that covers most of the ice, thick snow that lured her to the thinnest, most dangerous part of the lake. It's so distractingly beautiful, red on white, that she almost forgets it's *her* blood that's been spilled. That the ragged line that trails towards the broken ice must have dripped from her exposed wound as she tried to run to safety.

Her hand reaches and slips and reaches and slips but finds nothing.

She tries to scream. It's beyond her. The pounding inside her head and the stabbing sensation of the freezing water have stolen her voice.

Who'd hear, anyway?

She's alone, trapped in a frozen lake, nothing but birch trees and forest animals for miles; a whole lot of white nothingness.

She's not perfect. She's done a lot of stupid things. Things she regrets.

But she doesn't deserve this.

She didn't see this coming.

There are so many people she wishes she could talk to one last time. So many people she loves, people she hasn't told in a while.

She still thinks she'll be okay. This doesn't happen. Not to people her age. She can't just die. *Somebody* will find her and save her.

Her body starts to go numb. Her thoughts drift. Her scrabbling hand falls still.

The last thing she sees before the icy water claims her is a new snowfall.

It's breathtaking in its beauty.

Gentle, soft crystals fall on to her face. And fall and fall.

And fall.

London, England
Mid-December 2019

'Your first mistake, Alexander, was bringing them to a chophouse for lunch. These bastards don't want steak and ale, even if your hipster joint does serve chips in an aluminium basket and the table is reclaimed wood from the Tower of London. They want a Louis XIV dining experience: £400 bottles of port, ortolan birds eaten under white napkins, baba soaked in Armagnac.'

Alex stays mute as Charlie pauses his lecture to inhale a mound of Ossetra caviar, followed by a large gulp of Screaming Eagle wine.

'Lucky for you, the project manager phoned me. I got them into the Connaught for the chef's table. Focking steak. Christ, you're an amateur. We want them to stay with us when they get the contract. They'll need lobbyists all year round.'

Charlie claps Alex on the back with enough force – had Alex been choking – to dislodge the incriminating object.

'*Fucking* steak, Charlie,' Alex says, quietly. 'It's fucking with a U, not an O.'

'That's what I said.'

'And it was vintage côte de boeuf.'

'Old steak. Bloody hell.'

'The Cassidys will be lucky to get the contract, Charlie,' Alex says. 'I've thrown everything at it, but the government doesn't know what it's doing with the ports and it can't afford the technology these guys want to sell.'

'They're going to have to do something to keep the beggars out, Alex. It's the people's will. The PM has to announce a plan to deal with Brexit customs checks. Why not the Cassidys? Magic, contactless customs. Bloody geniuses, those brothers.'

'I think the PM's budget stretches to cardboard signs and black markers,' Alex retorts.

'We need more lubrication, you dry sod,' Charlie says, and stands up abruptly, off to locate Serena, the hostess.

Alex fills his glass with the dregs of the wine and surveys his work colleagues, all one hundred and twenty of them packing out the large, dimly lit cellar room of The Fig House. This is the annual Christmas party of Thompson, Mayle & Sinclair, or TM&S for those looking to save breath. But the only concession to Christmas the impeccably appointed Lebanese establishment has made is the table centre pieces: intricate berry garlands surrounding plain white candles. The room is still scented with the exotic musk of night-blooming jasmine; ornate copper amphora vases nestle beneath traditional arches, and the leafy plants lurking in corners are reminiscent of summers in cedar-lined gardens.

The firm's event organiser has chosen The Fig House because it's popular, not because it's seasonal.

Fock Christmas anyway, Alex thinks.

He had assumed when he started working in the Regency-era building that houses TM&S that he was the only one who hadn't come up through the Eton, Balliol ranks. This was mainly because every single person in his office spoke in the dreary, uniform drawl of the upper classes. He'd been wrong.

Take Christian in auditing, a working-class lad from Leeds. Annabel in accounts was born in a regular middle-class suburb of Newcastle. Neither of them started out a million miles from Apple Dale village, where Alex grew up. Christian and Annabel, though, have battered any Northern melody out of their speech. Unlike Alex, who is still mocked mercilessly for his accent. His nickname around the office is *Stainless Steel,* in honour of Yorkshire's gift to the industrial world and because Alex is not known for showing much emotion.

Charlie Mills' family started off in a working-class block of flats in the East End of London. But Charlie, Christian and Annabel's chameleon-like abilities serve them well in the business they're all in.

Lobbying.

The great skill of pretending to know everything so you can convince others, who are also only pretending to know what they're doing, that your way is best.

Alex is such a good lobbyist, he doesn't need to fake an accent. He just fakes everything else. His sister Vicky once told him he was the living incarnation of Don Draper from *Mad Men*.

Vicky has always had an unerring talent for articulating Alex's most secret fears.

Last month, Alex had been part of a team working on a contract for a private health insurance provider. Their job was to massage the figures in order to convince senior officials in the Department of Health that beds in the NHS were more costly to run than beds in private hospitals.

Alex, the son of a union-organiser postman and a village school teacher, had delivered the presentation smoothly. Only he could see his soul seeping out of his body as he spoke.

The Faustian bargain was signed when the department reps jumped all over the numbers, saying that they had been looking for exactly those kind of stats to back up a new policy direction. They'd all laughed and toasted their future partnership with coffee wheeled in by workers on minimum wage.

Charlie returns with an even more expensive bottle of wine.

While they don't share the desire to piss money into the wind, Charlie is still one of Alex's best friends. He's an interesting character. Charlie spent his first six years in a tiny council flat with his four brothers and sisters, all seven members of the family squashed into three small bedrooms. His entrepreneurial father, a Del Boy-meets-Alan Sugar type, had managed to progress from bus driver to coach driver to coach owner to coach-fleet owner. Charlie's father's empire on wheels paid for Charlie to go to Trinity College in Dublin, which was much easier to get into than the top English unis but carried just enough elitist cachet to have TM&S recruiters overlook the obviously absent blue blood.

Charlie is still likeable, despite his new-found snobbery.

Alex likes Annabel, too, but he can't stand Christian, who's rumoured to have screwed one of the interns on a promise of securing her a full-time position. Only the partners get to choose which of the interns gets to stay and it's rarely based on whether they're a good shag.

'You're very subdued, Alexander,' Charlie says.

'You know I can't stand these things, Charlie, mate,' Alex says. 'Sodom and Gomorrah were less hedonistic.'

'That's your problem, Alex. You just want to earn money. No idea how to spend it. So, what's the plan for Christmas?'

Alex picks up his refilled glass of wine and drinks deep.

'Home,' he says.

'Your lovely sister going to be about?'

'You've only ever seen photos of Vicky,' Alex says. 'I don't know where this obsession stems from.'

'Photos of her sun-kissed on a beach in Morocco in a string bikini, man,' Charlie says. 'I'm only human.'

'Put it like this – if she deigns to come home, I won't be letting you near her.' Alex swirls the wine in the glass. 'Anyway, I don't know what Vicky's plans are. Haven't talked to her in months.'

'She'll be home to keep the focus off you, don't worry,' Charlie says, but his thoughts are already elsewhere, on Serena, who's gliding past them in her tight white blouse and short black skirt, en route to sell another overpriced bottle of wine to one of their foolhardy colleagues.

Alex doesn't want to return to Apple Dale for Christmas. He's been trying to come up with an excuse for months but, ironically, the man who essentially massages the truth for a living can't conceive of anything credible enough to pull the wool over his parents' eyes. Nor can he say, *Folks, I can barely live with myself these days and I sure as hell can't live with seeing myself reflected in Dad's judgemental eyes over turkey and ham*.

He's simultaneously resigned to and bitter about the fact that Vicky is the shining light in the Evans household. Twenty-six-year-old Vicky, whose biggest achievement to date seems to be not getting pregnant while she screws her way around the world, and who only ever phones home to tap her family for cash.

Alex is the one who's got the big city job and an apartment in Marylebone. Alex is the one who's paid off his parents' mortgage.

So what if he made a mistake, once, when he was only bloody sixteen and barely knew he was born, let alone supposed to be protecting his future?

So what? Except his father won't ever let him forget it; then there's the fact he's only gone and become a sell-out, too.

Charlie pursues Serena for the rest of the night but it's Alex who ends up taking her home. Charlie Mills is a cocky chap with plenty of money, but Alex has plenty of money too and, ultimately, he has five inches' height on Charlie, his hairline isn't receding, he weighs about three stone less and is a good deal better-looking all round.

When the phone rings at 5.30 a.m., Alex wakes thinking it's his alarm. He's forgotten it's Saturday. He can't remember why there are black, lacy knickers on the floor, and the rain is so loud against the window of his top floor apartment, he's already talking himself out of his morning run.

Then he sees Ed's name flashing and answers the call.

'Dad?'

'Alex?'

'What's up?' Alex shimmies quietly into an upright position. Serena barely stirs. She's just as beautiful sans make-up, so much so Alex can forgive the fact her Bobbi Brown foundation is now spread across his 500-thread-count white pillowcase.

'You need to come home,' his dad says.

Alex blinks a few times, then tenses.

'What's wrong?' he asks. 'Is it Vicky?'

Of course he thinks of Vicky first. Why wouldn't he? Vicky's *employment* over the last few years has entailed bouncing from one dodgy tourist resort to the next. Vicky is the sort of person to see hitch-hiking as a cheap travel option, as though those nightmare stories involving missing backpackers could never apply to her.

'Your mum's in hospital. She's had a heart attack.'

Alex inhales sharply.

Mum's only fifty-five, he thinks. She's too young to die.

'Is she okay?'

Serena is waking now, her hand creeping across the sheet, trying to establish where she is without opening her eyes.

'She's fine. She's stable. But you need to come up here. Now.'

Ed hangs up.

Alex stares at his phone.

Why the urgency, if his mother is okay?

There's something Ed's not saying.

Alex shivers.

Is his mother fine . . . for now?

As he dresses, he rings Vicky's mobile. The line doesn't even connect, just goes straight to voicemail.

'Vicky,' he says, once the automated message service plays out. 'You have to come home. Mum had a heart attack. You need to get here, quick.'

He hesitates.

'This is my new number.'

Please, don't let me regret giving it to you, he thinks.

Koppe, Finland

'He's doing it again. Mom. Mom! He's—'

'I heard you!'

Agatha reaches into the glove compartment, rummages around until she finds some salted liquorice and tosses it into the back of the car. She turns her head to glare at all three children in the back.

'Olavi, stop biting your arm. Eat that instead. Onni, stop telling tales on your brother. Emilia, will you help me with these boys, please!'

Agatha's eyes return to the road, just in time to see the silver deer.

She lets the car roll to a halt on the compacted snow, not bothering with the brakes that will just make the vehicle slip and slide and possibly end up in the ditch that borders the forest.

They stop inches away from the reindeer, which stands completely still, eyeing the car's bonnet with equal parts disdain and disinterest.

Agatha's heart rate slows. Even the children stop squabbling and quietly observe the beast.

A rare glimpse of winter sun has broken through the clouds. It's unusually strong for this time of year, casting everything in a blinding white light, including the pale deer.

There's silence in the birch forest on either side. The trees nearest the road are bent double with snow, their branches like claws reaching towards the road.

'Why's he out in the morning, Mom?' five-year-old Onni asks, because even at this young age, he knows it's more common to encounter deer on the road at night.

'Maybe he likes being different,' Agatha says. She beeps the horn. The spell is broken. The deer gives her a mournful glance, then slopes back into the forest, taking his sweet time about it.

'Can we follow him?' Olavi asks and Agatha wishes she could say yes because anything that distracts her eight-year-old from arm-biting is a good thing.

'I've got to see Martti,' Agatha says. It's followed by a trio of resigned groans in the rear. They know and accept that Agatha has to work but they're also perfectly entitled to complain about having to sit in a boring doctor's office for half an hour.

One more year, Agatha tells herself. Then Emilia will be fifteen and she can watch the boys at home when Patric's unavailable and Agatha can't get another sitter. She's mature enough to do it now, but Agatha doesn't want to take the risk. Emilia has to be old enough not to panic if anybody unexpected calls on the phone.

Or if anybody unexpected turns up.

The doctor's surgery used to be in his house in the centre of Koppe, close to Agatha's home, but when Martti took over a few years ago, he opened up a more modern clinic on the other side of their small town. It's still close but Agatha has chosen to drive around Koppe, rather than through it, to get there. Everybody wants to talk to her since the news broke and they won't hesitate to stand in front of her car so she's forced to slow down, lower her window and give them updates. The town and its surrounds has a population of four hundred, though that can swell to over one thousand in residence on any given day, due to the tourists in Koppe Lodge and the Arctic Hotel.

The tourists come and go, but the residents are here all the time and they expect to be kept informed about what's happening.

The problem with a place like this – everybody knows your business. The positive in a place like this – everybody knows your business.

But, for now, Agatha needs to keep this business private, until she has decided how to proceed.

The secretary has hung *himmeli* from the ceiling in Martti's surgery and left straw out on the table in the waiting room for patients to have a go at making the traditional Christmas decorations themselves. Life can be slow-moving in the doctor's – sometimes the old women come in and just want to talk. Sometimes the old men, too. Or, sometimes, nobody wants to talk and Martti has his work cut out for him.

The boys fall to their knees to see who can win by weaving the most elaborate geometric shape. Emilia slumps onto the couch, tucks her knees up to her chin and opens TikTok.

'I'll be as quick as I can,' Agatha says, with insufficient conviction to fool even herself. None of the children respond, and in a fit of guilt, she hands Emilia twenty euro for *babysitting*, then says they'll stop at the garage for sweets on the way home. Emilia barely nods, already lost to the strains of a pop song and Addison Rae's slick moves on the viral video site.

Martti is in his office with Elon, the fisherman.

'Agatha.' Elon nods in her direction, then hangs his head. Agatha touches his shoulder gently, while exchanging a look with Martti.

'Quite a shock,' Martti says. 'But, thank God you found her, Elon.'

'Was expecting a couple of fat chars,' Elon says, unhappily. Elon's expression has always been one of inexplicable sadness, even when resting, but now he looks distraught. And like he hasn't slept all night. Agatha didn't either. They worked until the early hours and all of them were distressed afterwards.

Agatha wants to hug the mousy-haired man but she won't. Elon spends on average four to five hours a day ice-fishing alone on Lake Inari and lives as a single man in his isolated cabin outside Koppe. Even by Finnish standards, he's a man who's more comfortable in his own company.

Martti insisted Elon come to his surgery this morning. Elon had spent the longest time on the ice, and possibly the most traumatic. Agatha can tell from one glance at Martti that Elon's physical health is fine. His mental health is what's of concern. Elon is in shock, though he's not aware of it. But Elon won't take any drugs that Martti wants to prescribe.

Tomorrow, he'll be back out on the lake, fishing for char.

Elon leaves, promising them both that he's fine.

Agatha and Martti look at each other and shrug.

Most of the town elders still call Martti the newbie, even though he's been their doctor the last seven years and is in his forties. It doesn't help that he's so baby-faced, nor that his glasses are a little bit too large for his head, so he's constantly pushing them up his nose like a schoolboy at his desk.

Agatha knows Martti has dealt with death many times. Old

age. Vehicular accidents. Snowmobile tragedies. But, day to day, Martti's job is more run of the mill. Wart removal. Broken wrists. Concussion after a ski fall. Frostbite. Domestic violence injuries; there's a lot of that, come the long, harsh winters.

'How long was she in the water, doc?' Agatha asks Martti.

'Hard to tell, Agatha. Temperature being what it is. I'm sending her down to Rovaniemi. They'll do the post-mortem, give you something concrete. I suspect she's been there since she went missing, so, six weeks. There's nothing on her body that would indicate she was held captive first but let's leave that to the experts. Has her family been informed?'

Agatha nods. A family member will be needed to make the definitive identification but Niamh Doyle, the one who had reported her friend missing, was at the lake when they drilled out the surrounding ice of Elon's fishing hole and brought the woman's body fully to the surface. Luckily, Agatha had grabbed Niamh when she fainted, preventing the woman's head from hitting the ice and burdening them with a second casualty.

'What have they been told?' Martti asks.

Agatha sighs.

'What we can confirm as of now,' she says. 'That she was found in Lake Inari. Drowned.'

Agatha's district covers ten thousand square kilometres and several tourist resorts. To police all that, there's just her and two others based in Koppe, plus a couple of officers located in towns around the lake. Sometimes, it can take hours to get to a location, even in an emergency. Agatha was at the lake within minutes of receiving the call. A coincidence. Agatha and her junior, Janic, had been near that section of Inari when Elon made his discovery. Not that it mattered how quickly the police arrived. The woman had been dead for some time.

The young woman's family will want to know how and why she drowned, alone. Why nobody was there to save her. They won't understand that in Lapland, tragedy is always just a heartbeat away.

That sometimes, there's nobody to blame but yourself.

Though, in this case, Agatha isn't so sure.

Leeds, England

Alex spends twenty minutes trying to find a parking space at the hospital, increasingly frustrated with each wasted second. Eventually, he convinces the chap at the payment office to let him park up on the kerb beside it, because Alex is very good at convincing people to do things even when they know they shouldn't.

It's a short dash to the front door of the hospital through the driving rain.

His mother is on the second floor, which Alex learns en route is home to the Intensive Care Unit. This is why Ed sounded off, Alex realises. His mother might still be alive but she's not out of the woods.

Last year, Alex had tried to make his parents take out a private health insurance policy. They refused. One thing to have their mortgage paid off with their son's ill-gotten gains, quite another to jump on the two-tier bandwagon slowly chipping away at the NHS. Alex pointed out to Ed and Sue that it was no longer a slow chip under the current government; it was a sledgehammer. Their romanticised version of the National Health Service was dead and they would be too if they didn't take out a proper care policy.

His father is sitting outside his mother's room when Alex reaches the second floor. He's leaning forward on the chair, tilted at an angle that makes his son think he might tip over on to the floor if Alex doesn't get to him first.

Ed looks up at Alex when he feels the hand on his shoulder and croaks one word.

'Son.'

She's already dead, Alex thinks. He can see it in his father's eyes, in the hollowed-out, devastated expression on his face.

'I came as fast as I could,' Alex utters, a completely useless thing to say but something that he thinks he should.

He thinks of his sister Vicky listening to the two voicemails he left her. She'll be in an airport now, not even aware her mother is dead. She'll be crushed.

'She's in an induced coma,' Ed says, and cocks his head at the room behind them.

Alex, confused, looks in the window.

There's Sue propped up in a bed. She's hooked up to various wires; her blonde hair, normally curled and set, is flat against her head and the side of her face is bruised. But she is still very much alive. Alex looks back at his dad.

Ed's own dark hair has thinned since the last time Alex saw his father, though his beard is thicker than ever. They've always been hairy men, the Evanses. He remembers as a kid, his parents bringing them to Whitby beach, his father's bare chest covered in tufts of black hair as he carried both Alex and Vicky, one in his arms, one on his back. The strongest man we knew, Alex thinks. In every way. Something he admired as a small boy, hated as a teenager.

How could you ever amount to much, when your father was a giant?

Alex wonders what has happened to reduce Ed so, to take so much out of the man that he can't even stand up.

'What is it?' Alex asks. 'What have they said? Is she brain-dead? Is it something else? Did they find something else?'

'Your mum's fine,' Ed says.

He heaves himself to a standing position so they're face to face.

'The heart attack was brought on by the news. It's Vicky, Alex. She's dead.'

Alex blinks.

The world falls out from beneath his feet. Everything is moving slowly and quickly at the same time. Alex can hear his heartbeat, his breathing; feel his father's grip on his arm. But his vision is blurred, the lights overhead are buzzing, and the blood has turned cold in his veins.

'What did you say?' he asks.

'Vicky is gone, Alex.'

'She can't be gone. She's in Finland.'

'We got the call in the early hours. That's when your mother fell ill.'

'I don't understand. How did she die? What happened?'

Alex is unable to process the information.

'Was it a car crash? Did she fall?'

Alex is shaking Ed. He needs to know everything, right now.

'She drowned,' Ed says, without emotion. He's adjusting, burying his own feelings in order to respond to the violence of Alex's reaction. 'They say she was in the lake for weeks. We hadn't heard from her since September. We weren't worried. The last time we spoke, she said it was getting busier over there, there were loads of tourists. We thought, she'll be home for Christmas. You know what she was like. She wouldn't phone unless she needed something. God knows what they think of us, that we didn't even realise she was missing . . .'

Ed's head slumps.

Alex is frozen to the spot.

'She can't have drowned,' he whispers. He doesn't recognise his own voice.

He hasn't spoken to her in months.

Had she been trying to reach him?

Had she dialled his old number only to find it was out of service?

He'd deliberately not sent her the new one.

Alex almost retches.

'You're in shock,' Ed says.

Vicky, Alex thinks. The warm body next to his when they were small, the pest who was always telling tales to their parents. The little girl who once wrote an essay about how Alex was her role model because he'd done something nice for her that week. The teenager who nicked his cigarettes and took his first expensive car on a joyride just to push his buttons. The woman who could make him laugh and seethe in equal measure . . .

Vicky. Twenty-six-years-old, Vicky.

And even while he's trying to absorb the punch to the gut, Alex feels a rising anger.

This is so typical of his sister, to cause them all this pain, to take such risks that she's ended up bloody killing herself. How dare she? How could Vicky do this to them?

He turns away from his father, and without thinking, punches the wall.

It's only the fact it's some sort of cheap plastic divide and not actual concrete that saves Alex from breaking his hand.

The pain shoots through his knuckles and wrist and Ed grabs him before Alex can draw back his arm and add another dent to the first one.

'No,' Ed says.

Alex drops his arm. He doesn't need to do it again. The force was enough the first time to redirect what he was feeling from emotional to physical.

'I need you in control,' Ed says, cutting through the mists. 'I can't leave your mother.'

Alex swallows.

'They need a family member to officially identify the body.'

Alex looks at Ed. His father can't expect him to get on a plane, to go to a strange country, to function like a normal human being after what he's just been told.

Ed meets Alex's eye.

'Pull yourself together. You can fly out to Finland tomorrow. Bring her home. Bring my little girl home.'

Rovaniemi, Finland

The snow has been driven and piled into mounds around the car park of Rovaniemi morgue, so high they look like artificial walls. The one-storey morgue is almost hidden behind them.

Agatha left Koppe at 6 a.m. this morning, not long after her old boss and friend Patric arrived to care for the children. She'd driven the four hours to the Lapland capital sustained by coffee and home-made *korvapuusti*.

The morning is still gloomy; it suits Agatha's mood perfectly. Olavi had woken up three times during the night, screaming his head off, upsetting Emilia and Onni, though Emilia shrugged it off in true teenage fashion. Agatha had already been tired from the previous night, half of which had been spent on the lake. She'd needed eight, undisturbed hours.

Olavi had eventually fallen asleep in Agatha's arms, his lips clamped around the red mark on his upper arm, and she'd been too tired to even try to dislodge either him or his teeth. She blames the sugary treats they'd bought in the garage after leaving Martti's surgery and indulged in after dinner, but she knows his night terrors stem from something else altogether.

When Patric let himself in at 5.30, he'd woken Agatha gently, then carried a comatose Olavi back to his own bed, where Agatha knew he'd sleep peacefully for hours. Agatha, on the other hand, had no such luck.

The officer in the morgue reception remembers Agatha from her training period, and sends her straight down to the lab. Venla, the curly-haired pathologist, greets Agatha by handing her another coffee. Agatha realises she desperately needs to empty her bladder. She's unconsciously hopping from foot to foot.

'You didn't stop on the drive, did you?' Venla asks.

When Agatha shakes her head, Venla tells her the ladies is out of order but if she moves quickly, she'll get in and out of the men's before Leon, the caretaker, arrives for his scheduled 10.30 bowel expulsion.

'Regular as clockwork,' Venla says. 'If he ends up on my table, I'm going to do an in-depth study of his colon for science.'

Agatha urinates faster than she ever has, sees there's no toilet roll and thanks her lucky stars she has the constant Onni-ready packet of wet wipes in her handbag. Before she leaves, she hesitates, then charitably leaves a handful of wipes for Leon.

Venla is waiting for her with the fast-cooling coffee.

'I'll take you for lunch after,' she tells Agatha. 'We'll have a girly afternoon. God knows I need it, with the amount of testosterone around here. Not to mention it's a Sunday. You know my parents were obsessed with honouring the Sabbath? They'd spin in their graves if they knew I worked holy days. Where are you booked in tonight?'

'The Nordic,' Agatha says.

They talk as they walk down the dimly lit corridor and into Venla's lab. Agatha takes a breath when she sees Vicky Evans' naked body on the table in front of her, but Venla has been looking at the woman all morning and keeps speaking. Agatha has always thought that spending so much time with people who can't talk has made Venla very chatty with anyone who does.

'I'll get us a table at the Red Deer,' Venla says. 'It's around the corner. What time does the family get in?'

'This evening,' Agatha says. 'Just her brother. Alex Evans.'

She approaches the body while Venla picks up the file at her work station.

'I wouldn't like to be in your shoes,' Venla says. 'I presume he thinks he's bringing her home?'

Agatha nods.

Vicky was very beautiful, she thinks. Agatha is able to look beyond the damage that's been done to the body by the water. The victim's features are small and perfectly symmetrical, from her dainty little ears to her rosebud lips. Even the long post-mortem incision down her chest has been sewn back together in neat, exact lines.

Her hair has been shaved so Venla can examine the wound on her head. The woman had long brown hair when they took her from the lake, not unlike Agatha's own dark tresses, but much sleeker.

'It's as you suspected,' Venla says. 'That injury wasn't caused in the water. She was struck before she went in.'

'Could it have been a fall?' Agatha asks, a last-ditch attempt.

'No,' Venla says. 'She was hit with something metal. Once. It caused enough damage. Could have been the tip of an ice axe, from the shape of the wound. Right-handed attacker, and hit when she was facing him or her. Drowning was the cause of death but she had a subdural haematoma that would have resulted in death in any case.

I presume she was disoriented when she went under. Hopefully, she was so far gone, she didn't feel anything.'

Agatha shudders.

She reaches out and touches Vicky's face. Agatha doesn't want to imagine how it would have felt for Vicky to have been alone in the icy lake, so far from home, so far from her loved ones, knowing she was dying.

'I've got you, *rakas*,' Agatha whispers, stroking the cold skin of Vicky's cheek.

She turns to Venla.

'Any sign of sexual assault?'

'None. She was clean from the water. But there's no indication of any violence to the genital area and her clothes were intact. No trace of drugs in her blood. She was a very healthy, perfect young woman.'

'Too young,' Agatha says.

Venla is studying her, Agatha realises, and she blushes. She drops her hand and the pathologist turns away, pretending to be busy with her files.

'Is twelve too early for lunch?' Venla asks. 'I fancy a glass of Chardonnay.'

'Hm,' Agatha says. She's distracted. Venla looks up again.

'What's on your mind?'

'Her cabin in the resort,' Agatha says.

'What about it?'

'I haven't told you what we found there when she went missing.'

Koppe, Finland
Winter 1998

Kaya is cold as she mushes the dogs across the frozen lake. She left her reindeer boots at home.

In her rush to get out of the house as quickly and quietly as possible, she'd thrown on the nearest shoes, the ones she only wears inside.

If she'd taken the horse, it wouldn't have mattered. Galloping on the horse would have kept her warm. But she has to keep taking her foot off the back of the sled to help the dogs on inclines and her feet are starting to freeze. At this rate, she'll be lucky if she doesn't lose a toe.

Goddamn huskies, anyway. Just recently she'd had to tell a gang of tourists that the dogs aren't even indigenous to Lapland; they're just a fantasy construct the ever-growing numbers of holidaymakers expect to see. The trails the tourists are sent on at the husky farms are all freshly carved out each morning for the dog-led sleighs because the animals' little legs would just sink into the snow otherwise.

Horses, that's what real Laplanders use, when they're not in their cars or on snowmobiles or skis.

But if she'd taken the horse, her husband might have noticed when he went to close the stable. And if she'd taken the car or snowmobile, he would have heard. Exercising the dogs is Kaya's job, and they're always barking, so it didn't matter that they had yapped and whined when she'd hitched them to the sleigh and set off down the mountain. He'll be asleep when she gets back. He'll never know how long she was gone.

There's not a cloud in the sky and the fox fires are bright overhead, shades of vivid green against a background of a million twinkling stars.

Kaya can't spend any time appreciating them. They still hold magic for her, despite being a feature her whole life, but tonight she's too cold. Her breath forms short cloudbursts as she yells at the dogs.

And now Kaya can see the glow of the town.

At the edge of the lake, she follows the path that has been made throughout the day by the tourists tramping back and forth for activities on the frozen ice. It's not too dark. Lamps have been positioned to guide visitors for night activities. This part of the forest always reminds Kaya of *The Lion, the Witch and the Wardrobe* and the well-lit path through the Narnia snow on the other side of the wardrobe door.

Once she's near the town, she ties the dogs to a tree. She doesn't want them drawing attention to her when she's on the streets of Koppe. On foot, she can move about unseen.

She's shivering all over now and knows she needs to get her feet beside a fire.

She keeps to the shadows, avoiding the revellers spilling out from the bars serving après-ski beers and burgers.

Koppe is bursting with fake chocolate-box chalets these days, all designed to make visitors to Lapland think it's some sort of year-round Christmas-card idyll. They've no idea how brutal the winter is for those who aren't just here for a two-week holiday: the struggle to get through the long, dark months; the effort required to make a living from seasonal work to see you through a whole year, or to keep a farm from completely dying out over one particularly cruel season, as this one looks set to be.

When Kaya's working in the bar, sometimes tourists tell her they've been infected with Lapland madness and they plan to return in the summer. Autumn, she always suggests. In the summer, you'll meet the mosquitoes. Laplanders are used to them; tourists get eaten alive.

She skirts around some Germans in expensive ski gear and then cuts down a lane until she arrives at his house. Locals still live in town, even though there are three times as many tourists now as before and that number is growing. People seem to have found a happy medium. The tourists are shepherded unwittingly into the commercial bars and restaurants that provide the townspeople with jobs; the locals know the shops and social spots that don't charge through the nose.

Kaya thinks she would adjust, too, but she can't; she's stuck half the time up the side of a bloody mountain on a reindeer farm.

She knocks on his back door, three short raps.

He opens the door, curiosity on his face quickly turning to a frown.

'What are you doing here?' he hisses.

Kaya is taken aback. Last night, they were naked and entwined in each other's arms. Now he's glaring at her like she's something unpleasant he's just found on his boot.

'I need to speak to you,' she says.

'It's Wednesday night,' he snaps. 'You know she's here on Wednesdays.'

'But I . . .'

He looks over his shoulder, a noise alerting him.

'You have to go,' he says and he pushes her shoulder.

Kaya reacts with shock. He's never laid a hand on her that has been anything but inviting. He's never spoken to her in a tone that was anything but loving.

'I forgot it was Wednesday,' she says, weakly. She hadn't forgotten. She just needed to see him. 'I'm cold – can't you make an excuse for why I'm here? Can't I come in and warm up?'

He seems to be deliberating and Kaya knows it will be okay. He's just surprised to see her. She caught him off guard. She would be the same, if he arrived at her house when her husband was there. She doesn't even need to tell him her news tonight. She can tell him another time. Right now, she just needs some coffee and the heat of his fire.

'No,' he says. 'Go to the bar. We'll talk tomorrow.'

He closes the door.

Kaya stands there, stunned. From outside, she can still hear him. His wife is with him and he's telling her the person at the door was just a drunk tourist.

Momentarily, Kaya considers hammering on the door and drawing out his wife, telling her the truth – I'm not a drunk tourist, I'm the woman who's been fucking your husband for the last six months.

But if she does that, the vengeful satisfaction will be fleeting.

So, instead, she turns and slinks back into town, her tail between her legs and a gnawing feeling in the pit of her stomach that this is not going to go how she'd planned.

Her lover is not going to rescue her from her current predicament.

The way he'd looked at her when she had the audacity to call to his door on the wrong night.

It's entirely possible he'll kill her when he finds out what she's done.

Helsinki, Finland

2019

Charlie booked Alex a first-class flight to Helsinki on the company credit card.

It's not first class as Alex knows it, but he is grateful for the curtain that separates the front two rows from economy class; less so for the overly attentive air hostess. He refuses the complimentary champagne, which she takes as an affront, and the battle lines are drawn over lunch when Alex says he doesn't want the food. He wants a brandy. The air hostess consents to the brandy but only if he'll take the food. It's been paid for. It's been heated. No, they can't give it to another passenger. It might only be morning in Alex's brain but on this flight they're already operating two hours ahead and it's lunchtime.

Alex gives in because it's easier than fighting this little air-dictator. He remembers he hasn't eaten since yesterday, when his father made him swallow a limp ham sandwich in the hospital canteen before they returned to their small family home in Apple Dale. Alex kissed his mother before he left the hospital, for all the good it did. She wasn't the least bit aware of his presence. He's absolutely terrified she'll die while he's on this trip, organising the repatriation of his sister's body. How would he ever tell that story? How his family shrunk from four to two and he was with neither of his loved ones when it happened.

The dinner comes in a little tinfoil carton and the steam it emits when he opens it almost scalds his hand. Alex eats it all, with dessert, drinks the brandy, and then takes the glass of champagne and a coffee. He immediately feels sick as a dog. The air hostess looks smug in her pyrrhic victory.

They arrive in Helsinki and Alex is still oblivious to how woefully unprepared he is for this trip. The airport's heating system is pumping away and he takes off his sweater as he walks through the concourse towards the Schengen area zone to make his flight connection. On the other side of security, he notices a distinct change in the clothing of the passengers boarding the tiny plane for Rovaniemi. He's brought his Burberry cashmere coat, is wearing suit trousers and a shirt, and has a small overnight bag containing a pair of jeans, a spare shirt and a Ralph Lauren sweater. To be fair, he'd originally packed for an overnight in his parents' house. Not that he has a whole lot of Arctic-ready gear at his disposal. When Alex holidays, he gravitates towards the heat, not climates colder than what he already endures.

Everyone around him is dressed for a ski trip.

He's recovered from the sick feeling on the first plane and figures whiskey will keep him warm, so, once on board, he orders one and takes it with the complimentary glass of cloudberry juice.

It's not like he'll be here very long, he tells himself. Not that he knows how long it takes to bring a dead sister home from a foreign country. A couple of days, he supposes. Money is no obstacle and he guesses the Finns are good at this sort of stuff. Charlie spoke to the British Foreign Office and they were reassuring, apparently. They most likely wouldn't be needed but, of course, would be on hand should the family require it.

The police liaison, Agatha Koskinen, is waiting for him in the tiny airport, holding a card with his name on it. She's small, with dark frizzy hair; her face is round and kind, with the sort of eyes that make her look like a person who smiles a lot.

She's better dressed for the climate than he is. She's not wearing a uniform. Her attire consists of a padded knee-length jacket over a woolly jumper and jeans, and fur-lined ankle boots.

She takes one look at his thin coat and leather shoes and he can hear the *fuck* she utters under her breath.

'Do you have to wait for a bag?' she asks him, a hint of hope in her voice.

'No, but I would like to use the gents.'

He leaves her busily texting, while he goes to rid his bladder of whiskey and cloudberry juice.

In the spotlessly clean toilets, a man is helping an overexcited five-year-old wash his hands. The kid is bouncing on the balls of his feet.

'When do we see Santa? Will he come tonight *and* come again on Christmas Eve? Will he give me an Xbox? Are elves real?'

They're English, like Alex, but Alex says nothing. No matter. He's dressed like an Englishman.

The father smiles at Alex in the mirror.

'Already worth the five grand,' he tells Alex.

Alex nods, smiles wanly at the kid and leaves.

Outside, he can't spot Agatha but he can see the mother and daughter half of the English family waiting by the facilities. The little girl, no more than two or three, is spinning with her arms out wide, repeating the word snow, over and over, while the mother laughs.

And a long-forgotten memory hits him like a punch to the stomach.

Vicky at a similar age standing in a light snow flurry and spinning. A snow angel. The surge of warmth he'd felt for his little sister, even as a kid himself, witnessing her unbridled joy.

Alex closes his eyes. The memory felt like a leap through time. He can no more believe it was real than he can believe his sister is now dead. How can the memory be, if she is not?

'Sorry,' Agatha says. She's beside him. 'I brought the car closer to the door so you won't have far to walk.'

'Right. How cold is it, exactly?'

'Not as cold as it gets in January.'

Alex digests that.

They leave the airport and Alex – who thought he'd seen snow, growing up with bitterly cold Yorkshire winters – realises he's never seen snow as it should look. As they emerge through the doors, he can see mountains of the stuff in all directions.

The next thing he notices is that everybody around him is walking normally. He observes this right at the moment his shoes go from under him.

Everybody else is wearing snow boots, of course. Even the children have more balance.

Agatha reaches out and grabs his arm before he can fall.

And then the cold hits him. Alex has never felt anything like it. If he sticks his tongue out, it will freeze there. It's so cold, it's beyond crisp. It smells clean. Like burning-the-skin-off-his-face clean.

'I've organised some gear for you at the hotel,' Agatha says. 'We just need to get you there in one piece.'

'I . . . t-thank you,' he stutters, through chattering teeth.

Alex is filled with gratitude for this thoughtful gesture. He'd sell a kidney right now for a proper coat.

Agatha walks him to the passenger door and waits until he gets in before crossing around to the driver's side. Alex struggles with shaking fingers to pull on his seat belt. Once it's clipped, he puts his hands under his legs and rocks backwards and forward, trying to get the feeling back in his limbs. He'd been outside for maybe a minute.

Agatha turns the heating on full and they set off.

Everywhere, there are signs for 'Santa's Village'. Alex can see flashes of the neon-lit, tourist North Pole through the snow-covered trees.

Agatha takes a right at a crossroads and he realises they're driving in a different direction to the buses carrying families to their holiday destination.

'The morgue is closed but you can see your sister first thing in the morning,' Agatha says.

Alex swallows.

'I thought you might like to join me for dinner in the hotel this evening. I'm staying in the same one. You can order room service if you prefer. Of course, if you would like to walk around the town – once we have you kitted out – we can do that. Rovaniemi is . . . it's pretty, in its way. A lot more low-rise compared to what you're used to, I would guess. Ninety per cent of it was levelled in the Second World War so almost everything you see is relatively, well, new, I guess. This time of year, it's very Christmassy.'

'I'll stay in the hotel,' Alex says. Then, after a pause: 'It's very generous of you. To take care of me. I'm sure you have family at home or . . .' Alex trails off. There's a keyring dangling from the rear-view mirror; a picture of children in a small glass frame. But he doesn't have the energy for it, the small talk.

Agatha fills the gap.

'I'm staying there because I live up in Koppe. It's a long drive.'

'Oh. You're a police officer from where she was found? I thought you were a member of the Rovaniemi department.'

'No.'

Alex looks sideways at Agatha.

'So, you knew her?'

A pause.

'I probably saw her around town, the odd time. I'm not in the Lodge much, not unless it's to deal with a problem. I don't tend to eat or drink there. Tourist prices. When her friend reported her missing, I saw plenty of photographs, so I feel like I know her better than I did.'

Alex bristles.

Six weeks. That's how long Vicky had been missing, according to his dad.

'Why weren't we informed that she'd gone missing?' he asks.

Agatha hasn't taken her eyes off the road.

'It wasn't clear she *was*. Adults can come and go as they please. There was no indication of foul play. Her friend didn't come into the station for two weeks. Even then, it was with reluctance. Nobody wants to go to the police for something that doesn't feel essential. Guides in the resorts – it's clichéd, but they're often free spirits. Adventurous sorts. And of course – nobody came looking for her. Her family, I mean. We didn't have details for you. She hadn't listed a next-of-kin for the resort. That was unusual. And it would be more usual for *you* to come to *us* if she was actually missing.'

'You found us quick enough to tell us she was dead,' Alex says.

'Different protocols,' Agatha says.

'Six weeks,' Alex says. 'She was missing six weeks and you don't sound like you were particularly concerned.'

'I was. But not enough to contact the British embassy. In the absence of any contact from her family and without any evidence Vicky had come to any harm . . . Alex, I'm sure you're aware of what it takes to officially pronounce somebody missing? Six weeks might seem like a long time to you, but in reality, it's not. Not for an adult.'

'But her friend was obviously concerned. Which friend was it?'

'Niamh Doyle. Irish woman. Like I said, she was reluctant to even report it. At first, she assumed Vicky had left but would get in touch. After a while, Niamh tried to call her. I think what worried her most was the fact there were no updates on Vicky's social media. That didn't alarm me. When people choose to go off the radar, for whatever reason, they don't tend to maintain their presence on Instagram. I opened a file, just to be on the safe side, and we did talk to people in the Lodge and around the village. But, then we were moving into December and once it gets close to Christmas . . . It's Koppe's busiest time.'

Alex, already on edge, is annoyed now. He can feel it brewing inside him. That old yet familiar feeling he's learned to suppress. He wants to snap at this woman, at her calm, measured tone. He wants to ask if Vicky was forgotten about because this town, Koppe, has to make a buck in December.

But he doesn't. Because while he's angry, he knows it's a displaced, redundant anger. He's furious that his sister is dead. Not that he hadn't been informed she was missing.

He can't be angry at that. He should have already known. As Agatha says, he should have been the one to report her missing.

So he swallows his rage, but he knows the policewoman can sense it because she sets her lips in a thin line and says, 'I'm very sorry.'

Aren't we all, Alex thinks.

'She stopped leaving her next-of-kin details in workplaces,' he says, after a few minutes have passed. 'Several years ago, she got drunk and had an accident off the back of some bloke's moped in Italy. The cops rang my folks; they nearly had nervous breakdowns. Vicky reckoned if anything like that happened again, she'd be the one telling us the story, in her own time, when it was less alarming. Stupid, but logical, in her head. She knew we were all concerned about her living like she did. She didn't want to give us more cause to say "I told you so".'

'Ah,' Agatha says.

Alex looks out the windscreen. All he can see in the beam of headlights is snow. Everywhere. There might be life up here, but there's no sign of it on this lonely road. It's so deserted that he's surprised when they come upon the low-roofed town and its blocks of bars and restaurants.

Rovaniemi.

He glances sideways at the policewoman. She looks deep in thought.

One of Alex's skills is reading people.

And he can tell, in this instant, that there's something Agatha is holding back.

★

In the Nordic Hotel, he opens his room door to a ridiculously large suite. Charlie has gone all out. The partners might pull him on this one, but Charlie will quote the stats of the business Alex brought in this year. Somewhere down the line, they'll deduct it from a bonus, but Alex will worry about that then.

Alex drops his overnight bag on the floor, removes the bizarre soft toy – a husky he can buy for twenty euro, apparently – from the bed, and falls on to it, staring up at the softly lit ceiling.

Euros. He has none. Never even thought to change any at the airport. He arrived in Finland in a pair of impractical leather shoes and a Burberry coat with sterling in his pocket. He's less prepared than he'd be for a quick trip to Brighton beach on a wintry day.

He'd like to stay on the bed. Just getting here has taken every ounce of strength. But he sits up, undresses and stands under the rainfall showerhead in the modern, black-tiled bathroom, then pulls on a fresh shirt and jeans.

In the bathroom again, he pours a glass of ice-cold water from the sink and pops two aspirin. His reflection in the mirror shows bloodshot eyes and pale skin. He looks like shit.

He's typing a text to his father to say he's arrived safely when there's a knock on the door. He opens it to find Agatha standing there, holding several bulky bags.

'Thermals, snow boots, a proper coat, a hat and mittens and a wool sweater. I guessed your size for my friend; I think I got it right. The boots should be too big anyway. You need to wear two pairs of socks with them.'

'Mittens?' is all Alex can think to say.

'Better,' Agatha says. 'Your fingers will keep warmer together than if they're separate.'

'Okay?'

'Dinner?'

Alex nods.

He will go through the motions. Eat, drink, sleep. And tomorrow, he'll arrange the coffin and flight to bring Vicky home.

The hotel restaurant's interior is dark. Black leather couches, teak walls, tables lit with single candles perched in pine cone settings. Alex can't even read the menu. Agatha orders for them both, a burger for herself, local fish for Alex. He thinks she said perch but he was busy forming questions in his head.

She asks if he wants any alcohol. He declines. He's had plenty in the last forty-eight hours and he's conscious he doesn't want to drink his way through this trauma. He works with several people who can only be described as high-functioning alcoholics. He won't be one of them.

'I hope you don't mind,' Agatha says, sipping from the glass of red the waiter brings her. 'I've three kids at home; it's very rare that I'm away from them for a night.' She blinks, then adds quickly: 'Not that this is a special occasion.'

Alex shrugs.

'You don't look old enough to have three kids,' he says.

It's her turn to shrug.

He'd place her at his age.

Early thirties, three kids and a police officer. She either has a very supportive partner or she's some kind of superwoman.

The food arrives. Alex hasn't timed it so, but Agatha has just taken the first bite of her burger when he realises he can't just go through the motions.

'How did it happen?' he asks.

Agatha puts the burger down and he can see her chewing and swallowing as fast as possible. He's worried she might choke. He keeps talking, to give her time.

'Vicky likes to live on the edge. Scuba-diving. Abseiling. Mountain-climbing. But she's never so much as broken a bone. Not even when she went off the back of Romeo's moped in Italy. But I assume she got unlucky, that the ice was too thin . . .'

He stops, reads Agatha's frown.

'It was an accident, wasn't it?' he says, even while he thinks, well, of course it was. She was on a frozen lake on her own in the middle of nowhere and she drowned.

Agatha hangs her head, then lifts it and meets his eyes.

'I don't think it was,' she says.

Alex feels the blood drain from his face.

Agatha pushes her barely touched plate aside.

'I'm sorry. I should have told you this earlier. You seemed tired and . . . shaken. I wanted to make sure you had some food inside you and you got some sleep. That was stupid of me. Of course you want to know what happened. We . . . we believe she sustained an injury to her head before she went in the water. That she was hit with something.'

'Are you saying my sister's death was intentional? That she was murdered?'

Agatha nods. Alex's throat constricts.

'By who?'

Agatha shakes her head.

'We don't know. Yet.'

'Has she been in the lake the whole time?' Alex asks, thinking fast. He still can't absorb what he's just learned. 'Was she killed immediately, I mean? When she went missing? Or was she . . . was she put there after?'

Agatha opens and closes her mouth. The smell of Alex's food rises from his plate. Perch. A lake fish, he remembers. He feels bile rise in his throat and he swipes the plate away with force.

Agatha jumps. A handful of diners look over.

'Sorry,' Alex mumbles. 'It's just, my mother had a heart attack when she heard the news. That's how I found out. I went up to see her and they told me Vicky had drowned. I don't . . . I don't understand what's going on.'

'That's a lot to deal with.' Agatha tilts her head, sympathetically.

'I need facts,' he says. 'What happened to my sister? Who would have hurt her? Do you at least have a suspect?'

Agatha hesitates, then leans closer, before speaking quietly.

'When we contacted your family, the only information we had for certain was that your sister had drowned,' she says. 'And I'm told by the medical team that is, in fact, the official cause of death. Her body was found in Lake Inari by a local ice fisherman. Elon. He's a good man and he held on to her arm until we got to her and broke through the rest of the ice. It took hours. He never let go.

'I noticed she had a head wound when we got her out of the water but it was entirely possible that had happened by accident; that she'd hit her head going in, or on something under the water, which would have caused her to become disoriented and not aware of what was happening. All these guides are trained to manage ice-breaks and submersion. The pathologist confirmed for me this morning that the angle and depth of the wound indicates it was inflicted. Vicky might have fled from her attacker and gone through

42

the ice or her attacker might have put her in the water. There was no indication she'd been . . . interfered with, before she died. It's difficult to establish the exact time of death because of the circumstances, but the medical examiner indicates she did most likely die around the time she went missing.'

Agatha pauses, takes a breath.

Alex takes a sip of sparkling water. His mouth is so dry, he can barely feel his tongue.

'We're looking for suspects,' Agatha says. 'But, so far, there's no obvious motive for murder. We started interviews at the Lodge yesterday. They're ongoing.'

'Did you check her phone? Her emails? You said there was nothing on her social media, but have you got into her accounts?'

'Her phone is missing and the signal is dead. It might have gone into the water with her. We haven't been able to access admin of her social media yet to check direct messages or deleted posts. Permission for that takes longer than it should. We did get into her email account. We were able to guess the password. It was her name and birthday. Common enough. There was nothing of concern. Do you happen to know what password she might have used for her social media accounts? When we tried to use her email to reset her social media passwords, it wouldn't respond so she may have set them up from an older email account.'

Alex shakes his head. He wonders why Vicky wouldn't have just left her passwords saved on her laptop. That niggling feeling is back, like there's something more he should be asking, or something Agatha is not telling him.

And he's suddenly, acutely aware that he has a piece of information that, by the sound of things, Agatha doesn't.

He's not sure why exactly, but he doesn't say anything.

Not yet. He wants to know what he's dealing with first.

'So, there's an investigation,' Alex says, instead. 'Who's leading it? Can British detectives come over?'

'We can liaise with the English authorities, of course,' Agatha says. 'This is an area with a lot of tourism and we have had deaths in the past where foreign affairs departments and police forces have been consulted and kept abreast of case developments. But I will lead the investigation. Unfortunately, this all means we can't release her body as quickly as we would have liked—'

'*You're* leading the investigation?' Alex says, incredulously. 'But you're . . .'

Agatha waits.

'You're too young.'

'I'm thirty-five,' she says, 'and I am the chief of police in Koppe and the surrounding area. I have two officers serving directly under me—'

'Two officers?' Alex feels the anger he swallowed earlier resurfacing. 'How are you going to undertake a murder investigation with a team of three?'

'– And officers in surrounding areas, plus we will have the full support of headquarters here in Rovaniemi.'

'I'm sorry, but that's ridiculous,' Alex says. 'I thought you were a liaison officer. We're sitting here, having dinner, and my sister's killer is . . .'

He can't even finish. The kindly woman in front of him looks like she's been slapped but he feels no remorse. Everything he's buried for the last day and a half has finally erupted. He doesn't care any more if Agatha is not the correct target or if he's out of order.

Alex can feel the familiar anger he usually keeps checked coursing through his blood in hot bubbles. He just wants somebody to tell him this is all a bad dream and Vicky is fine, she's alive, they got it wrong. He wants to see Vicky, and when he does, he's going to yell at her but then he'll tell her he loves her, he never stopped, that no matter what was said or done, she's his sister.

He'll apologise for not having called her, for making sure she couldn't call him. For his great sin of assuming he had the luxury of time and that those months he chose to freeze her out didn't matter.

'You can't solve her murder,' he snaps at Agatha. 'She was missing six weeks and you didn't even know anything was wrong.'

'Nor did you,' she says and even though her face immediately fills with regret, the damage is done.

Alex stands and walks away from the table.

And when he's in the lift, he thinks again about what Agatha said. How the police had examined Vicky's email account.

Vicky had two email accounts.

The one she used for the world and the one she used when she contacted him.

Is there something in the second one that might tell Alex what happened?

Alex wakes abruptly from sleep, gasping for air. He thinks he may have dreamt about Vicky, that he might even have imagined her drowning.

He rubs his chest until his heart slows down and the tightness there subsides.

He sits up in the comfortable bed and reaches for his phone.

His father picks up after two rings, sounding tired. Immediately, Alex remembers that Finland is two hours ahead of England.

'Were you asleep?' he says.

'It's 4.30 a.m.,' his dad replies.

'I'm an idiot. I'll phone later.'

'I wasn't sleeping, really. And I've the alarm set for five. I'm going in to your mother. Have you—' His dad falters. 'Have you seen her?'

'Dad—' Now it's Alex's turn. How can he phrase it?

'What is it?'

'The policewoman who met me. She said . . . it wasn't an accident.'

There's silence down the phone for a few seconds.

'Vicky was always taking risks,' Ed says, breaking it. 'I've been reading up – those lakes can be thin in parts—'

'I know,' Alex says. 'That's what I thought. But—'

'No. It's not possible.'

'Somebody killed her, Dad.'

Alex delivers this news with shame, like it's his fault.

Ed breathes deeply for a few moments.

'Do they know who?' he says, at last.

If Alex had a name, he'd have already dealt with the bastard.

'No. Or not that they've told me.'

'So, there'll be an investigation?'

'Yes.'

'By the Finnish police?'

'Yes.' Alex sighs. Up to last night, if you'd asked Alex if he had a problem with the Finnish police, he'd have said, of course not, I'm sure they're up there with the best. Nordic countries are like that, aren't they? Civilised. Efficient.

46

But now his sister is dead. Murdered. And Alex wants the comfort of speaking to English detectives, to a police service he understands and can navigate.

To his father he says: 'I'm sure they know what they're doing.'

His father doesn't answer.

'I'm going to stay here,' Alex rushes to add. 'They're not releasing her body yet. I'm going to find out what's going on.'

'Good. Don't let them fob you off. You find out the truth.'

Alex nods agreement on his end of the call.

'And Alex,' Ed adds, a note of caution in his voice. 'I understand what you might be planning. I'm thinking the same thing. But, when you do find out who hurt her, let the police do their job. Don't go thinking you can sort this with your fists. Do you hear me? That fucker should live with what he's done.'

Alex takes a deep breath.

'For fuck's sake, Dad.'

'In the hospital,' Ed says. 'You lost your temper. You hit the wall.'

'You'd just told me my sister was dead.'

His father says nothing and Alex lets it go. This is old ground. He's not doing this now, nor should he have to. He's a grown man, with a successful job and life, and he won't let his father revise that.

They say goodbye with the rest unspoken.

It takes a full five minutes before he calms down.

He dials Charlie next.

Charlie is already up, on his way into the office. Alex can hear the sounds of London rush hour in the background.

'Alex, boy. Desperate. Just desperate. Did everything go okay with the flights and hotel? Everybody's asking for you. This close

47

to Christmas, too. And such a lovely girl.' Charlie takes a breath. 'Alex, I'm just curious, mate, do you know where you left the full Cassidy file? Actually, don't worry about it. I'll find it. What can I do for you? You need tickets? Undertakers?'

'She was murdered, Charlie,' Alex says.

'Fuck me.'

Charlie falls uncharacteristically silent.

'I'm going to stay here, ask around,' Alex adds. 'The cop in charge is barely out of uniform by the looks of it. Dropped the bomb last night while she was eating a burger.'

'Bloody hell.'

'I'm due a few weeks' leave.'

'The partners will understand. If you're back after New Year's, nobody will bat an eye . . .'

Alex grimaces. He can't imagine returning to normality, or a time beyond this.

'What else?' Charlie says. 'You want a PI? I know a few. A pal of mine, her husband was screwing his secretary. She got a lovely little dossier compiled on him before she dragged his arse to court.'

'I'm okay, for now. The Cassidy file is on my desktop. You know the password.'

'Tough times, Alex. If you need anything, I'm a call away, right? Money, contacts, whatever. Just say. I'll get on top of the Cassidy stuff. Elicit some sympathy in government ranks for your current predicament. They have to give port control to somebody. You leave it to me.'

Alex hastens the goodbye. He couldn't give less of a fuck about his clients or government contracts. When he hangs up, he stares blankly at the 4K images of Lapland showing on loop on the OLED TV screen.

Agatha meets him downstairs at the breakfast buffet. Alex mumbles an apology for storming off at dinner; she dismisses it with a wave and apologises in turn for her lack of tact.

Order is restored, but he still doesn't mention Vicky's second email account. His amateur hacking attempt before bed last night was unsuccessful and he's determined to check that account before he alerts Agatha to its existence. As far as he knows, Vicky only used it for him but what if he's wrong? What if she was communicating with others?

He waits for a coffee from a machine that looks like it was designed by NASA while she piles two plates with various pastries.

'I'm not hungry,' Alex says.

'You have no appetite,' she tells him. 'It's not the same thing. I ruined your dinner last night, so you haven't eaten. Breakfast is important.'

The hotel agrees, Alex thinks, as he looks around the huge buffet area, which features all manner of cereals, pastries and hot foods, not to mention a collection of ice buckets filled with champagne bottles for early morning mimosas.

'Food is a practical requirement here,' Agatha says. 'Dieting is for people who want to freeze to death. I always have grain bars in my pockets.'

Alex doesn't reply that anything he eats now will most likely come back up when he lays eyes on his dead sister.

They take a seat in one of the comfortable booths and Alex glances at the cover of the national newspaper. It's all in Finnish;

he can't understand a word and doesn't recognise any of the people photographed.

'Is it in the paper?' he asks Agatha.

'Not yet,' she says. 'We get a lot of accidents in Lapland this time of year. Tourists mainly, but also locals. The national newspapers don't tend to cover them, unless they get a statement to say it's more serious. Which we haven't issued yet.'

'Why don't they cover accidents?'

Agatha cocks her head sideways. She appears to be waiting for Alex to run the calculations.

'Bad for tourism,' he says.

'People don't realise that when they come here, they're only ever moments from death.' Agatha sighs. 'The weather, the landscape, the wildlife. It's not always hospitable. If ever. It's one thing staying at the Christmas villages. But people who stray further up . . .'

'Why do they come? Don't answer that. Adrenaline junkies.'

'Lapland madness, they call it. You come here, you enjoy the extreme sports, you celebrate in warmth and luxury after. Sleep in an ice igloo. If you're lucky, you'll see the fox fires light up the sky.'

'Fox fires?'

'The *revontulet*. The Northern Lights.'

Alex stares into his coffee. He takes a bite of a little bun. It's warm, custardy and has a distinct cinnamon taste.

'I'm going to stay for a while,' Alex says, after a moment.

'In the hotel?' Agatha asks.

'No. In Lapland. I can't bring Vicky home yet, so I may as well talk to the people who worked with her. See where she lived. Collect her things.'

Agatha puts down her coffee cup and stares at him.

'Alex, I'm not sure what's going through your head but you can't run your own investigation into your sister's death.'

'I never said that.'

'But I strongly suspect it's what you're planning. You do not trust that I can do my job. You think I need a big team, like you're used to in England. You expect an army of officers combing crime scenes, and press conferences, and everybody she worked with to be pulled in for interrogation—'

'Are you saying they won't be?' Alex interrupts.

'Of course they will, they already are, but you don't understand this place, you don't know what policing is like here. Lapland is vast but it is not very populated. And your sister was murdered weeks ago – already this is a different type of case. We can't rely on DNA, because she was in the water. We don't have CCTV up here. People forget things when they are not in the immediate past. This won't be like investigations you might be used to, but it will be effective.'

'How many murders have you solved in Koppe?'

'None.'

'Excuse me?'

'In Koppe, none. In Rovaniemi, I was on nine murder cases, most of them domestic violence-related. Alex, we don't get a lot of murder over here. And we've never had one in Koppe in the years I've been in charge.'

'Until now.'

'Until now,' she repeats.

'And you wonder why I'm not brimming with confidence.'

He puts his coffee down.

'I'm ready to see her.'

★

Venla steps into the corridor when Alex is in with his sister. She and Agatha lean out the window, taking short puffs of a shared cigarette. Agatha used to smoke all the time, but she won't around the children. She doesn't drink much around them either; doesn't want them thinking she too might not be able to control herself. They've had enough of that in their lives.

But right now, she needs a bloody cigarette.

'He isn't crying,' Venla tells Agatha. 'But he's simmering. Looks the sort to hold it all in until he has a breakdown in about ten years' time because somebody's made him a sandwich with the wrong filling and it's the final straw. He's got a lot of rage in him. I can tell.'

'And he's coming up to Koppe,' Agatha says.

'Oh dear.'

Venla takes a drag from the cigarette then hands it back to Agatha. 'A Brit who doesn't trust the locals. Why am I not surprised?'

'If your sister died over there, would you just leave it to their police?'

'Magnanimous of you,' Venla says. She turns and rests her butt against the windowsill, heating her cheeks on the radiator that sits below it. 'I suppose the Brits know what they're doing, don't they? I've streamed *Luther*.'

She looks Agatha dead in the eye.

'He can solve my imaginary sister's death any day.'

Agatha gives Venla's shoulder a gentle dig.

'Hey, I never even asked yesterday,' Venla says. 'How are the kids?'

'Good.'

Agatha pulls up a recent photograph on her phone.

'God, Emilia is all grown up. She looks so like you.'

Agatha smiles, then frowns.

'Olavi is biting now.'

'Other parents complain?'

'No. He's biting himself, not other kids, thankfully.'

'He'll forget, eventually,' Venla says. 'They all will.'

Venla knows the family's story. When Agatha came down for Venla's fortieth last year, the pathologist tried to convince Agatha to apply for a police transfer with a foreign force; Venla knows that Agatha won't ever really feel at peace while the ghost that haunts her and the children still knows where they live.

But Agatha can't leave. Lapland is her home.

'Hey, I mean it,' Venla says. 'They're great kids and they have you. They'll be fine. You all will.'

Agatha shrugs. Can anyone forget trauma?

Will they ever be allowed to?

Inside, Alex is standing beside Vicky and thinking he will never recover from this moment.

They've always looked alike, he and his sister. Dark-haired, dark features, good cheekbones.

This thing in front of him is not his sister. It's not just the shaved head – which is something Vicky would do for a dare – or the off pallor of her skin and blackened, frostbitten extremities.

It's her stillness. He can't ever remember Vicky being this still. She was effervescent. She was always active. Couldn't sit in one place.

Her very essence has been extinguished.

She'd have fought very hard to stay alive. Vicky loved life. Every dangerous thing Vicky did, every adrenaline shot she chased, it was all so she could *feel* more. Whoever did this robbed her of something to which she'd clung dearly.

He feels a fury so great it threatens to overwhelm him. He sways on his feet and brings his face closer to hers.

'I'm sorry, Vicky,' he whispers. 'I'm sorry for cutting you out.'

He hopes she can hear him.

It's light by the time Alex and Agatha leave the morgue and set off on the road for Koppe, on the shores of Lake Inari. It's the first time Alex has seen any daylight – if that's what this gloom is, in Finland. When they left the hotel this morning, it was still dark.

For the first hour of the drive, he says nothing. He's still thinking about what he's just seen.

But, eventually, he begins to notice the landscape.

'There are so many trees,' he says, without even realising he's spoken aloud. He thinks they're trees, anyway. They're so heavy with rime and freshly fallen snow, they look almost like sculptures. He can't understand how they haven't snapped under the weight of what the weather has thrown at them.

'Yes, but they're all the same,' Agatha says. 'Birch. Spruce. Birch. Pine. Birch. Until you get to the top of Lapland, where there are hardly any trees at all. But, yes. Almost three quarters of Finland is covered in forest. It's sort of what we're known for.'

She waves at a passing vehicle on a tight stretch of the road. Alex has no idea how she can drive with such confidence in such conditions.

'It looks different in the light, doesn't it?' she says. 'Enjoy it while it lasts. This time of year, we're lucky if we get five hours of daylight and even then, most days it's just dull.'

'Does it get depressing?' Alex asks.

Agatha shrugs.

'We're used to it. You know Rovaniemi is the gateway to the Arctic Circle? The line runs through the Santa Village. By the end of summer, we're so tired of having endless days and no nights that it kind of balances itself out. Technically, we have eight seasons in Lapland. But people only ever really think of the Arctic Circle as having summer or winter.'

'That Santa Village,' Alex says. 'Do the locals like it, or does it drive everybody nuts?'

'It provides jobs,' Agatha answers. 'Up here, the choice is tourism or mining. The village is nice. Magical. But there are more . . . exclusive versions. Kakslauttanen is incredible. It has fields of glass igloos so you can sleep under the Northern Lights. It's magical.'

'But expensive?'

'Everything is expensive. We want tourism, but the right sort. And Christmas is our Mecca. Santa is Finnish, of course.'

Alex glances sideways at Agatha.

'You don't believe me,' she says. 'But it's the truth. *Joulupukki* comes from a fell called Korvatunturi. He lives there with Mother Christmas and makes toys in his workshop with his gnomes.'

'Not elves?'

'Pfft. American concoctions. Like that red and white suit. Everyone knows *Joulupukki* dresses like a goat. He's traditionally a symbol of fertility. Horns on his head and everything. And real elves don't work with Santa. They have their own magic.'

'That goat suit must come as a shock to the families who buy those two-night packages,' Alex says, dryly.

'We tone it down,' Agatha says, smiling. 'You know, we get half a million letters from 198 countries delivered to the Arctic Circle post office every year. So, we have proof. We own Santa.'

She says this deadpan. Alex looks back out the window. He's fairly certain he read recently that the real Santa Claus, St Nicolas, came from Turkey and is buried in Ireland. Santa's tomb probably wouldn't make as good an attraction as this snowy wonderland, though.

'Christmas was Vicky's favourite time of year,' he says. 'When the rest of the world caught up with her . . . *joie de vivre*.'

Agatha is looking at him now; he can feel her gaze.

'So,' she says, 'when was the last time you spoke to your sister?'

It's seamless, the segue from tour guide to detective.

'Five months ago,' Alex says.

He's thought of little else but how long it's been since he last spoke to Vicky.

'What did you speak about?'

He looks out the window again.

'We were talking about a gift for my parents. It was their anniversary. It was a short call. She made a suggestion about what it should be and said she'd give me the money when she was home. She always said that. Never did. She wanted to send them on a cruise. And I told her I didn't mind subbing her on regular gifts but this was a step too far. It wasn't even an important anniversary. She got mad. We had a go at each other. She hung up. I didn't bother calling her back.'

Agatha nods.

'I see. You weren't to know what would happen.'

Alex swallows down the guilt.

'We have her phone records,' Agatha says. 'I can't see your number on them, so she didn't try to ring you, either. These things happen with siblings. Petty squabbles. Trust me, I know.'

Alex sighs. He'll have to tell her the truth.

'My number isn't on those records,' he says, 'because I lost my phone in August and I ended up changing networks. I didn't give her the new number, the number you have for me.'

'Oh,' Agatha says.

'So, you'll have to check the records again before you know if she tried to call me. For my old number.'

Agatha says nothing. They both know what that means. That his sister could have needed him but she wouldn't have been able to get through.

'I'm sure if there was anything urgent, she would have contacted your parents,' Agatha says, after a few awkward moments have passed.

'Unlikely,' Alex replies. 'She only ever rang home when she needed a loan. She was surprisingly thoughtful, in a twisted way.'

He takes a breath.

'We weren't estranged, you know. I wasn't . . . I didn't think it would mean this much, not giving her a blasted phone number. I just needed a break. Vicky was . . . she was very loveable, in so many ways, but she never really grew up. I think it's being the youngest, being the pet in the family. Cute when they're small, not so cute when they're full-grown adults. And she was prone to disappearing off the radar herself. It wasn't unusual for months to pass and not hear from her. The first time she did it, we were all annoyed. When somebody does that a few times, you stop giving a shit. You get tired of being the one they can contact whenever they want.'

He stops talking. He sounds defensive. He is defensive.

They fall quiet again.

'Maybe it's not my place to say this,' Agatha says. 'But she seemed to be doing okay up here. She had friends. You shouldn't feel guilty for looking out for yourself. You weren't responsible for her.'

Alex tries to absorb the balm she's offering.

'She mentioned a couple of friends, earlier in the year,' he says. 'I've seen pictures on her Instagram, too. Looked at them on the way over. A couple of lads: Nicolas and Florian? And that woman she was friendly with. Niamh.'

Alex never spent time on social media, so the pictures were new to him. He'd pored over Vicky's pages, scanning everybody's face, every location shot she took, trying to immerse himself in his sister's life.

'When she disappeared, I mean, she didn't turn up for work, correct?' Alex says. 'Why weren't they more alarmed? She must have had some sort of routine.'

Agatha is quiet. Alex stares at her, wondering what she's not telling him.

'It's like I said,' she says. 'The guides, they come and go. She didn't hand in her notice. That happens sometimes.'

She sounds cautious in her reply. Alex knows now there's more.

The keychain is still dangling from the rear-view mirror and Alex watches it spin. Three children.

'Those are your kids?' he says.

She nods.

One of the kids looks to be in her teens. Maybe they just start younger over here, Alex thinks. All those dark nights. Nothing to do but make babies.

'Did Vicky give you any indication anything was wrong when you talked to her that last time?' Agatha asks.

Alex narrows his eyes.

'She sounded . . . excited,' he says. 'Particularly so. Like she was in the mood for celebrating. Hence the suggestion of a big present for our folks.'

'No hint that she'd fallen out with anybody?'

'Nothing like that. Do you think it was somebody she worked with who did this?'

'I don't know. While I was down in Rovaniemi, my officers finished questioning the Lodge staff. Like I said, we have a last known sighting for Vicky and we're assuming she died that night or very soon afterwards. So, those immediate hours after she was seen have become very important. And everybody she worked with has given us an alibi.'

Agatha seems to hesitate.

'There were a lot of tourists in the resort last month.' She sighs. 'It was at capacity. Cheaper in November than December.'

Alex thinks about this.

'Tourists,' he says. 'Does that mean—'

'Yes,' she says. 'If it was a tourist, he or she could be long gone.'

'He or she? Could it have been a woman?'

'I can't rule it out.'

They don't talk for a while. As they drive, Alex realises how sparsely populated this part of the world is. He's never seen anything like it. They pass through what Agatha tells him is euphemistically referred to as a town, and stop for coffee and the facilities. It has a small garage and three or four houses, from what Alex can see. He buys a blue paper-wrapped chocolate bar labelled with the name Karl Fazer. He needs a sugar hit to go with the strong coffee. He tries to use his card at the till, but Agatha won't let him, tapping hers instead.

Back in the car, they don't see another house for an hour.

She seems unaffected by the driving, used to the long distances and eerie emptiness of the surrounds.

Alex starts to drift into a semi-sleep, lulled by the repetitive scenery of trees and snow, snow and trees.

He opens his eyes when the car slows and sees that they're approaching another town. A sign tells him that it's Koppe.

The town is situated in a valley, mountains on either side, and the road begins to descend towards it.

The few outlying houses give way to a K-Market, some more low-lying buildings – lights already glistening in their windows to ward off the oncoming winter night – and then, below the town and beyond the tree line, he glimpses Lake Inari.

It's huge; a great frozen expanse of nothingness.

A billboard tells him Koppe is populated with four hundred people, but the large hotel they pass on the hill down has him guessing there are a lot more people in residence.

'Here we are,' Agatha says. 'Koppe. Almost the edge of the world.'

Alex looks at the dots descending down one of the slopes at speed and realises they're skiers. And then he sees a sign telling them where to turn for Koppe Lodge and the tourist cabins.

Something is niggling at Alex. Something he can't put his finger on, but something he knows he's forgotten to ask because he's tired and he's still in shock.

Something that doesn't add up in what Agatha has told him about his sister going missing.

Koppe
1998

The next time Kaya sees her lover is at work. He's sitting with friends tonight, at a table across from the bar. He doesn't really belong in that circle but he's good at acting like he does. He tries to catch her eye while she's serving a group of customers. The group consists of more of the ubiquitous developers, up from Helsinki. This lot have visited several times in the last couple of months. They're almost regulars at this point but they still don't know Kaya's name; they don't even acknowledge her existence when she serves them. Kaya, like all the other locals, is just another face that can be roped into serving the many tourists these men want to attract to the area, while they live in their nice apartments in Helsinki and private villas out by the lakes below the capital.

He comes to the counter when she's free, to the side where they normally take in the dirty glasses. She can tell he's been contributing plenty to the bar's profits tonight. His eyes are glassy; he smiles at her but it's lopsided.

Almost a week has passed since she turned up at his house looking to speak to him. Almost a week since he left her standing in the cold on his doorstep, refusing to even allow her in to dry off and warm up.

She's thought of him every second since but she knows he hasn't thought about her. He's thinking about her now, though. She can see it in the way he's drinking her in as she bends over to fill the glass-washer, her skirt riding up her thighs at the rear.

His wife is tending to her invalid mother up in Riutula.

He expects Kaya to come home with him tonight. He expects her to allow him to fuck her, even after how he treated her.

'Kaya,' he whispers, his voice silky and familiar. 'Aren't we friends any more?'

She shrugs. She's not so good an actress that she can pretend his slight to her didn't happen. She's still stinging. She's only twenty-two and some hurts are worse than others.

'Kaya, pudding.' He gives her the puppy dog eyes that always work, the look that leaves her begging for him even when she knows everything between them is so wrong.

'I'm sorry,' he says. 'I freaked out. You know how much I worry. For you and for me.'

It sounds like he means the apology.

Or Kaya wants to believe him so badly, she's happy to fool herself that he does.

'I know,' she says, quietly. 'I shouldn't have come to your home.'

He shakes his head, makes a little admonishing gesture with his finger, then winks as he strokes his chin.

'Not that I don't like it when you're naughty,' he says.

She feels her insides melt. Is that all it takes, she chides herself. Him turning on the charm, him wanting you again?

Yes, she's sorry to admit. She so badly needs to feel wanted, she'll forgive almost anything.

Not that she won't make him work a little harder. She'll expect him to worship her. She'll want him to say all the right things. But she needs things to be okay between the two of them. For everything that's to come.

She'll go home with him after her shift. Her husband is always asleep when she gets in, anyway. His day on the farm starts in the middle of the night; when she's on night shifts in the bar, their paths barely cross and he's used to her 'working' late.

She always has time to wash the scent of her lover off her body before her husband can sniff him on her.

Yes, she'll go home with this man who's causing her so much turmoil. She'll let him take her clothes off and she'll let him fuck her and when he's happy, when he's sated and lying in her arms, she'll ask him if he's noticed the changes in her body, if he's already sensed the difference.

His wife can't have children.

Kaya wonders if that's what will tip it for him. The chance to be a father.

Once he's on board, he'll protect her from her husband.

He'll protect her and he'll protect his baby.

The child that is a ticking time bomb in Kaya's womb.

Koppe

2019

Agatha has left Alex in a cabin up at Koppe Lodge. She'd phoned ahead earlier and Harry promised he'd organise a nice one. Even though it's Christmas, the Lodge has space. December prices are astronomical; most tourists try to have their Santa experience in November or even January, when everything is that little bit more affordable. Then the locals get some respite, until the schools start to take their midterms in February and families from the rest of the country head north for winter fun.

For now, Koppe Lodge is crowded but not as crowded as it can get. Not as full as it was when Vicky Evans went missing.

Agatha knows Alex needs to do this for himself and his family; come to Vicky's workplace, ask her friends what they know and size them up. Agatha would do exactly the same. She understands that Alex is driven by guilt – guilt because he couldn't save Vicky, guilt at not giving her his phone number, at not having even thought about his sister until he realised she was dead.

And guilt is an emotion Agatha understands very well.

But the police chief in her knows he has now become a problem she has to contain. Family members are always a difficulty in murder investigations. At best, a hindrance, at worst, capable of destroying a whole case.

She has to keep him happy, though. Perhaps if he feels he's conducted his own little investigation he'll go back to England and leave Agatha to do her job, instead of complaining to the Met and trying to get them involved.

And he might actually be of use. From the soft interviews they conducted with Vicky's colleagues when it was indicated the woman might have gone missing, and then the formal interviews when her body was discovered, they've learned little of note. Everybody liked Vicky, allegedly. Nobody had reason to attack her.

Agatha knows it takes a while before the mud-slinging starts in murder cases, especially mud aimed at the victim, but so far there's no inkling of anything being amiss.

It could have been a random attack. That would make Agatha's job very difficult.

But there's that little piece of information she's held back from Alex which makes her think otherwise, which makes her think Vicky's killer was somebody who knew her, even temporarily. She will tell Alex what it is, if he doesn't find out for himself first, but for the moment she's trying not to overburden him. The last thing she needs is him seeing every person in the Lodge as a potential murderer.

She's just let herself in the door when Patric appears in the hallway, tea towel slung over his shoulder. He has completed most of the housework while he was watching the children, even though Agatha keeps telling him there's no need. Patric is retired now, or supposed to be, but he's one of those men who needs to be busy.

He still gets up early in the morning and he always has a list of jobs to do, but he's also always willing to help Agatha when she asks. Mainly with the children. She does ask for advice about cases, but they've both erected a Chinese wall of sorts. She needs to prove she can do the job without the old chief watching over her shoulder. He wants to show he trusts her.

'You have a visitor,' Patric says, as Agatha kicks off her snow boots.

'Oh?'

'In the kitchen. Agitated.'

Agatha's stomach clenches and it must show on her face because Patric quickly adds:

'A visitor from the Lodge.'

'Ah. Okay. The kids were all right last night?'

'Emilia did her essay, Olavi played Xbox and Onni built something very impressive with your cushions and bedspread. We had pizza. And they all slept through the night and got off to school fine this morning.'

'You are so good to us, Patric.'

'You lot keep me young.'

Agatha kisses Patric on the cheek – the strands of his straggly white beard tickle her – and thinks, I don't know what I'd do if anything ever happened to you.

Then she walks through to the kitchen.

Niamh Doyle is there, pacing. She doesn't see Agatha immediately, and Agatha watches her for a few moments.

If handed a box of colours and told to draw an Irish person, this is the version that Agatha would sketch. Red hair, green eyes, a smattering of orange freckles across her nose. Agatha's never been to Ireland. She can't imagine they all look like this, no more than everybody in Lapland fits the Hollywood-projected Sami look. But she does think the Irish tourist board could get good use out of Niamh Doyle.

As she paces, Niamh lifts the end of her hair and sticks it in her mouth, chewing the strands. Agatha winces. It reminds her of Olavi and his many, many anxious habits.

'Hi,' Agatha says.

Niamh stops pacing and drops her hair.

'You're back.'

'We made good time. What can I help you with?'

Niamh stares at her like it's obvious.

'What did they say in Rovaniemi? What happened to Vicky?'

Agatha takes a deep breath.

'I can't discuss this with you, Niamh.'

'I was there when they pulled her out! I told you she'd gone missing, didn't I? I said, she wouldn't just go off like that, she'd have been in touch by now. Nobody believed me!'

'After two weeks,' Agatha reminds her. 'You didn't report her missing for two weeks.'

Niamh flinches.

'I wanted to before but . . . I didn't want to be alarmist.'

Agatha knows, from the inflection on the word, that somebody put 'alarmist' in Niamh's vocabulary. Niamh didn't think she was being alarmist in the slightest until somebody told her she was.

I wonder who, Agatha ponders.

'I have a right to know,' Niamh says. 'She was my friend.'

'Technically, you don't have any rights,' Agatha replies. 'Only her family do.'

It's unkind, but it's true.

Niamh's face falls. Her lip trembles.

'Please,' she says, in a small voice. 'She looked so . . . I can't stop thinking about her. I've been on the lake almost every single day since she vanished. All that time, her body . . .'

Niamh trails off.

Agatha hesitates. Everybody will find out anyway, she reasons. Especially with Alex staying up in the Lodge.

'It wasn't an accident,' she says.

Niamh looks like she's going to faint again. Agatha watches the various reactions flash across her face. Shock, denial, a hint of begrudging acceptance, because it had already crossed Niamh's mind.

'She was one of the safest guides,' Niamh says, shaking her head. 'I knew something was wrong. From that very first morning. We were both on early shifts and I should have seen her out and about. I didn't, none of us did, and I thought, maybe she's ill, or hungover, but . . .'

Niamh's features contort, like she's swallowing bile.

'But everybody told me I was overreacting,' she says. 'Because of what we found in the cabin.'

'Because of the cabin,' Agatha echoes.

The thing that seemed so innocuous but is now so very important.

It was less what they'd found and more what they hadn't found.

Vicky's cabin was spotlessly clean. All her belongings were gone. Had been since the morning she vanished. To Harry, the Lodge manager, the cleared-out cabin had seemed evidence of an errant employee who'd upped and left without even handing in notice.

To Niamh, it had always felt off, and she said her concern had only grown as the weeks passed, which contributed to her arrival at Agatha's station to report Vicky missing. Followed by Harry, who reluctantly admitted that he too had grown concerned because Vicky was still owed wages and hadn't come looking for them, a reference, anything.

The empty cabin had caused a problem for Agatha. If Vicky's place had been abandoned, all of her belongings in situ, she'd have been a lot more concerned.

But now, Agatha knows that the likely explanation is that somebody killed Vicky and got rid of her belongings, including her laptop and phone, to make it look like Vicky had left, something that indicates a very malicious level of planning.

'Who did it?' Niamh asks.

'I don't know,' Agatha says.

Niamh sinks into a chair.

'Her brother is here,' Agatha tells her. 'He's staying in the Lodge. He wants to talk to the people who lived with her. He hadn't seen her in a while.'

'I . . . of course. I'll talk to him.'

Niamh is still staring at the floor, trying to process what she's learned.

'Are you going to question *him*?' Niamh asks.

'Her brother?'

Niamh meets her eye.

'Not her brother, for fuck's sake. You know who.'

Agatha takes a deep breath.

'I will be questioning everybody of relevance,' she says.

'That's not what I asked!'

Niamh crosses her arms and glares at Agatha.

'If Vicky was murdered . . . we all know who did it. I was only here a few days and people were warning me about him. Don't you think something should have been done by now? If he's killed *again* . . .'

Agatha flinches.

This is her greatest fear. Everybody jumping to conclusions. It's the last thing she needs. People acting as judge and jury. Small town like this. Tempers and emotions running high.

It can lead to bad places.

'We don't know who did it,' she says. But even to her, it sounds weak.

She's going to have to sound a whole lot stronger to convince a town that already suspects the local bogeyman and is baying for blood.

Alex's meagre assortment of belongings disappear in the large drawers in his new living quarters. It's a luxurious affair: log walls and wooden-beamed high ceilings; a dining area with high-backed, brown leather chairs flanking a large fireplace; a king-sized bed placed in a glass dome extension so he can watch the stars at night. He reckons it probably costs close to a thousand a night to stay here, but they're rolling out the full dead-sister treatment.

Alex takes a deep breath. Every time he thinks of his sister as dead, it hits him anew.

He wants to examine her stuff. The police probably have her laptop, and he knows her phone is missing but he wants to see those call records; he wants to find out if she needed to tell him anything before she died. If there's some clue to what happened to her.

He opens his own phone and his email. He searches for the last email from the address she kept and used solely to wind him up.

There's nothing there since earlier in the year, when she'd sent him a singing happy birthday card.

Nothing from her regular, respectable email either.

He'll have to tell Agatha about the second address. He doesn't know why he hasn't yet, only that it has something to do with him not fully trusting her. For Alex, people have to earn that. He doesn't just give it, even to those in authority. Especially to those in authority. When you work in a job like his and you've seen behind the curtain the way Alex has . . .

Alex shakes his head and puts his phone down. He's going around in circles.

He imagines for a moment how the police chief must see him. Impulsive. Foolish. Naïve. All the things he's not, all the things he's so carefully ironed out of his character. Alex is a cynic now. Life, his job, and, quite possibly, Ed made him that way. Ed is cynical. About government, about the system, even about the machinations within his local union branch. He's had good reason to be, most of the time. Alex has never met a union man who couldn't be turned by a promotion and a bonus, or by the massive skeleton in his cupboard.

He bundles up in his new warm clothes and leaves the cabin. He glances at the little push-sleigh beside his door. Even as he's wondering why they've left him a kid's toy, an elderly couple pass by; the old lady is sitting in the sleigh, the husband is pushing it. The pair of them living their best lives in bright red snowsuits.

Alex steps off the cabin's porch and his new boots sink into the foot of snow that's collected there. He trudges in the direction of

Vicky's workplace, taking giant, moon-landing-spaced steps to try to make progress.

He passes children building the biggest snowman he's ever seen, rolling the two separate body parts with enviable focus. Their cheeks are flushed, their eyes glistening with excitement, and Alex feels a pang of envy for their unencumbered lives. A few days ago, his biggest worry had been trying to worm out of Christmas dinner with his family. What a problem to have.

He rounds a tall mound of snow and, out of the corner of his eye, spots something that brings him up short.

People are running down a long wooden deck, some naked, some in swimsuits, to climb down into a large open hole in the otherwise frozen lake, steam erupting from their bodies as they hit the water. They're shrieking with laughter, their skin is mottled pink, their breath forms clouds in the air.

He shakes his head and continues to the main building. It stands like a black oasis in the middle of a white desert; a log cabin constructed of burnt teak, with a church-like roof and large glass windows through which Alex can see holidaymakers in various colourful wool sweaters.

Once inside, it's all hustle and bustle. The bar and restaurant on the left provide a symphony of clinking glasses and delicious aromas. To the right, there's the hum of conversation in the lobby area, where more tourists are toasting their Christmas breaks with glasses of white wine and tall beers.

Passages lead off to various parts of the building, all of them posted with 'North Pole'-type signs. Ski gear is one way; horse-riding this way; snowmobile and ice activities another.

Alex stands on one of the giant mats inside the front door, an attempt to soak up the water trailed in by people's boots. As soon as he's partially dry, he moves to the reception counter and waits behind a small group of Americans, all wearing bright blue overalls and helmets, as the man at the desk tells them their guide will meet them at the snowmobile shed.

'Is this dangerous?' one of the group members asks. 'Are you sure the teenagers are okay doing it?'

Some chuckles from the adults and embarrassed groans from the teenagers.

'It's perfectly safe,' the receptionist replies, in what Alex thinks is a German accent. 'If you fall, the kill switch will stop the machine, and remember, you'll only hit snow. The guide will explain. But make sure not to go off the track. We've had one machine go underwater already this year. They are very expensive pieces of equipment. And be careful on the turns to *not* follow your instinct. Lean against the turn. And don't put your leg down to stop the vehicle. They're heavy and the metal at the side will slice right through if it falls on you. Even bone.'

There's deathly silence from the American tourists, until one of them breaks it with a nervous laugh. The German receptionist smiles, but Alex knows he isn't joking.

The group moves off and Alex approaches.

'Can I help you, sir?'

Alex thinks the fresh-looking face and tight blond crew cut is familiar, and then he looks at the man's badge. Florian. One of Vicky's friends.

'I'm Alex Evans. I'm here to . . .'

The man in front of him, already pale in skin tone, whitens.

'*Gott*. Yes. Vicky's brother. We heard you were coming.'

73

'Yes. Thanks for the cabin. I don't know how long I'll be here . . .'

The Florian guy is staring at him, opening and closing his mouth, trying to figure out what to say next.

'We're, uh, we are all so sorry for your loss.' Florian has landed on the typical response. 'We cannot believe it. Vicky was very dear to us.'

'Strange, nobody reported her missing for a while,' Alex says and then bites his tongue as the man in front of him visibly wilts. 'Sorry,' Alex says. 'I'm still tired from travelling and it's been a terrible shock. Is there any chance I can see where she stayed? If it's still empty? I don't know if the police have all her belongings . . .'

It might be Alex's imagination but he thinks Florian's blinks are slower and his cheeks have coloured. The man is either thinking of a way to break something to Alex, or to keep something from him.

'Perhaps you would like to meet some of her friends first?' he says.

A delaying tactic, Alex thinks. But, fine. He does want to meet Vicky's co-workers.

'Sure,' he says.

Florian steps into a back room and says something to somebody partially hidden behind the door. Another man emerges. Mid-forties, handsome in a Nordic-giant type way, wavy blond hair, high cheekbones. He frowns at Alex before walking to the far end of the reception desk, as Florian comes out from behind it.

Not a friendly guy, Alex thinks, but it's strange he wouldn't at least acknowledge Alex and his loss, if he works here, too.

Florian leads Alex through the bar. They pass a giant, fragrant Christmas tree and arrive at a snug by a roaring fire. Several people are huddled in a circle by the grate, all of them holding glasses filled with a honey-coloured liquid. They're all youngish, twenties, and wearing a uniform of black waterproof trousers and khaki-green polo shirts. Their heads are bowed but their glasses are raised.

They look up at Florian, then see Alex behind him.

'This is Vicky's brother,' Florian says and before anyone can say a word, Alex realises he's arrived in the middle of a toast to his sister. One of the women shoots up and approaches him, her arms outstretched. Alex flinches as she envelops him, her thick blonde hair swishing against his face, the overpowering smell of Chanel tickling his nostrils.

'We are all so sorry,' she says, another German accent. 'We just heard. We thought she'd moved on to another resort. She was such a good friend.'

Alex pulls away. He doesn't recognise this woman from Vicky's photographs. Her name tag says Beatrice and he doesn't recognise that either.

He scans the crowd, looking for any faces that might be familiar. A guy by the fireplace meets his eye and stands. I know him, Alex thinks. Nicolas. Brown hair, glasses, looks like a Calvin Klein model dressing down. He had his arm around Vicky's shoulders in one of the pictures and Alex wondered if they'd a thing going on.

Nicolas offers his hand to Alex and Alex shakes it, wondering if that hand played a part in killing his sister.

'Hey, man,' Nicolas says. He could be Finnish or from any of the Nordic countries. He sounds like a European who learned English in America. 'Sorry for your loss. Vicky was . . . she was special.'

Alex nods, embarrassed at being the focal point of their outpourings.

'Have the police told you anything?' Florian asks. In an instant, the atmosphere changes from polite condolences to barely concealed morbid curiosity.

'Just that she was murdered,' Alex says, and he can feel the group recoil at hearing it spoken aloud so bluntly. 'They won't be releasing her body for a little while so I'm going to stay a bit. It would be nice to see where she lived and know what her life was like here. If that's okay.'

'Anything we can do,' Nicolas says, stiffly. 'We let her down.'

Alex meets the other man's eye again. He thinks he can identify genuine pain. It's like looking in the mirror. But is it regret or remorse on Nicolas' face?

Alex glances around.

'Is Niamh here?' he asks.

Florian is about to answer, but Alex realises somebody has just approached from behind and turns to see the red-haired woman from Vicky's photos, the one who reported her missing.

'I'm Niamh,' she says.

She looks as shaken as Alex feels.

'Um, you've met everybody?' she asks. 'Florian, Nicolas, Beatrice.'

She points at the ones standing, then to the ones still sitting.

'And this is Leon, Melanie and Liz. There are more of us and everyone knew Vicky, but we still have to work. We have about twenty guides here at any given time.'

'Are you the manager?' Alex asks. She looks young but she speaks with such authority, he can believe she is.

'No. That's Harry. He's on reception, you must have seen him when you came in? Big blond.'

Alex frowns. Why didn't the manager make it his business to

greet him? And he wonders why Niamh utters Harry's name in a tone she hasn't applied to the others. There's history in that name. For her, anyway.

'Alex, we're going to have proper drinks for Vicky tonight,' Florian says, his voice full of apology. 'Later, when we're all finished work. You're very welcome to join us?'

The others nod eagerly and Alex doesn't say no, though he can't quite say yes.

Niamh puts her hand on Alex's back and guides him away from the group at the fireplace. It's proprietorial but it doesn't bother him. He needs some time to try to come to terms with how many people Vicky would have been in contact with.

Niamh walks him to the bar where she gets two cups and fills them with coffee.

'I'll show you Vicky's cabin after we've had these,' Niamh says.

Alex nods.

She hands him the cup. He sees her hands are trembling.

'I'm sorry I didn't report her missing straight away,' she says. 'It's just, it was the perfect storm. We were on different shifts for a few weeks and I guess it was so busy here, we weren't checking in with each other much. Then, well, it did look like she'd simply decided to leave . . . I was worried, but I was more hurt she hadn't told me she was going, to be honest.'

Alex realises, in that moment, what's been niggling at him.

'What about all her stuff?' he says. 'If she was murdered, all her things must have still been here, right?'

Niamh looks at him blankly.

'Didn't Chief Koskinen tell you? Vicky's cabin was empty. *None* of her things were there.'

Alex tries to absorb this.

'What do you mean, empty? Where are her things?'

'We don't know.'

Alex closes his eyes and pinches the bridge of his nose.

'Hold on,' he says, when he opens them. 'If she was murdered, and her stuff is gone, does that mean whoever did it came here and . . .'

He trails off.

'She might have met somebody, packed and left?' Niamh suggests, sounding completely unconvinced.

Alex raises his eyebrows.

'You were friends, weren't you?' he says. 'Why would you even think she'd go without telling you?'

Niamh shrugs, helplessly.

'Why would I think anything else?' she says. 'Her stuff was gone and . . . it's not the first place your head goes, is it? To thinking that somebody has been murdered.'

Alex looks over at the group sitting by the fireplace. Vicky's work colleagues. People who'd have had access to her cabin, he presumes.

'Alex,' Niamh says, and he has to lean in to hear her. 'Will we find out who did this?'

He nods.

'Good,' she says. She takes another sip of the coffee. When she places it down, she grips his arm. Her hand is small but her grip tight.

'Whatever you do, don't wait for the Koppe police to solve it, do you understand?' she whispers. 'This isn't like home. Up here . . . some people are untouchable.'

She finishes the last sentence with a shudder.

Alex is about to ask her more but she puts a finger to her mouth, releases his arm and turns towards the bar counter.

Alex looks behind him to see what made her fall quiet.

Harry, the manager, is approaching the group gathered by the fireplace.

He glances over at Alex and Niamh.

Alex senses something from him.

Hostility.

And he wonders where that comes from.

Alex is able to walk to the local police station using Google Maps on his phone. He can't understand why 4G in the Arctic Circle is so damn good and yet half of Yorkshire struggles to get decent broadband. He's wearing all his thermals but the cold still bites at his exposed cheeks and the part of his forehead not covered by his hat.

How, he wonders, can anybody live, let alone thrive, in this sub-zero climate?

He suspects the beauty of the place has a lot to do with it.

It doesn't mean a lot to him – this is where his sister was murdered, after all – but even he can see that Koppe is Christmas-card pretty. White houses striped with black wooden beams, topped with Toblerone roofs; lamps in windows already glowing against the dark; snow falling gently on to windowsills and porches. Alex checks his phone. It's 4 p.m. but already it feels like deep night.

Under street lanterns, he passes brightly dressed tourists carrying ski equipment. They seem unaffected by the freezing weather; their cheeks are pink from the cold but they're all chatting animatedly about their day on the slopes. A door opens to his left and he smells beer and charred steak and glimpses revellers already warming up after a day outdoors.

An older man greets him in the reception area of the police station, which is in one of the chocolate-box houses but with a plaque outside announcing it as Koppe police headquarters.

The officer is bald but has a thick grey moustache. He looks reassuringly in charge. Alex knows the thought that pops into his head is misogynistic but he wonders why this guy is on reception and Agatha is the boss.

There's a little kid sitting behind the counter, maybe five, staring at Alex with uncensored curiosity. Alex thinks he recognises him from the keyring in Agatha's car.

'You're the Brit,' the kid says in perfect English.

'Deputy Onni, get the chief,' the policeman says.

The kid gets up and runs down a corridor.

Alex waits, staring at the officer, who stares back.

Agatha arrives and lifts up part of the reception counter for Alex to walk through.

'Thank you, Jonas,' she says to the older man, as she sees Alex through to the corridor. 'You're okay to watch Onni some more?'

The kid has appeared again, staring up at Alex, all big eyes and perfect baby teeth.

Jonas grunts and Agatha leads Alex on.

They enter an office and Agatha closes the door.

Alex hasn't seen a single other officer in the place.

'Does he ever shut up?' Alex says, nodding back over his shoulder to indicate he means Jonas.

Agatha snorts.

'You're settled in?' she asks.

'I've been to Vicky's cabin,' Alex cuts her off.

Niamh had taken him there after their coffee.

Alex hadn't been able to get to the police station quick enough . . . once he'd seen it.

'Ah,' Agatha says.

She sits in the chair behind her desk. Alex takes the seat facing it.

'You didn't tell me all her belongings are gone,' he says. 'That's why you didn't take it seriously, when she was first reported missing.'

She nods, purses her lips.

'I was still concerned,' she says. 'But yes, it was difficult to look beyond that fact.'

'Have you found her things?'

'No.' Agatha frowns.

'But you've examined the cabin again.'

'As soon as we found her. Jonas printed it. It was still empty.'

'Did you find anything?'

He can sense her hesitation, but she continues to answer his questions.

'Nothing unexpected, though the lab in Rovaniemi is running all the fingerprints. Vicky had a few parties in her cabin so we picked up a lot of sets. Which means most of her colleagues will appear in the results.'

'Blood?'

'Nothing more than trace in the bathroom. Could be from anything. Nicking her leg when shaving, a paper cut . . . The cabin hadn't been cleaned. It meant there was no dilution but, still, we didn't pick up on anything. She wasn't killed there.'

Alex sits back.

'And you didn't discover anything interviewing her co-workers?' he asks.

'Nothing of note,' Agatha says. 'We did initial interviews when Niamh reported her missing. And more since she was found, of course. We will do repeat interviews. You needn't worry about that.'

There's something she's not telling him. Alex can practically feel it vibrating between them. It dawns on him, suddenly, what it is.

'You already suspect somebody,' he says.

Agatha draws her lips into a tight line. Alex watches as she deliberates whether she should be forthcoming. He decides to throw all his cards on the table.

'The best way to stop me causing a ruckus here is just to keep me in the loop,' he says, hoping that does the job he intends and doesn't, instead, just piss her off.

Agatha raises her eyebrows and says nothing for a few seconds. He starts to wonder if she's decided to clam up.

'A name has been mentioned, in relation to the night before she went missing,' she says.

Alex sits up.

'Mentioned in what capacity?'

'She was seen in the company of an American tourist who was staying at the Lodge. They spent some time together and on that last night they were at a bar in town before returning to the Lodge bar. They were with a group, but then the two of them went back to her cabin.'

'Who is he? Have you arrested him?'

She says nothing. Alex's stomach knots.

'He's not here, is he?' he says, quietly. 'This is what you meant when you said whoever did it could be long gone.'

'He returned to the United States before we started our inquiries. Alex, that doesn't mean we're not going to pursue the matter. If he was involved, his leaving the jurisdiction makes this harder, but it won't protect him. And he is also just one avenue of investigation.'

Alex is filled with a feeling of frustration unlike anything he's experienced in a very long time. It courses through him; even his ears are tingling.

'What's his name?' he says.

'I can't tell you that.'

Agatha's posture is tenser now. Perhaps she can sense how dangerous he's become, armed with this little bit of knowledge. Alex feels it himself. He knows, without a shadow of a doubt, if that guy was standing in front of him now, he'd beat him to a pulp to get to the truth.

Before Alex can push further, Agatha places a sheaf of A4 pages in front of him.

'Vicky's phone records,' she says. 'Can you tell me which of those is your old mobile number?'

Alex swallows and looks down at the first page. The records show calls as far back as June. He sees his number printed on the tenth of that month. He remembers the call. Vicky had phoned looking for a loan.

And again on the fifteenth. Because she needed more money than she thought.

Then, on the first of July, she'd phoned to talk about their parents' anniversary.

His last call with her.

Something had changed in those two weeks. She'd gone from

asking to borrow money to suggesting they both spend a lot on a present.

He goes through the records wordlessly until he gets to the days before Vicky died.

She didn't try to phone him in August or September.

But then . . .

There it is.

His number. He blinks.

Agatha is watching him, waiting.

'That's my number,' Alex manages to choke out. 'She did try to get in touch.'

Three times, in the last week of October, the week before she went missing.

This number is no longer in service.

Agatha turns the pages around to face her, but not before Alex spots something else.

Another number.

His heart slows.

'I wouldn't read too much into it,' Agatha says, in a tone that tells him this is just to placate him. But he can hear the concerned note underneath. Why did Vicky not bother trying to contact Alex for months and then make a sudden flurry of calls a week before she died?

'She might have just wanted to say hi,' Agatha continues. 'Would, um, three times in a week be normal for her if she was trying to get hold of you? Had she done something like that before?'

'She'd ring plenty, if she needed something,' Alex says, his voice small.

Agatha looks at him.

'Maybe she just wanted another loan. It might not be related to what happened to her, at all. Wouldn't she have rung your parents to get your new number if she really needed you?'

Alex hesitates.

'No,' he says, sighing heavily. 'Like I said, she didn't like to bother them. And she especially wouldn't have wanted them to know I'd changed my number and not given her the new one. They already knew, though. I'd told them. I told them if she rang looking for me to tell her to piss off.'

Agatha looks down at the desk. Which is just as well because Alex can't meet her eyes.

'Tomorrow,' he says, 'I want to see where she was found.'

Agatha doesn't answer immediately. He knows she could tell him she's too busy to chauffeur him around Koppe on the murder trail of his sister but he suspects that she'll keep extending the hand. And he's right. She nods.

He stands up and moves to her office door.

'Wouldn't it be convenient,' he says, 'if it transpires it was an American tourist?'

'What do you mean?'

'What you said, about tourism. If it was an American who killed a British tour guide, well, that stops Koppe from being tarnished, doesn't it? It's still a safe place to holiday.'

Agatha's face creases in anger and it's the first time he's seen her look really unhappy with him.

'I've already told you, whether Vicky was killed by an American or a local is irrelevant. When people come here, we need them to know they have nothing to fear. Not through crime, anyhow.'

'Right,' Alex says. He studies her for another few seconds, then leaves.

She seems sincere, he thinks.

But Niamh's warning about the effectiveness of the local police is still ringing in his ears.

Outside, Alex breathes in the ridiculously cold air until his lungs sting.

Vicky might have just been ringing for money. Or maybe she wanted to make up and had been pissed when she finally realised that Alex must have changed his number.

But, she would have known she'd see him at Christmas. She could have had it out with him then.

There's no way she'd have rung his office to have a fight with him.

She knew how professional he was in work.

And yet, that's exactly what Vicky had done a couple of days before she'd died.

She'd phoned the offices of TM&S.

Koppe

1998

Kaya is half covered by the blanket, one leg and arm under, one leg and arm on top. Her hair is splayed across the sofa cushion; her right breast is exposed. The firelight behind her sends shadows dancing over her skin.

She knows she looks beautiful – he's seen her lying like this before and told her she's impossible to leave, that he has to lie back down with her. She remembers that time, her laughing, him telling her she'd be the death of him as his body hardened against her touch. Her husband has never made love to her twice in a row.

She's not sure her husband has ever made love to her, at all. Not like this.

But her lover is no longer looking at her with lust.

He's standing in the doorway staring at her, face aghast, abject shock in his eyes.

'No,' he says, just one word. He turns and leaves the room. Moments later, she hears the shower.

Kaya stays perfectly still; so still, she can hear her heart pounding in her chest.

I'm pregnant, she'd said. I'm carrying your child.

He'd jumped up as though scalded and fled to the door.

Minutes ago, he'd been inside her, whispering in her ear, the two of their bodies moving in sync.

Now, a valley stretches between them.

Is it mine? he'd asked. What if it's his?

It's not. It's yours. I love you. We can be together.

No.

Kaya is not a fool. She knows what this means.

Another woman might con herself into thinking he's just in shock, that he can be brought around.

Kaya knows better. She knew it when he rejected her the night she arrived at his door, the night she put his marriage in jeopardy.

In that one word – 'no' – he's given her his answer.

It's only ever been about the sex for him. All the I love yous and the whispers about staying together forever, they were said in passion. They were never meant to mean anything.

The fire is making the skin on her back tingle and the rug and blanket are still warm, but Kaya feels terribly, terribly cold. She sits up, finds her pants where they'd been discarded. She reaches for her bra, her thermal tights, her work blouse and the jeans she brought for the drive home.

She's dressed by the time the shower stops running.

She's almost made it to the door when he appears.

'Where are you going? Wait. I can drive you up the mountain. It's too cold for the snowmobile.'

He can't meet her eye.

She shakes her head.

'I don't need you to drive me. You've been drinking.'

'It never worried you before.'

'I was never pregnant with your child before.'

He flinches.

'We have to talk.'

'About what? You've made your feelings clear.'

'I don't know how this happened, Kaya.'

'You've been sticking your dick in me every week for the last six months. It's called biology.'

His face fills with embarrassment, then irritation.

'It hasn't happened for my wife,' he says. 'I thought – I thought it was me. And I supposed you were on the pill.'

'Congratulations. You're fertile.'

'Kaya, you need to get rid of it.'

She's already at the door, her coat on.

'Kaya, are you listening to me?'

She stops, turns, stares at him.

'I'll decide what I'm going to do,' she says. 'Whether that suits you or not.'

The scales have fallen from Kaya's eyes.

He's standing in front of her, his skin blotchy from the hot shower water. His stomach is a little flabby over his groin; his penis hangs limply between his legs. He's trying to project anger but sounds desperate, and yet, he thinks he's in control of the situation.

'And what about your husband?' he snaps. 'What do you think he'll do to you?'

'I guess I'll find out,' she says, managing to keep the fear from her voice as she turns to the door.

'Kaya!' He roars at her. 'Don't even think about walking out that door. We didn't agree to this. We both knew the score.'

He starts to cross the room. He looks so furious, she thinks he's about to hit her.

She doesn't wait. She throws open the door and runs.

He's naked, he can't follow.

By the time she's at the snowmobile, her whole body is shaking. I'm a cliché, she tells herself. As old as time. Pregnant and rejected by my lover. Left with the decision of whether to cuckold my husband or deal with my lot alone.

She takes the track towards the lake.

Out of the frying pan and into the fire.

Koppe

2019

Agatha has always enjoyed Patric's company. When they worked together, certainly, but maybe more so since he's retired.

Patric, at sixty, could have stayed on in his job as chief of Koppe police, but Agatha's predecessor wanted to pass the baton on. Now he talks as if his time in charge was another era.

What Agatha has always liked about Patric is that his years in the force didn't have a detrimental affect on him. Patric doesn't dwell on the horror and Agatha knows that he's seen plenty of that.

Patric, like Agatha, makes a point of highlighting the lighter side. He knows Agatha pulled a body out of the lake a few days ago. He was there, after all. In a town like this, those situations are about all hands on deck. But he doesn't ask her immediately what's happening. Instead, as she follows him through to his kitchen, he asks her if she's heard that the bar on the road to Neilim is closing.

'I'd forgotten it was still open,' Agatha says.

'That bar stayed open through the Second World War,' Patric says. 'My father used to drink in it, when he was driving the trucks.'

'Why's it closing now?'

'People come to town to drink.' Patric shrugs. 'It's easier, when everything is concentrated. Look at us in Koppe. A choice of bars. Big changes.'

'Makes policing a bit easier,' Agatha says. 'And we may have a choice, but we all still end up in Elliot's, don't we?'

Patric smiles.

'I got a call from the owner of the Neilim bar once,' Patric says. 'A few locals had got rowdy with some miners that had stopped in. Bit of a brawl had broken out. A couple of the miners were Russian. Age-old. I told the owner I wouldn't be there for three hours. I was dealing with some guy who'd knocked his wife's teeth out.'

'What did the bar owner do?'

'He rang the bell and told them to drink up, that it was closing time. It was only five in the afternoon. They were too pissed to notice. They reacted like sheep, emptied their glasses and left. Beat the crap out of each other on the road outside but it wasn't his bar that got smashed up.'

'Russians should know better than to go into an isolated bar full of Finns.'

'You'd think.'

They've taken seats at Patric's kitchen table; the old linoleum tablecloth is covered in circular marks made by hot cups over the years. Patric fusses at a pot of coffee and places two slices of home-made blueberry pie beside the coffee mugs. He's an excellent cook.

'Any word on the American?' he asks.

Agatha smiles.

'I suppose Jonas has been talking.'

'You know he can't keep a secret.'

They both laugh. Jonas wouldn't tell anybody if he was having a heart attack. Her other officer, Janic, though . . .

'Eat,' Patric says, nodding at the pie. 'You're skin and bone.'

'Oomf. I'm trying to lose a few pounds. I can't even feel my bones any more, I've so much cushioning.'

'You're too skinny, already. It's all the worrying.'

Agatha raises her eyebrows.

'And have you had something to worry about, lately?' Patric probes. 'Beside this case? Anything you need to tell me about?'

Patric knows everything. He knows that when the phone rings or there's a knock on the door, Agatha's first reaction is always panic.

'Not a thing,' she says, and that's true because there have been no calls or door knocks.

She just knows there will be, eventually.

'And the children?'

'I think they're okay. I hope. There are little flare-ups. But it's been two years.'

Patric nods then picks up her fork, cuts off some pie and holds it to Agatha's mouth until she's forced to eat, like a child.

She takes the fork and pretends to poke it at his eye.

'Enough, old man. I need your advice.'

'Leave this shithole and move to Helsinki.'

'So you've said, many times. You also made sure I was appointed to this job, so it's a little contradictory.'

'But you should be doing a better job in the capital. You're too smart for this town.'

'Apparently not. I've managed to track down the American. I'm just . . . not sure. Something doesn't add up.'

'You've interviewed him already?' Patric asks.

'Not properly. Spoke to a member of the police department where he lives. He has no record – one of the cops even knows him, says he's a good kid.'

'What are the chances of you finding the one person in America the cops have intimate knowledge of in a good way?'

Agatha laughs.

'He's from a small town, albeit in a big country. New England, seaside place.'

'So, what's not adding up?'

'He's at home and is acting normal. After murdering a young woman and dumping her body in a lake? And clearing out her cabin to fake her disappearance? Is he a complete psychopath?'

'You think they don't exist? And you don't know how he behaved for the day or two he was here after she disappeared. The fact he's acting regular at home might not mean anything. Maybe he's convinced himself it's all a bad dream now. It *could* have been an accident, you know. He might not see himself as a murderer. Just a guy who made a mistake. Seems to me, leaving her in the lake the way she was . . . it was amateurish.'

'I know,' Agatha says. 'But I feel like I shouldn't close off other avenues. We're going to speak to the people he was here with, too. If he was behaving strangely, then they should have picked up on it.'

'And what other avenues do you think you should be on?' Patric pours more coffee. Agatha takes a tentative sip, aware this is her sixth or seventh cup of the day and Patric makes it strong.

'One of the woman's friends said something,' Agatha says. 'About . . . about everybody knowing who killed her.'

Patric shakes his head, slowly.

'For God's sake,' he says.

'I know,' Agatha agrees. 'But should I . . . do you think I should interview him?'

Patric stands and walks to the sink. He pours the dregs of his coffee out and she can see his shoulders tense. He takes a few moments then turns around.

'For twenty years,' he says, 'every time something happens, his name comes up. A tourist missing for a few hours. A crash on the motorway. An accident on the slopes. Someone losing a cat. I'm so tired of it. Twenty years of people telling me I should arrest him for so much as the wind changing. Twenty years of people assuming they know how to do my job.'

'But . . . there has been reason to be suspicious of him,' Agatha says, cautiously.

Patric looks at her, like he's disappointed.

She exhales, a troubled sound.

'You want my opinion?' Patric says. 'Interview him, if you think there's a need. But Agatha, the man deserves some peace. I'm ashamed of how this town has treated him over the years. Me included. I would hate to see you pressured down the same path.'

Agatha listens and she hears what Patric is saying. He's right, of course he is. She just wanted to come and check.

Whoever murdered Vicky Evans, she will find them. Whether it was the American or somebody closer to home.

But she can't help the growing feeling in her stomach that something very bad has happened in Koppe. Is happening in Koppe.

Again.

Alex takes a slice of pizza from one of the many laid out on a long banquet table at the top of the hall.

He's in a giant vaulted room, reminiscent of some sort of royal dining area. Koppe Lodge is a series of separate buildings, he's learned. The main building contains the reception, bar and restaurant, and is the starting point of all the planned activities, including buses to the ski chairs.

Behind the Lodge are the saunas. Alex has never seen such an array of options for sweating to death. That building leads to the frozen lake, part of which has been kept ice-free so the tourists can have a dip after their eucalyptus sauna, or whatever else they've been enduring.

Beyond that building and across a little bridge is Santa's house, a quaint white and red wooden affair. Alex has seen children leaving there, gifts in hand. Then there's this communal dining hall, a huge building with giant entrance doors and a roaring log fire at its far end. It wouldn't be out of place on a *Game of Thrones* film set, Alex thinks.

Alex sees some of the staff gathered at the far end. They're all in what he now realises is the uniform of the activity guides. There are other staff in the Lodge, but these are clearly the ones who knew his sister best.

He eats the pizza slice without tasting it, though he is aware of it being slightly bitter. He glances at the sign in front of the plate he chose from. Reindeer pizza. Delightful. He wonders how much Rudolph he'll end up eating on this trip.

He walks to the end of the hall.

Niamh is at the table facing away from him; he spots her by her red hair. She's sitting beside the manager guy, Harry, Alex realises. They're hunched in a heated conversation – their body language marks them apart from the people they're sitting beside.

Niamh turns away from Harry, spots Alex, and slides off the bench.

'Come and join us,' she says.

Alex follows her, registering that she doesn't return to where she had been sitting but instead escorts him to the far side of the table. He tells himself it's because there isn't room for two to sit where she was, but a little part of him wonders if she's keeping him away from this Harry guy – or if Harry wants Alex kept away from him.

When Alex sits down, it's next to Nicolas.

'You've met most of the guys,' Niamh says, taking a pew on his other side. 'We're more or less the full guide contingent.'

She throws out some more names around the table. Alex nods at them in turn. With the exception of Harry, they're all in their twenties, early thirties at most. All of them look fresh-faced, healthy, outdoorsy types.

'I'm Harry, the manager.'

It speaks. Alex looks at the man and detects a Finnish accent, which he's starting to get more of an ear for.

'Harry's from Koppe,' Niamh says. 'One of the only locals.'

'You hired my sister?' Alex says.

'No,' Harry says, quietly. 'The owner does the hiring. I just manage the place.'

'You do the firing, though,' Nicolas says. 'Don't you, Harry?'

It sounds like a loaded statement.

'It was a ten-kilometre detour and one of the snowmobiles ended up in the lake.' Harry sighs.

Somebody leans over Alex's shoulder, places a bottle of something called 'Lapin Kulta' in front of him.

'Harry fired a new guide yesterday,' Nicolas says, bringing him up to speed. 'Just because the poor chap got a few tourists lost. It's not like they got frostbite or anything.'

'Safety first,' Harry says. He smiles; it looks more like a grimace to Alex.

'That's the motto around here, is it?' Alex says.

The group falls silent.

A woman down the far end of the table sits forward. Alex can see her properly now. Long blonde hair, big blue eyes. In London, she'd be on the cover of a magazine. In Koppe, she probably spends her days encased in oversized overalls, chaperoning wealthy tourists on sleigh jaunts.

'Vicky once brought a team on a cross-country ski and lost one of the group in the forest, remember?'

Fond smiles around the table greet her anecdote.

'She said he was picking berries,' the woman continues, 'and she forgot to count when they moved on. She only realised when they'd gone a couple of Ks that he wasn't with them. She didn't tell anybody he was missing, just brought them on a loop trail. Everything looks the same to them, they'd no clue. But then she spotted his tracks and realised he'd followed them. So, she brought the team back on another loop. But the guy had got to where they turned around and followed their tracks back down. And this went on until she figured out they were chasing each other in circles and she turned her group around, said they were going home and met the guy coming up on his third lap.'

'Vicky wasn't fired, just so you know,' Nicolas says. 'Too pretty to lose her job, eh, Harry?'

'Nobody complained,' Harry says, and he shrugs. Alex notices a faint softening in his expression.

It continues like this. The guides take turns to talk about their memories of Vicky.

Alex should be taking comfort from it, but instead he finds their tales excruciating.

They're doing what people do when somebody dies, he realises. They're making a saint of his sister. And he knows that's one thing Vicky wasn't. She was real and flawed and messy.

It's in the flaws and the messiness that he'll find out what caused her death, he thinks.

He notices Harry and Niamh stay quiet. Maybe Harry has no stories about her, Alex thinks. He's sure Niamh does, but he suspects, like him, she doesn't want to reminisce, not when she's still getting her head around the fact Vicky is gone.

The night wears on. People drink more. Harry leaves, the guides seem to relax more without the manager present, and a bottle of whiskey appears on the table.

Alex finds himself alone with Niamh as others drift away from the table.

'I know you all knew her,' Alex says. 'Maybe better than I did, these days. But this . . . eulogising. It doesn't sound like Vicky.'

Niamh smiles thinly.

'No,' she says. 'But what are people going to say? Sorry your sister died but this one time she phoned in with a hangover pretending she was sick and I had to do her bloody job for her, the bitch?'

'If that's all she did,' Alex says.

'Vicky wasn't an angel,' Niamh says, nodding. 'I'm telling you that as her best friend here, and I guess you already know. She could be blunt. A little selfish. But she was also kind and funny and, well, she was up for anything. I liked that.'

Alex takes a sip of beer.

'What you were saying earlier,' he says. 'About not trusting the police. What do you mean?'

Niamh glances around, warily.

'Ignore me,' she says. 'I was just ranting. It's . . . well, up here, tourism is everything. You know what I mean?'

Alex does know. The message is as subtle as a brick.

'The police think a tourist might have done it,' Alex says. 'An American.'

Niamh sucks in her cheeks.

'Hmm.'

'You know who he is?'

Her eyes fall from his. She knows.

He's surprised by her reticence, especially after her earlier forth-rightness. He wonders if somebody has had a word with her in the meantime.

'Please,' Alex says. 'I'd just like his name. He's not here any more, so it's not like I can confront the guy.'

'Fair enough,' Niamh says. 'I'm just not sure it's going to be any help. His name was Bryce Adams.'

'Bryce Adams. So, was she seeing this guy?'

'She spent some time with him. He was only here for a fortnight. Good-looking. Not very smart. But, cute. In an American-foot-baller kind of way. We get a lot of them over here – very rich, very into a more exclusive experience. It's far more expensive to come to Finnish Lapland than to hit the slopes in, say, France. Plus, they get all the adrenaline-junkie shit here. Climbing ice waterfalls. Driving Audis over frozen lakes. Snowboarding. You name it.'

'Right. And this Bryce Adams guy, he was into the extreme?'

'Yeah. He and his friends. And then at night, they hung out with Vicky and Beatrice and a couple of the other girls. I asked Vicky if she was into him, but she laughed it off. She was with him the night before she disappeared, though. Lots of people saw her go off with him. Then she was gone. And he left a couple of days later.'

'Did you see him, after?' Alex says. 'Did you ask him any questions?'

'No. I was busy and . . . well, like I said. When we saw she'd cleared her cabin, it was hard not to think she'd just left. That's what others said to me, anyway.'

'Others like who?'

'I don't know. Everybody. Anyway, no matter what I thought, I couldn't start interrogating guests.'

'But this Bryce guy was definitely the last known person with Vicky?'

Niamh shrugs.

'I don't know,' she says. 'It seems that way.'

'Did he seem the type to you?'

'The type to kill somebody? I mean, is there a type? Would so many girls get killed if there was a type we knew to watch out for?'

'Fair point,' Alex says.

Niamh sighs.

'Sometimes these guys, they come over and they get all pumped up. They drink too much, they think they can fuck all the tour guides. They can cause a bit of trouble but we've never had this before.'

Alex grits his teeth.

'Do you know where he was from?' Alex asks.

'They were wearing Patriots jerseys in the bar one night,' Niamh says. 'So, I'm guessing Boston or somewhere near there.'

Alex absorbs this. It's a start. Massachusetts is a big place, but a name and possible state is better than no name and fifty states.

Niamh downs a shot of whiskey. She's drinking too much, Alex thinks. He barely knows her, but he can see in her face she's not enjoying the alcohol; she's using it to numb herself.

He wonders how he'd have felt had he witnessed Vicky being taken out of that lake.

'Where are you from?' he asks, trying to distract Niamh from the whiskey and himself from his thoughts. 'Sorry, I haven't asked you anything about yourself. I've also been meaning to thank you—'

'Honestly, don't,' she says, quietly. 'Don't thank me. She was my friend. In as much as you can be in one of these jobs. I used to work in Thailand, a rep at a beach resort. I hung out with a couple of girls for an entire summer, thought we'd be mates for life. I haven't spoken to them, bar the odd comment on their Insta pages, in about three years. But Vicky was different and I suppose, even if we did go home eventually, Yorkshire's not that far from Dublin. We probably would have met up.'

'Dublin?'

'Yeah. Though, I haven't been home in a few years. Not properly, not for more than a week here or there. Don't really get on great with my family, you know.'

'Vicky was never home,' Alex says.

Niamh frowns.

'You look surprised,' he says.

'She talked about you all a lot. I assumed – well, I know she was here all this year – but I presumed you were close. She was much fonder of all of you than I am of my lot.'

Alex swallows. He takes a sip of beer to wash down the lump in his throat.

'She tried to ring me,' he says. 'A few times, the week before she died.'

Niamh stares at him.

'I think she needed me,' he adds.

'Don't blame yourself,' Niamh says. 'Blame the person who killed her.'

'If I can find out who that is and why they did it.'

Niamh nods sympathetically, but he notices she looks away quickly.

He follows her eyes. She's looking over at the other guides, now lounging around the fire at the end of the hall.

His gut is telling him there's more that Niamh isn't telling him. That she has more to say about Vicky.

Nobody wants to add to your pain, he thinks.

And that's quickly followed by: *Vicky, what the hell were you up to over here?*

Agatha can hear Olavi moving before she sees him. She's sitting up in bed, Vicky Evans' case file on her lap, the photos from the lake and the morgue splayed across the crocheted bedspread. She's been wondering how many officers she can bring in from surrounding areas to help blitz through Koppe on a door-to-door. If they can't send help, she'll have to go cap in hand to Rovaniemi and that will entail ceding some control of the investigation.

She's also been wondering why Vicky was so eager to get hold of her brother in the week before she went missing. They're still making their way through the other numbers on Vicky's call log but Alex's is the only one she attempted more than once. There's an English landline in the records that Agatha now knows belongs to a lobbying firm in London. Where Alex works, Agatha suspects, though he didn't mention it. He might have missed it, amid the shock of seeing his old mobile number there. Agatha wants to give him the benefit of the doubt. She doesn't want to think that she also has to contend with Vicky's brother keeping secrets from her.

Had Vicky been in debt of some kind? Her bank account details had come through this afternoon. The balance was healthy – very healthy, in fact – and she had no credit card bills outstanding. It didn't look on paper like Vicky was in need of cash. She seemed to have been saving a regular amount every month since summer – €2,000 every four weeks, almost all of her monthly salary. Agatha wonders if that had something to do with her suggestion of an expensive anniversary gift for her parents. Had her argument with Alex inspired Vicky to live frugally and put proper money away so she could prove him wrong?

Was that why she'd phoned him? So she could tell him she'd enough saved to pay her way?

Olavi comes in just as Agatha grabs the last close-up photo of Vicky's head wound and stuffs it into the folder.

His eyes are barely open, the top of his arm is a furious red and he's sniffling.

She lifts up the bedspread and he climbs in, wordlessly, lying with his face away from her as she spoons his back and strokes his hair.

'The bad dream?' she asks him.

He nods.

She looks over his shoulder at the top of his arm. The mouth shield is working; the skin is sore but at least it's intact.

'You're safe here, my darling,' she says. She smells his hair. It's getting darker every year. Olavi was practically blond when he was born. He still uses the same baby shampoo as Onni, even though she's told him, at eight, he can use a more grown-up version. She thinks Olavi is unconsciously trying to stretch out his childhood as long as possible. Perhaps if he has another few years, he can block out the trauma he experienced early on.

'Nobody is coming,' Agatha whispers. 'It's just us four. You, me, Emilia and Onni, okay? We'll always be together.'

'You promise?'

He already sounds half asleep again, safe and warm in her bed.

'I promise.'

Agatha's tired, too. She's starting to drift off, thinking she must remember to turn off the bedside lamp, when Olavi speaks again.

'I saw Luca.'

Agatha's whole body is at once awake and alert. She tries not to react, not to jump up from the bed to check the doors and windows. She concentrates on keeping very still and her voice very even, though her mouth is dry and her heart is thumping.

'When?' she says.

'Last week.'

'Where?'

'Outside school. When we were playing.'

Agatha's mind races frantically through the timeline. Last week . . . it's about a week since the biting started up again.

Now it makes sense.

Last week. She had been in town, right up until she'd had to go down to Rovaniemi, and she hadn't seen Luca. Does he really mean last week? Olavi still gets time mixed up. Sometimes he'll say, *remember yesterday*, and he'll be referring to something that had happened days ago.

'What were you playing?' she asks him.

'Helmi let us build a snow fort. She said we could put pine cones in it for the elves.'

Agatha remembers. It was a mild day and Helmi had let the children outside. She'd confessed to Agatha that evening that she'd hosted a birthday party for her sister the night before and had a wine headache, so she had needed the fresh air as much as the kids. Agatha had seen the children in the yard when she'd passed by on the way to interview one of the local Sami herders about a lost, possibly stolen, reindeer. She hadn't stopped; didn't want to get stuck there talking to Helmi or have Olavi begging her to climb into his fort.

That was seven or eight days ago. If Agatha had been around, Luca would have known to hide. Then, when Agatha was out of sight, Luca must have emerged . . .

Agatha feels sick. She doesn't even think to ask Olavi if he's sure. She knows the children fear Luca's return but they've never gone so far as to have dreamt it up. The last time any of them had seen Luca, they'd seen Luca. It hadn't been a figment of their imagination. And it had thrown their lives into disarray.

Agatha won't let it happen again.

Alex wakes early, his head still fuzzy from the night before. He hadn't meant to fall asleep straight after returning to the cabin, but a combination of all the travelling, the Arctic air and the beer had knocked him out. He sees his phone on the pillow across from him and vaguely remembers he'd been looking up something just before he fell asleep.

Bryce Adams. The American.

Alex sits up. It's 7 a.m. He has fifteen work-related emails – he can already see Charlie responding to the Cassidy account ones and looping Alex in. There's a text from his father, which must have come in last night. Two words – *any news?*

No news is good news, right? Except in this instance.

Alex gulps down half a bottle of water and opens Facebook, an app he has an account on but never uses.

There are too many Bryce Adamses to count.

Alex opens Instagram. He doesn't have an Insta account and has to set one up to view other users' photos and comments.

Hundreds of Bryce Adamses.

He googles the name and Boston.

Too many hits.

To hell with this, he thinks.

He phones Charlie.

Wakes Charlie.

'What? Oh, thank my lucky stars, Alex boy. Must have knocked the alarm off. Late night.'

'Sorry,' Alex says. 'Charlie, that help you were offering me?'

'Wait. Pen. Need pen. Have to write this down. Think I'm still drunk. Might need a reminder.'

Alex listens to Charlie scrambling for the back of some receipt or other, then for a pen.

'I need to find a Bryce Adams. A Yank. Might be from Massachusetts, or might just have a thing for the Patriots. Travelled to Lapland in late October, early November. In his twenties, bit of an adrenaline chaser.'

'This is fun. I feel like a PI. Hey, do you think private investigator sounds sexier than lobbyist?'

'Everything sounds sexier than lobbyist. Charlie, you know this social media shit. How do I get Facebook and Insta to let me into Vicky's accounts? If I contact them—'

'You'll die of old age before they respond. You're better off hacking in. Take a guess at her password.'

That hadn't worked for the police, Alex thinks.

'By the way,' Charlie says. 'Closed the Cassidy account late last night. Government is giving them the Channel ports. You're welcome.'

'What do you mean, you closed it? They didn't make a decision to give that port contract in the last forty-eight hours. If it's closed, it's a miracle and it's because of the work I did.'

'Listen, there's no need to get upset, I'll make sure the partners know you had a hand.'

'Jesus Christ.'

'You're not gonna lose it, mate, are you? Is *Stainless Steel* about to crack?'

Alex takes a deep breath. Ruthless fuck.

'Charlie, shush. Tell me, who would have been working in reception in October?'

'Our reception? Bloody hell, man, don't you notice these things? Josephine, the blonde. She's been there since summer.'

Alex thanks Charlie and hangs up. It's too early to ring the office.

He sighs and sends his father a text – *No news, anything from Mum?* – and heads to the shower. When he returns, his father has typed back, *No news.*

At the station, a different officer, young with Elvis sideburns, tells Alex that Agatha isn't in work yet. He helpfully gives Alex directions to Agatha's house, which is just a street away from the station.

Alex can't imagine a situation in England where he'd be sent to the chief of police's home, even in Apple Dale, which is a relatively small village. But he doesn't question it. It's the exact convenience he needs.

He walks past a couple of sports shops on the main street en route to Agatha's and thinks he ought to buy some more appropriate clothing. Agatha's thermals and winter coat are doing their job but Alex still only has the bare minimum to wear over the thermals. Plus, Agatha hadn't taken it on herself to buy him underwear, which brings its own problems.

At a stall selling hot chocolate and gingerbread men, Alex asks where he can find a shop to buy regular, non-ski clothes. The stallholder frowns, then suggests Alex go to the K-Market on the way into town. Or, he could call into the Versace store a few streets down. Alex is mind-blown. A supermarket or the local Versace outlet. How very ski resort.

The police chief's house is a small chalet with the same pointed roof as its neighbours and fairy lights strung around the inside of the frosted windows. He has to knock several times on Agatha's front door, inhaling the scent of the pine wreath hanging from a nail in front of his nose, before it's opened; a tentative gap, through which a dark-haired teenage girl peeks out.

'Is Agatha here?' he asks.

'Who are you?' she says.

Another face pokes through the gap lower down – the fairer-haired little boy from the police station.

'It's the man whose sister died,' the kid says.

He reaches past his sister and pulls the door open completely.

'Onni!' she snaps.

It's quickly followed by a roar, this time from Agatha.

'Emilia! Onni! What have I told you about the door!'

Agatha appears. Alex has only known her the last thirty-six hours or so but this is the first time he's seen her properly ruffled. More than ruffled, in fact; she looks scared.

She catches sight of him on the porch and her countenance changes instantly, from fear to confusion, but in her eyes he can still see the remnants of whatever had passed through her mind when she saw the open door.

'I'm sorry to disturb you at home,' he says. 'The guy at the station . . .'

'No. It's fine. Sorry, I didn't mean to shout.'

She's speaking more to the children than him. Behind her, he sees another kid emerge. He's aged somewhere between these two, definitely too old to be sucking his thumb, which he's doing right now.

He's still in his pyjamas. They all are, Alex realises. Agatha is wearing a large sweater over a pair of check bottoms. He's embarrassed; he'd presumed she'd be at the station by 8.30 a.m. but he's gone and woken the whole family, by the looks of things.

'I'm running late,' Agatha says. 'Please. Come in.'

Alex follows Agatha through to the kitchen.

'Emilia, make Alex some tea or coffee. I'll get dressed. Um, we can go straight to the lake, but I have to bring the kids somewhere afterwards, so they'll be in the car.'

'Mom, you said we were staying home—'

The teenager, Emilia, addresses Agatha, but Agatha cuts her off.

'Not now, Emilia.'

Alex has always very firmly placed himself in the category of not-a-dick but he's also never been in the category of brother-to-a-murder-victim before and he can't help but feel impatient at this woman's disorganisation. At the station yesterday, she'd impressed him with her preparedness for his questions. Now, he's having very unkind thoughts about mothers of young children being given important jobs.

Vicky would have torn him a new one if he'd uttered that thought aloud.

'Sure,' he says, mentally planning the call home to get hold of somebody in the Met.

Agatha hesitates and he can tell she wants to defend her situation. Instead, she bites her lip and rushes from the kitchen.

Fifteen minutes later and after a lot of kid-wrangling on her part, Alex and Agatha are in her car and heading on the road out of town to see where his sister was found dead.

Alex looks over his shoulder at the three kids in the back. The girl is on her phone, the two boys on tabs.

The middle kid, the one whose name he doesn't know, speaks without even looking up.

'Do you know how to play Roblox?'

'I do not,' Alex says.

'What do you know how to play?'

'Poker,' Alex says without hesitation. 'And Call of Duty.'

'Is that the one with the sex workers and car thieves?' the teenage girl asks.

'Emilia,' Agatha says.

'Sex workers?' Alex repeats.

'Prostitute is an offensive term,' Emilia says. 'Though I suppose in that game, they're called hoe—'

'Emilia!'

Alex almost smiles.

The car falls silent again.

'That's Grand Theft Auto,' Alex says, after a few minutes. Agatha grimaces. The kids giggle.

They've been driving for fifteen, maybe twenty minutes.

Alex might be imagining it, but Agatha seems to be relaxing the further they get from town.

'It's a long way,' he says.

'Not much further.'

'I guess I thought it would be closer to the resort,' he says. 'How come she was this far away?'

Agatha glances in the rear-view mirror at the kids, then makes a face at Alex that tells him to hold off until they've arrived.

She pulls off the road and they descend around a hair-raising bend, made more terrifying by the fact the ground beneath them looks and feels to Alex like sheer ice. Worse, Agatha drives like she doesn't expect to meet anybody, taking the turn wide.

'You're a skilled driver,' Alex says. 'I can't even see where one lane starts and another ends.'

Agatha shrugs.

'Winter tyres,' she says. 'Plus, it's deserted.'

'But you get some traffic, right?'

'Of course, but everybody takes it easy. That's why it takes so long to get anywhere. Crashes are one of our worst fears, to be honest.'

'What do you mean?'

'Some of the resorts use tour buses; there might be twenty or thirty on board. If one crashes somewhere outside a town, it could be a while before we hear about it and then it takes a while to get to them. And if they're not already dead in the crash . . .'

'The cold gets them,' Emilia says from the back. 'You should never leave your vehicle. Not while it's still warm.'

She sounds deadly serious. Something in her knowing tone makes Alex shiver. He wonders how young is too young up here to learn about such awful things. Or whether that kind of warning is fed to kids with their mother's milk.

They arrive at their destination and park up. Agatha leaves the keys in the ignition and the heating on as she and Alex get out of the car.

'It's taken us a while to drive here,' Agatha says, as they walk in the direction of the lake. Alex can see its frozen mass through the thin, leafless trees that poke up from the snow. 'We'd have been here quicker by snowmobile,' Agatha continues. 'Everybody crosses their nearest section of the lake in winter, you see. Very few drive around it.'

They clear the reedy trees and arrive at the lake's edge; Agatha walks straight on to the snow covering it.

Alex hesitates. It takes a couple of seconds for her to realise she's not with him.

'What are you doing?' Agatha calls back.

Alex stares at the thin layer of snow in front of him.

'It takes getting used to,' he says. 'The notion of stepping on to a lake.'

'But you're already on it,' she says, confused.

Alex frowns. He looks down at his feet again, kicks away some of the snow, realises that there's packed ice beneath.

'We're *parked* on it,' Agatha continues.

'What?'

Alex glances back at the car.

'But the trees,' he says.

'They're in the water,' Agatha says. 'Alex, parts of this lake are so thick, they race cars across it. You've seen the advertisements. The big hotel in Koppe is hosting an annual Porsche event as we speak.'

'But Vicky . . .'

'Six weeks ago. Inari had only started to freeze. The ice was still thin in parts.'

Alex takes that in. If his sister had been on the lake six weeks later, does that mean she'd still be alive?

But of course not. She didn't just drown. She was attacked.

He follows Agatha. Daylight has arrived and now he can see how isolated they are. He does a 360-degree turn – all he can see for miles is the open expanse of the lake and the surrounding trees. You could scream yourself hoarse out here; nobody would hear you.

They walk for a couple of minutes until they arrive at some markers on the ice.

'This is where she was found,' Agatha says. 'But that doesn't mean it's where she went in. The lake is over one thousand square kilometres and she could have floated from anywhere. She could have been over the other side when she went in.'

'It feels so isolated.'

'Well, you know. Everything *is* up here. Next stop east is Russia.'

Agatha points in the distance, then pivots and nods back in what Alex thinks might be the direction of town.

'Through the trees over there, can you see it?'

Alex squints but he's not sure what she's looking at. She pulls a small pair of binoculars out of her coat pocket, focuses them and hands them to Alex.

He looks through the sights and spots a rooftop.

'That's the dining hall at the resort,' Agatha says. 'There are trails on the lake where they take the snowmobilers and cross-country skiers. Vicky was scheduled to check the cross-country trails early that morning. I don't know if she ever did. Certainly none of the other guides saw her.'

'So, she could have been attacked at any time, anywhere,' Alex says, quietly. 'Which means, you really do have no murder scene.'

He knows enough to understand this is a problem.

'Precisely,' Agatha says. 'I have to build this case based on verbal evidence. I need people to talk.'

'And what if they lie?'

'I'm very good at being able to tell when somebody is lying,' Agatha says. 'Eventually.'

'Eventually?' Alex snorts.

'Yes. I've found, Alex, that a lot of people are good at telling a lie once. Twice even. But it takes a lot of skill to continue lying. To be consistent with the detail.'

Alex shakes his head.

'You don't believe me,' she says.

'I work in a business where people lie for a living,' Alex says.

'Yes, but I'm sure everybody is expecting everybody else will lie,' Agatha says.

Alex shrugs. She has him there.

'I'm sorry,' he says. 'I don't know what I thought I'd see coming out here. It felt important.'

Agatha glances at the markings on the ice.

'I would have done the same,' she says.

Alex wants to move his feet to walk back to the car but he can't seem to make them work. There might be nothing here now, but it's hit him: this is where his sister's body was brought back up on land. If that fisherman hadn't been here, how long would Vicky have been underwater? Would she have ever been discovered? What if her body had got caught in reeds?

He shudders, unable to expel the thought from his mind.

'This lake is sacred to Sami people,' Agatha says.

'They're the indigenous population?' Alex says.

Agatha nods.

'You're not Sami?' he asks.

'No. Janic is. You met him in the station this morning. Inari, the town further up, houses the Sami parliament. We've a few Sami working down here but they mainly farm reindeer. They've been very badly treated by Finnish people and non-Sami Laplanders over the years. Tend to keep to themselves.'

She hesitates, reluctant to make him leave but clearly eager to get going.

'Will we?'

Agatha nods in the direction of the car.

Alex crouches down. He touches the ice.

Then he stands and makes himself walk.

As he follows Agatha, he feels a buzzing in his pocket. He takes off his mitten, feels the bite of the cold on his fingers almost immediately. He reaches inside the pocket of the coat for his phone, which buzzes again with a second text message. They're both from Charlie. The first is a screenshot of a photograph from Instagram that Alex hasn't seen before. It's a picture of Vicky and a man. They're both smiling; the man has a mouthful of blinding white teeth and both are wearing the ubiquitous blue ski suits he's seen on half the tourists at the Lodge. They have sun visors pushed up on their heads and the man has his arm around Vicky. Alex squints at the photograph. In the upper left corner, he sees the Insta handle name for Bryce Adams from Georgetown. The second message says: *Found your boy, that's him in the pic. Haven't got number for him yet, try a DM?*

'Something important?' Agatha has halted her progress and is studying his face.

Alex looks up.

'Just home,' he says.

'Don't take your mittens off too much,' she says. 'Or have your phone out for long. The cold saps the battery. Even if it is mild today.'

'This is mild? I can't feel my face.'

'This is practically balmy, my friend.'

In the car, the temperature had said minus seven.

'I'll be right behind you,' he says. 'I'll send a quick reply.'

If Agatha is wondering why he wouldn't wait until they were back in the vehicle, she doesn't say. She cocks her head, examines him with that knowing gaze of hers, then turns and walks back.

Alex opens his new Insta account, briefly wonders how he already has five followers, and uses it to search for Bryce's account. From there, he sends a quick direct-message request.

His fingers are trembling. Mostly from the cold, but partly adrenaline.

Then, before he returns to the car, he stares one last time at the spot on the lake where Vicky was found.

Koppe

1998

Kaya mainly draws from memory, but sometimes she gets lucky. Today, there's a skulk of foxes out. Only the kits. Their parents are busy hunting.

She watches them through the trees, their fur white and soft as they gambol through the snow.

It's the smallest that has caught her eye, though, the one that's still blue-grey. He's a little apart from his siblings, not taking part in the nipping and play-fighting.

It's this one Kaya has chosen to draw. The outsider.

She supposes she's always felt that way herself. She has never quite fit with people the way she's supposed to, her husband included. She doesn't even know why they married. He was just there. They'd come up through school in Koppe together, though he didn't hang around the town much. He was always working on his parents' farm, or out herding when there were even more deer. This farm. He was quieter than her peers and Kaya probably thought that meant he was different, too. Unusual. Mysterious. She read in a magazine once that the red flags you see in the first days of a relationship are usually the same red flags that cause a break-up. And she'd realised early that her husband's silence wasn't mysterious. He was just dull.

When she turned sixteen, she let him take her virginity out on the island on Inari. It felt risqué. The Samis' beloved island, rumoured to have been a place of ritual and sometimes sacrifice. But the excitement was all in her head. In reality, it was a stiflingly hot summer's eve, her back was scratched by the twigs on the ground beneath her, he'd sweated all over her and the poking he did between her legs left her less breathless and more just sticky and in pain.

Four years later, they were married. He'd asked and Kaya had said yes. Why? Because she could. Because there weren't a lot of guys her age in Koppe. Because he was big and strong. Because he wanted her. Yes, he was dull. But being alone was worse.

Her parents were devastated by her choice of partner. His mother, already three years dead, wasn't there to see the wedding. His father barely caught the ceremony, before a heart attack took him, too. So the first year of their married life was spent with Kaya adjusting to the fact that at twenty, she was now a farmer's wife. Getting married so young felt daring. Being stuck halfway up the mountain hadn't been part of the plan.

But she adjusted and she was willing to give it a go. She might have been playing at housewife, but she found, oddly, that she was quite good at it.

A year later, she had come to the realisation that settling for boring wasn't just a temporary arrangement. There was no excitement in her husband; moreover, he was now too fond of the drink to be of any use to her. A few months after that, she was fucking somebody else. She was only young, after all.

Now, at twenty-two years of age, Kaya is unhappily married, carrying somebody else's child, and that man doesn't want her either.

Her mother always said Kaya only had one foot in this world, the other in her fantasies. Drawing has always helped. On the page, she can create something real. Something beautiful. It comes naturally to her. Teachers had told her that. You should go to Helsinki, Kaya, they would say. Go to art school. But she didn't take their advice. Now all she has to show for her dreams is her drawing book, the few sketches that hang in the bar and the odd painting her husband lets her frame.

Kaya looks up and realises the kit is staring straight at her.

They gaze at each other for a few seconds. Kaya's heart rate and her breathing slow down.

She wonders if he can sense the baby growing inside her. If he knows that she's already a mother. Animals are intuitive like that. She's already noticed the reindeer and horses are more gentle around her. Not the huskies. They don't seem to care; they're just bundles of endless yapping energy.

Maybe it's not too late. She could go to Helsinki, have the baby, try to manage alone. Nobody knows her there. They wouldn't know what she'd done, the mistakes she'd made. They wouldn't judge.

But that chance to start again would also mean she'd be on her own. No money. No family. No friends.

She hears a noise on the porch behind her. She's been so focused on the young fox, she didn't even hear her husband come out of the house.

He's looking down at her drawing book. Kaya doesn't move a muscle. She's praying he doesn't want to look at the other pages.

There are pictures in there she doesn't want him to see.

He gave her this book, but she knows, in his heart, he considers her art a silly hobby. Sometimes, with drink on him, he goes further and tells her how little talent she has, because if she had any talent then she wouldn't be there, would she? She wouldn't be with him, on this useless reindeer farm in the middle of nowhere. Kaya might not understand everything but this she does: her husband places little value on himself and, therefore, little value on her for choosing him.

She braces herself. She can't smell alcohol, but that doesn't mean anything. She must always be prepared.

'That's beautiful.'

His words are so unexpected, they provoke more of a reaction from Kaya than if he'd hit her.

'What?' she yelps.

'Your drawing. It's very beautiful. You've captured his eyes perfectly.'

Kaya looks at her page, then back at the forest. The foxes are already gone, disturbed by the sound of humans talking.

'I . . . thank you.'

'You should put it in a frame,' he says.

Kaya doesn't know what to say. He hasn't let her hang anything in months. Said the house was starting to look like a cheap-ass art gallery.

'Thank you. I will.'

She feels his hand on her shoulder. His hands have always been rough, strong, even when they were only teens. They attracted her to him. She'd forgotten what his hands felt like. She'd become so used to yearning for her lover's hands.

'We've both been working hard lately,' her husband says.

Kaya nods without speaking.

'Let's treat ourselves,' he says. 'Let's go to town, have a nice dinner. Act our age.'

Kaya swallows. She manages to nod again. He squeezes her shoulder. She places her hand on his, squeezes back.

Then he completely shocks her as he leans down and kisses her head.

'I'm sorry this is so hard,' he says.

He leaves. Kaya is too stunned to react.

Was that – was he being nice to her?

She slams the book shut and sits perfectly still.

Maybe this can be fixed. He had so much thrust on him with the farm when his father died. Within a year, he'd had to sell half his herd and he still struggled to pay the hands he'd brought in to help take care of the rest. He must be terrified, a lot of the time, trying to make it all work. But they've made it this far. Things seem to be going well, the reindeer are selling. She hears him saying things like that, when she lends him half an ear.

She's only five, six weeks gone, at most. If she slept with him tonight? If they had sex now – would he ever know?

For the first time in a long time, Kaya feels something blossoming inside.

Hope. She feels hope.

Koppe

2019

Agatha doesn't want the children out of her sight, but at the same time she can't do her job with them in the back of her car all day. She brings them to school late but she asks Helmi to keep an eye on the little ones and tells an irritated Emilia that she has to stay in at break time.

When she gets to the station, Lassi Niemenen, the owner of Koppe Lodge, is waiting for her.

He stands when she enters reception and follows her to her office, grumbling all the way.

'You summon me here, then you're not around when I arrive,' he says. 'I'm a very busy man, Agatha. And I've a council meeting today.'

'I was on police business,' Agatha says, though she's just back from the school. She holds open the door to her office and lets him walk in ahead of her. He doesn't thank her and she notes with no small degree of satisfaction that the bald spot on the back of Lassi's head is marching on.

She's never liked Lassi. He's in his late fifties now and still considers

123

himself some sort of stud. His hair – at the front, at least – is too long for a man his age and he wears his dark beard in a distinctive goatee fashion that makes her think of the devil. She's certain he uses hair dye, too.

Lassi has a reputation and he's very happy with it. He's slept with half of Koppe, by his account, and he always makes sure to hire the best-looking girls in the Lodge. Lassi is also married, though for the life of her, Agatha can't understand why his wife hangs on.

He tried it on with Agatha once. When she rebuffed him, he moved on to her sister and got luckier there. Of course he did; Agatha's sister never had any taste in men.

Now, when Lassi looks at her, sometimes Agatha thinks he's imagining her sister and it makes her skin crawl.

'So, what do you need?' he says, checking his watch like he's the busiest man in the world.

'Vicky Evans was murdered,' Agatha says. 'I'm sure the Koppe grapevine has been in action.'

She knows her junior, Janic, will have told his mother, who will have told her neighbours, who in turn will have spent the night on the phone to everybody in Koppe. That's not to mention Niamh Doyle telling everybody at the Lodge, and Alex's presence there.

'I heard. Terrible business. But, she'd left the Lodge, hadn't she?'

Lassi is already sitting. He shrugs – the very act of it makes Agatha want to punch him in the face.

She takes a deep breath, and her own chair, and faces him.

'Her stuff was packed up and taken from her cabin. We don't know if she was the one who removed it.'

'Well, who else would?'

'Whoever killed her.'

Lassi laughs. Agatha bristles.

'I don't see what's funny,' she says.

'Oh, come on. What you're suggesting is nonsensical. Somebody murdered the girl then came and packed up her belongings? She was hit on the head, wasn't she? Doesn't exactly sound like the work of an organised killer.'

'Really?' Agatha says. 'How would you kill somebody?'

The smile slides sideways off Lassi's face. His eyes become slants as he stares at Agatha.

'Isn't it more likely she left the Lodge to be with some guy or other and they fell out? I've heard a rumour she was seeing one of the tourists. Some American. Maybe she thought he'd take her home with him. You know what these girls are like. He probably dumped her stuff in the lake and you haven't found it.'

'Vicky Evans was a British citizen. She didn't *need* to find herself a Western boyfriend to rescue her. Not like some of the girls you hire.'

This is old-trodden ground for Agatha and Lassi. She's convinced some of the temp staff he's had in have been illegals. They never stay long enough for her to prove it. But she keeps watching. She knows Lassi's Lodge is in competition with the ski hotel. He never lets on but it has to be affecting his business. The hotel offers better packages, is more affordable, and it's bigger, able to carry loss leaders. She's positive if Lassi has found ways to cut corners on expenses, he's cutting them.

'The girls I hire are all above board,' Lassi says.

He shrugs and again she feels that familiar crawling on her skin.

This is a man who places all 'girls' in the same two categories, Agatha thinks.

Fuckables and unfuckables.

'Did you have much contact with Vicky?' she asks.

'She was a nice kid, I recall.'

'Twenty-six when she died. Hardly a kid.'

'You get to my age, everyone under forty is a kid.'

What does that make you? Agatha wants to say, but doesn't.

'So, this nice kid, as you call her, is working in your Lodge. She disappears, without notice or any indication of where she's gone, and it takes two weeks before one of her friends comes to see me. Nobody in any official capacity at the Lodge was concerned.'

'Isn't hindsight a wonderful thing, Agatha? It can take something innocent, like a girl moving on from her job, and make it appear sinister in the blink of a retrospective eye. Ask any business owner. Employees leave. Sometimes without notice. You're only ever a job to these people. There's no loyalty. Even when you pay them well and give them good conditions, they've free will. Should we assume that each time an employee departs from the payroll, they've been murdered? You certainly didn't. From what I've heard, you were no more concerned than anybody else.'

'Don't you all refer to yourselves in the Lodge as one big happy family? If your sister or daughter suddenly didn't come in to work, wouldn't you be concerned?'

He's smirking at her now. Agatha knows it's because he's thinking of her sister and how utterly unreliable she always was in any and every job. Agatha doesn't react. She just sits there, unblinking, and waits for his answer, refusing to let the colour that's rising up her neck go any further.

'Well, I don't have any sisters or daughters,' Lassi says. 'And as I said, I agree this is a terrible business. Hopefully you catch the

American guy. I am very concerned, Agatha. Don't think I'm not. News like this is extremely bad. You and I both know it's important that everybody sees Koppe as a safe destination.'

'Heaven forbid your business is affected,' Agatha says.

'Which would you rather?' Lassi snaps. 'Skiers on the hills or excavation machines? You know how badly those corporate types want access to our mountain? Koppe is built on money, Agatha. If you only knew the sort of offers I've seen made to the council for mining licences . . . people could be tempted, you know.'

Agatha feels her jaw clench. She counts to ten, calms herself down. To acknowledge Lassi as some sort of saviour of Koppe is something she just can't do.

'So, for the record,' she says. 'You had no interaction with Vicky, other than hiring her? You didn't see her afterwards?'

Lassi stares at her.

'I *saw* her,' he says. 'But I didn't *see* her, if that's what you're getting at. I'm a married man.'

Agatha swallows the snort that threatens to expel itself.

'If that's all,' Lassi says.

He stands up.

'How did you know about the American?' Agatha asks.

'What?'

'You heard a rumour she was seeing an American tourist. From whom? It's not like you to be hanging around with the staff at the Lodge.'

Lassi hesitates.

'I saw them in Elliot's bar that night. Vicky, a few others from my staff and the group of Americans staying there. I was at the poker night. All night. Ask Elliot.'

Elliot, owner of the most frequented bar in town and one of Lassi's inner circle.

She watches Lassi leave.

She knows he's lying to her.

She'd lay money on Lassi having tried it on with Vicky Evans.

But did he do more than that?

Back at the cabin, Alex checks his new Instagram account. There's still no reply from Bryce Adams. Alex wonders if he'll even see the message; whether people notice DM requests from those they're not following on Instagram. The guy has fifteen hundred followers; maybe his inbox is full of messages from people he actually knows. Plus, Alex wasn't exactly direct. *We have a mutual contact, can we speak?* What else could he have said? *I think you might have murdered my sister, or at least fucked her the night she died. Give me a call?*

Alex didn't want to mention Vicky at all, in case he scared the guy off.

But now, he has nothing. Not even an indication the message has been read.

He dials reception at TM&S.

'Hello, you're through to the offices of Thompson, Mayle & Sinclair. Josephine speaking. How may I help you?'

'Josephine. Hello. This is Alex Evans.'

There's a sharp intake of breath.

He can barely picture the face of the woman on the other end of the line. He has a vague memory of a blonde at the reception desk, but most of his interactions with reception have been via the group secretary upstairs. Also, unlike Charlie, Alex doesn't mentally note the dimensions of every woman he meets.

'Mr Evans. I was so sorry to hear your news.'

'Thank you. Josephine, can I check something with you?'

'Anything.'

'My sister placed a call to our offices on 30th October. I never got the message or, if I did, I don't recall the details. I know it's a long shot, but do you remember taking the call?'

'Of course!'

Alex blinks. He wasn't expecting such an emphatic yes.

'I was literally only telling somebody that I'd spoken to your sister, Mr Evans. She seemed like a lovely woman.'

'Right. I see. Why was there no message for me?'

'She didn't leave one. She actually asked that I didn't disturb you when you returned to the office either. You weren't here, you see. You were at a meeting.'

Alex frowns.

'Did she tell you why she was calling?'

'No, I'm afraid not.'

'She didn't sound upset or anything, did she? Did she happen to mention a guy's name – a Bryce Adams, maybe?'

Josephine falls quiet and Alex imagines she's thinking hard. Anybody who can remember a call from over six weeks ago, when that person probably handles hundreds of calls a day, is a conscientious individual.

'She sounded absolutely fine,' she says. 'Maybe a little . . . I don't know, embarrassed? When I said you were out, she was relieved, I think. As though she regretted calling the office, to be honest, and not your mobile phone.'

Alex hangs his head.

Vicky *wouldn't* have phoned his office unless she really needed him.

But he's no closer to knowing what she wanted.

'Oh,' Josephine exclaims. 'She did say one thing.'

Alex sits up.

'She said she'd send you an email instead.'

Alex thanks Josephine quickly and hangs up.

And checks his emails, again.

Nothing.

She was going to send him an email, so why didn't she?

He'd received nothing from her regular account. Nothing from the account the police don't yet seem to be aware of.

Alex shivers.

He stands up and turns the heating dial on the wall up a few notches. No matter what he does over here, he can never get properly warm. He doesn't know if he's just not made for this temperature, or if the tiredness and perhaps the erratic eating is messing with his body's reaction to the cold.

When he can feel the warmer air starting to circulate through the cabin, he returns to the glass dome that houses his bed and sits back down. Somebody made up the bed while he was out. The black fur-like blanket has been straightened out over the crisp white duvet and sheets, and a little box of chocolates wrapped in a gold ribbon has been placed on one of the decorative cushions.

Alex sits on the edge of the bed, phone in hand, and logs out of his Instagram. Then he opens a fresh Instagram sign-in page.

He enters Vicky's regular email address.

Under password, he tries her name and birthday and a '1'. His name and birthday. Combinations of their parents' names and birthdays. He tries their ages, their home village. He tries Finland. Lapland. Other places she's lived over the years.

Then he falls back on the bed and closes his eyes, hoping if he relaxes, something will just come to him.

And, miraculously, it does.

How could he have forgotten?

Vicky started using a particular password in her teens. He used to mock her for it. Her first pet's name, her age when she got him and an exclamation mark. Her first pet was a hamster called Teddy, gifted for her eighth birthday.

Nobody could understand why she called that hamster Teddy.

Alex feels the pang of a memory again. That hamster died with a kernel of corn stuck in its mouth and he'd nearly died laughing when he'd seen the thing, its legs and arms splayed, the corn stuffed half in, half out of its jaw. But Vicky had been devastated, so Alex had taken a new pair of trainers out of their box, filled it with straw, dug a hole down the back garden and conducted a funeral. Because, while he was the typical big brother, he wasn't always a shit one.

Alex sits up, types in *Teddy8!*

He's in.

Alex throws up a silent prayer of thanks to a God he doesn't even believe in.

He scrolls through Vicky's Insta account and sees some new pictures in her drafts and archives, including the one of her and Bryce on the slopes that Charlie found on Bryce's account. Alex squints at the photo. His sister's eyes are glistening but – is he being paranoid or does she look uncomfortable? Is that unhappiness in her glance?

He can see that she and Bryce follow one another so he opens up Vicky's DMs and types in Bryce's name. There's no existing conversation there.

Alex types: *Hi, can we talk?*

He throws his phone on the bed and stares out the window, trying to plan his next move. Outside, several people pass by on horses. They're laughing and calling out to each other as the horses' nostrils blow clouds into the air and their tails brush white dust.

Her second email address, the one she used to torture him with.

Could she have used Teddy8! for that one, too?

Alex is thinking about trying it when his phone buzzes beside him.

It's an Instagram message from Bryce Adams.

Vicky, babe, how are you doing? Still freezing your ass off? Tell me you want to take me up on my offer, New England for the holidays. I'll send you an American Airlines ticket. Come on!

Alex reads it, his heart sinking.

The guy is either very clever, or very ignorant to the fact he's just received a message from a dead girl.

Alex starts to type.

The older officer on reception, Jonas, lets Alex go straight through this time. He finds Agatha in her office.

'I don't know why I'm surprised,' Alex says, angrily. 'Of course you're here, sitting behind your desk, doing nothing.'

He knows he's come in like a bull in a china shop but it's too late to rein himself in now. He's furious.

'Excuse me?' Agatha looks up from her laptop.

'I've just spoken to Bryce Adams.'

'You did what?'

Agatha glares at him with such ferocity, Alex almost hesitates to go on, but he can't stop himself.

'You haven't even interviewed him! He had no idea Vicky was

even dead. Just how serious were you taking him as a suspect? Or was he just a convenient diversion?'

'What were you thinking? I told you, you cannot interfere—'

'It seems very much like I must. Look, I'm happy to let you do your job if you're doing your ruddy job. But you said this guy was a suspect and then I find out he hasn't even been contacted?'

Agatha crosses her arms. She studies him with a quiet stillness that immediately makes Alex feel embarrassed at his outburst. He starts to clench and unclench his fists, a method he learned years ago to release tension and regain control.

'There's a reason we haven't issued a press statement about Vicky's death yet,' Agatha says, slowly. 'We didn't want the international papers to pick up on the death of a foreign national here. It's big news. It travels. So, if Bryce Adams killed her, he had no way of knowing we'd found her. We've been in contact with the police in his home town. They have been keeping tabs on him. His ignorance meant they could study his movements and behaviour. Listen to him with his pals in a bar to see if he was boasting. Get warrants for his emails and phone. Wait to see if he slipped up and mentioned something happening with Vicky. All this before bringing him in for an interview.

'Now, he knows her body has turned up. At best, you'll have put him on his guard. At worst, you've just given him a head start to get halfway across the United States.'

Agatha pauses to let what she's said sink in.

Then she picks up her phone. Alex realises his error with lightning speed. He listens as Agatha speaks in rapid Finnish into the phone. The only words he picks up are 'American' and 'police'.

'You can leave now,' she says, her hand over the receiver.

Alex swallows his pride and retreats through the office door. As he walks down the corridor he can hear her switch to English.

'Yes, Agatha Koskinen in Koppe here, we spoke yesterday. I'm sorry, I think the time difference . . . Yes, I need to speak to you about Bryce Adams . . .'

Jonas wordlessly lets Alex out from behind the reception area.

Alex opens the police station's front door and walks out into the freezing cold. He stands on the porch, rubbing his hands together absent-mindedly as he tries to rationalise his actions.

He's started out on to the main street, his shoulders hunched, when he hears the snow crunching behind him.

It's Agatha; she's followed him outside. She's coatless and wraps her arms around herself, shivering as she speaks.

'Well, you're an idiot, but not a dangerous one,' she says. 'The Americans say Bryce Adams just reported to his local station and wants to make a statement. He's going in with his lawyer. Turns out, as soon as you spoke to him, he realised he'd be a person of interest. But he's claiming he had nothing to do with Vicky's death.'

Alex stares down at his feet, or what he can see of them.

'Sorry,' he says. 'It was . . . impulsive of me.'

Agatha says nothing.

'He answered a message from Vicky,' Alex adds, looking up. 'He thought she was still alive. I'm sure of it.'

'We'll see,' she says. 'Alex, can I give you some advice?'

He finds a spot somewhere over her shoulder and stares at it, too embarrassed to make eye contact.

'I can't make you go home. I even understand why you want to stay. And I sense you're not the sort who can easily be dissuaded from trying to find out what happened to your sister. But, please, allow me to do my job. Don't second-guess me. Just because in your head this is some backwater, that doesn't mean I'm not equipped to conduct this investigation professionally.'

'I've apologised—' Alex begins.

'And I accept. You have a right to be informed of developments, but if you insist on rushing at things hot-headed, then I will request a liaison officer from Rovaniemi be assigned to deal with you and your embassy. My job is to solve Vicky's death, not put out your fires. Look . . .'

She hesitates.

'It's been a very stressful few days. Why don't you take a couple of hours to relax? Look around town, go for a sauna, something. Clear your head. Spend a little time understanding what Vicky did here. Maybe then you'll start to see this place a little clearer, too.'

Alex takes a deep breath.

Agatha turns and walks back to the station.

Alex heads in the direction of the Lodge.

Do what Vicky would have done.

It's not a bad idea. If he puts himself in his sister's shoes, he might find the steps she walked that led her to her murderer.

He has, in his rush to confront Agatha about Bryce Adams, completely forgotten to check Vicky's second email account with the password he has remembered.

Early evening, and Alex finds himself sitting in a dimly lit wood-burning sauna at the Lodge, which he's been told by Florian is the most traditional type of sauna.

This isn't the first time Alex has been in a sauna but he's wondering right now if it's the hottest. Sweat is dripping from every part of his skin – from his forehead on to his eyelids, from his neck and down his back – on to the wooden bench on which he sits.

There's a large stove in a pit in the middle of the room, the coals resting on top. Alex watches as a completely naked man stands, pours water on to the coals with a ladle from a bucket, then starts wildly swinging a towel around his head to make the steam circulate faster. Alex is oddly transfixed by the man's penis as it flaps between his legs and is amazed that nobody else is fazed.

Every other Finnish person in the sauna is naked, but there are tourists, like himself, who are wearing swimwear. And most of them are drinking beers. Alex can't decide whether it's genius or imbecilic to mix alcohol with this heat.

The door opens and somebody enters. He doesn't see it's Niamh until she's sitting beside him. She's wearing a swimsuit, her red hair roped in a plait that hangs down her back, and he can't help but appreciate the curves of her figure. Alex might have other things on his mind, but he's still a man and still alive.

'You enjoying this?' she asks him, quietly.

'It's like a meeting with the partners in my job,' Alex replies. 'I'm sweating and uncomfortable and it feels like it will never end.'

She smiles.

'How long have you been in here?'

'About five years. Or maybe minutes.'

'Give it five more. Then you'll need to cool off.'

She hands him a glass of iced water with mint leaves and berries floating on top. He drinks it, gratefully.

'You have to keep hydrated,' she says.

'Why are saunas such a big thing here?' he asks.

'I don't really know. They're obsessed. Two million in the country, they say. For a population of just over five million.'

'Why so many? *How* are there so many?'

'A lot of businesses have them. A lot of private homes, too. Some people sacrifice a bedroom to have a sauna.'

'You're kidding me?'

'Nope.' Niamh smiles. 'I know. London is like Dublin. Bedroom numbers are everything. But these people like to have solo saunas. I guess it has a lot to do with what they say about the Finns.'

'What's that?'

'An introverted Finn looks at his shoes when he's talking to you. An extroverted Finn looks at your shoes. They like their own company. They're quiet. Shy. Private.'

Alex eyes the naked man.

'Nudity in saunas is very normal,' Niamh says, grinning. 'It's only us non-Continentals that are total prudes.'

Niamh pauses.

'Time for some cold air,' she says.

Alex helps her down off the bench and they leave the sauna.

Even though the door brings them directly outside, the cold doesn't hit Alex straight away, his body is so hot.

'Come on,' Niamh says.

He follows her down a deck; Alex realises too late that she's leading him to the lake.

They stop at the end of the pier-like walkway. It's dark, but lights are dotted along the ice path and around the pool of water.

He watches her descend a few steps into the water, holding on to a rope, until she is submerged to her neck.

Alex frowns. He can't understand why she'd bring him here,

why she wouldn't see the significance of it for him. Unless she's just not thinking at all. This place is still a job to Niamh, after all. She's probably stopped seeing it as anything other than a series of tasks every day.

'You have to do it,' she says, her lips trembling. 'In and out. It's a rite of passage.'

She clambers out and hands him the rope.

'The steps are slippy with ice,' she says. 'Just hold the rope and don't let go.'

He takes a good grip and, before he can talk himself out of it, lowers his body into the icy-cold water.

The pain is instant. It takes all his willpower to continue, to make his whole body go under the surface. His breaths, already shallow, start to shorten until he's gasping.

When he's in it up to his neck, Alex can no longer see Niamh, or anything around him.

It's not just the piercing cold.

His head is filled with thoughts of Vicky.

This. This is what it must have felt like. Her last moments, in this lake.

He dips his head under.

In an instant, the world goes silent, but just as suddenly, the rushing starts in his ears. He's in agony. Panic courses through him. He reaches to pull himself out with the rope and realises it has slipped from his hands. He didn't even feel its release.

He opens his eyes, the water assaulting his eyeballs like shards of glass. He can't see anything except blackness.

Alex is in full terror mode until he feels his arm being gripped and he's pulled to the surface. His foot hits one of the steps as he moves; he was still standing on them and didn't even realise. He'd lost all sense of where he was.

He emerges, coughing and spluttering, his heart racing. Niamh is standing on the steps beside him, her face ashen, her hand still gripping his arm.

'Why did you do that?' she asks, her voice filled with distress. 'Why would you do that?'

Alex can't answer her. His teeth are chattering too badly.

Later in the bar, dried and dressed, Niamh hands him a hot juice of some sort and some sugary biscuits that she orders him to eat.

'I wanted to feel it for a moment,' he tells her. 'I'd no idea how disorienting it would be.'

'I'm sorry. I wasn't thinking. I forgot . . .'

'It was horrible,' he says.

He can't think of any other way of describing it, no descriptive noun that would capture it better. It was just horrible. Completely.

'I hope,' he says, and his voice chokes a little, 'I hope she was already unconscious when she went in.'

Niamh is staring at the bar counter. She's crying. She roughly brushes the tears away when she realises he's watching her.

'I shouldn't be doing this in front of you,' she says. 'It's just every time I think about it . . . I feel so *angry* at Vicky for dying. Does that make any sense?'

'Yes,' Alex says.

'It does?'

'I'm angry all the time. When I'm not sad and confused, I'm angry.'

'Alex, I . . .'

She trails off. He waits. She visibly swallows.

'There's something I've been keeping from you,' she says.

Niamh is still looking down at the bar counter.

'Everybody is keeping something from me,' he tells her.

'It's not exactly about Vicky,' Niamh says. 'Except . . . except I think it could be.'

Niamh glances around them. There are a few tourists in the bar, but none of the guides, and nobody appears to be paying them any heed. Still, Niamh is cautious.

She looks furtively at Alex.

'Have the police mentioned Miika Virtanen?' she says.

'Who?'

Niamh hesitates again.

'Maybe I shouldn't say anything. Look, talk to the police. Ask them to tell you.'

'Niamh.'

'I . . . I just think he might be a person of interest.'

'Who is he? Does he work here?'

'No. Not here. He lives here, though. In Koppe.'

She glances at Alex, her face a little fearful.

'I don't want people to think I'm causing trouble,' she whispers. 'This is my job. I don't want to lose it. This is a small town and we guides, we're just meant to smile and do the work. But if you're looking for somebody to blame . . .'

'Who is this Miika? Did Vicky know him?'

'I don't know,' Niamh says, even quieter. 'She would have known *of* him. We all do. If the police *aren't* looking at him, you should ask why.'

Koppe

1998

Kaya's mother places the plate of joulutorttu Kaya has brought with her on to the counter and smiles her thanks. Kaya knows the Christmas cakes will stay there and that Karla will offer guests her own version. She taught Kaya well, but not well enough; Kaya's attempts will never match the sugary concoctions her mother bakes.

'You must remind me to give you my new glögi recipe,' Karla says. 'You'll enjoy your glass even more on Christmas Eve, trust me. I take it you'll be coming with us to the cemetery, after? We can put fresh candles on Mummo's grave.'

Kaya nods, half-heartedly. She plans to honour the tradition with Miika this year and go to his parents' graves with him so he doesn't have to go alone. She's already planned their special dinner. Roast pork, scalloped potatoes, carrot casserole and mashed rutabaga. She won't be with her parents this Christmas Eve but she doesn't want to let them know yet.

'So, my darling,' her mother says. 'Tell me all your news. How are things at the bar?'

She pours Kaya some coffee and pulls up a chair at the kitchen table. There's a plate of biscuits beside Kaya but she can't bring herself to eat one. Her appetite is veering wildly between needing to consume everything and being absolutely unable to stomach the thought of food, let alone the real thing.

Karla pushes the plate closer to Kaya and Kaya reluctantly picks up a biscuit. She nibbles on the side of it, so her mother is pleased, and tries not to vomit when the taste hits her tongue.

'No real news,' Kaya says, determined to keep talking so she won't have to eat. 'It's busy with Christmas coming. It feels like there are more tourists this year.'

'There are more every year,' Karla says. 'Have they given you a pay rise? If you're busier, you should get more money, no?'

'I get paid plenty, Mom.'

'Pfft.'

Karla leans over and brushes Kaya's hair from her face. Kaya knows, because she's been told all her life, that she and her mother look alike. Older relatives pretend to do a double-take every time they see Kaya; then they make a production of saying, *Oh, is that you, I thought it was your mom!* Sometimes, Kaya worries her mom forgets that Kaya is indeed a separate person. She fusses over her too much, is always telling her what she should be doing, what she should be saying. She's never trusted Kaya to live her own life properly. Not ever.

'Tell me your news' is always the opening gambit for 'tell me what I have to correct you on, now'.

'You need more money so you can start saving,' Karla says.

Kaya sighs.

'Why do I need to save, Mom? Miika has sold a lot of meat this year.'

Her mother looks into the distance.

'You know, I always hated reindeer,' she says.

'What?' Kaya almost chokes on a laugh.

'Their stupid big eyes and those silly antlers. I never understood why our lot didn't just leave them to the Sami. We don't need them now. We can buy beef in the supermarket and the last pair of good winter boots I bought were from the sports shop.'

'Mom!'

Kaya shakes her head in amazement. She's not surprised at her mother's latent racism. Ever since she could comprehend, Kaya has known there's an us and them when it comes to Sami and non-Sami. Miika has Sami blood in him. His grandfather. It's part of the reason her parents never liked him. Kaya thinks her mother's outburst might have more to do with that than reindeer. To hate reindeer, to be honest, borders on blasphemy round these parts.

'I think their eyes are nice,' Kaya says, but her mother is already shaking her head dismissively.

'Anyway,' Karla says, 'you need to think about money for when you leave.'

Kaya stares blankly at her mother.

'Oh, come now,' Karla says. 'You must be planning to, eventually? Nobody is going to judge you, Kaya. We've all seen the marks you think you're hiding so well.'

'Mom,' Kaya whispers. 'I don't want to talk like this.'

'I can't even talk about my own daughter's husband?' Her mother's nose wrinkles in distaste. 'If you can't discuss this with me, who can you talk to, Kaya? I know you've no friends. You never really did and it's not like he lets you mix with anybody. As soon as he could, he had you up that mountain—'

'His father died. We had to take over.'

Karla opens her mouth to speak but Kaya places a hand on her mother's arm.

'It's got better,' Kaya says. 'Really. He's been treating me very well. He just lost his temper a few times. He was working hard and—'

'If a man hits you once, he'll hit you again, Kaya.'

'You would know.'

Kaya instantly regrets it. She stares down at the table. She and her mother never speak about Papa's tempers. They're so rare these days, anyway. He doesn't have the same pressure on him now he's close to retirement. Kaya doesn't think Papa has hit her mother in years.

Does she blame her mother for her own warped sense of what a marriage should be? Would any of Kaya's friends have stayed after their husband hit them a first time?

But it's never as straightforward as you think, is it? That's what Kaya tells herself. She might have grown up in the nineties, listened to pop music and watched American films, but Koppe is still a small place. A lonely place. It's not like there's a huge selection of men.

As though her mother is reading her mind, Karla reaches over and takes Kaya's hand.

'Do as I say, not as I do, child,' she says. 'You don't need to live my life.'

'I'm not,' Kaya says, softly. 'It's different.'

'Then why do you look like death? Look at your cheeks. Not an ounce of colour. I know your head is usually in the clouds, Kaya, but you have to come down and deal with reality sometimes.'

Kaya swallows. She does look peaky. She's barely eaten today and last night, for some reason, she couldn't sleep. Insomnia on top of morning sickness. It's draining. But she can't tell her mother yet. In Kaya's new arrangement of dates, it's too early to have morning sickness.

'I have a cold, Mom,' she says. 'I swear, Miika hasn't laid a hand on me in months.'

Karla doesn't believe her.

But she nods and smiles.

Because, Karla, like Kaya, knows that when a woman has made her mind up, there's no changing it.

Even if it means the death of her.

Koppe

2019

Patric has brought over meatballs for Agatha and the children, and more of his blueberry pie. He stands over Agatha as she heats the meatball sauce on the hob. He's making sure she doesn't burn it, even at this ridiculously straightforward stage, while simultaneously ordering the children to set the table. Emilia, Olavi and Onni always do exactly what Patric tells them. Agatha is not surprised. He might not be the boss any longer, but he still has the boss voice.

'I thought you guys deserved one decent meal that's home-cooked and not take-out,' he says.

'You got them pizza the other night,' Agatha cries, defensively.

'A treat night.'

'Yes, well, I made them a perfectly acceptable breakfast this morning.'

'You gave us cereal, Mom,' Emilia says.

'With fresh milk,' Agatha retorts.

Agatha spots Patric slip Emilia a twenty before the kids leave the kitchen. He's not staying for dinner. He has a hot date. Agatha knows he's been chatting up Cecelia, who runs the restaurant at the Lodge and lost her husband last year. Cecelia is in her sixties now, but she's still a big, beautiful woman. She'd been Cloudberry Queen many years ago, even won at national level. Something she likes to remind people of, frequently.

'So,' Patric says, when the coast is clear. 'Tell me.'

Agatha had asked him to pop by this evening. He knows something is wrong.

'Olavi says he saw Luca.'

Patric straightens up.

'I thought you wanted to speak about Lassi.'

Agatha rolls her eyes.

'Don't tell me he's been complaining to you that I asked him a few questions? Is he ever going to come to terms with you retiring and me being the boss?'

Patric leans against the kitchen counter, his ear cocked to make sure none of the children are coming up the hallway.

'Forget him. I'm surprised you could concentrate on anything today.'

'I still have a job to do,' Agatha says.

'Nobody has mentioned seeing Luca.' Patric shakes his head, thinking. 'Surely if somebody as infamous as that was hanging around town . . . You know you're safe, don't you? No matter what happens.'

'It's not me I'm worried about,' Agatha says. She stares at the kitchen table, and the four place settings. Once, there would have been five.

Now, the fifth person is the one who fills her nightmares.

'If Luca is back, I'll find out,' Patric says.

'Thank you. For everything.'

'You've nothing to thank me for.'

He helps her dish out dinner, then he leaves with a reassuring pat on her shoulder.

The kids pile in and Agatha is distracted by the boys squabbling over who has the larger portion of food.

Just passing on the information makes Agatha feel a little better. For so long she kept everything silent about Luca, about how hard things were and how poorly Agatha was managing. She knows now that silence is power. Patric will help, she thinks. Patric will keep us safe. The whole town will.

The kids scoff down the meatballs, then seconds, while Agatha pushes a couple around her plate, only managing a few bites. She takes a thin slice of the pie – all that's left, really, after the children got their mitts on it – and toys with that too. She's well aware she's counting down the seconds to them retreating to their rooms so she can pour herself a large glass of wine and try to unwind.

She gets her wish at 8.30 and slumps into a chair in the sitting room, Vicky Evans' file on her lap. The two officers secured from the nearby town of Sellaniemi have been helping with interviews around town all day and Agatha is catching up on the statements. Town will be easy compared to driving around the wider area and knocking doors. It can take an hour to get from one house to the next.

Agatha wraps a blanket around her shoulders and sips white wine while reading through the typed-up notes. So far, everything matches the statements made when Vicky disappeared. No inconsistencies, yet. Harry, the Lodge manager, was the very last person to see Vicky, when she entered her cabin with Bryce Adams, the night she seems to have vanished. But plenty of people in Elliot's had seen her with Bryce and the other American tourists leading up to that. Everybody seemed happy. There were no arguments, no apparent danger.

Agatha flicks to the statement emailed over from the States a couple of hours earlier. In it, Bryce Adams confirms he went back to Vicky's but denies they had sex.

Agatha scans the transcript of his interview.

I got the impression Vicky was a nice girl, up for a laugh and a flirt, but that maybe she acted a little more fun than she was? Like, she wanted to have this reputation as a party girl but she wasn't really into me. Sure, I could say she led me on a bit. I thought we were going back for – you know. Sexual intercourse. I think she considered it, too, but changed her mind. I didn't react angrily to that. I know most guys would, but my mom reared me well, and all through school and college I've been taught when a girl changes her mind, she changes her mind. I've even taken a pledge. No means no. We had a few drinks and I left. I didn't see her again but she was very much alive when I left.

Bryce's friends confirmed that he had rejoined them in the Lodge bar at 11 p.m. There was some mocking that he'd been very quick in Vicky's place.

Agatha frowns. On the one hand, she struggles to imagine a young man taking it well if Vicky invited him to her cabin and then told him she didn't want sex. On the other, if he went into her cabin at 9.30 p.m. and was back in the bar by 11, was that enough time to attempt to have sex with her, be rebuffed, fight over it, attack her and dump her in the lake? And then to return, clear out her cabin, head to the bar and act perfectly normally for the night?

He'd gone back to his shared cabin around 1 a.m. Maybe, just maybe, he'd waited until his roommate was asleep and gone back to

Vicky's cabin. There were too many *what ifs* with that hypothesis, though.

Agatha shakes her head. She takes out the full medical report Venla has emailed and confirms, again, what she already knows.

No sign of sexual assault to Vicky's body. She might have had consensual sex before she died, but it would be impossible to tell. If Bryce had killed Vicky because she'd refused to have sex with him, he'd have been more likely to rape her, then kill her.

Agatha is taking another sip of her wine when there's a loud knock on her front door.

She jumps so hard, the wine glass hits her teeth and some liquid spills on to Vicky's case file.

Agatha stands up; her heart is racing.

Without hesitating, she goes to the locked safe under the stairs and reaches for her weapon before heading to the door, just as the knocking starts again.

She'll use it if she has to, she tells herself. If it's a choice between Luca or the children, she'll use it.

Through the chained crack in the door, she sees Alex Evans.

She throws the door open and stares at him.

Her annoyance must show on her face because Alex looks taken aback. Then she realises what's caused his reaction. She's brandishing her service weapon.

Agatha lowers her arm.

'So, not much crime around these parts?' Alex says, and Agatha almost laughs. It's partially relief flooding her body that he's not who she thought he was. But it's also the look on his face.

'I can come back,' he says, contrite. 'I shouldn't have come to your house. Again. I apologise.'

'Why wouldn't you come to my house?' Agatha asks. 'It's the time of the night that's the problem. You ever heard of calling ahead?'

She stands back and cocks her head to indicate he should come in.

They sit on the partially sheltered deck at the back of the house. She's lit the stove and given him a blanket for his knees because he looks terrified at the prospect of sitting even half outdoors. He has a glass of wine to match hers.

He's staring up at the sky. The night is cloudless, the stars in their millions.

'It's beautiful,' he says. 'You don't get this in the city. You don't even really get it in Yorkshire. The towns are too big. Too much light pollution.'

'You might get lucky,' Agatha says. 'We could have an aurora tonight.'

She sips her wine. It's helping her to relax and she reminds herself that the amount she drinks is a perfectly normal volume for a grown woman. She's not dependent on alcohol. She just likes it.

She's not Luca.

'Is there any news about your mom?' she asks.

'She's still in an induced coma,' he says. 'The doctors think she's going to be okay.'

'How is your father coping?'

'In his usual way, I'd imagine. Telling the doctors how to do their jobs, knowing better than everybody else.'

'Does he work?'

'He's a postman but he was the top guy in his union back in the day. When he gave speeches, Christ, it felt like the earth was quaking. He doesn't do it as much now. He's handed over the reins.'

'Old age?'

'More fatigue. Too many years under right-wing governments. Mum made him retire. She thought . . .' Alex snorts. 'She was worried the union would give him a heart attack.'

Agatha can appreciate the irony. She hopes his mom is doing okay. It would be too much, to lose both the women in the family so close together.

'A postman,' she says. 'But you didn't follow in his footsteps.'

'No.'

There's something there, Agatha thinks. Something between father and son. Some wound that has yet to scab.

'I wanted to make money,' he says, shrugging.

Agatha studies him.

'I don't think money is everything to you,' she says. 'Maybe you just like your job?'

Alex frowns.

'I don't,' he says. 'I don't even know how I ended up in it.' He hesitates. 'I suppose I was flattered into it. Very important people who did very important things wanted me to join them. They saw something in me that I'm not sure I even saw in myself. They were willing to give me a chance when . . . well. It is what it is.'

It is what it is. Agatha likes that saying. She might steal it. She'll use it when somebody from town comes in to complain about one of their neighbours. *It is what it is. What do you want me to do?*

'What about you?' Alex asks. 'Your parents? Were they cops, too?'

'They're dead,' Agatha says. She stares into her wine glass. 'Anyway, what was it you wanted to talk about tonight?'

Alex doesn't speak for a few seconds, probably thrown by her diversion. Agatha slows her breathing. She won't talk about herself. She never does. She has too much to hide.

'Miika,' Alex says.

Agatha breathes out.

'Miika,' she parrots. 'Miika Virtanen. Who told you about him?'

'Does it matter?'

'It matters what you were told. How lurid was the tale? Was it accurate, or recounted with the usual local colour? I've heard stories where he has fangs and only comes out on a full moon. Some say he drinks the blood of young virgins. Some say he's a dirty pervert. And some say he's just an oddball reindeer farmer from up the mountain.'

Alex stares at her. Agatha takes a sip of wine and swallows.

'Ah,' she says. 'You were just told to ask about him. I see. One of the staff at the Lodge, then. Of course they assume the local bad guy must be involved. Because the murderer couldn't be someone more sinister, like, say, somebody they know.'

Alex says nothing.

Agatha sighs. She stares up at the stars.

'Miika is our town rumour,' she says, after a minute or two has passed. 'He's very real, don't get me wrong. But the stories that have grown up around him are just that. Stories.'

'So he does live here? In the town?'

'He lives up the mountain. Alone.'

'Why do they talk about him?'

Agatha turns and looks at Alex.

'His wife disappeared.'

'Disappeared, disappeared? As in, she didn't just up and leave him?'

'No, she disappeared. Twenty-one years ago. People looked for her but, nothing.'

'So, why is he considered a monster?' Alex says, and she can tell from the tone of his voice he already knows.

'People presumed he killed her,' Agatha says.

'Did he?'

'How would we know? Her body was never found. There was no evidence.'

'He still lives here? Even with all the speculation?'

'Sure he does. The man says he has nothing to prove. Nothing to hide. But he only comes down from the mountain to do business. He doesn't socialise down here.'

'Why would people assume he'd killed her?'

'He's weird.' Agatha sighs. 'That doesn't mean anything more than what it is. For all we know, his wife had an accident somewhere, slipped down a gully and was never found. Or maybe she's living happily in Helsinki under another name. We don't know.'

'Why was his name mentioned to me, then?' Alex says. 'If this happened years ago, why would anybody presume he has anything to do with Vicky?'

Agatha glances upwards again. She can see it starting, the shifting of the sky. She can smell it, hear the static.

'Because . . . some things have happened here over the years,' Agatha says.

'Things like what?'

Agatha doesn't answer. She points up at the sky. The air is crackling.

Green is the first colour to shimmer. It comes in a line at first. It starts to build quickly towards the curtains effect. Tonight, the lights will be strong. Agatha knows the signs.

She watches Alex's eyes widen.

'It's slow,' Agatha says. 'That's what you're thinking. But what you see on TV, that's the speeded-up version. The lights last for hours, most of the time. All night.'

Alex doesn't respond. She can tell it's taken his breath away. It always does, the first time.

They watch as blue waves begin to creep through the green. The colours form a magnificent kaleidoscope, long streaks pulsing against the cold night sky.

'It's . . .' Alex seems to struggle for the right words. 'I've never seen anything like it.'

'You're lucky to see it like this,' Agatha whispers. 'I've heard of some tourists hiring helicopters to get to see the lights when there's cloud cover.'

They both watch for a couple of minutes.

'What was his wife's name?' Alex says, breaking the silence. 'This Miika guy.'

'Kaya,' Agatha says.

Alex nods, his eyes still on the aurora.

'And what bad things have happened here over the years?'

'This really isn't a conversation I should be having with you.'

'Why not?'

'I'm the chief of police and you're a foreign citizen.'

'But you don't want to have the Met breathing over your shoulder,' Alex says. 'Which is why you're doing your best to keep me happy.'

Agatha looks at him sharply. He's perceptive, she'll give him that. Agatha takes a deep breath.

'I suppose there's nothing I can tell you that you won't be told in a far more salacious fashion by somebody else in town,' she says.

'And arguably, it's better you give it to me in the professional, understated manner you seem to specialise in.'

Agatha almost smiles. Then her face grows serious again. She's still reluctant to throw fuel on the fire.

'What is it?' Alex prompts her.

Fine, Agatha thinks. She'll roll the dice and see how they land.

'Kaya wasn't the last woman to go missing,' she says.

Alex follows Agatha through a door in the kitchen and down into the basement. It's dark; she's told him the light on the stairs is broken but there's one below and she knows where the cord is by touch.

'You waving that gun around tonight,' Alex says. 'These missing women . . . Is there a link?'

'What? Oh. God, no. That's nothing to do with these cases. It's just . . .' She doesn't finish.

Just what, Alex wonders.

She tells him to wait on the bottom step then feels her way into the middle of the room. He hears a snap; light floods the basement and he can see her standing in the middle of the room holding the light cord.

The next thing he sees is the wall. There are pictures and marker lines and threads and maps.

It's Agatha's version of an FBI case board.

'I don't want the kids seeing some of the images in my case files,' Agatha says. 'So I keep them down here and the door locked.'

'Makes sense.'

Alex crosses to the wall. She's written three names at its top and, underneath, triangles of information spell out the facts of their disappearances.

Alex scans the dates.

'Cold cases,' he says.

'Cold but open,' Agatha says. 'The case files in the station are slim and sit in a drawer. But I put up this board when I took over in Koppe. It's just a reminder, because it's years since I've been able to dedicate any time to them. Sometimes, I google their names to see if anything pops up. And every time a body is found, anywhere in Finland, I wonder. Proper investigations were conducted into each of them but . . . nothing.'

She pauses.

'Alex, none of these women disappeared in the same circumstances as your sister. Vicky's body was found. These women just vanished off the face of the earth.'

'Couldn't that be just luck?' Alex says. 'Her body surfaced – these others didn't?'

'Some of it is luck, but also, her body was unimpeded. I told you how big Inari is. If you wanted somebody to disappear, you would bring them to the middle, weigh them down, and in all likelihood, we would never see them again. Whoever killed your sister made an amateur error. And Alex, I'm certain that if there was stupidity involved at that point in Vicky's murder, there was stupidity involved at other points. Which is how I think I'll catch her killer.'

Alex considers this.

'Is that what you think happened to these three?' he says. 'That they were weighted down in the lake?'

Alex looks at the names again. Then he studies the photos. Three women, all different ages, could even be different nationalities, they look so unalike. He points to the first one.

Kaya Virtanen.

'Twenty-two years old,' Agatha says. 'Last known sighting, working in a local bar, though her husband, the infamous Miika, always maintained she left the house the next morning to return to town and that was the last he saw of her. That was 1998.'

Agatha lifts a finger to her chin and starts to tap it as she stares at the photo.

'When my old boss – he was chief at the time – when Patric began to suspect something had happened to her, the locals were already whispering that Miika had done away with her. But there were other rumours, too. A foreign businessman had taken an interest in her; someone overheard him say he was going to, in his words, "screw her". She was seen knocking him back. I looked up the guy; he was charged with sexual assault in the States a few years ago. There was also talk she might have had a boyfriend. A couple of townspeople said they'd seen her car leaving late a few nights, long after the bar had closed.'

'Your lot ever find a boyfriend?'

'No. But, you know, affairs happen. Small town, long nights, a tiny populace. With so few members of the opposite sex to choose from, people settle and then get itchy feet. She married young. Always a problem.'

Alex glances at Agatha. He wonders if that was a problem for her, if that's why she's rearing three children on her own.

Agatha points to the next picture.

'Mary Rosenberg, twenty-nine. Canadian. Went missing in 2007. She was staying in my friend Becki's place. Well, her mother's, actually. Henni runs a sort of exclusive resort, up the lake a bit. For private bookings.

'Mary's mother was Finnish, her father Canadian; she liked to spend the winters over here. There was talk of her almost making the Olympic skiing team back home but she had an accident in her teens and damaged her back. She came here to ski for fun and give a few lessons. That day, she went out on a cross-country ski and never returned. Becki and Henni were immediately worried. Then her fiancé in Montreal grew concerned when she didn't return his calls and flew over. Her clothes and belongings were still here but she was gone. There were searches all over.'

The last picture.

'Hilda Paikkala, thirty-six, lived in the next town over. 2014. Seen by her neighbours walking along a road out of town. She had a bag on her back and she had friends living in the next village. I was working here by then, back from my stint at Rovaniemi. We assumed at first she'd had an accident en route. The roads and surrounding woods were searched. But when her body wasn't found, people started to wonder whether somebody had offered her a lift. A car was spotted on the same route hours later; a man and a woman allegedly arguing in the front seats. They never came forward, so the speculation persisted. They could have just been tourists arguing over a missed road.'

'But you thought somebody picked her up and killed her?'

Agatha shrugs.

'Three women, their bodies never found,' Alex says.

'And we don't know if they were involved in accidents or if something else happened.'

'But now, Vicky.'

'Like I said, it's not the same.'

'Only because her body turned up.'

'And also because her room was cleared, Alex. All of these women disappeared and the places where they were staying were left like the *Marie Celeste*. Hilda took only a small bag, enough to stay with friends for a few days. Mary just had her day gear. Kaya had her bag and purse.'

'Maybe there were too many questions asked before,' Alex says. 'Maybe this time, he thought clearing her room would make people believe she'd left. It almost worked, didn't it? Maybe this Miika guy has been knocking off people for decades. What if he's getting clumsy because he's got away with it for so long and that's why he didn't put rocks in a bag with Vicky? Don't serial killers take bigger and bigger risks? Isn't that what they say?'

'Alex, if Miika wanted to kill his wife and properly cover it up at the time, he could have done that to begin with. He could have got rid of all Kaya's belongings and then told people she'd left him. Her family claimed she wasn't happy with him but her mother also told Patric that Kaya refused to admit she was unhappy. So, it would have added up if she was too ashamed to tell anybody and just left. But Miika wouldn't let it go. He reported her missing and insisted the police look for her. Yes, serial killers will often look for attention but generally they start out very anonymously. They don't insert themselves into the initial investigation. That's something *they* say, too.'

'So, why did the townspeople assume he'd killed her? He's weird, fine. But to think of him as a serial killer?'

Agatha sucks in her cheeks.

'They knew Miika was capable of violence.'

Alex bristles.

'He was the quiet sort,' Agatha continues. 'He didn't mix much, but he'd been involved in a couple of fights in town and Kaya was seen with bruising. It was enough for Patric to bring him in and make his life very uncomfortable. But Patric was also the first one to accept Miika hadn't done anything.'

'Why, if Kaya was never found?'

Agatha shakes her head.

'If you knew Patric . . . I trust his judgement.'

Alex lets out a deep, troubled sigh.

'Do you think my sister is going to end up as one of these unsolved cases? Another name on your board?'

Agatha doesn't answer him straight away. Alex turns and stares at her.

'Do you?'

'I can never promise, with absolute certainty, that I will solve a case,' she says. 'Look at their pictures. Do you think I want this board here? Kaya's parents phone and ask for progress reports once a year. They moved to Rovaniemi – they couldn't stay up here, living with the thought that the man whom they believed murdered their daughter was still here, still free.'

Agatha bites her lip.

'Mary Rosenberg's fiancé married another woman and every now and again he sends me an email asking if there's news,' she continues. 'And I think of Hilda every time I pass the café where she worked. It's the same for Patric, but worse. He was the lead on all these cases. Nobody remembers all the ones he solved, all the people he did help. They just remember the failures. And they can't get their heads around them either, so local people look to what they can understand. Miika Virtanen hit his wife. His wife vanished. Miika must have killed her. Oh, somebody else has gone missing. It must have been Miika.'

'You're a local,' Alex says. 'Why don't you think like that?'

'Sporadic serial killers operate in patterns,' Agatha replies. '1998, 2007, 2014. And now 2019. The gaps are too wide, too irregular. They mean nothing. Most serial killers might leave a break at the start but then, when they're active, they become chaotic. They lose the ability to restrain themselves. And they usually have a type. These women had nothing in common. They were different ages, looked nothing alike. The only thing that links them is that they all disappeared in my jurisdiction. But in the jurisdiction next to mine, two guys went missing a few years ago and were never found. They were climbers, so everyone assumes they fell somewhere and their bodies were lost somewhere hard to reach. And they were men, so nobody else could have been involved, right?

'An old lady disappeared the year before. Told her family she was going out to the shop and that was that. But when it's women of a certain age, people arrive at less sinister conclusions. She got cold and disoriented and fell into a hole. Nobody would snatch an old woman, would they?'

Alex says nothing for a few moments. He looks at the board.

'So there's no pattern,' he says. 'But like I said. What if these are the only ones you know about?'

'It's a small population,' Agatha replies. 'We'd know if there were more. And if tourists were going missing all over the place, we'd especially know. I don't think these women are linked to your sister.'

'So, why tell me about them at all?'

He's frustrated now. He can see the sense in what Agatha is saying but, still . . .

'Because you've already been told Miika's name and this is next,' Agatha says. 'They'll tell you all about his other *victims*. And I want you to have some context, to understand that the police here are not incompetent fools. There is absolutely nothing connecting Miika Virtanen to your sister.'

'Have you questioned him?' Alex asks.

Agatha looks away from him. He waits for her answer.

'I have no reason to,' she says.

Her answer is adamant but, even still, Alex can hear something. Uncertainty.

Agatha might not think there's a serial killer operating in Koppe, but nor is she convinced there's not.

'You're not sure,' Alex says, and looks her dead in the eye. 'You're not sure if there's something more sinister going on here. This board in your basement all these years. There must be other unsolved cases. But you have *their* faces up here. Together. You put them together for a reason.'

Agatha starts to shake her head but then she pauses and looks back at the board. He can see the movement in her throat as she swallows.

'None of it indicates a serial killer,' she says, quietly. 'And I haven't been hunting one. But the single most important thing I've learned over the years is that being sure of something doesn't make it so. I could be wrong.'

Alex can tell it's taken her a lot to admit that in his presence.

He looks back at the board.

'My sister had a second email address,' he says.

Agatha spins around to face him.

Alex doesn't look at her.

'I think she might have tried to send me a message. Why was she trying so hard to get in contact with me before she died? What if she knew she was in danger?'

Koppe

1998

The bar owner has introduced a range of American beers and Kaya is struggling to find the brand the men at the counter want.

It's busy tonight; the Helsinki businessmen are back and the Americans ordering the Sam Adams cream stout are with them. Kaya has been listening to them on and off all night, as she's fetched their beers and served them chicken wings and sides. One of them started a conversation with her about the fries, telling her he'd never tasted anything so good. She'd begun explaining that Lappish potatoes are the best in the world, because of the midnight sun, but then realised he didn't want an actual conversation with her, just to stare at her breasts.

The men are discussing a new hotel on the side of the mountain. The idea is it will lead straight out to the ski slopes, and chairlifts will be built to bring residents back up to the hotel after they've been in the town. One of the Helsinki men has pointed out that the local council will have to be soothed – a lot of trees will need to be felled for the development. But they can use the wood in a sustainable fashion: he says sustainable in a way that implies it's the most useful word in the English dictionary. Plus, a friend of his can contact the council and make enquiries about locating a mine in the area. Everybody knows the mountain is rich with chemical elements. When it comes to debate at council, the politicians will be faced with a choice between a rock or . . . well, smashed rocks.

Kaya supposes they don't think her English is good enough to fully understand what they're saying, but she understands perfectly.

She is, however, too happy to care.

The last few weeks at home have been good. Miika hasn't been drinking as much. Kaya doesn't know if it's a decision he's actively taken or if it's because the farm is busy right now. He's got a new meat order from a couple of local restaurants and it looks like they'll actually make some decent money this winter. He's talking about expanding the herd again. He's still doing most of the butchering on his own, but he's also thinking about bringing in a couple of Sami men at the weekend to help with that, too.

It's the first time in a long time she's seen him so relaxed and she's even more convinced that his bad behaviour has been a result of stress. She can forgive him for that.

Last week, he went to Rovaniemi and came home with a new scarf and hat for her, pretty red wool and delicately designed. It's two weeks until Christmas and he could have kept the gifts until then, but he gave them to her.

He's been enjoying her body, too. Not like when they were teenagers – all amateur, rough fumbling – and not like after they were married, when she often felt like a piece of meat.

She's giving herself to him and he's noticed. He likes it.

She's started to change; she feels more fleshy, more curved. It's the baby growing inside her, but she tries not to think about it.

She won't break the news to Miika until it's time. Her clothes are starting to strain a little, here and there, but she's pretty sure she can hide it a while longer. Her skirts are easy to let out but she might need to go up a blouse size sooner rather than later.

Kaya hums along to the tune playing on the radio while she cleans the bar counter.

One of the Americans is back, the guy who was staring at her cleavage. She doesn't like this man. He has a look on his face that reminds her of a wolf. The way he studies her, she reckons he'd eat her if he had half the chance. They get like this, a lot of these businessmen. Think they can come to these provincial towns and take what they want. Land. Business. Locals.

Kaya pours him the spirit he asks for and his fingers touch hers as she places the glass on the counter. It sends an unpleasant electric current through her. She knows everyone is watching them. His friends, the other bar patrons. Looking to see if she reacts, if the guy will get lucky or if she'll tell him where to go.

She's stretching up to put the bottle of whiskey back on the shelf when he speaks.

'What time do you finish?' he asks.

Her blouse slips out of her skirt with the stretch and Kaya is conscious her skin is on show now. She blushes and tucks it back in, hastily.

'Why do you ask?' she says.

'I could give you a ride home.'

'My husband will do that,' Kaya says, and it's true; Miika is coming to collect her. Her car engine stalled last week and Miika has been dropping her into work while she waits for it to be fixed. She could have taken the snowmobile but she's told Miika she hasn't been feeling well. What she hasn't told him is she's not sure if all the bouncing around on the snowmobile will harm the baby.

In any case, having Miika drive her in has been useful. Miika turning up when Kaya is in the bar has helped to keep her ex-lover at bay. She's glad of it. She's doing her best to ignore him, like they never happened.

'Surely you're too young to be married,' the American man says. He's still watching her, staring at her and the glimpses of skin between the buttons on her blouse. Kaya is increasingly uncomfortable under his gaze. She feels like the reindeer must when buyers come to the farm and examine them, checking the density of their fur, the solidity of their antlers. This guy would grab her if he could, and from her eavesdropping, she knows the group are staying in Koppe for the next two weeks. That means this guy, in her bar, every night. She wishes her co-worker would return from his break and take over. She could feign some excuse and go hide out back for a while.

'Let me buy you a drink, anyway,' he says. 'We could have a bit of fun, hey? Just a little. All innocent.'

'No, thank you,' she says, sharply.

Movement catches her eye. She looks over to the corner of the bar, near the door, and realises her husband is standing there. He must have arrived a few minutes ago and he's watching the American guy. She's not worried at what he'll think. She knows Miika can see the stranger is upsetting her. Her face is flushed and her body language is doing its best to repel the unwanted attention.

He crosses to the bar and Kaya joins him, a grateful, relieved smile on her face.

'You're early,' she says.

'I thought your boss might let you off,' he says. He glances sideways at the American, who slinks back to his table as Kaya's smile grows wider.

'Did you tell him you haven't been feeling well?' Miika asks.

Kaya shrugs. She has been exhausted the last few days. Utterly and completely. But she's managed to drag herself into work each evening, her face pale, her eyelids heavy; she's even covered for some of the other girls who are off with less serious issues – like hangovers. Of course she hasn't said anything to her boss. She can't.

'We're too busy,' she says. 'But it's nearly closing. Sit here at the bar and I'll get you a coffee.'

Miika sits up on a stool. He looks over at the table of businessmen. Kaya smiles again. Miika is huge, practically a giant of a man, compared to those soft-handed fools. Lately, Kaya has been reminding herself that Miika was the strongest guy in her class and how she used to enjoy the feeling that nobody would ever harass her when he was around. She'd become too used to fearing his strength. Not any more.

Kaya likes this possessive side to Miika. She feels protected. Wanted.

She moves about behind the bar, conscious her husband's eyes are on her and enjoying every moment.

Maybe tonight, she thinks. Maybe I'll tell him tonight I'm pregnant with his child.

Koppe

2019

Alex is so wound up after leaving Agatha's that he doesn't head straight to his cabin. He stops in one of the bars in town and sits at the counter, where he orders an old-fashioned. He looks around, wondering if this is the bar the girl Kaya worked in.

He's given Agatha Vicky's handle for her second email account. But he didn't tell her he might have guessed at Vicky's password for that account. Alex wants to check it first in case there are any emails that Vicky wanted for his eyes only.

That bloody user handle, though.

It always amused him how Vicky could return to acting like a little girl when she came home for holidays in their parents' house. It's not like their parents were daft and didn't know their daughter was a bit wild. They'd seen the pictures on her Facebook page. Foam parties in Ibiza. Skinny-dipping in Portugal. They knew she worked in nightclubs and as a holiday rep and had lots of boy-friends. She wasn't an innocent.

Their parents didn't, however, know just how lacking in inno-cence their favourite child was.

Alex did, though. He knew all about those six months when she made plenty of money.

VoluptuousVicky@poledancers.com

Vicky's assigned email when she worked at the exotic dance club in Marbella. Strip club, for want of a better name.

Vicky wasn't ashamed of what she'd done. Alex knew he shouldn't have been either; he didn't own his sister. But, truthfully, he *was* embarrassed. It mortified him, that his sister had resorted to that type of work. And she knew that, so she goaded him with it, always emailing him from that address to provoke a response. Insinuating, in her way, it was his fault she'd done it at all. It was Vicky at her worst. You won't lend me money. Fine, I can earn it myself.

When she'd claimed to have money last summer, enough to pay her half of their parents' anniversary gift, he had assumed the worst.

That's why he'd blanked her. Out of anger. He was sick of subsidising her lifestyle, then being emotionally blackmailed when he didn't.

Alex sighs and looks around.

Over in the corner, he spots the Lodge manager, Harry. He knows Harry has seen him, but he doesn't acknowledge Alex. Harry, instead, angles his body away, so he's facing the older man in his company, a guy in an expensive shirt, with a vain goatee. The stranger glances at Alex, a peculiar look on his face. As though he knows something Alex doesn't.

An older man with bushy brown hair comes out from behind the bar and joins Harry and the stranger. He deals from a pack of cards but he too glances over at Alex.

Alex feels his pulse quicken, and immediately talks himself down.

I'm being paranoid, he tells himself. They're curious about me because of Vicky. It's normal.

He turns back to the bar. The TV screen mounted above the optics is showing a recent American football game, the Ravens versus the 49ers.

The whole bar, in fact, is a love note to the United States and all things international. The English-written menu offers burgers, pizza, chicken wings and bratwurst. The bottled beer in the fridges is a mix of American, German and Finnish beers. And the barman had given him his old-fashioned without blinking, even using an appropriately high-end bourbon.

Where am I? Alex wonders.

He takes out his phone and is about to try Vicky's email address when he sees he has a missed call from his father. He dials back.

'Alex. Any news?'

'Still nothing,' Alex replies. 'But . . . there's definitely something off.'

'Off, how?'

'Vicky wasn't the first woman to go missing around here.'

Silence. Then:

'What does that mean? How many women have gone missing?'

Alex stares into his glass.

'Three,' he says. 'Over a long number of years and none of them were found. Now, Vicky. I'm asking questions. I don't know if it means anything.'

He listens to his father's heavy breathing.

'If you smell something is off, something is off,' his dad says, after a few moments. 'Do you think the police are hiding information?'

'It's the police telling me this,' Alex says.

'Well, at least there's that. Wouldn't trust our own lot.'

'How's Mum?' Alex asks.

'They're waking her up tomorrow. They say things look good. Alex—'

Alex waits.

'I almost wish they'd leave her under another couple of days. It will be like living through it again.'

Alex understands and he's glad he's not there for it.

'As soon as she wakes,' he says, 'get on the phone to me.'

'I will. As soon as you find out anything there, do the same. And I'm, eh, sorry.'

'For what?'

'When I said you needed to keep your temper in check. I shouldn't have said it.'

'It doesn't matter,' Alex says, when they both know it matters a lot.

'Right. Goodnight, so.'

Somebody has sat down beside Alex. The bar counter is full of empty stools but this chap has settled himself close enough to Alex for their elbows to touch. He's in his sixties, maybe, and looks like he's employed to play Santa in one of those tourist villages.

'That looks good, what you're having.'

He points at Alex's drink, then nods to the barman.

'Can I help you?' Alex asks.

The man studies him.

'Isn't it me who can help you?'

'Excuse me?'

'You're Vicky Evans' brother, aren't you?'

Alex tenses.

'Who are you?'

'Time was, I would be the one dealing with your sister's case.'

Alex hesitates.

'Patric?' he asks.

Patric nods.

'Let me get you another one of those. You look like you need it. And I just had a date that didn't go too well, so I guess I need one, too.'

Alex doesn't protest.

'So,' Patric says. 'You're gonna solve your sister's murder.'

'I never said that.'

'Do you trust Agatha to do her job?'

'No offence but, from what I heard tonight, the local police don't exactly have a sterling record when it comes to young women around here. You've lost a few, now.'

'No offence, eh?'

Alex shrugs. He's only met the guy; he doesn't care if his feelings are hurt.

'Agatha is a better chief than I ever was,' Patric says.

'Terrific,' Alex says. 'That means, one way or the other, I'll get justice for my sister. But, between you and me, mate, she didn't look too on top of things tonight. She opened her door waving a gun at me.'

Patric narrows his eyes.

'Did something happen? Was she okay?'

'She was fine. I think you're missing the point.'

'Even police officers have lives of their own,' Patric says, quietly. 'Was there anybody else there when you arrived?'

Alex frowns. The other man seems particularly anxious.

'Like who?' he asks.

Patric tugs at the whiskers in his beard.

'Has she mentioned Luca?' he asks.

Alex shakes his head.

'No.'

'Then it's not my place to say any more,' Patric says.

Alex takes a sip of his drink and, in his head, starts to add up the parts. Agatha living on her own. Her jitteriness this morning when the kids answered the door without her, then the gun this evening. Plus, she brought the kids in the car with them to the lake, like she didn't want them out of her sight.

Patric might not be giving a lot away but it doesn't take a rocket scientist to work out Luca must be Agatha's ex, possibly an aggressive one at that.

'I called over to Agatha tonight to ask her about this Miika guy,' he says.

Patric takes a sip of his drink. He doesn't speak for a minute or two and Alex begins to grow uncomfortable in the silence.

'This was where she worked, you know,' Patric says, eventually.

Alex blinks.

'Kaya?' he says, stunned at the coincidence. There are at least ten bars in the town, and even though he had mused about it, he's genuinely surprised he wandered into hers.

'Kaya,' Patric repeats, and in the way he says the name, Alex knows in that instant the man is haunted by her. 'Pretty girl. Knew her most of her life. Her parents blamed me, for not finding her. The whole town had the case solved, convinced it was Miika.'

'You weren't, though.'

'From the start, I *knew* it was him.'

Alex stares at Patric.

'Excuse me?'

'I wanted it so badly, I made it him,' Patric says. He shifts uncomfortably in his chair. 'I'm going to tell you this because this whole town is prepared to send you off hunting a man who doesn't deserve it. And I helped cause this problem. I wanted Miika Virtanen to be guilty because it made sense. And if he was guilty, he could tell me where Kaya's body was so I could give her back to her parents.'

'And how do you know you were wrong?'

Patric faces the bar again.

'When I was finished with him, he still had the same story.'

Patric looks down at his knuckles and Alex, suddenly, understands.

Patric lifts his glass, drains the drink. Alex does the same.

'Agatha is better than me,' Patric says. 'And she'll do it the right way. Whoever it is, the person who did this to your sister, she'll find him.'

Alex absorbs this.

'Thank you,' he says, finally.

'For what?'

'For feeling it. For that girl, I mean. Whatever guilt you're torturing yourself with, I bet her family would be glad to know you did what you could. If you could tell them.'

Patric shakes his head, unwilling or unable to accept the absolution offered by a stranger.

'You should go home,' he tells Alex.

'I'm not leaving Koppe,' Alex says.

'I mean home to the Lodge. Don't sit here drinking all night. The morning is wiser than the evening.'

'Say again?'

'Finnish wisdom. I think you'd say, everything will be clearer in the morning.'

Patric gets off his stool, throws a note on the counter and grips Alex's shoulder.

Alex bows his head, a little acknowledgement.

As he watches Patric leave, he realises he can feel eyes on him.

Alex turns. Harry and the two other men are still sitting in the corner, ostensibly playing cards. All three have been watching him and Patric talk.

Alex stares back, until they look away.

Back in his cabin, Alex barely pauses to take off his coat before opening up Hotmail.

He types in Vicky's email address, then the password he suspects she used.

Bingo.

He's into her account.

The messages in her inbox are old and mainly from the manager of the club she worked in when she was exotic dancing. There are a couple more that Alex has to back out of straight away. Emails from pervy customers talking about what they were thinking when Vicky was dancing and how they'd like to meet up in person.

Alex shakes his head. How could his sister cope with that shit? Of course that was Vicky, wasn't it? Thinking she could handle anything and anyone.

He opens her sent emails. It's possible, he knows this, that she might have sent him an email and that he'd deleted it without even reading it. He can't remember doing that, but if he'd been drunk and had seen a message from that email address come in . . . yes, in a fit of anger, he might have just got rid of it and forgotten all about it.

There are no recent sent emails. None from around the time she went missing.

The last email she sent him, that he definitely did see, is still there.

Alex checks the inbox again but there's nothing. He checks the trash. No emails of import there, either.

So, why did she tell Josephine in TM&S she was going to email Alex and then not send anything?

Next morning in the breakfast hall, Alex spots Vicky's friend Nicolas.

He's been sensing that some of the guides in the resort are avoiding him in one-to-one settings. He doesn't know if this is a natural reaction, not wanting to be around somebody else's grief, or if there's a more sinister reason.

He gets talking to Nicolas as they fill their plates. Small talk, about Finnish food.

While standing, Nicolas makes Alex try something called a Karelian pie, a small soft cake thing, smothered in butter and loaded with scrambled egg. Alex has only just swallowed the strange-tasting concoction when Nicolas starts to heap rye bread and cheese on to his plate.

'I draw the line at burnt bread,' Alex says.

'It's not burnt. It's just black.'

'You got any plans this morning?' Alex asks.

Nicolas frowns.

'Work,' he says.

'Right.'

Nicolas cocks his head.

'You can come with me if you're at a loose end. But we've got to keep an eye out for Lassi.'

'Lassi?'

'The owner.'

Once Nicolas has kitted out Alex in a pair of the ubiquitous blue overalls, they prepare to leave. On the way out through reception, Alex spots the older man he saw in the bar last night, talking to Harry.

'Who's that guy?' he asks.

'*That's* Lassi,' Nicolas tells him.

'He's Harry's boss?'

'Yep.'

'So, he's the one who does the hiring?'

'Yep. He's on the local council too, got a lot of sway. So, if you lost your job here, you'd want to be careful because, chances are, he'd make sure you weren't hired anywhere else in town, either.'

Alex narrows his eyes at Lassi. The other man is busy with a customer and doesn't notice.

He looks the sort, Alex thinks, to seduce young women, his money giving him all the confidence he needs.

Had he tried to make a move on Vicky and it had gone badly?

Outside, in temperatures of minus ten, Alex is fully appreciative of his thermals and the extra merino wool socks and heat pads that Nicolas gifted him in the equipment room. Alex picked up a couple of extra sweaters in a shop in town but he's still running to catch up with how he should have packed for this trip.

Nicolas, it transpires, is in charge of the husky sledding, and this morning he's smoothing out the route for this afternoon's tourists.

They walk towards an enclosure, following the sound of barking and yapping dogs. For some reason, Alex has an image in his head that huskies are practically wolf-sized. He's astonished to see they're not much bigger than the average dog and not all of them are white-furred and blue-eyed.

'We use a mix of dogs,' Nicolas explains. 'To be honest, we take what we're sent from the local commercial husky farm. They do the larger tours; we're just a small offshoot. But the farm is also owned by Lassi.'

'He's quite the entrepreneur.'

'Yep. But he's still struggling, I reckon. That hotel up on the mountain has really dented his business. He has to – how do you say it? – juggle a lot of balls to keep it all going.'

Alex presumes he's going to sit in the sled while Nicolas does something . . . leads the dogs on or whatever. Instead, Nicolas points to the sled handlebar and the skis that jut out to the rear.

'Something fun for you,' Nicolas says. 'So, stand on the skis. Hold on to the handlebar. That footrest in between your skis is the brake. It will slow the dogs down. Just take your left foot off and put it on the brake, but make sure you keep your balance on the right ski when you do. You don't want to fall. Also, don't jump off. If there's nothing stopping them, the dogs will run like crazy and I'll end up in a ditch with my neck broken. Whatever you do, keep your hands on the handlebar. Don't try to touch stuff as we pass; the dogs might speed up and you'll lose your fingers. Good to go?'

'I'm sorry, what? You'll have to run through all that again—'

Nicolas is already loosening the rope tying the dogs to the fence pole.

'Hold her steady so I can get in the sled,' Nicolas says.

'Christ,' Alex says, jumping on the right ski and balancing his foot on the brake. As soon as Nicolas is in the sled, Alex takes off the pressure.

The dogs take off at a pelt and Alex almost loses his balance.

'I don't know the way,' Alex shouts.

'The dogs know the way,' Nicolas calls back.

For a few minutes, Alex concentrates on the dogs. When he realises they can't go much faster and, in fact, have settled into a rhythm, he begins to relax. He even gets the hang of using his foot to help the dogs up the inclines. Then he starts to enjoy the passing landscape. It's serene; unblemished white snow as far as the eye can see, dense spruce to either side.

'I'm starting to think we've been approaching dogs all wrong in Britain,' Alex says. He's freezing, yet exhilarated.

'It's not for me,' Nicolas says. 'I don't even like dogs.'

'And they put you on husky duty?' Alex says. 'Where are you from, anyway?'

'Moscow.'

'Oh.'

'You thought I was Finnish.'

'Sorry. All the accents are blending into one,' Alex says.

'Netflix English, we call it. I'm a mongrel. Finnish mother. I try not to mention my dad too much around here. Harry has a Russian father, too, but he grew up here. Can't imagine that was easy. His parents didn't work out. I'd bet any time his mother and father fought, she called him the Russian invader . . .'

Alex smiles.

They travel in silence for a few minutes. Then Nicolas speaks.

'I know you'll be wondering about me,' he says. 'And all of us who worked with your sister. Vicky and I were friends. There was nothing more. I'm gay. I don't mention that much, either. Wouldn't have been a good idea where I grew up and the habit stuck. So, I wasn't some broken-hearted lover of Vicky's. And we never fell out over anything. But, she wasn't universally adored, like people are saying. And . . . I didn't think it was strange that she'd left.'

Alex tightens his grip on the handlebars.

'What do you mean?' he asks.

Nicolas hesitates.

'Vicky was a good-looking girl. She got a lot of attention. Not always from the right people. And that kind of woman can also make other women jealous.'

Alex frowns.

'Other women like who? Niamh?'

'No. Vicky and Niamh were never in competition for any guys. Niamh has her own little crush going on and Vicky had no interest in him. Niamh is devastated about Vicky.'

'I know,' Alex says. He wonders who Niamh has a crush on, but it's irrelevant in the scheme of things.

'Look,' Nicolas says, shrugging. 'Vicky and Niamh were like those popular girls in school. Fun, flirty. Tight with each other. And take Beatrice, for example. Every time a hot guy stayed in the Lodge, Beatrice had to wait and see if Vicky or Niamh wanted him first. And then just Vicky, because Niamh stopped chasing tourists after a while. That must have stung.'

Beatrice, Alex thinks. He remembers how the woman had accosted him with warm wishes that first day he arrived, the uncomfortable feeling he'd had of overfamiliarity.

'You hardly think this Beatrice killed my sister because Vicky was more popular than her?' Alex says.

'I haven't a clue, my friend,' Nicolas replies. 'Vicky was struck on the head, wasn't she? Girls – they can be vicious. But, look. I'm just using that as an example. Maybe there were a few things on Vicky's mind. Guys harassing her. Other girls being jealous. Or maybe she thought Harry was going to fire her ass. She wasn't the best guide and she did miss a few shifts here and there. Whatever it was, I got the impression that Vicky *was* thinking of moving on.'

'They asked everybody for alibis,' Alex says.

'I know. I wasn't here the night she disappeared. I spent the night in the hotel on the slopes. I was with somebody.'

Alex digests this, the fact Nicolas feels the need to tell Alex exactly what his alibi is. He's also trying to figure out if the chap is genuinely trying to be helpful by telling Alex his feelings about Vicky and Beatrice, or if he's stirring some shit.

Alex lands on the side of helpful. There's nothing in Nicolas' tone that feels malicious or trouble-making. He's just telling it how he saw it.

Alex is so focused on his thoughts that when he shifts his leg weight, he forgets his foot is actually on the brake, slowing the dogs down. The dogs feel the jerk and take off. The side of Nicolas' face bangs off the sled; Alex is thrown but he manages to get his foot on the ski. Luckily, the dogs aren't as energetic as they were at the start and their pace evens out.

'Sorry,' he says.

'It happens,' says Nicolas.

They ride in silence for several more minutes.

Alex spots the Lodge through the trees and realises they've done a short loop and are doubling back. A delivery van has pulled up to the rear of the Lodge; a large man in a blue puffer jacket and trapper hat is taking a box of goods out of the back.

'Have you heard of this Miika guy?' Alex asks.

'He only delivers every second week.'

'I'm sorry, what?' Alex says.

'Miika. Over there.'

Alex stares over to where Nicolas is pointing. The man at the delivery van has turned towards them. His movements are slow, measured. He stares over for a moment, then walks towards the service door to the Lodge's kitchen.

The dogs veer right, towards their enclosure.

'That was Miika?' Alex says, his heart racing. 'The guy who lives up the mountain? The one they all think murdered his wife?'

'Yeah. If you had venison this week, it came from his farm. Can't let a missing wife get in the way of a good produce deal.'

Alex has forgotten how cold he is. Inside his suit, he's sweating.

That man was huge. He could see it, even with the jacket and the way he slouched. Miika gripped that box and lifted it with ease, when anybody could see how heavy it was.

Is that the man who murdered his sister?

When they arrive back at the dog enclosure, Alex instinctively wants to race to the Lodge to confront Miika, but Nicolas tells him to keep his foot on the brake until he's tied the dogs back up.

Alex waits impatiently for the other man to give him the nod. He's about to be liberated when, from within the folds of his outerwear, he hears his phone ringing.

Alex pulls off his leather over-gloves and then his right mitten, unsticks his pocket velcro and searches for the phone, frustrated by all the layers.

It's his father calling and Alex just answers it in time.

'Dad, I have to—' he begins to say, but he's interrupted.

'Alex,' his mother croaks.

Alex stands deadly still, forgetting everything for a few seconds bar what it's like to hear his mother's voice. Nicolas looks at him questioningly.

'Mum? Are you okay?'

'I'm okay.'

She doesn't sound it. She's alive, she's talking, but Alex knows his mother will never be okay.

'Oh, Alex,' she says.

'It's okay, Mum,' he says. 'I'll be home soon.'

'No,' his mother says, and Alex falls quiet. 'Your father told me where you are and what you're doing. You do this, pet. Find out who hurt my little girl.' She breaks off with a weak sob. Alex waits, listening, a lump in his throat.

'I'll be here,' his mother says, when she recovers herself. 'I'll be waiting for you. And Vicky.'

'I'll do my best,' Alex says, weakly.

He can hear his mother's pause.

'Your best has always been good enough,' she says.

They both know that's not true, Alex thinks, but his mother cuts into his thoughts.

'I know you think you let us down, Alex,' she says. 'You were only a kid. Sixteen. You show me a lad up here who hasn't got handy with his fists at some point in his life.'

'It was more than that, Mum.'

'I know, son. But it feels important to tell you how little that matters and how much I love you. I know you still carry it. I wish I could have told Vicky that anything in the past . . . it was irrelevant. It's my job to love you anyway.'

They say nothing for a few seconds; Alex listens to his mother's ragged breathing, knowing each word must be a strain for her.

'Alex, you meant the world to her, you know that,' his mother says. 'She always looked up to you.'

'I wasn't a good brother, Mum. She didn't even have my phone number when she needed me.'

'I know that, pet. She wasn't always a good sister. Or a good daughter. Vicky wasn't perfect. But she was ours and we were hers.'

Alex blinks away the tears that threaten to break free from his eyes.

They talk for a couple of minutes more.

Alex is shivering by the time he hangs up. Nicolas doesn't ask who was on the phone. Alex's side of the conversation gave it all away. They walk back towards the Lodge in silence, the tall Finn/Russian lending Alex support by his presence.

When they arrive, Miika's van is already gone.

Alex is fairly certain guests aren't supposed to be in the kitchen of the Lodge but nobody is paying him any attention.

It's a large area, filled with sparkling clean stainless steel units and the bustle of lunch preparation. Every cooker ring is heating a pot, every counter is topped with chopping boards and trays of diced and julienned vegetables and other ingredients.

At the centre of this hive of activity is a large woman in a chef's apron, her hair pinned in an industrious bun, her glasses steaming from the heat.

She looks at him blankly when he stands in front of her, momentarily trying to establish whether he works for her or is lost.

'Are you Cecelia?' Alex asks. Nicolas had told him who to ask for.

'Yes?'

'Can I talk to you? I'm a guest at the Lodge.'

'No, no, sorry. No guests in here. You –' she points to one of her worker ants – 'take him back to the restaurant.'

'My sister Vicky was a guide here.' Alex uses the magic words.

Cecelia's face registers this, then fills with distress.

Before Alex knows what's happening, she's enveloped him in a tight embrace and he's almost gasping for air. The woman's arms could crack walnuts.

She stands back then, without a word.

'Thank you,' Alex says, and he means it. There's something . . . maternal in Cecelia and after the conversation with his mother, Alex needs that.

Before Cecelia can offer to feed him up, which Alex knows is coming, he speaks.

'I wonder if I can ask you a few questions—'

'Absolutely. She was such a good little worker, you know. Unlike some of the others. She was always happy to roll her shirtsleeves up and pitch in, even if it wasn't her job.'

Alex nods in appreciation. He'd never thought of Vicky as a hard worker. Turns out, there's plenty he didn't know about her.

Cecelia leads Alex to the side of the kitchen, away from the many listening ears.

'I wanted to ask you about the guy who delivers your venison. Miika Virtanen?'

The older woman's eyes darken.

'Him?' she says. 'What about him?'

'I heard some tales about him,' Alex says.

'Of course you did,' Cecelia says, eyeing him shrewdly. 'Most tourists wouldn't be bothered by local gossip. But you're not a tourist, are you?'

Alex shakes his head.

'It was a little strange to see him delivering goods here,' he says.

'That's Lassi for you. Our lord and master. He'd do a deal with the devil if it meant a discount. Lots of men round here will buy from Miika. I suppose *they* don't feel threatened by him. I won't deal with him when he comes here. I get one of the lads to take the boxes.'

'You believe what they say about him, then?'

'What *they* say about him, *Pulu*?' Cecelia says. 'I am *they*. We all know what he did.'

'To his wife.'

'To his wife –' Cecelia lowers her voice – 'and to the others.'

She glances around, but Alex senses she isn't worried in the slightest about anybody listening. She's queen of all she surveys in the kitchen. She might be worried the boss or the owner might wander in, though.

'Is it possible,' Alex asks, 'that he might have had something to do with what happened to Vicky?'

Cecelia doesn't answer immediately. Alex can tell that, while she's the sort who considers it her God-given right to speak her mind, she's aware in his presence that this isn't historical or some-thing that's happened to somebody else. When she answers him, her tone and words are measured.

'I can't say yes or no,' she says. 'What I will say is that, just as a matter of routine, I would ask him where he was the night your sister vanished. But I don't see how Vicky would have come across him. Miika is only in town when he's delivering, twice a month at most.'

'But,' Alex says, 'he delivers to this Lodge. Isn't it possible she might have encountered him if she helped you out in here the odd time?'

Now Cecelia frowns.

'Well, yes,' she says. 'But it's normally the boys I ask to take in deliveries. Not that I'm sexist – I'm stronger than most of these little things – but it's just what you do, isn't it?'

Cecelia places her hands on her hips, deep in thought. Then she turns around and bellows.

'Beatrice!'

Alex is surprised to see Beatrice emerge from behind a counter at the far end of the kitchen. She must have been there all along but he hadn't spotted her.

She walks towards them, her face contorting into that sympathetic expression she had when he first met her. It only serves to make Alex feel uncomfortable.

'Hello, Alex,' she says.

'Beatrice helps out when I'm under pressure, too,' Cecelia says. 'Beatrice, you were in here a good bit with Vicky. Do you ever see Miika, the guy who does my venison deliveries?'

Beatrice hesitates.

'You can speak freely,' Cecelia says. 'I don't care what your opinion is of him.'

'The weird guy from the mountain?' Beatrice says. 'Not really. I was warned to avoid him when I started working here. He is only down once or twice a month, yes?'

'Did you ever see Vicky talking to him?'

'Only that one time.'

Alex tenses up; he can see Cecelia does the same.

'When?' Alex asks.

'A couple of months ago. I saw Vicky talking to him outside but it wasn't for long. She said he asked her if Lassi was here. Vicky wasn't bothered by him. She'd heard the tales, too, but she said it was all . . .'

Beatrice trails off.

'All what?' Alex presses.

Beatrice glances nervously at Cecelia and then back to Alex.

'All *stuff and nonsense*. I told her she was being stupid. I mean, there's no smoke without fire, is that not the saying? But she just laughed. She always knew best. Thought she did, anyhow . . .'

Beatrice stops. She looks at Alex, mortified, then down at the ground.

'Thank you, Beatrice,' Cecelia says, her tone colder now. 'Could you bring those trays of *graavilohi* out to the ski party?'

'Sure,' Beatrice says, and scarpers.

Cecelia looks at Alex.

'She's not as clever or as nice as your sister was.'

Alex says nothing. He agrees.

'Maybe Vicky saw Miika for a moment or two,' Cecelia adds. 'But I'm sure it's just like Beatrice says. She answered his question and that was that.'

'You're probably right,' Alex says.

They look at each other. Cecelia's face is full of pity.

He imagines locals like her are already speculating that Miika, the monster who lives on the mountain, has struck again.

But now Alex has proof that the man did in fact talk to his sister, that he must have known who she was.

He wonders whether the police are even aware.

Before Agatha leaves the station, she braces herself, picks up the phone on her desk and dials one of the only numbers in the world she still remembers off by heart.

When her call goes straight to voice message, she doesn't know if she's grateful or annoyed. She'd prepared herself to have the conversation, argument, or whatever it could be called. But she didn't want to have it, not really. Now, though, as she listens to the automated voice message, she wonders, what does this mean? That the person on the other end can't hear the phone? Or can't come to the phone? Or is ignoring the phone?

At the beep, Agatha takes a deep breath.

'Olavi saw you. I don't know what you're playing at. I warned you, Luca. Stay away. If you love them, if you ever loved me, just stay away.'

She hangs up the phone, pulling her fingers back quickly, like they've been singed. Agatha doesn't know if Luca will try to ring back, which is why she has used the station phone. She's long since blocked Luca from her mobile. And her email. And Facebook.

Outside, in reception, Janic is struggling with a string of fairy lights, trying to unknot them with the intense focus of a kid trying to build the *Millennium Falcon* with two thousand pieces of Lego.

'Gotham City all safe, Janic?' Agatha says.

He looks up, confused. Agatha nods at the fairy lights.

'Thought we should have a little bit of Christmas,' he says, defensively.

'That little bit of Christmas will take until next year to unravel.'

Agatha reaches under the counter, takes out the petty cash box, opens it and hands Janic a fifty-euro note.

'Go to the store and get new lights and a small tree. I don't want people calling me the Grinch.'

'That's not what they call you.'

'Oh? What do they call me?'

Janic's eyes widen in panic.

Agatha smiles.

'And when you've decked the place out, maybe do a little bit of police work.'

'Yes, Chief.'

Agatha leaves the station.

After working herself up to make the call to Luca, then failing to connect, she now just wants to forget about it.

She is, in fact, already regretting it.

Outside, Agatha takes one of the snowmobiles. She plans to travel across Inari and it's quicker that way.

She passes by the slopes, already dotted with skiers descending from the hotel and taking the lift back up. She remembers when those hills only contained trees. She likes the large, wooden-styled hotel – it's pretty, inside and out – but it has also taken over the town like it was always there and part of her resents that.

The journey only takes minutes along the edge of the lake. Agatha enjoys the cold on her cheeks under her visor. She's always felt more comfortable on the snowmobile than on skis. Odd, because every

Lappish child is practically born with them on their feet. But Agatha always wanted to go faster. She still remembers her mother screaming at Agatha and her sister to slow down whenever they took off from the house on the snowmobiles. The girls never obeyed. They liked to race each other. The seeds of competition to be the best, the fastest, the biggest risk-taker were sown early in their household.

The red wooden house stands where it has always stood, at the edge of the lake, its deck stilts currently encased in several metres of ice. Agatha remembers calling out here as a kid, when her friend Becki used to invite her on sleepovers. They'd hike for miles through the forest then return, sweating, and cannonball from the deck into the lake.

Becki still lives in the house, with her mother, though she and Agatha don't spend as much time together as they'd like and certainly not as much as they did as children. First, Agatha had to go to Rovaniemi for training. Then, when she returned, it wasn't long before she became police chief and had to manage that as well as being a single mom. And Becki's mother, Henni, has grown older and more cantankerous, which means Becki spends a lot of time with the tourists they take in, making sure Henni doesn't rile the people who pay their bills.

There isn't an awful lot of time for hanging around on Becki's deck, drinking to the changing seasons and chatting about life.

But Agatha is proud of her friend and happy to see the red house is still doing what it always did. People imagined the hotel and the many holiday cabins in town would put Henni's place and Lassi's Lodge out of business. But the Lodge kept going and the red house has endured too, with its quaint charm and more intimate Lappish experience.

When Mary Rosenberg stayed with them back in 2007, it was her third or fourth winter there.

Something about talking to Alex last night, showing him her case board in the basement, has unsettled Agatha. Everything she told Vicky's brother was true. She doesn't think there's a serial killer operating in Koppe. She doesn't want to think it. People go missing all the time, for lots of reasons.

But, can you ever rule something out?

It has bothered Agatha over the years.

Sure, there's no pattern.

But there are three missing women.

Becki hears the snowmobile and comes out onto the deck to see who's calling. She's wearing an oversized cream woollen cardigan, tied at the waist, and her beautiful blonde hair is swept into a full ponytail. She was always a stunner and, if anything, has got better-looking in her thirties. Agatha swallows her little pang of envy. You shouldn't be jealous of friends, she tells herself. And what do looks matter to Agatha anyway? It's not like, even if she had any, she'd be in a position to try to use them.

Becki smiles when Agatha takes off her helmet.

'At last,' Becki says. 'I thought we'd get all the way to Christmas before I saw you.'

'I'm sorry,' Agatha says, automatically. 'It's been crazy with this case . . .'

'You don't need to apologise to me, I'm the one who should have called by to see you and the children. I should be far more help to you than I am. Come on in, I've just taken cookies out of the oven and I've a pot of hot chocolate on the stove. My God, I've just heard myself. I sound like a proper little homemaker.'

Agatha parks up the snowmobile, then walks up the steps to the rear of the house, kicking snow off her boots as she goes. Inside the back door, she changes into slippers and removes all her damp outerwear.

The inside of the wooden house is a Christmas wonderland. Most Laplanders decorate tastefully for Christmas, simply, wooden ornaments and candles taking centre stage. But the tourist destinations always try to meet international expectations and Becki has a nine-foot fir in the centre of the high-ceilinged dining room, twinkling with thousands of lights and ceramic baby angel Gabriels tooting horns.

'Understated,' Agatha says. 'I sent Janic to the store to get some fairy lights before I left the office. I see, now, I should have sent him here for inspiration.'

Becki cheerfully ignores her.

When she's settled Agatha on a comfortable settee with a fur blanket over her knees, Becki pours them both hot chocolates and puts a plate of cookies on the coffee table.

'Do you have many staying at the moment?' Agatha asks.

'Just one family for Christmas. One very wealthy family. They're out hiking with Mom at the moment. You should have seen their faces, this little old lady telling them she'd be their guide.'

'They don't know your mom,' Agatha says.

'She'll leave them for dust.' Becki cocks her head. 'But at least she'll keep them on the straight and narrow. They wanted to go looking for Sami people. Take pictures. Went on like they were hunting trolls. They nearly died when I told them the driver in the Adidas tracksuit who brought them here was a Sami man. Anyhow, you didn't come out here to check up on me. What's on your mind? You have your chief of police hat on.'

'Am I that obvious?'

Becki tilts her head.

Agatha smiles and takes a sip of the hot chocolate, savouring its warmth.

'Mary Rosenberg,' she says.

'I thought she'd be playing on your mind. Mine too. When I heard a body had been found in the lake, I figured it would be that girl from the Lodge. Too weird, otherwise. But, you never know. Every time I hear something, that's where my mind goes. I know there were others, but she's the one who stayed with us so she's stuck with me.'

'It's been twelve years, now,' Agatha says. 'I'm just wondering if there's anything you or your mom remembered afterwards that we might look at now in a different light.'

'What sort of light?' Becki sits forward. 'The police were sure it was an accident.'

'Yes,' Agatha says. 'I remember.'

She'd been training in Rovaniemi at the time. Becki had rung with the news – she'd been quite distraught, Agatha remembers. They'd searched and searched for Mary.

Patric had told her, on the one-year anniversary, after Agatha had returned to Koppe, that he'd been convinced the lake would thaw that summer and Mary's body would be found. It was unusual that somebody so familiar with the countryside would fall foul of it and yet an important reminder that it could happen to anybody. Even the most experienced skiers.

It was only when Mary stayed disappeared that the rumours started.

'But she never was found,' Becki says, sadly.

Agatha shakes her head.

'Becki, I'm sure you've heard that Vicky was murdered.'

'Obviously,' Becki says. 'The phone lines started buzzing with that one as soon as you got back from Rovaniemi. But what are you saying? You think Mary might have been murdered, too?'

'I don't know,' Agatha says. 'I just need to make sure that's not what happened.'

Becki studies her. Agatha can see her friend is considering something.

'There was something that I always thought strange,' she says.

Agatha puts down her hot chocolate.

'It might be nothing,' Becki continues, 'but I found her fiancé a bit odd.'

Agatha frowns. She wasn't expecting this.

'Her fiancé?' she says. 'The guy in Canada?'

'Did she have more than one?'

Agatha rolls her eyes.

'But he wasn't here,' she says. 'He never came over with her. He only arrived after, didn't he? To help with the search.'

'Oh, I know that,' Becki says. 'I don't mean he flew here and he killed her. That's why I didn't mention it, at the time. What I mean is, he never stopped calling.'

'When she went missing?'

'Yes. But before, too. He was always phoning her. Phoning and emailing. He seemed really possessive. I used to think, that's the reason she comes here each winter. To get away from him.'

Agatha remembers the guy. He'd come over for the one-year anniversary of Mary's disappearance. Agatha had stood at the lake with the locals, Mary's fiancé among them, as they tossed white winter roses on to the ice.

He'd been distraught. When Agatha took over, Patric told her that part of her job would be dealing with relatives who'd lost loved ones over the years and never got a resolution. Agatha had taken a couple of calls from the fiancé. He'd always seemed charming. Sad, but soldiering on.

'Maybe he was just concerned about her being over here on her own,' Agatha says.

'Maybe. I'm sure you're right.'

Becki doesn't sound convinced. And Agatha knows how important it is never to dismiss somebody's gut feelings.

'What are you thinking?' she asks. 'Is there something you're worried about?'

'I just wondered, well, I always thought – what if Mary wanted to get away from him? You remember that movie? *Sleeping with the Enemy*?'

'Julia Roberts?' Agatha says, her eyebrows raised.

'Yes. She fakes her own death to get away from her husband.'

Agatha half smiles.

'I remember it was a great movie,' she says.

'You're laughing at me,' Becki says, smiling. 'I know. It sounds ridiculous. I'm letting my imagination run away with me.'

'I'm not laughing at you,' Agatha says. 'It's just, I know it's actually a lot harder to disappear yourself than how they make it look in those movies. Mary's picture was in all the papers . . .'

'All the Finnish papers,' Becki says. 'What if she'd left Finland?'

'Her stuff was still here, though, wasn't it? Her passport, her clothes.'

'Yes, but no money. Her purse was gone.'

'That's hardly that unusual,' Agatha says.

'On a cross-country ski? Was she going to pop in somewhere for a cola? And she brought a bag of supplies on the trip. What if she'd put a change of clothes and some essentials in it? A fake passport . . .'

Agatha narrows her eyes. Becki shrugs.

'It's just a theory,' she says.

Agatha sits forward and places a hand on Becki's knee.

'Becki, I want you to be completely honest with me. Have you got a fake passport, a grab bag and some money, and are you planning to do a runner on your mom? It sounds like something you've fantasised about and I know she can be a pain in the ass . . .'

'Agatha, I can assure you, if she ever gets too much for me, I'll just shoot the old trout.'

They both laugh but Agatha's brain is already running double time and she goes over what Becki has said and the possible avenues it offers up.

When she's leaving, Becki grabs Agatha's hand and asks her if everything is okay at home.

Agatha smiles so hard her jaw clenches.

'Of course,' she says. 'Why do you ask?'

'You looked like a ghost when you arrived and you still look like a ghost,' Becki says. 'And it's not just your case. Spill. Luca?'

'Maybe,' Agatha says, reluctantly. 'I'm not sure. I'm trying to stay focused on work but . . .'

Becki purses her lips.

'Why don't you all come here for Christmas Eve?' she says. 'Stay a few nights. You're allowed time off, aren't you? The American family are nice, you'll get on with them. And you know our place is big enough; you could take the attic rooms and see nobody, if you wanted. Or, I could pay you to wear traditional garb and pretend to the Americans I've caught a real Sami family.'

They both laugh.

'Actually,' Agatha says, 'if you aren't too busy, would you object to me sending the kids up for a sleepover, sooner?'

Becki studies Agatha. Agatha tries to look relaxed, like her stomach isn't churning with fear every waking moment.

'They can stay with me as long as you want,' Becki says. 'You know they'll be safe here and I can keep them very, very busy.'

Agatha squeezes her friend's hand, unable to express her gratitude with words.

When she leaves, Becki waves until Agatha can't see her any more.

And Agatha realises, as the snowmobile puts miles between her and Becki's house, that the prospect of getting the children out of Koppe town has left her feeling more relaxed than she has since Olavi told her his secret.

Koppe
1998

Kaya is deathly, deathly tired, but still she fills the bucket with lichen and walks towards the reindeer enclosure. Miika had to drive all over Lapland yesterday during a blizzard and she knows he, too, is exhausted. He's been so good to her lately, she wants him to know that she can be good back. That between them, they can make this marriage work.

Last night, while he slept, she sketched him. Even after all these years, it's the first time she's drawn her husband. He was sleeping so peacefully. Just this big mound in the bed, his chest rising and falling in a steady rhythm. She'd never watched him in slumber before. Normally, after work, she'd get in the bed beside him, close her eyes and only wake when he was already gone.

Her lover always wanted her to draw him. He would shower her with words of praise and admiration, so eloquent in his flattery and, now she knows, lies. She did draw him, but not with the same love she drew Miika last night. It's funny, how quickly you realise lust was only ever that.

There was something very intimate about drawing Miika while

he was dead to the world. Something so trusting; him lying there, exposed, vulnerable, and her capturing every line of it.

It made her feel protective. Maternal even. This is her family. Miika and their child.

She hasn't told him about the baby yet. There hasn't been a chance. He's either been tired or working. But today, he's home.

She'll do his chores and let him sleep. Then, later, she'll make him his favourite meal, poronkäristys, and pour him some of that nice sweet wine he likes from Germany. It's always tickled her that her husband likes wine that tastes to her like dessert. Her lover was very different, preferring the tang of ale or the sting of whiskey. Miika loves whiskey, too, but thankfully he hasn't had too much of it lately. She couldn't bear it if, just as everything was coming together, he decided to start drinking properly again.

She has no lover to run to, this time.

Kaya shakes her head. She won't think of that man any more. He had the smallest of chances to redeem himself. If he'd left his wife and come found her, grovelling on his knees, she'd have forgiven him. She might have left Miika for him. But now the die is cast and she hates him, hates having to see him when she's in work. She wishes he was dead.

Kaya lets herself into the enclosure and begins to scatter the lichen around the ground. Most of the reindeer nuzzle against her legs then get to eating. Except for Pukka, who wants Kaya to feed him from her fingers, the way he likes it.

Kaya giggles as his tongue tickles her hand. She forgets the pregnancy nausea, the tiredness, all her little stresses and worries, as she feels the heat of the animals' bodies around her, watches their breath snorting into the frozen air and thinks: this is my life, it's what I want.

When she returns to the house, she scrubs down the kitchen and polishes all of Miika's mother's old ornaments in the sitting room. Then she goes to the bathroom, takes off her clothes and runs a bath.

Under the hot water, she runs her fingers over her stomach, which seems to have stretched even more. She lets her hands slide over her breasts, realising that they, too, have swollen further. Her hair, when she washes it, feels thicker than ever, and softer, too.

Kaya is standing naked in the bathroom when Miika comes in. She's drip-drying on to the towel as she applies cream to her face in the mirror.

She turns. He's staring at her, his eyes travelling over her body. He says nothing and Kaya starts to blush. She's been feeling something towards him lately – lust. She hasn't felt that way for him in a long time. Even when she started having sex with him so she could convince him the baby was his, it was just out of necessity.

Now, though, her eyes are drawn to Miika's strong body and his large hands. She thinks: I want them on me. I want him on me. She can hardly think for how much she wants him.

'Do you want me to stay like this?' she says, coyly.

He looks up at her, then. There's something strange on his face.

'You're pregnant,' he says.

Kaya almost panics before she remembers it doesn't have to be a secret any more. She was going to tell him, anyhow.

'Yes,' she says, beaming.

'How long?'

'A few weeks, I think. It must have been that first time after so long . . .'

He looks down at her body again.

'Are you glad?' she asks. Something in his demeanour has changed. The air is bristling with it.

The desire she was feeling is seeping from her body as fast as the heat from the bathwater.

Miika turns and walks out of the bathroom.

Kaya stays standing there, very still, her heart racing. She doesn't understand what's just happened. Is he angry at her? Does he not want her to be pregnant?

She reaches for her towel, wraps it around her body and sits on the edge of the bath.

Then, a horrible thought hits her and she starts to tremble.

Maybe Miika is not going to be the fool she needs him to be.

Koppe

2019

The roadside café where Hilda Paikkala worked before she went missing is not far from Becki's, so Agatha takes a small detour before heading back into Koppe.

Anywhere else, the police might not presume that the people who'd worked in the café five years ago still worked there, but not around here. Jobs aren't easy to come by this far north and, mostly, once you get one, it's a job for life. Not to mention, this business is family-run.

Agatha parks up near the petrol pumps beside the café. There are a couple of large trucks pulled in on the other side of the road, hauliers stopping for fuel and sustenance before continuing the long, arduous drive down to the capital. Most of them are coming or going from Sweden, crossing the border at the top where the two countries meet. Agatha knows the vast majority of drivers will have been on the road since last night. Sometimes they pull over and sleep in the cabins behind the driver's compartment. It's a legal requirement that they don't drive for longer than a set amount of hours. The distances they cover are vast and conditions up here are ripe for lulling people to sleep.

But she also knows that some of the truckers have bosses and companies that don't write decent pit stops into the schedule, and so a few of the drivers in the café will be mainlining coffee before hitting the road again for another long shift.

The bell tinkles on the door as Agatha steps in and pulls back the old, chequered curtain to enter the building. She removes her gloves and coat; the owner has the heat dialled up, maybe to encourage customers to stay a little longer.

There are a handful of men sitting at the tables, consuming bowls of coffee, sandwiches and cakes. They look at her with mild interest; something in her demeanour reveals she's police and they all lower their gazes. The last thing they need is her stopping them as they're getting into their trucks to ask to look at their itineraries and tachographs. She'll be able to tell with a glance if they've slept since they left Helsinki or Stockholm or whether they should be sleeping here before driving on.

Agatha heads straight to the counter, ignoring the drivers.

A young, raven-haired woman is there, taking a tray of tired pastries from behind the glass display and replacing it with a fresh one. She smiles at Agatha; they know each other, mainly to see around. Agatha has never had much call to come to the café; there's rarely trouble here. The truckers save that for the pubs, when they're rested and drink has been taken.

But the woman remembers Agatha from years back, when Agatha was helping Patric with the investigation into Hilda's disappearance. Agatha was just the deputy then and this woman, if she recalls correctly, is the owner's daughter and somebody who worked alongside Hilda.

They'd been friendly, despite the age gap. The woman – Anna, that's her name – was only eighteen at the time and Hilda was in her thirties. But she'd found Hilda great fun and latched on to her.

'Chief,' Anna says. 'It is chief now, isn't it?'

Agatha smiles.

'The last three years,' she says. 'And let me guess, you're the boss now, too?'

Anna snorts.

'Not a chance. Dad's out back, doing a stocktake. Which is code for playing online poker. Luckily, we have him on a limit. Otherwise my *inheritance* would be gone from underneath me. Can I get you a coffee?'

Agatha laughs at the tone Anna uses for the word inheritance, and politely declines the coffee.

'Do you need to speak to Dad?'

Agatha had already thought about this on the way over. The café owner hadn't been entirely helpful when Hilda disappeared. He seemed to know very little about his employee, other than the fact she was a good worker and had never caused him any problems. Agatha had called in a couple of times since, and the old man never had anything to add to his original account.

Hilda had left work the evening before she disappeared. She had a few holiday days owed. She told her employer she was going to visit friends the next day in a town upcountry. That was the last conversation they had.

'Actually,' Agatha says, 'I wouldn't mind chatting to you this time.'

'Me?' Anna asks, curiously.

A trucker comes to the counter to pay his bill. He keeps his eyes down, avoiding Agatha. He throws down the exact amount on his bill and a couple of twenty-cent coins.

'Is that your tip?' Agatha says.

The guy looks up at her, alarmed.

'Uh.' He mumbles something, then fumbles in his pockets. He pulls out a couple of two-euro coins and places them gently on the counter.

'Thanks,' he says, then leaves.

Anna looks at Agatha.

'Can you stay?' she says. 'The guy only had a cheese sandwich.'

Agatha smiles. It can't be easy, being in your early twenties and working in a place like this, with men who are either monosyllabic or trying it on.

'I guess you want to ask about Hilda,' Anna says.

'What gave me away?'

'Nothing else has ever happened here. Nothing we're associated with, anyway. And with the girl from the Lodge . . .'

'I've no updates,' Agatha says. 'But, you know, it's still a live case.'

'I always thought that was just one of those things the police say to placate families.'

Agatha's jaw twitches. How right Anna is.

'Hilda didn't really have any family, though, did she?' Agatha says.

'Nope. Some people in Helsinki, but nobody she ever really talked about. She had friends, though. She was very bubbly. She got on with people. Well able for working in here with all the guys who pass through. She taught me everything I know.'

'Is there anything that you've thought of over the years that might have seemed important afterwards? Anything she said in those few weeks running up to her disappearance, any periods of time when she was a little off or acting unusually?'

Anna narrows her eyes, giving Agatha's question real consideration.

'Well, I wasn't here a whole lot,' she says. 'As you know. I was in and out of school and really just helping out. She always seemed fine to me. If anything, I would say she was really happy before she disappeared. Like, really.'

'Happy? Not just in her normal way? Your dad always said she'd a smile on her face and was a good worker. Her friends didn't think there was anything going on with her, but then, they said they hadn't seen her much, that she'd been working a lot. They were looking forward to her visit.'

'Not happy in her normal way,' Anna says, slowly, and Agatha can see she's thinking hard. 'I would say she was practically glowing.'

Agatha frowns.

'Why?'

'I don't know. Like – she had a secret or something.'

'You never mentioned this before.'

Anna smiles, shyly.

'To be honest, I don't think I understood before. I kind of do now.'

'What do you mean?'

Anna glances over her shoulder at the set of curtains behind the counter. Agatha guesses she's checking her father isn't about to put in an appearance.

'I met somebody, in my last year in college,' she says. 'We were just friends, but it's grown into something more. I'm engaged. I haven't told Dad yet. He'll say I'm too young, that the whole point of sending me to college was to get out of here, but I plan to do both. Matt is from Austria – we're going to get hitched and travel through Europe before getting proper jobs.'

Agatha tries to look supportive.

'That sounds fantastic,' she says. 'I'm very happy for you.'

Anna's smile falters.

'You're not, really,' she says. 'You think I'm too young, too.'

Agatha shakes her head.

'What does it matter what I think? I was never lucky enough to meet anybody like that. It wouldn't have mattered to me if I'd been twenty-three or thirty-three, I'd have jumped at the chance.'

Anna relaxes again.

'Well, I'm not stupid enough not to realise how it looks,' she says. 'Which is why I haven't told anybody. Nobody who'd judge, anyway.'

'And you think that Hilda might have had a secret like that?'

'Yeah. I do.'

Agatha doesn't get it. Hilda wasn't a girl in her early twenties. She was a woman in her mid-thirties. Why couldn't she just come out and say if she was with somebody? Why stage 'a visit' with her friends, all to spend a few days with a guy? And why not return? Had she run off with him? Or had he hurt her? Why was he a secret in the first place?

Unless there was a reason she was keeping it private.

If it was somebody she shouldn't have been with, Agatha thinks.

'But she never mentioned who,' Agatha asks. 'You never caught sight of a picture on her phone or heard her talking to anybody who seemed special?'

Anna shrugs.

'She flirted with every guy who came in here. That was her way. It would have been hard to know if one of them was more special than the other, and I guess that's how she was around all the men she met. But I do think there was somebody. I think she was happy because she was in love.'

Agatha thanks Anna and they make some small talk for a couple of minutes before Agatha leaves.

She stands outside, breathing in the cold, fresh air for a few moments after the stuffy heat of the café.

She's not entirely sure what she's doing, dragging up all this history.

What she had told Alex wasn't a lie. The chances of these three vanished women being connected is slim, let alone their cases having anything to do with Vicky Evans.

And yet . . .

None of Hilda's friends had ever mentioned a boyfriend.

In any investigation, there can be a dripping of information over time. And Anna has mostly been down in Helsinki, so Agatha's not annoyed with herself for not unearthing this possible nugget sooner.

But she is curious as to what it means. It might be nothing. Hilda had her eye on somebody or had started seeing somebody – maybe even a married guy – but then she went missing and he couldn't come forward.

Or, he was involved in her disappearance.

In which case, it means everything.

And that niggling in the recesses of Agatha's brain – that tiny suspicion that she had never allowed to take hold – is starting to sound louder.

What if these women are connected?

What if Vicky's death has opened a Pandora's box?

★

When she returns to the station, Agatha finds Janic and Jonas eating chicken rolls and playing cards.

'Seriously,' she says, dumping the bag of cookies in front of them, the ones Becki sent back with her, 'are you already on Christmas holidays, Janic? There's nothing pressing for us to do, no?'

Jonas doesn't respond, he just starts to quietly, slowly, gather all the cards. Janic jumps up, full of guilt.

'I was just taking a break,' he says. 'We've done the door-to-door around Koppe. There's nothing new to report. I spoke to Rovaniemi as well, that Venla one in pathology. She said you have the full report and she has nothing to add. And I had to go over to the other side of the mountain today. Somebody said there were scouts out there.'

'Scouts for what?' Agatha says.

'The usual. Mining.'

Agatha raises her eyebrows. Everybody knows Koppe is safe from mining scouts, the well-paid reps who come to Lapland to source lands for industrial exploration. The village has secured its economic success via tourism and most of the council members are actively invested in the hospitality industry. Plenty of business people have come to Koppe in the past, just like in other parts of Lapland, looking to win mining licences, but most of the actual mines end up in poorer, less scenic parts of the country.

She doesn't know if Janic's source got it wrong or if he was skiving this morning.

'Sit down and finish your lunch,' Agatha says. She meets Jonas' eye. The quiet man gives her a hint of a smile. He knows her well, whereas Janic can only see her as a boss. To be fair, it's probably the best thing. He's the sort who'd take advantage, otherwise. His mother spoils him. If she didn't, she'd have told him to shave those sideburns by now.

'When you're finished, I want you to check something for me,' she says.

Janic grabs a pen and pad and looks at her, eagerly.

'Mary Rosenberg,' she says. '2007. I want you to recheck whether her passport was picked up leaving Finland. It was followed up at the time but maybe somebody missed something.'

Before Janic can finish writing the name, Jonas leans back in his chair, reaches over to his desk and picks up a file. He hands it to Janic, who stares at it, confused, then hands it to Agatha. Agatha glances at the name on the white sticker on the cover – it's Mary Rosenberg's file. Jonas had already pulled it out.

'Hilda Paikkala, too?' Agatha says, and like magic, Jonas produces a second file.

'Great minds,' Agatha says, while Janic looks between the two of them, completely bewildered.

He might be practically mute, but anybody who knows Jonas is aware of how useful he can be. Had he wanted to progress in the police, he could have. He has a good head on his shoulders. Good intuition.

And he's just compounded Agatha's fears. If he too has started thinking about these cold cases and a possible connection to the new case, then maybe the path Agatha is testing her toes on isn't entirely off course.

'Any luck getting access to Vicky Evans' second email account?' she asks.

Janic shakes his head.

'I tried coming up with the password but nothing. I've contacted the server. They're usually quicker than the social media sites, so we might get lucky.'

Agatha purses her lips.

She has an inkling that Alex Evans could make a good guess at Vicky's password. Maybe he already has and he's just not telling her.

'Visitor,' Jonas warns her, and Agatha looks over her shoulder at the front door.

She's expecting it to be Alex and it is Alex.

'We need to go up and see Miika,' he says.

'Alex, as we discussed—'

'I saw him this morning at the Lodge. He was delivering food. You tell me this guy is some kind of urban legend but it's not like he's just lurking up in the hills, is it? He does business with the Lodge and I've checked in the kitchen – Vicky did have an interaction with him. They were seen. Maybe it happened more than once.'

'Are you doing the very thing we agreed you wouldn't do? Are you interrogating people?'

Agatha dumps the files on the reception desk.

Alex spots the names on the two front covers, then looks to her.

'You're wondering, aren't you? You're wondering if it's the one guy.'

'I wouldn't be doing my job if I didn't look at every angle, including the absolutely most unlikely ones. Come on, then.'

Agatha hasn't taken her coat off. She might as well get this over with.

Even though it's exactly what he came and asked her to do, Alex remains rooted to the spot. He'd probably been expecting admonition, not cooperation.

'We'll go see him,' Agatha says. 'But *you* have to keep your mouth shut.'

'You're letting me come?'

Agatha pauses.

'Here's how I see it: I bring you. You listen. You're happy. I don't bring you. You go find him on your own. You cause untold problems. Am I right?'

Alex's face tells her everything she needs to know.

Agatha sighs and points the way back out, as her deputies watch on, bemused.

Agatha takes the snowmobile again, making Alex sit on the back.

'You ever been a passenger on a motorbike?' she asks.

'No, but I've driven one.'

'This is a hundred times safer,' she tells him. 'There's a speed limit set on the ones in the Lodge, so the tourists don't kill themselves, but they can go a lot faster. I won't push it to the limit, don't worry. Just hold on to the sides and if you get anxious, tap my shoulder. Oh, you've no back trouble, do you?'

'Why?'

'Just asking.'

Agatha smirks. Alex is such a cool customer. It's nice to have the upper hand for once.

She looks up at the sky as she helps fasten Alex's helmet. She doesn't like how the air smells or the taste of it on her tongue. There's a heavy snowfall coming. Hopefully they'll get up and back before it lands. Still, when she sees Janic emerge from the station, she calls over to him.

'If I'm not here at school time, will you pick up the kids?'

Janic looks up at the clouds and nods. Agatha jumps on the snowmobile.

She's suddenly, uncomfortably, conscious of Alex's legs flanking her. He's a tall man – quite a handsome man – and while that hasn't escaped her notice, she's been more than aware of the reason for his visit and how she must behave towards him. Not to mention, he's been a thorn in her side.

Now, at close quarters, she feels the smallest of butterflies in the pit of her stomach and immediately quashes them.

It isn't just that it's entirely inappropriate.

She'd promised herself, for the kids' sakes, no men. No boy-friends or part-time lovers or any complications that could distress them or cause any instability.

She takes off, going a little faster than she normally might because she's nervous about the weather. They cross the lower end of the lake then start into the forest on the other side. The ride is a lot bumpier here than on the smooth surface of the lake and she hopes Alex is coping. He doesn't tap her shoulder, even when she's dodging in and out of trees as they climb the mountain. Agatha knows it's scarier as the passenger, when you can't see the swerves coming and you aren't holding on to the handlebars.

The journey takes just under half an hour. Agatha pulls up at the sheds beside Miika's reindeer enclosure. She gets off then helps Alex climb down.

'Fuck,' he says, when he's on steady ground. He looks at her with the expression of a man who can't believe he's still alive. 'Fuck.'

'And I'm the sensible driver in our station.' Agatha shrugs.

He rubs his lower back.

'Sore?' she asks.

'I tensed,' he answers. 'Going through that forest, I thought I was going to fall off.'

'It's the quickest way. We'd still be in the car circling the lake. Higher up, they've built a road across, but it's still not as fast. So, this is your first sight of a proper farm. What do you think?'

Agatha sweeps the air with her hand, covering Miika's house, the sheds surrounding it, and the reindeer enclosure.

Alex steadies himself and it's then he notices the animals. She enjoys seeing the look on his face: it's the same for everyone the first time. Reindeer are practically mythical creatures to non-Nordics, especially in their natural habitat. Agatha has only ever seen them as working animals, but she still enjoys witnessing the enchantment in others.

Alex walks towards one and holds his hand out. The reindeer sniffs, hoping for lichen. Finding nothing, he snorts and lopes off, but not before Alex gets to run his hand along the beast's back.

Alex turns back to Agatha and for a moment she can imagine what he was like as a child. His eyes are bright, his cheeks red dots on pale skin; he's just seen his first reindeer in Lapland. She's glad she's given him this tiniest moment of respite from grief.

'Their fur, it's so thick,' he says.

'Each individual hair is hollow inside,' Agatha tells him. 'It both insulates and cools them. And when they're killed, every part is used.'

'I thought there'd be more. If it's a farm.'

'There'll be hundreds more out on the mountain. But you must never ask a reindeer farmer how many are in his herd. It's considered very rude.'

And just like that, Alex's eyes travel to Miika's house and darken.

The snow has started to fall now; Agatha notes the swirling patterns and knows what they mean. She also sees smoke pumping from Miika's chimney. She expects him to be in, but it did occur to her at a certain point on the trip that spontaneity is never a good idea when you're travelling miles and a heavy snowfall is due. Like all the houses round here, Miika's home will be unlocked and they can take shelter, but still, she should have checked.

Maybe, she thinks fleetingly, she didn't want to warn him they were coming.

'You ready?' she asks Alex.

He nods and leaves the reindeer. He's shivering again – she reckons from a combination of the cold and the adrenaline leaving his body after the ride. Agatha thinks that if the stress of this trip doesn't age him, the extreme weather will.

They step on to Miika's porch and knock on the door, while kicking the snow off their boots. The house is as Agatha remembers it: a basic wooden chalet with a dark pointed roof. She and her sister, along with half the kids in their class, used to come up here in their late teens, with bottles of alcohol and hearts full of daring. They did it more after Miika got rid of the dogs and wasn't alerted to the teenagers' presence so quickly. Far more exciting to try to catch a glimpse of the man, unseen.

This was the house where a woman was murdered, after all. That's what the grown-ups said.

The poor man, Agatha thinks. Teens can be cruel. Especially when the townsfolk, who are supposed to keep a rein on them, don't care about the man that they're torturing.

It's half the house it once was. Literally. Miika's father and his brother split the house in half when they both got married. His brother rolled his on logs towards the other side of the mountain. Agatha likes telling tourists that the term 'moving house' comes from actually *moving* house.

There's no answer at the door and Agatha calls out. She's rethinking her strategy, until she hears movement over by one of the sheds beside the reindeer pen.

Miika emerges, his apron covered in blood, a large knife in his hand.

'Nothing suspicious there, so,' Alex mutters under his breath.

Agatha raises her eyebrows.

'He's butchering meat,' she says.

She takes a step off the porch and calls to Miika in Finnish.

'I just wanted to have a chat, if that's okay.'

Miika takes a look at Alex and then back at Agatha. When he answers her, it's in English.

'It's about that girl, the one you found? I had nothing to do with that.'

Agatha can practically feel Alex react adversely. She knows Miika, knows his ways and that the man has no time for small talk. Of course, he'd just come out and say it. But to Alex, it must sound defensive.

'We'll just take a few minutes of your time,' she says. 'If you'd be kind enough to offer us a hot drink?'

Miika rubs his hands down on his apron, which has started steaming. The blood from the reindeer is still hot and it's reacting with the cold air. Agatha glances at Alex.

She can read his thoughts.

Vicky's brother has Miika hung, drawn and quartered.

★

Alex is reluctant to go into this man's house, but he's even more reluctant to let Agatha go in alone. She keeps looking at him like she's surprised by his hostile reaction to Miika. He wants to ask her how he's supposed to react to this giant of a man, already suspected of murdering his own wife and two other women, and who may have killed his sister. It doesn't help he's had to wash blood off his knife and himself before he can put the kettle on.

They sit around a table in a small sitting room that's also a kitchen, on hardback chairs fashioned sometime in the 1930s. Alex is pretty certain very little has been modernised in this house since it was built. He can't see a TV, for starters. He thinks of his own apartment, of the underfloor heating and voice-activated controls in every room, the flat-screen that can slide back into a cabinet in the wall, the speakers in the ceilings, the automated temperature adjustments in the shower, and the fridge that informs him when he's running low on milk and mineral water.

On the wall in front of him, there's a framed front page of an extremely old newspaper. Alex doesn't understand the Finnish headline but he can tell by the old-fashioned photograph that it's men panning for gold in a river.

Pioneers. That's what this cabin and the whole countryside remind him of. People brave enough to find new ground and survive in difficult circumstances.

He'd die if he lived out here, and he doesn't mean that in a snowflake, can't-exist-without-his-appliances way. The cold and the boredom would kill him. From his recollection of Agatha's murder wall, Kaya was a young woman. How on earth had she coped?

While they wait in silence for the kettle to boil, Alex looks around the room some more, observing the antiquated dresser, topped with a tray of dusty glasses. There are several picture frames, and while some contain photographs, there are also drawings, including one of an Arctic fox. They're detailed, intricate, and very skilled. He wonders if Miika has hidden artistic talents or if the only thing he's hiding is a penchant for murdering and disappearing women.

'You've heard all about it, then,' Agatha says, when Miika puts mugs of instant coffee down in front of them.

'I heard. I presumed you'd be up before now.'

Miika sits down. It evens the score a little but he still has a few inches on Alex, something Alex is not used to. But it's less the height of the man and more his girth. He's twice as wide as any man Alex has ever seen, and none of it looks like fat. He can understand, wrongly or rightly, why Miika causes such fear and rumour down in the town.

'I didn't know if I'd reason to come up,' Agatha says, shrugging. 'Did you know Vicky Evans? She worked in the Lodge.'

Miika glances at Alex, but he doesn't ask who he is. It's plain that he's already guessed, given he and Agatha are conducting their conversation in English.

Alex wonders why Miika's not railing against his presence. Is it because he has nothing to hide? Or because he has, and playing the innocent is all part of the fun?

'I didn't know her,' Miika says. 'She could have been any of the ones who work down there. When I go in, I keep my head down and I don't speak to anybody. Especially not the women.'

Agatha doesn't immediately say anything. Alex sees she's distracted by something outside the window. He follows her gaze. The snow is falling heavily.

Agatha turns back to Miika.

'Somebody in the Lodge said they saw you talking to her.'

Agatha takes out her phone; pulls up an image. Alex catches a glimpse. It's one of Vicky's Facebook pictures; a recent one. She's in snow gear, but her dark hair and broad smile are visible.

He holds his breath as Miika looks at the photo.

'Maybe,' he says. 'I was looking for Lassi. I asked a girl. I didn't want to, but there was nobody else around. It must have taken all of a few seconds. Could have been her.'

'Then, there have been times you've spoken to women in the Lodge,' Agatha says. Her tone is gentle to Alex's ears but he gets the implication and so does Miika, because he's glaring at Agatha with his head cocked, a belligerent look on his face.

'I go to the Lodge kitchen,' he says. 'I drop off my delivery. Four times a year, I take payment from Lassi. He tries to avoid me, every time. Makes excuses. The cheque had an error on it. He accidentally left the email to his bank on draft. Nonsense. There's usually one of the kitchen hands there; I can ask them to run in for me. I don't talk to the women in the Lodge, if I can help it.'

Agatha and Miika stare at each other for a few moments. Then she puts her phone away.

'So, were you delivering to the Lodge around the time she went missing?' she asks.

'What was the exact date?' Miika asks.

Agatha tells him the date in November when Vicky was last seen. Miika stands and crosses to the cabinet, taking out a small diary and ledger. He sits back down. Alex notices how the whole house seems to shake when Miika walks.

'I drove down to Rovaniemi,' he says, pointing at an entry in the diary and showing it to Agatha. 'I had to buy some equipment for the farm that they don't deliver. I went down that morning and I wasn't back until the following night.'

'Did you stay in a hotel?'

'Stayed in my truck. Have a bed in the back. Took it down instead of the car because I was bringing the equipment back up.'

'But people would have seen you down there? That day and the next?'

'I'm hard to miss.'

He's got that right, Alex thinks.

Part of him is still hopeful. Slept in his truck? In this weather?

'I might get the names of those shops you called into,' Agatha says.

Miika shrugs. His dark eyes narrow then and he rests his chin on his hand.

'How do you know when she was killed, though?' he says.

'Excuse me?' Agatha responds.

Alex tenses.

'You know when she went missing, but I'm guessing the lake left you unsure about when she died. The water, the temperature. Somebody could have taken her and held her against her will.'

Jesus Christ. Alex feels the shudder run right through him, from the back of his neck all along his spine and down his legs.

Miika is calm. Completely lacking in emotion. Alex looks to Agatha, expecting her to react angrily.

'That's true,' Agatha says, her face betraying nothing. 'Though I'm going to guess, if you weren't here the night she disappeared, you couldn't have taken her, Miika.'

'Sure,' he says. 'But what if I told her to wait somewhere for me? What if she stayed here for a while?'

The hairs on Alex's neck are standing.

He's toying with them. The psychopath is fucking toying with them.

'You could have done that,' Agatha says. 'In which case, you wouldn't mind me looking around?'

Miika glances at Alex.

'Be my guest,' he says, holding out his hands.

Agatha takes a sip of coffee – her and Miika's eyes are locked. It's like a battle of wits, Alex thinks. A part of him doesn't want to be left sitting with the guy at the table alone. He wants to search this house, too, see if there's any evidence of Vicky being here.

But he senses Agatha wants him to stay. She wants to nose around on her own.

Alex feels something nagging at him. It started when Miika was speaking. He can't put his finger on it but it's there . . . somewhere.

As Agatha heads into one of the bedrooms, Alex stares down at the chipped wood on the cheap table.

'So, are you the boyfriend?' Miika asks.

Alex frowns. The man's voice has completely changed now he's talking to Alex alone. He sounds . . . softer. Less threatening.

'Brother,' Alex says. He still can't keep the hostility from his voice, regardless of the other man's altered demeanour.

Miika says nothing. Then he exhales, heavily.

'Sorry for your loss,' he says. 'I had a sister. She died when I was a kid. Only a baby. Went into the lake. My parents got her out in time but the cold was in her lungs.'

Alex doesn't know how to respond. He's hardly going to say 'thanks for the condolences'.

'You've heard the rumours about me?' Miika says.

Alex nods.

The other man nods, too, and stands. He crosses to the cabinet, picks up one of the framed photographs, brings it to the table.

'Kaya,' he says, and hands it to Alex.

Alex looks at the young woman in the photograph. She's pretty in an unconventional way. Slavic-type, high cheekbones, full lips and masses of dark hair. But it's her eyes that grab Alex. Deep, thoughtful eyes, the sort that you know are hiding secrets. Kaya was already dreaming of being somewhere else when this photograph was taken, he thinks.

'The drawings are hers,' Miika says. 'She was always drawing. Even in school. She was talented.'

'Did you kill her?' Alex asks.

Miika stares at him.

'My wife or your sister? Or both?'

Alex shrugs. He places the picture frame down on the table between them, eyeballs Miika. The man could floor him with one swipe, even if Alex tried to hold his own. Maybe Agatha would get her gun out in time, maybe she wouldn't. But Alex refuses to be cowed by this man, regardless of what he might have done – because of it, in fact.

'I killed neither,' Miika says. 'Kaya left, like I told the police. There was nothing unusual; she didn't take anything with her. Well, bar the one thing that she always had on her, but I told them that too. And she never came home. Did I hurt her? No. Did somebody? Yes. I believe they did.'

Alex frowns.

'What do you mean?'

Miika seems to hesitate. He sips his coffee.

'When they couldn't get me to confess, they decided Kaya must have had an accident. They didn't look at anybody else. Made sense. They protect their own in this town. The ones who they think are worth protecting. I never fit that description. Never have been accepted, really. Neither fish nor fowl. Got Sami blood in me, so reindeer-farming is in the family. Lots of people round here don't like the Sami. But I'm not pure Sami so the Sami don't have much time for me either. Think reindeer-farming should be their sole preserve. Law says anybody can do it, though.'

He points at the old newspaper article on the wall.

'See that? That's my uncle. He moved house, gave up farming. Thought he'd try his luck at gold-panning in Ivalojoki River. Big thing, here, panning and mining for gold. But he never made his fortune, not like the guys back in 1868. My father, though, he did okay on the farm. You don't get far dreaming, that's what he always said. Kaya never understood that. All she did was dream.'

Agatha slips outside now, glancing quickly at Alex as she goes. Alex figures Miika feels freer speaking in front of him. And maybe Agatha is counting on that.

The front door and porch doors are only open together for a second but the gust of snow that blows in tells Alex that a blizzard has hit. He looks back at Miika.

'You don't think Kaya had an accident?' Alex asks.

Miika shakes his head.

Alex backtracks.

'What did she take with her? You said she always had this one thing on her.'

'She had her coat and her purse, obviously. We had no mobile phones then. But she took her drawing book. She was very protective of it, kept it safe here unless she was sketching in it. It was very precious to her. A leather-bound journal. Small. I'd bought it for her.'

'Why didn't the police believe you?'

Alex thinks of the old chief, the man he'd met in the bar the other night. They were only together a short time but Alex had been begrudgingly impressed by the man. Patric, that's his name. Could he have been so inept that he didn't bother pursuing the real killer, after failing to pin it on Kaya's husband? Or was it, as Miika is implying, more to do with corruption, *letting* somebody else get away with it?

'I had . . .' Miika trails off. He stares into the fire that's burning fiercely in the stove.

'I was not always a good husband,' he says. 'People knew that. Kaya's parents knew that. I am ashamed of things that I did. I can say I was young and I was under pressure, but they're just excuses. I hit my wife. Several times. Always after alcohol. So, when I reported her missing, at first, Patric looked. Then, when he couldn't find her, he assumed I was lying. No matter what I said, or how I protested. Because he knew, like everybody, that I'd been violent with her. Patric made his point. Perhaps I deserved to be punished for being the man I was. But I'm not a murderer.'

'Those other women who went missing over the years, though,' Alex says. 'People think . . .'

'I know what they think. I can't stop them thinking those things.

So I just go about my business and keep my head down. I didn't kill your sister. I don't even remember meeting her. And I've suffered enough for Kaya. I'm not suffering any more. I'm not keeping my head bowed while another death is blamed on me.'

Alex studies the other man. Really studies him. He wants this guy to be guilty. Just like Patric did. So he can *know*.

But Alex can't see deceit in Miika. He can see guilt – the man clearly feels intense guilt. Of course, if he was beating up his wife, and then she disappeared, that's probably natural.

'Do you think somebody could have murdered your wife and those other women?' he asks. '*And* my sister?'

'I don't know about that,' Miika says. 'I just know, if they suspect me of doing every bad thing that has happened in this town, and I haven't done those things, that doesn't mean somebody else didn't.'

Alex nods. He thinks the same.

'Why are you telling me all this?' he asks. 'Why are you happy to talk to me and not Agatha?'

Miika snorts.

'Why do you think?' he says. 'You're an outsider. She's not. Maybe you'll judge me. Maybe you won't. She can't help it. She'll judge whether she wants to or not.'

The doors open again and Agatha comes in.

'No secret cells or underground torture rooms?' Miika says.

Agatha raises her eyebrows.

'The weather has taken a bad turn,' she says.

'I can put on some food,' Miika offers. He turns to Alex. 'You ever try blood pancake?'

Alex has no desire to try blood pancake but he tries to look semi-enthusiastic.

Agatha's phone is ringing. She takes it out.

'It's the station,' she says.

Alex watches Miika light a ring on the gas stove as Agatha starts to speak in Finnish.

Miika puts a pan on the ring and takes a jug of something from the fridge. Alex stands and walks over to the wooden countertop, feigning interest. The jug is full of blood. So, blood pancakes are no exaggeration, he realises.

'Do you have any idea who?' Alex says, his voice low. 'If somebody is killing women up here, do you know who it could be?'

Miika pours blood into the pan and lets it form a flat circle. Alex watches it bubble.

'You've gone from thinking I might have hurt your sister to asking me to help you?'

'I don't care how it looks,' Alex says, truthfully. 'I just want to find out who did it.'

Miika shakes the pan as the blood turns black.

Alex waits impatiently.

'Like I said,' Miika says. 'They protect their own. They watch out for themselves. Certain people around here, they want to protect their reputations. Some would say, they *are* the town.'

Alex studies Miika.

And then, out of the blue, it hits him. What Miika had said that jogged his memory.

Lassi's emails to the bank were left in *drafts*.

Alex needs to check Vicky's email drafts. Why the hell hadn't he done that?

Agatha's voice is growing louder. Both Miika and Alex look at her. Alex notices how pale she's turned; her voice is fraught. He can't understand anything she's saying but he can hear one word.

Luca.

She hangs up the phone.

'We need to go,' she says.

Alex glances out the window. It's a snowstorm like he's never seen, a hurricane of white.

'What about the weather?' he asks.

'You can stay,' she says, already pulling on her coat. 'Or you can come with me. It's up to you. I'm leaving now.'

Alex looks at Miika's pan and grabs his coat from the back of the chair. If she reckons she can get them back in that weather, he trusts her.

He glances at Miika one last time.

He doesn't think the man has told them everything. But he's right about one thing. Alex came up here thinking he might be facing his sister's killer. Now, he's not so sure.

Outside, the snow is swirling thick and fast. The light of the day, already dull, has been vanquished, but it wouldn't matter if it was 1 p.m. or 10 p.m., Alex can barely see his hand in front of his face in the blizzard.

'Are you sure about this?' he calls to Agatha. She doesn't reply; he thinks she's nodding. Either way, Alex is man enough to admit he is utterly terrified as he climbs on the back of the snowmobile.

They take off at speed and soon Agatha is navigating her way back down the mountain. She appears to be doing it by memory because Alex checks over her shoulder a couple of times and can see absolutely nothing.

He finds if he leans his head against her back, he's sheltered from the worst of the storm. It occurs to him that if they crash and die, the last thing he'll have done is be within centimetres of this woman's body and he barely even knows her.

He does know that, whoever this Luca guy is, Alex feels a lot of aggression towards him and that's a thought that solidifies itself as they hare down the mountain, his spine feeling more bruised every time it's slammed against the back of his seat.

He was right to trust Agatha, though. She gets them back to Koppe in one piece.

They both go into the police station, though it's clear Agatha has no intention of staying put. Patric is there and he seems to be a calming force. He says something to her in Finnish that instantly soothes Agatha.

'Will you get him back to the Lodge?' she asks Patric in English, nodding at Alex. Alex feels like a ten-year-old and is about to point out if he survived the trip down the mountain, he can handle the ten-minute walk to where he's staying. But it's not the time. Agatha looks almost faint with worry.

She rushes from the station and Alex is left looking at Patric.

'We'll take my car,' Patric says.

The blizzard seems to have eased a little as they set off. Patric is quiet. When they pull up at the Lodge, Alex turns to him.

'Is everything okay?' he asks. 'With Agatha, I mean.'

On closer examination, Alex can see that Patric, too, looks a little shaken. Maybe that's why he answers Alex frankly, as opposed to telling him to mind his own business.

'She'll be fine,' he says, 'once she sees the kids are fine.'

'What happened?'

Patric sighs.

'Janic picked them up from school and brought them back to the station. He only planned to stay there a couple of minutes before dropping them over to mine. I often help Agatha. I've known her, and those kids, all their lives. But Janic got caught on a call. Another call came in and Emilia answered the phone. She thought she was helping. It was Luca.'

Alex doesn't reply for a few seconds.

'He's the ex, right?'

'The ex?' Patric repeats. He turns and looks at Alex.

'Yeah?' Alex says, uncertain now. Patric is staring at him, quizzically.

'The kids' dad?' Alex adds.

'No,' Patric says, shaking his head. 'Luca is Agatha's twin sister.'

Alex blinks, too confused to immediately formulate his next question. He'd made the classic assumption. But Luca is as much a girl's name as it is a boy's.

'Sorry,' Patric says, catching himself. 'Like I said before. It's Agatha's business.'

Alex doesn't ask anything more.

He stares out the window at the Lodge, about to get out.

'Where were you, anyway?' Patric says. 'This afternoon.'

'We went up to see Miika.'

Patric frowns.

'Hell. Why does nobody listen to me? The man deserves some peace.'

Alex shakes his head.

'It wasn't like that,' he says. 'It wasn't an interrogation. And . . .' Alex hesitates. 'I believe you. I don't think Miika had anything to do with my sister. In fact, I'm not sure if he had anything to do with his wife's disappearance, either.'

Patric raises an eyebrow.

'That makes two of us in the whole town,' he says. 'Three, when Agatha is being sensible.'

Alex shrugs.

'What convinced you?' Patric asks.

'I don't know. It felt like he was telling the truth. Maybe I'm just easily fooled, but he looked me in the eye and said he hadn't touched my sister and I . . . I believed him.'

Patric studies him. Alex maintains eye contact.

'Maybe you might tell that lot in the Lodge the same thing,' Patric says. 'Some of the female staff are saying he shouldn't be allowed to do business down here.'

Alex looks back at the resort, lit up against the dark night. The snow is still falling, but lighter now.

'They can only trade on rumours when they don't have the facts,' he says.

'Is that aimed at me?' Patric says. 'Agatha told me what you think. That maybe there's a serial killer up here. You're wrong. Nothing about any of the women who went missing around here ever said serial killer to me. Including your sister's death. It's not my case, but in my opinion, whoever killed Vicky knew her. Somebody cleared out her room. Somebody who knew what cabin she was in.'

With that, Patric releases the door lock.

Before Alex gets out, he turns to Patric again.

'This Luca. Is Agatha safe around her?'

Patric's lips form a thin line, telling Alex everything he needs to know.

Alex gets out and watches Patric drive off into the night.

Then he looks back at the Lodge. Through the glass windows of the bar, he can see somebody looking out.

It's Harry, the manager.

Agatha has filled bowls with popcorn and chocolate to accompany an entirely age-inappropriate action movie for the boys in the sitting room. They're aware something is going on but are happy to play oblivious if it means being spoiled rotten.

She and Emilia sit in the kitchen. Emilia stares blankly at the hot chocolate in front of her.

'Do you want to talk about it?' Agatha says.

Emilia shrugs.

'It's okay,' Agatha says. 'I'm not angry. You answered the phone in the police station. It should have been safe for you to do that. It shouldn't have been Luca.'

'She sounded . . . she sounded good,' Emilia says.

Agatha considers this before responding. Luca has sounded good before, then come into their lives and wreaked complete havoc.

'Did she say anything to upset you?' Agatha asks.

'No. She just asked how we all were. She said she misses us all.'

Agatha bites her tongue so hard she almost draws blood.

She misses Luca, too. She misses the idea of what Luca should be. Their parents died, one after the other, a heart attack and then cancer. It was the sort of tragedy that should bring siblings, especially twins, together. And with three kids, you need siblings, right? All that work, a sister would be so much help.

But Luca had never been easy to be around.

'Why did she ring?' Emilia asks. 'Does she want to see us again?'

Agatha shakes her head. There's a knot in her stomach tight enough to hang herself with. If she hadn't phoned Luca, Luca wouldn't have phoned back. Agatha has done this. She invited her in.

'Will she come here anyway?' Emilia adds.

'No!' Agatha says, too quick and too loud. She repeats it, but calmer. More like the adult Emilia needs.

'I'm not letting her come here to disrupt our lives again,' Agatha says.

'Last time was very bad,' Emilia says, her voice small. 'I'm sorry. I know she's your sister. It's just . . .'

Agatha puts her arms around Emilia and pulls her in until Emilia's head is tucked under Agatha's chin.

'It's okay, baby,' she says, fully aware that Emilia is weeks off turning fifteen and is no more a baby than Agatha was at that age. It doesn't matter. Sometimes kids need to feel cherished.

'If you want us to see her, we will,' Emilia says. 'But I'd rather not. And I don't think Onni and Olavi—'

'You are not going to be seeing my sister,' Agatha says, emphatically.

They're disturbed by a knock on the door. Emilia tenses, but Agatha strokes her cheek.

'If Luca turns up here, I'll deal with her,' she says.

Emilia looks reassured and that's all that matters. She doesn't need to know that Agatha is beyond terrified at the prospect of her sister coming back to Koppe, that Luca has always been able to catch Agatha out and can rain destruction just by breathing.

How many times has Agatha wished her sister would just die?

How often has she hated herself for that very thought?

But it's justified, isn't it? She's been grieving her sister for decades. And there's no worse grief than grief for a loved one who's still alive.

Janic is at the door, his face full of apology.

'I'm so sorry, boss,' he says.

Agatha steps on to the porch, even though it's freezing, so the kids won't overhear.

'It wasn't your fault,' she says. 'Patric says you were on a call.'

'Jonas had gone to help some tourists find their cabin. They were drunk, as usual. I turned around and Emilia was . . . all the blood had left her face.'

Agatha shakes her head, again.

'It's okay,' she says. 'Did she try to phone back?'

'No,' Janic says, adamant. 'I took the phone when I realised; I read her the riot act but she hung up. I, eh, hope that's okay.'

Agatha smiles, thinly. They're all on her side, she reminds herself. Hers and the kids'. They all know what Luca is capable of. It's not like years ago, when it would be Agatha's word against Luca's. Luca, the party girl, the fun-timer, the one who could cause mayhem then smile innocently and say, *Who, me?* And everybody would smile and say, *Oh, don't be so serious and sensible all the time, Agatha. Lighten up. Like Luca.*

Until Luca kept crossing lines, showing how little she thought of all their good opinions.

'With everything happening,' Janic continues, 'I forgot to tell you why I was on the other phone when it happened.'

'Oh, yeah?'

'I was trying to track down Mary Rosenberg.'

'You find something?'

'No. I did a check with passport control. Nothing was missed the first time. She may have used a fake document, but Mary Rosenberg didn't leave the country on her own passport, I confirmed that much. No, the thing I discovered was about the other one. Hilda Paikkala.'

'They logged her passport?' Agatha is confused.

Janic shakes his head. Agatha can tell he's brimming with excitement at his discovery – he's practically designing himself a badge that says he's a proper detective.

'I was on the phone to the Swedish police,' he says. 'And I made a breakthrough.'

The bar in the Lodge is packed to the rafters. Most of the customers have gathered around the huge Christmas tree and the fire. Glasses of mulled wine clink in toasts; the aromas of ginger and cinnamon are strong in the air.

Alex has to think for a moment – what is it, a week until Christmas? Will he be home by then? He can't leave his parents alone in Yorkshire, one child dead, the other trying to find her killer, and his mother still recovering in hospital, no matter what his mum says.

But he's no closer to knowing what happened to Vicky.

If this was work, he'd have a clear goal and a deadline, and if the target wasn't met, the project would be dropped. Losses cut. Alex is ruthless when it comes to walking away from problems in his world. Successful lobbyists know when they're winning and when they're losing and it isn't always in the campaigns expected to go well. Sometimes the most difficult job gets the quickest result, like the Cassidy contract Charlie has allegedly brought home.

Alternatively, something that should be a slam-dunk can limp on for an age until either the company that's hired Alex runs out of resources or TM&S itself calls time.

Alex doesn't know if this is something to call time on yet. And he feels guilty for even letting the thought cross his mind. This is his sister he's thinking about giving up on. Not a contract.

Alex takes a seat at the bar. Florian is dealing with a group of middle-aged German women at the far end, so there's nobody to serve him.

He opens his phone, goes back into Vicky's second email account and straight to her drafts.

His heart stops.

It's there. An email to Alex, written on 30 October.

At once, his palms are clammy and his blood cold.

The email is brief. A few short paragraphs.

Alex, tried to ring your office today. Need to talk. I'm not earning money how you think. Look, I found out something and I said I wouldn't tell anybody but I know you know the value of shit and I think this thing—

Fuck it. Why am I even writing this? You changed your number and didn't even give it to me. So what if I was back dancing again? Like you never did anything wrong? You've done way worse than me. We both know it.

I'm wasting my time. What would you know about metal, anyway.

I'm scared about what I'm doing. Alex, I'm fucking scared.

The email was never sent.

It's like a bolt to his heart.

That last line. She was scared.

What had she been doing?

What did she mean by metal?

He reads and rereads the email until he's disturbed by the feeling of somebody in his space.

When he looks up, Harry is standing in front of him.

'Are you okay?' Harry says.

Alex blinks. He shuts down his phone and swallows.

'Yes.'

'Drink?'

Alex swallows. He's trying to think straight, trying to work out what Vicky meant.

But he also wants to talk to Harry, to find out what he knows about Vicky.

Alex takes a deep breath.

'You've been avoiding me,' he says.

'Excuse me?'

'I've been here a couple of days. You manage this place. You were my sister's boss. But you haven't voluntarily sat down with me once and spoken with me. And I'll have a sparkling water, thanks.'

Harry keeps his eyes on Alex as he takes the bottle of Evian, twists the lid and puts it on the counter beside a tall glass with ice and a slice of lime.

'I don't know what to say to you,' Harry says.

He turns to serve a customer who's rocked up beside Alex. Alex stares down the end of the bar. The owner, Lassi, has joined Florian to chat with the German women. He's all cheesy smiles and expensive aftershave charm.

When Harry's done with the other customer, he comes to stand in front of Alex again.

'How badly do you need these platitudes? *Sorry for your loss*. Hearing it over and over, it doesn't really make any difference, does it?'

'I don't want platitudes,' Alex says. 'I want to know what happened to her. So, do you have anything to tell me that can help?'

Harry glances left and right down the bar. There's nobody immediately to either side of Alex.

'No,' Harry says, stiffly. 'Look, I was . . . I liked Vicky.'

'Liked her how? Were you seeing her?'

'No. I wasn't seeing her. That would have been inappropriate. I was her boss.'

There's something in how he says it that leaves Alex unconvinced.

'The night she went missing, where were you?' Alex asks.

Harry looks up. Niamh has come into the bar. She looks over, sees them together and frowns a little, then walks over to a tourist group.

'Somewhere I shouldn't have been,' Harry says, his eyes still on Niamh.

Alex narrows his eyes.

Niamh.

Alex wonders what the age gap is there. Harry looks to be about early forties, maybe? And she's early twenties.

Not to mention, staff.

'Anybody can fuck up,' Harry says, like he can read Alex's mind. 'Niamh is the first and last employee I've been with. I've already told the police. And my boss. She initiated it. I was drunk. I'm not . . . I know how it looks.'

'Did you try anything on with my sister?' Alex asks.

He watches as Harry's hands tighten on the dishcloth he's holding, his knuckles turning white. This is a man capable of violence, Alex thinks. And a man used to controlling it.

He recognises the signs.

'No,' Harry says.

Alex thinks he's lying. He's pretty sure there's more that Harry is not telling him.

'Did you see *anybody* try anything on with her? Like, somebody else she wasn't interested in?'

Harry shakes his head but not before his eyes dart quickly to the right. Alex looks up the bar. Florian and Lassi are alone; the German women have returned to their table. Alex isn't sure which one Harry's eyes betrayed but it was one of them.

Alex slips off his stool and walks to the top of the bar. The scent of pine needles from the Christmas tree is so strong up here, it tickles his nose.

Florian leaves to bring a drink to a customer's table but Lassi observes Alex's approach. When Alex is beside him, Lassi flashes a wide smile, revealing perfect white veneers that are too large for the man's mouth.

'It's Alex, isn't it?' he says. 'How are you doing, son?'

Alex doesn't get to reply; Lassi keeps talking.

'I was very sorry to hear about your sister. I'm told she was an excellent worker and got on with everybody. Especially the tourists.'

There's something in the intonation of the last sentence that makes Alex pause. Is this guy *mocking* Vicky? Implying something sordid?

Lassi gestures to Alex to take the bar stool beside him. Alex stays standing.

'Didn't you know my sister personally?' he says.

The other man blinks, calmly, his face giving away nothing.

'I'm sad to say I didn't. I own a couple of resorts across Lapland, it's difficult to stay on top of all the staff.'

There it is again. *Stay on top of.* Alex doesn't know if he's being paranoid or if Lassi is deliberately baiting him.

'That's not to say she wasn't a cherished employee,' Lassi adds. 'I wouldn't want you thinking that. I do remember she was a very pretty girl.'

Lassi's smile is broad and full of teeth.

Alex realises the din in the bar has faded in his ears; it's just him and this man, and every part of his being is telling him Lassi is a deeply unpleasant character.

'Let me buy you a drink,' Lassi says, still smiling.

'No, thank you,' Alex says. 'I already have one.'

'Well, for you, everything is on the house here. We're like family in Koppe Lodge and Vicky was one of us. I might not have had the pleasure of her company much, but our young folk are important to me. We feel your loss. I hope you're enjoying your stay in the complimentary cabin?'

Alex feels the hot rush of bile at the back of his throat. Lassi is smiling amiably – and maybe an objective observer would say his words were just ill-chosen, not malicious – but this is not a good man, Alex's gut tells him. Lassi has done bad things in his life. Alex doesn't know how he knows, but he knows.

He feels an incredible urge to hit him. He pictures himself letting go, just really letting go and pummelling this man's face to a bloody pulp.

He has to breathe deeply, clench and unclench his fists. This is the closest he's come in a long time to losing it, he realises. And he's tried so hard for so long to control himself. To be a better man.

He can't waste all that on this guy. All it would take is one punch – all it ever takes is a punch – and Alex would regret it.

Instead, Alex comes close to Lassi, so close he's breathing on the man's skin.

'When I find out who hurt her, I'm going to kill him,' he says.

Because that, he knows, is true.

Then he forces himself to turn on his heel and walk away, heart beating hard in his chest, tears rising in the corners of his eyes. As he exits the bar, he knows that every single employee is watching him leave and has witnessed the interaction, too.

He's almost back at his cabin when Niamh catches up with him.

'Wait,' she says, gasping for breath. He stops and watches her trudge through the deep new layer of fallen snow until she's level with him.

'What were you and Lassi talking about?' she says.

'Nothing,' Alex spits. 'Why? Is there something I need to know about him?'

Niamh lowers her gaze.

'You were happy to give me a steer about that Miika guy,' Alex says. 'So, if you think you can still be of help, then tell me what you know. You were her friend, weren't you?'

'Of course I was her friend.' Niamh hesitates. 'But I'm also an employee.'

'Are you seriously telling me your job means more to you than helping me discover who murdered my sister?'

Niamh hangs her head. Then she shakes it.

'Come on,' Alex says. 'I'm fucking freezing.'

They walk towards his cabin.

Koppe

1998

Kaya doesn't care if his wife is there. She doesn't care if somebody sees her call to the house. She doesn't care if they have a screaming match on the street.

She needs help. She needs his help. He got her into this mess. He can help her get out of it.

The wind bites as she emerges from her car and tries to pull her hood up. She'd told Miika she was going shopping. He didn't answer her. His silence over the last twenty-four hours has practically thrummed between them.

Kaya walks quickly down the lane to his house. She doesn't go round the back; she steps right up on to his porch and hammers on the front door.

He opens it, surprise on his face.

When he sees her, the surprise turns to fear.

He pulls her into the house hurriedly.

'What are you doing?' he asks. 'She's just left. Did you see her leave?'

He's hoping Kaya will say, 'Yes, I watched and I waited until your wife left.' Some indication that she didn't just arrive, not caring whether her lover's wife was there or not.

Kaya shakes her head and walks past him, through to the kitchen. She sees the bottle of whiskey on the counter. She badly wants to pour herself a glass. Would a drop hurt the baby? Does it matter? She's not sure she can even keep the child now.

She lifts up the bottle, then puts it back down as quick. She's being stupid. She can't think that way. It's her baby, no matter what happens.

'Kaya,' he says, his voice thick with anxiety. 'What is it? Why are you here? I was just about to go to the bar . . . poker night with the guys . . . this isn't a good time.'

'He knows,' she says.

She watches her lover pale – no, she wouldn't even describe it as pale, he's actually turned green.

'You told him?' he says.

'No, I didn't tell him.'

'Then how does he know?'

'I don't know. I just . . . He does.'

He's regaining his colour a little. He takes a seat at the table, indicates she should do the same.

'Miika couldn't know,' he says. 'We've been careful. I'm assuming you told him about the child. Is that what you mean? He knows you're pregnant?'

He nods at her stomach. She winces at how he utters the word 'child'. Like it's a thing removed. Something repellant.

'He guessed,' she says. 'He saw me, getting out of the shower. And then he wouldn't talk to me. I was going to tell him. I hoped he wouldn't work out the dates. But he took one look at me and

I swear, he was calculating in his head. He spends his days on the farm. He sees life and death all year round. I should have realised, he knows pregnancy—'

'Kaya, he's not a goddamn gynaecologist. He can't figure out the day you got pregnant just by looking at you. And what of it? I assume you've been sleeping with him if you thought you could pull the wool over his eyes.'

'I wasn't,' Kaya says, quietly. She'd managed to rebuff Miika plenty over the months she'd been cheating on him. Her hours in the bar helped. He was usually asleep by the time she got home.

'But I did, again, a few weeks ago,' she says. 'I thought I'd have enough time. I'm twelve weeks now. I didn't realise I'd show so quickly. He's not an idiot. He can tell I'm closer to three months than six weeks.'

'So that was your plan? Christ. Why didn't you just do what I said? Have you any idea of the mess you've caused for yourself?'

Kaya grips the edge of the table. She needs to put her hands somewhere so she doesn't hit him.

'The mess I've caused for myself? Don't you mean for us?'

Her lover stares at her with an expression that drips condescension.

'Exactly what purpose do you hope to serve by telling him you were with me, Kaya? Do you think I'll leave my wife? That we'll set up a happy home somewhere? That's not going to happen. You'll be alone. I'll spend a few weeks in the doghouse but my wife will forgive me. You know why? She'll forgive me because there'll be a child and she'll want that baby in our lives. We'll fight for custody of it. You'll lose it. You'll have lost your husband. You'll have lost your home. And you'll have lost your reputation. I might not be the most popular man in this town, Kaya, but I'm still a man. You'll be known as the one who tried to wreck a marriage, just because you couldn't keep your own. You'll be known as a slut.'

Kaya is shaking by the time he's finished.

'You wouldn't take my child,' she says.

'You go shooting your mouth off about this, just watch me. I'm not sacrificing my whole life because of a fling.'

'You're a bastard,' she says, her voice trembling.

He shrugs. There's a flash of what she thinks is contrition across his face and she imagines, for a moment, that he's being hard on her because he thinks it's the only thing that will work – that he doesn't believe these things he's saying. That he wouldn't put her through all that.

'What do you expect me to do?' he says, angrily. 'You scratched an itch. That's all. I'll never leave her.'

Tears flow from Kaya's eyes. She wants to lash out at him, to cause him as much pain as he is causing her, but she knows that everything he says is true. This can only end badly for Kaya. And she has nobody to blame but herself. Isn't that all he was to her, too? A good fuck? Somebody who made her feel good?

Would she have ever looked at him if she'd been happy at home?

No. She wouldn't have. It was the illicitness of it that appealed to her. The feeling she was doing something forbidden. It was never meant to be forever. She had known that, no matter the fairy tale she told herself.

'What do you suggest I do?' she says.

Her head is hanging low so she doesn't see him come around the table and kneel in front of her. His expression is softer now. He tries to take her hands; she pulls them away.

'You know what you have to do,' he says. 'Go home. Book an appointment. Get it sorted. Beg him for forgiveness. Tell him it was a stupid mistake. That's if he even cares once the baby is gone. And if he's still angry, leave him. Go stay with your parents. I can give you money to start again somewhere else. Things like this happen, Kaya. It doesn't need to be a disaster. You don't have to make it a disaster.'

He makes it all sound so easy. And it is. For him. No matter what happens, he'll be okay, she thinks. This won't ruin his life. Not like hers.

'What if I don't want to get rid of it?' she says. 'What if he forgives me and we raise your child as mine and his? Could you live with that? Could you live with seeing your son or daughter and them never knowing about you? That dry bitch is never going to give you a child. This is your last chance. You said you thought you'd end up divorcing her eventually. Take this. Take this moment.'

He stares at her stomach and for a moment, she thinks her words have landed, that somewhere deep inside, beneath his anger and resistance, he realises there's an opportunity in front of him.

But then he looks up and she can see in his eyes that he has nothing but contempt for her.

'I'd be very careful about what you do,' he says. 'You're already afraid of Miika, Kaya. You've no idea what I could do to you. I might separate from my wife. But if I do, it will be because it's my choice. Not because you forced it.'

He gets up off his knees then and glares down at her.

Kaya can't meet his eyes.

His words, the way he's staring at her.

She's suddenly absolutely and utterly terrified.

Koppe

2019

Alex realises when they get to his cabin that he hasn't eaten since breakfast. His stomach betrays the fact to Niamh and within moments she's on the phone to the Lodge kitchen. Minutes later, a guy arrives at the door with a foil-covered tray and a bottle of wine. Alex hadn't even thought of room service, despite the fact there's a thick leather-bound menu sitting on the locker beside his bed. Champagne under the Northern Lights seems to be the house specialty.

They sit in the armchairs by the fire and Alex swallows some of the creamy concoction on the plate, realising he's even hungrier than he thought.

Niamh's not eating, busying herself instead with uncorking the wine and pouring two large glasses.

'Lassi,' Alex prompts her. 'Lassi and Vicky.'

'There was no Lassi and Vicky,' Niamh says. She takes a large gulp of wine. 'But I'm sure he wishes there was.'

There's silence for a while, as she watches him eat.

'He has a reputation,' she adds. 'Not a pleasant one. We've all had to deal with him. Some give in but there's a way of managing guys like him and most of us are fine.'

'What are you saying?' Alex says. 'Fucking him is part of the job?'

'God, it's never that overt. He doesn't force anybody. Haven't you lived in the real world long enough, Alex? He's rich. He's powerful. But he's not a beast. He plays to his strengths and some girls play that game, too. Others, well, it's about resisting but not making a man like him feel rejected.'

'Mind games,' Alex says.

'That's what being a woman is.' She sighs. 'Endless fucking mind games.'

'Did you play along or win the game?'

Niamh angrily bangs her glass down on the table. Alex jumps. He can see she's furious with him.

'I'm sorry,' he says, contritely. 'I'm not judging. Just . . . asking.'

Niamh still looks annoyed, but it slowly leaves her face.

'Forget it,' she says. 'I just . . . I don't screw around. I can manage Lassi.'

Alex holds his hands out in apology.

'How did Vicky handle him?'

'Not well,' Niamh says, quieter now. 'Vicky told him to take a run and jump. Which was neither giving in nor playing along.'

Alex can hear the words coming out of Vicky's mouth, can picture her face as she said them.

He remembers a holiday together. Him, twenty-one, Vicky, fifteen. One of the last his parents roped him into. The ferry to France, a campsite in Brittany. Some Italian guy, good-looking, fancying his chances with Vicky.

Alex can imagine that some girls her age would have been flattered by the attention. The Italian was handsome enough to catch their mother's eye, let alone a fifteen-year-old with raging hormones. He'd spotted the guy sidling up to Vicky on the far side of the pool, as Alex was getting a drink at the bar. All smiles and Mediterranean charm. Alex had said he'd watch Vicky while their parents enjoyed a meal on their own in the campsite restaurant.

He'd put his drink down and rounded the pool at speed, just in time to see Vicky's big smile as she said, *I'm fifteen – what are you, some kind of fucking paedophile?*

Then she'd turned, dived under the water and swum to the middle of the pool. Alex had nearly fallen into the water, he'd laughed so hard.

Alex is still lost in the memory when he realises Niamh is staring at him.

'That's very Vicky,' he says.

'Lassi was annoyed but . . . also intrigued,' Niamh continues. 'I guess he saw her as a bit of a challenge. I've heard Lassi talk about horses that need to be broken in. How, once their spirit is broken, you can get a good ride on them. I'm not sure he discerns between fillies and women.'

Niamh looks nauseated and Alex feels the same way.

'He made out to me that he barely knew her,' he says.

Niamh looks him straight in the eyes.

'He's a liar,' she says.

Alex studies her.

'You really don't like him,' he says.

'I hate men who think women are just there to be used,' she says.

'So, why didn't you tell me he was harassing Vicky?' Alex asks. 'Why send me on a wild-goose chase after this Miika guy who, by the way, doesn't seem to have had anything to do with her?'

Niamh doesn't answer for a moment. He can see the firelight dancing in her green eyes as she looks at him: she's hurt.

'I didn't know it was a wild-goose chase,' she says. 'All I know is he's the guy all the locals have been talking about and yet, as far as I could see, the cops had no interest and hadn't even mentioned him to you. Jesus, Alex, you're not the only one wondering what happened to her. I've spent every day since they found her asking myself if I should have done things differently. If I should have reported her missing straight away. If I could have helped protect her. I'm looking at everybody, wondering who's capable of what. All. The. Time. Even when I know these are people I've worked with for years; people I like.'

Alex believes her. He can see the rings under her eyes and can imagine the sleepless nights she must be having.

He takes a deep breath.

'Except, you don't like Lassi.'

'No. But I'm not telling you he's a killer, either. You asked me about his relationship with Vicky. It irritated her, the way he kept coming back. He's like that with all of us, but he's not here *all* the time. You're only seeing him about the place now because Christmas is coming and the rates here at Christmas time . . . the tourists in the Lodge at the moment are the cream of the crop. They are people Lassi wants to return every year. He's trying to market himself as more exclusive than the hotel on the mountain. They're stealing his business. He has to work hard to keep it.'

'The police haven't even mentioned him,' Alex says. 'They never mentioned Miika or Lassi. The only person they've even considered is this Bryce guy from the States.'

'Lassi has an alibi. Elliot, he runs the American-themed bar in town, runs a poker game. It was on that night – the night Vicky was in there with the Yanks before they all came back to the Lodge. Lassi and Elliot and a few others played poker late into the night, apparently. And then Lassi went home to his wife.'

Niamh snorts after the last word.

Alex sits back. He drinks his wine and absorbs what she's told him.

'If you don't think Lassi is involved in what happened to Vicky, why did you run after me when I left the Lodge?'

Niamh narrows her eyes.

'I ran after you because you looked upset. I was no use to Vicky. The least I can do is try to be of use to you. But if I'm not, if I'm upsetting you, just tell me to fuck off and I will.'

Alex shakes his head, softly.

'You're not upsetting me,' he says.

Niamh visibly relaxes.

'I'm sure Lassi wasn't involved in what happened to your sister,' she says. 'I can't believe anybody from here hurt her. But I also know Lassi isn't a good man. He's not a two-dimensional baddie. He does good things for Koppe, even I can see that. He gives a lot to charity. He seems to love his wife, despite what he gets up to. And he's actually a generous employer, his reputation with women notwithstanding. But he can be mean. Rude. And you don't need or deserve that shit.'

Niamh shudders. Alex wonders if perhaps she wasn't as capable of dealing with Lassi as she wants him to believe.

'I heard you have an alibi for the night Vicky went missing, too,' Alex says, carefully. 'Harry.'

She blushes, then.

'It won't be happening again. Harry has this thing about not sleeping with staff.'

She rolls her eyes.

'But you like him,' Alex says.

'Sure. And he likes me, he's being a dick. It's just a pity he couldn't have been a dick that night because if he'd said no, then I might have been out with Vicky. Maybe I'd have got with one of the Americans, too, and we'd have all gone on somewhere together.'

'Did you do that much?'

Niamh smiles.

'We were a good team,' she says. 'We weren't sleeping around. But sometimes, we'd get drunk with a gang and end up in each other's cabins for the night, laughing at the funny things that had happened over the evening. God, I miss those nights. I wish that had been one of those nights.'

Niamh stares into the fire. The logs crackle; Alex thinks he can smell pine but it's probably still the smell from the Christmas tree in the bar, stuck in his nose.

'When you were with Harry, did you fall asleep at any point or is he a really special sort of guy?'

Niamh raises her eyebrows.

'I slept.'

'Any chance he could have left and come back without you noticing?'

'Jesus. No. Of course he didn't. Harry would *never* do something like that.'

She's properly angry again, Alex realises. It's as defensive as he's heard her and he wonders if she truly believes Harry is incapable of doing something bad or . . . if she just doesn't want him to be.

'What about Beatrice?' Alex asks.

'Beatrice?' Niamh snorts. 'Why would she hurt Vicky? She barely knew her.'

'Nicolas implied she was jealous of Vicky.'

'Bloody hell. Lots of girls were jealous of Vicky. *I* was jealous of her. She was stunning. Funny. Smart. I'd have fucking died for her hair, instead of my carrot top. Being jealous is not enough reason to kill somebody. Beatrice is the jealous type, but if jealousy was enough to make Beatrice kill people, she'd never have made it through secondary school.'

Alex picks up his wine glass. It's empty. Niamh leans across and tops him up. Alex realises he's had more than her and the alcohol's hitting him harder. He's tired. So bloody tired.

'Agatha has nothing,' he says. 'And she's got family stuff going on. I think she wants to find Vicky's killer but . . . is she giving it her full attention? Do you know anything about this sister of hers? I get the impression she's trouble. Not the trouble I'd guessed at, though. I thought Luca was the father of Agatha's kids.'

'The father of her kids?' Niamh says, frowning.

Alex shrugs.

'Single mother. I joined up the dots, but in the wrong way.'

'She's not a single mother, though,' Niamh says. 'Well, I suppose she is, but not in the way you think.'

'What are you talking about?'

'Those kids who live with the chief aren't hers. They're her sister's.'

Alex sits forward.

'Excuse me?'

'Harry told me. Agatha has custody of them. I don't know Luca, but Harry does. He says she's a psycho.'

Alex shakes his head, confused. He hadn't seen anything between Agatha and the kids to make him imagine they weren't hers.

He thinks, if I haven't noticed that, what else have I failed to notice?

Have I already missed who killed Vicky?

Niamh picks up the poker and leans across to stoke the fire.

As she stretches, Alex nods at the tennis bracelet on her arm.

'Vicky had one like that,' he says.

Niamh touches the bracelet. She smiles, fondly.

'It *is* Vicky's,' she says. 'She gave it to me for my birthday. I told her she was a tight bitch. And she reminded me that I stole a bottle of vodka from behind the bar for hers. We were always broke. Neither of us ever had a penny.'

She laughs. Then, suddenly, Niamh's face fills with pain. She starts to unclasp the bracelet.

'Jesus,' she says. 'What was I thinking? You should have it. I'm sorry – I should have realised immediately.'

Alex puts his hand gently on hers.

'No,' he said. 'It's yours. I only noticed it because I bought it for her. She never liked it. Sorry, I probably shouldn't say that. I'm sure she meant well, giving it to you. She said at the time, what was it . . . oh, yes. *You buy for me the things you think I should have, not the things I'd like to have.* The bracelet was too minimalist for her.'

'But all her stuff is gone,' Niamh says, helplessly. 'Please, I'm sure she did love it. It's a beautiful bracelet. Take it. To remind you.'

Alex looks down at her fingers, resting gently on the bracelet. He can tell it means a lot to her. He can tell his sister meant a lot to her and he's glad Vicky had somebody like this over here, so far from home.

'I want you to keep it,' he says. 'You were a better friend to her than I was a brother.'

'That's not true.'

'She wanted to tell me something, before she died. But she couldn't get hold of me.'

'What did she want to tell you?'

'I don't know.' Alex frowns. 'But she was scared.'

Niamh shrugs, helplessly.

Alex sighs. Then it hits him, what she's just said.

'The pair of you were always broke, you say.'

'All the bloody time.'

'Did you notice . . . did Vicky seem to have more money since the summer?'

Niamh scrunches up her face as she concentrates.

'I . . . yes, now that you mention it. She bailed me out a few times and said I didn't need to pay her back. We'd take care of each other when we could, but . . . yeah. That was weird.'

Alex mulls on this. Vicky was always broke, Niamh had said. That fits with Alex's long experience of his sister.

But over the summer, Vicky had had money.

Where did she get it from?

Agatha tells the kids to wait in the car while she calls to Alex's cabin. She knocks on the door and waits.

When it opens, Niamh is standing there. Agatha says nothing for a moment, taking in the bare legs under the T-shirt Niamh is wearing and the tousled hair. Within seconds, Alex appears behind her.

'Sorry for the interruption,' Agatha says, 'but I've arranged an early meeting.'

'Somebody of interest?' Alex asks.

Agatha nods.

'Give me two minutes.'

He disappears inside.

Niamh shrugs, looking a little embarrassed but not really. Agatha doesn't blame her. She used to have a life once, too.

'I'll wait in the car,' Agatha says with a tight smile. 'You should close the door. All the heat is getting out.'

Agatha glances at Niamh's bare legs again. Niamh smiles and closes the door.

There goes that little fantasy, Agatha thinks, remembering the feel of Alex's legs on either side of her on the snowmobile yesterday.

Not that it could have ever come to anything, anyhow.

Agatha sighs. She really does get all the luck.

The kids are antsy in the car and Agatha hands out the rest of the salt liquorice from the glove compartment. She'd explained the plan this morning. Emilia's not entirely happy. She wants to see her friends in the run-up to Christmas. She'd thought a trip to Rovaniemi was on the cards. Now, she's being sent somewhere even more isolated.

Olavi and Onni are fine. They love Becki, and Becki's mum, and news of the American family has them even more excited. Thankfully, that's what swung it for Emilia in the end, discovering that the Americans have a teenage son.

The door to Alex's cabin opens and he trots over to the car.

The second he's in the car, the kids launch themselves.

'Is that your girlfriend?' Onni asks.

'Who?'

'The one who opened the door with no clothes.'

'Onni,' Agatha hisses.

'She had *some* clothes on,' Alex says. Agatha raises her eyebrows and Alex smiles apologetically.

'She's not my girlfriend,' Alex says.

'She's just a hook-up, right?' Emilia says.

'What's a hook-up?' Onni asks.

'An F-buddy,' Emilia says.

'Emilia,' Agatha hisses and puts the car in drive. 'Stop using those terms around your brothers. Stop using those terms, full stop, or a TikTok ban is coming your way.'

'Why don't I just curl up and die of boredom,' Emilia drawls.

'We'll put that on your tombstone,' Agatha retorts. She turns to Alex. 'I apologise. We're in peak teenage mode this morning.'

'We were all teenagers once.' Alex shrugs.

'I don't ever want to get old,' Emilia says.

Agatha and Alex exchange a glance.

'How's your arthritis and Alzheimer's this morning?' Alex says.

Agatha smiles, gratefully.

'I can't remember,' she says. 'How's your incontinence?'

'Do I smell?'

Emilia glares at them in the rear-view mirror.

They arrive at Becki's and Agatha asks Alex to wait in the car while she runs in with the kids and their bags. She almost does it in one trip, too, except Olavi remembers he's left his charger in the car, then Emilia wants her AirPods from the glove compartment and there's one almost-disaster when Onni can't find his soft elephant, but they find it in Olavi's bag.

Alex says nothing when she returns to the car and they get going again.

'Sorry,' she says, unprompted.

'It's no problem.'

He's not so uptight today, she thinks, and that's followed by, maybe he just needed to get laid to help him relax.

Don't be a bitch, Agatha chastises herself. So what if he found solace with someone. If anybody deserved a break . . .

'So, who are we going to see?' Alex asks. Agatha has been so busy having a conversation with herself, she has to reset.

'Oh. A member of the Swedish police.'

'Why?' Alex asks.

'Hilda Paikkala. Something came to our attention when Janic was redoing the passport checks.'

'Something like what?' he says.

'That's why we're going to talk to this officer. She told Janic a little on the phone but I want to speak to her in person so I'm positive we're talking about the same Hilda.'

'Is it a long drive?'

'Two hours, maybe.'

'Barely anything,' Alex says, wryly.

Agatha smiles. He's getting the hang of things up here.

'Why are you bringing me?' Alex asks.

'Because I think you'll be interested in what this cop has to say. I'll let her explain it when we're up there.'

They drive in silence for a few minutes.

'You and Niamh,' Agatha says. She can't help being nosy. Even if she is turning into a dried-up old spinster.

'It's nothing.'

'Charming.'

'I don't mean it like that. I just mean, she has a thing for somebody else.'

'Harry.'

'She told you?' Alex says.

'She's his alibi.'

'Why did you say it like that?'

'Like what?'

'She's *his* alibi. They're each other's, surely?'

Agatha frowns. She hadn't deliberately phrased it that way, but she can hear how it sounds.

Revealing.

'Do you think he's lying?' Alex asks.

'How could he be?' Agatha says. 'He has an alibi.'

She purses her lips. She can feel Alex staring at her but she says nothing more.

Does she suspect Harry? She's known him a long time. He always struck her as a nice man. A little misguided at times, but that's mainly because he shows such loyalty to Lassi.

Maybe, Agatha thinks, she just suspects everybody. Vicky didn't hit herself on the head. And some of the alibis for her closest co-workers are thin. Nicolas was staying in the hotel with a *friend*. But the room was in the friend's name and the guy had already left before he could be questioned. Nicolas was seen up there, that was true, but had he stayed there all night? Beatrice had gone back to a cabin with one of the American tourists. He confirmed it; he also confirmed she returned to her own bed sometime in the early hours. He'd walked her there and returned to his lodgings, but she could easily have left again. Florian was on the night desk at the Lodge. Several tourists confirmed they had dealt with him during the night but there were periods when he could have been away from his post.

If Agatha had an exact time for Vicky's death, she could conceivably chip away at everybody's alibi in some shape or fashion.

Halfway towards the town where they're meeting the Swedish contact, a place just inside the Finnish border, Agatha pulls in at a service station and buys them both coffee and fat buns.

An hour later, an hour of small talk, which Agatha senses they're both using to steer clear of more important conversation, they arrive at the meeting place. Officer Hermansson is already there. Hermansson is younger than Agatha expected, and Agatha's half waiting for Alex to roll his eyes and comment on the average age demographic of everybody involved in his sister's case. But he shakes the blonde female officer's hand and offers to get more coffees. Hermansson already has one, and Agatha and Alex don't really want any more. So they sit in front of the young officer and listen as she talks.

'I only started as a sergeant in the Láhpo police station two years ago,' Hermansson says. 'If I'd been there when your girl Hilda went missing, the name would have stayed with me but, as it was, it's just pure coincidence it meant anything to me when your colleague sent out the bulletin yesterday.'

'So, you're not from the passport control office?' Alex asks.

'No. Láhpo is the nearest border town with a police station. As a Finnish citizen, Hilda Paikkala wouldn't have needed a passport to cross into Sweden.'

Agatha nods.

'When Hilda went missing originally, there was a passport check at the airports,' she says. 'But Patric also checked land border crossings. He sent out a bulletin to border towns in Sweden. Anyhow, when I asked Janic to redo the passport checks for Hilda and Mary, he also copied Patric's first move and went to the border town stations to recheck on Hilda. We have a lot of interaction with these stations and sometimes it's just quicker to do this sort of thing at a local level, rather than through Interpol.'

'Láhpo received that original bulletin,' Officer Hermansson says. 'And I saw in our file that Chief Koskinen checked in when she took the job three years ago, to see if there was any update. Unfortunately, our old boss passed away shortly after that, or it would have struck a chord with him when Hilda's name eventually cropped up.'

'I should have checked again,' Agatha admits.

'Well, your officer checked yesterday. And Hilda only came to my attention last year.'

'Wait,' Alex says. 'You're saying Hilda is alive?'

'I don't know if she's alive right this minute,' Hermansson says, 'but I can tell you she was alive and in Láhpo in July 2018, four years after she went missing from Inari.'

Hermansson lets the information land with Alex, in the same way it hit Janic and then Agatha when he told her.

'Tell him how you came across her,' Agatha says.

'Drugs ring,' Hermansson says. 'It was the big case when I started in my station, January 2018. A cross-jurisdiction investigation, spanning five years. Swedish hauliers going in and out of Russia. They were buying the drugs in Russia and then bringing them down through Sweden, across from Malmö into Denmark and on to wider Europe. I came in at the tail end but my boss made sure I was involved. One of the things he had me do was go through all the loose ends, such as the people the gang leaders used for small jobs, so when we did a big sweep, we'd pick up everybody. Sometimes, when you take the head off the snake, it leaves room for a new one. The bosses didn't want any wannabe replacements emerging.'

Agatha nods. She knows the story of this particular gang bust. The Finnish police had kept a close eye on it. Then and now, most of the drugs that come into Finland come from the top down: Sweden and Russia.

'Hilda Paikkala was in a relationship with one of the drivers,' Hermansson says. 'She was doing paperwork for the gang. I found photos of her with her boyfriend in their office, her name on fraudulent accounts sent to the bank, her handwriting on a lot of the tax files they kept. They were passing themselves off as a legitimate haulage company, after all.'

'You're absolutely positive this was her?' Agatha says. 'It wasn't just a Finnish woman with the same name?'

Agatha doesn't think that is the case: Janic had spoken to Officer Hermansson at length on the phone, but Agatha had still wanted to meet her in person, to be sure.

'We never picked Hilda up,' Hermansson says, cautiously. 'Or the boyfriend. But several of our confidential informants confirmed her name and identity as Hilda Paikkalla, of Finnish nationality. It didn't matter too much in the end. We didn't arrest everybody and she seemed like an unlikely person to take over the gang. It would have been too big a leap, accounts manager to drug dealer.

I reckon she and the boyfriend ran as far and as fast as they could. If they went through Denmark, they could be anywhere by now. But then I saw the email come in from your colleague asking about Hilda Paikkala. Just to be sure, I checked the original bulletin and the photo against the one I have from our case.'

Hermansson places a picture on the table. It shows a near middle-aged woman, attractive, her arms around a large man with a huge red beard.

'We took this from the office when we raided it,' Hermansson says. 'It was pinned on the wall beside a Chinese take-out menu. It matches our surveillance photos of one of the drivers and of a woman we saw going in and out of the office.'

It's a picture of Hilda, looking older in this photograph than the last one Agatha has of her, the last picture Hilda posed in with her friends.

'It's like seeing a ghost,' Agatha says. 'I've had this woman's face on a case board since I took over as chief in Koppe.'

'Every one of my bosses seems to have one,' Hermansson says. 'A person who goes missing and never turns up. Unfortunately, because Hilda wasn't arrested, we didn't have her name officially recorded and the bosses didn't log her ID with Interpol. She wasn't nearly as important as some of the others who got away and we'd have had a hell of a time proving guilt in her case, anyway. She could have claimed she was duped into signing the fraudulent accounts by the boyfriend. If we'd picked her up or registered her, you'd have seen the flag.'

'Why didn't you contact Finland to see if she'd returned here?' Agatha asks. She's trying to keep the frustration from her voice. Five years. That's how long she and everybody else thought Hilda Paikkala was missing, presumed dead.

To think that all that time the bloody woman had been living in Sweden.

To think that all that time, she was another noose that had been hung around Miika Virtanen's neck.

'We *did* contact Finnish authorities,' Hermansson says. 'That is, I did. But I went straight to Helsinki. I didn't know at the time about the bulletin from here or where she was from. I should probably have taken a leaf from your officer's book and gone direct to you guys, or at least to Rovaniemi, but I was still new and green and I thought I should do things properly.'

Agatha's jaw clenches.

'When was this?'

'August 2018.'

Agatha can feel the heat of Alex staring at her and she knows how this looks. She is suddenly deeply regretting bringing him on this little factfinder. It had sparked something in her, his interest in old cases that she's long sought the truth about. But now she remembers what he is. The brother of a victim whose case is very current and she's no closer to solving. And he has just witnessed her, inadvertently, solve another case. One that makes her and her force look like bumbling idiots. She can imagine that memo arriving in Helsinki and it being filed under *who gives a fuck?*

'Sorry I can't help with your Mary Rosenberg case,' Hermansson says. 'But, maybe it's the same deal. Maybe she just went somewhere and hasn't turned up yet. You might get lucky with her, too.'

Agatha smiles through gritted teeth. The only one they know for certain did turn up was Vicky Evans. Nobody is going to get lucky with that one.

★

'I know how this looks,' Agatha says to him as they drive back towards Koppe.

'I didn't say anything,' Alex says.

'You didn't have to.'

'I was the one who started speculating about the possibility of a serial killer. I was wrong.'

'You weren't the only one speculating.' Agatha sighs.

Alex looks out the window for a while, watching as the landscape changes from the large, open snow plains to forest-lined road again. He doesn't think he'd ever get tired of this scenery if he lived up here. He can see how some people might find it tedious – the same sort of trees, the ubiquitous white. But to his eye, it's a winter wonderland. Funny, how a covering of snow can make anything look beautiful.

'It doesn't mean the theory is entirely wrong,' Agatha says. 'We know what happened to Hilda. We still don't know where Mary is, or Kaya. Though, your sister's case is obviously the most important.'

'To me,' Alex says.

'I appreciate you saying that,' Agatha says. 'But, while I owe as much to Mary and Kaya's families, Vicky is the only actual murder case I'm investigating and the most recent. I don't want to go down a rabbit hole of *what ifs,* but you were right to ask the question about a possible link and it had crossed my mind.'

Alex shrugs. He has something on his mind. Agatha has trusted him this morning. Bringing him to this meeting with her – it showed she's been listening to him. He needs to start trusting her.

'I found something,' he says.

Agatha waits for him to fill her in.

'I figured out the password to her second email account.'

'Ah. And you've looked in it?'

'There was a draft email. I'm going to forward it to you and I was going to tell you the password today. She wanted to talk to me. She doesn't explain in the message but . . . she says she was scared.'

Agatha's brow furrows.

'Read me the email,' she says.

Alex opens his phone and reads the message, all of it.

'You said she kept that email address just to wind you up,' Agatha says. 'But that email . . . she was being serious.'

'Yes, but she didn't follow through,' Alex says. 'She started to tell me something and then lost her temper. I don't know what she means when she says I know nothing about metal . . .'

Alex trails off. Agatha has a look on her face.

'What did she mean by metal?' she asks him.

'I don't know. Maybe she meant mettle. It's – it means ability to cope. Not metal as in iron or something.'

'Are they spelled the same?'

'No. She spelled actual metal. M, e, t, a, l. *What do I know about metal?* Well, more than most. I grew up in an area renowned for bloody steel.'

Agatha's frown deepens. Then she purses her lips.

'I wish you hadn't checked her emails without me,' Agatha says.

'It just suddenly dawned on me, what the password would be,' Alex lies. 'And I only saw the message last night . . .'

That part, at least, was true.

'What do you think she was scared of?'

'That's what we need to find out.'

Alex senses Agatha has more, but she doesn't add anything.

'It's not like Vicky to be scared,' he says. 'But, according to Niamh, my sister might have had some funds. Which fits with her suggesting we spend all that money for our parents. I think she might have done something stupid to make some cash. And maybe it backfired.'

'Like blackmail?' Agatha says, thoughtfully.

Alex nods.

That's what he fears.

Agatha falls quiet. He can see she's deep in thought.

'Thank you,' he says. 'I know you're doing your best. And . . . with a lot on your plate.'

Agatha's breath catches. Alex watches her, sees that she's trying to keep her face placid.

'What did Patric tell you?' she asks. 'I'm guessing you spoke when he drove you back to the Lodge.'

'He didn't tell me anything. He's very loyal to you.'

'Somebody told you something,' Agatha says.

'All I know is you're having trouble with your sister . . .'

Alex trails off.

'It's not my business,' he says. 'I just want you to know, I appreciate you have problems, too.'

'Thank you,' Agatha says.

Alex doesn't expect her to say anything more. He's wondering how they'll fill the remaining hour's drive when she starts to talk.

'We're twins, you know,' she says, suddenly. 'Luca and I. And she was always the fun one. The adventurous one. A bit like you and Vicky.'

'It comes naturally to some people,' Alex says.

'Yes, and sometimes you have to be more responsible to balance everything out.'

Alex nods in agreement.

'Did you have to be more responsible?' he asks.

'Our parents died in our early teens. Dad had a heart attack, Mom had cancer. It was rough but we weren't particularly close. They were older when they had us. Not really able for kids. Then, Dad was always working and Mom was quite . . . um, she was narcissistic. Luca gets a bit of that from her. We never felt we could grieve for Dad. Our mother owned that space. And then everything revolved around her illness. I'm not saying we didn't miss them when they were both gone, but we were surrounded by aunts and neighbours and we were okay. We had each other. I took it okay, anyway. Luca, not so much. She was always a bit wild. Without any parents . . .'

Agatha turns her head to look at Alex.

'I don't know why I'm telling you all this.'

'I've been thinking the same,' Alex says. Then, quickly, when he sees her expression, 'I mean, why I feel it's easier to talk to you. I think it's because we're strangers and we've been thrown together in odd circumstances. You've had to deliver news to me that's immediately made us intimate acquaintances. Plus, you know I'm going to leave and we never have to see each other again. Not to mention, we nearly died together on that snowmobile.'

Agatha laughs.

'We were in no danger of dying,' she says. 'You're right, though. It's easier, sometimes, to be in the company of strangers. I don't talk about this stuff. I don't have to. Growing up here, everyone knows your business. All of it. All the time. It's . . . it can be oppressive.'

'I get it. My village was similar. Not as small but . . . yeah. You get into a bit of trouble, good luck to you, hoping people will forget about it.'

It's Alex's turn to stop talking. He's not sure how much of this he wants to tell her; whether she'll think less of him if she learns certain things about him.

She doesn't press him.

'I take it Luca was a hellraiser,' Alex says, deciding to keep the focus on her. 'And you were the sensible one.'

Agatha's expression falters. Alex misses her smile immediately. When she laughs, really laughs, it transforms her entirely. She has a pleasant face, anyway, when she's relaxed, but there are little worry lines on her forehead and around her mouth, which seems to be pinched a lot of the time in concern. But when she's happy, she's captivating. Even with her hair in that frizzy ponytail, her big woollen jumper and jeans, and wearing not a scrap of make-up.

He's aware the more he's in her company, the more he likes her. Respects her, too. He's also aware that he's not planning on forming any attachments while he's here. Which is why he gently, but firmly, rebuffed Niamh last night. Niamh is not into him. She's just looking for somebody else to help her numb the pain of losing Vicky and probably figured he'd be in the same boat.

He's acutely conscious that, having seen Niamh in a T-shirt at his door this morning, Agatha will have assumed that Alex was with her. She won't know and he won't tell her that, actually, Alex conked out in the armchair sometime in the early hours and woke to find Niamh equally comatose on the end of his bed. A second bottle of wine and the hours of talking had done them both in.

'That's not the half of it,' Agatha says, responding to his statement. 'The kids, you know . . . they're Luca's.'

Alex isn't able to feign surprise.

'Somebody told you that, too,' she says. 'Did they tell you how they ended up living with me?'

'No,' he says, truthfully.

Agatha sucks in her cheeks.

'Luca had them all with different dads,' she says. 'It started in our late teens. She'd drink, take drugs. I was training to be a cop and she was smoking weed and popping pills all day long. We went from being different personality types to polar opposites. People in town started to realise, too. Luca would have these huge highs then these horrible lows.

'Usually it was only me who saw the lows. But they got worse as the years went on. She started picking fights with people. Stealing from the bar she was working in. Putting it up to Patric and the other cops. Then she got caught off her face on a nicked snow-mobile in the middle of the lake. She nearly killed somebody. And as for her boyfriends – the badder the better.'

'Easy to attract the wrong sort of guy when danger is your stock in trade,' Alex says.

'Stocking trade?'

'It's an expression. Stock in trade. Your modus operandi. Behaving a certain way brings certain people to you. Moths to the flame.'

'I couldn't have put it better. She was the flame and they were throwing themselves at her. Of course, I didn't realise what was going on with her but Patric did. To me, she was just Luca, maybe a more extreme version of herself. But Patric saw that she needed help. That she was . . . unstable. Then, suddenly, she was pregnant with Emilia. I've an idea who her dad is. A good-time guy, lives in Rovaniemi, comes from money. I was training there at the time, so I knew of him. He wanted nothing to do with his baby, anyway.

But Luca wanted Emilia and she tried to clean up her act. Managed it, too, for a while. Then she was back to her old self, boozing, causing fights, sleeping around again. It's honestly a miracle she didn't get pregnant more than she did. By the time she had Olavi, Emilia was living with me. Then she tried again and had the two of them with her, but they lived close by so I could keep an eye.'

Agatha pauses. She's delivering the story in a matter-of-fact tone, but Alex can imagine how painful those years were, watching her sister go up and down. With kids thrown in, it must have been torturous.

'Emilia and Olavi ended up back with me just before Onni came, and then I had all three. Onni was three days old when I took him home from the hospital. She had some dickhead pretend to be a visitor and take her out clubbing while Onni was left in his cot. Then she threatened to have me arrested for stealing her kid. She assaulted a nurse in the hospital for letting me in – held a syringe to her throat.

'Eventually, she realised she had a choice. Jail or psychological evaluation. So, she went to a doctor. And then it was the five of us, all trying, while she did her therapy. But then I found out she'd stopped going, had stopped taking her medication. She was taking drugs all right, just not the proper ones. I had to have her taken away to rehab. Forcibly. At the start, she used to send me the most poisonous letters. She was going to get out. Kill me. Kill the kids. But then she got better. Or so it seemed.'

Alex is holding his breath. The story is already horrific but he knows it's going somewhere worse by how low Agatha's voice has become. He can barely hear her over the car's heating system.

'The eldest kids had already had so much disruption in their lives.

Every time they were with me, they had stability, but then they'd go back to her and it would be okay for a while but end in disaster. I can't even bear to repeat the details. At least Onni was saved that, but he still saw her madness. She turned up once to see him when he was two, with a stolen Xbox for his birthday present, which she'd missed by months. She didn't bring anything for the other two. Eventually, she agreed I'd adopt them. She told them, right out, she'd never wanted them. Which was a lie, but, anyhow. They were calling me Mom by then. I didn't think I'd ever forgive her for that but at least they had me. And I explained to them that the thing about my sister was, she wasn't bad. She just did bad things. I'm not making excuses for her but she's never been a well person. I realised that, too late.'

'She scares you,' Alex says, tentatively. 'I could see it when you opened the door the other night holding that gun. You were ready to use it. Are you afraid she's coming back to hurt the kids?'

'The last time she came—' Agatha says. She trails off, takes a deep breath. 'Are you sure you want to hear all this? It's so goddamn depressing.'

Alex shakes his head.

'It's your story. And I appreciate you trusting me enough to tell it.'

Agatha sighs, heavily.

'It's certainly a story. The last time I saw Luca, well . . . She turned up at the house while I was working, claimed I'd agreed she could bring the kids out for a treat. Patric was busy, so I'd asked an older teenager from town to babysit because I was stuck. The girl really didn't know better. Emilia sensed it was wrong but she didn't know enough to say no. She didn't realise she could. They got in the car with Luca and Luca drove them out to the lake. It was January and she said she wanted to bring them skating. At the lake, she launched into this rant and had a go at them for *choosing* me. The kids were terrified. They didn't know what to do or say. And then Luca started snorting coke. She offered it to the kids.'

Agatha takes a breath.

Alex almost wants to take her hand. He can hear the horror of the memory in her voice but she's still speaking calmly, still driving smoothly. She's come to terms with this, he thinks, and he feels admiration for her.

'Luca got so wasted that she passed out. The engine was off. She'd no phone. Emilia didn't know what to do, but she knew enough to stay in the car. If they'd left the car . . .'

Alex can almost feel Agatha's shudder.

'It took us nine hours to find them,' Agatha says. 'They were all nearly frozen. They almost died. She claimed she hadn't intended to hurt them, but I don't know. I just don't know.'

'Christ,' Alex says.

Agatha's hands are tight on the steering wheel.

'She's barred from seeing them,' Agatha says. 'And she's kept to it. I thought . . . I thought even she had realised she'd gone too far. But now, I think she's trying to come back again.'

Alex shakes his head.

'I don't know what to say,' he says.

'We all have our crosses,' Agatha says, shrugging. 'Look at what you have to deal with right now.'

Alex considers this.

'It's not the same,' he says. 'I feel grief, and yes, I feel guilt, but even when she was driving me nuts, I loved Vicky and I know she loved me.'

Agatha smiles tightly.

'Remember that,' she says. 'Because if that's how you felt, she would have known. You always know. I loved my sister once, and Luca loved me, too. But, life changes.'

They fall quiet for a while.

'Let me buy you a drink when we get back,' Alex says, breaking the silence.

'I don't need pity,' Agatha says, sharply. 'That's not why I told you about her.'

'I know that. I'm not offering you pity. I want to say thank you for all the work you're doing.'

'It's my job.'

'I've a job, too, and I know the difference between doing it with my heart and doing it with my head. We didn't get off to the best start, you and I.'

'Because you thought I was incompetent,' Agatha says.

'Harsh. But on the nose. Things have changed, though.'

'You're still a pebble in my shoe,' Agatha says. 'Are you like this in your job? Relentless?'

'That's pretty much what my job is.' Alex sighs.

They go to the same bar where Alex had sat a couple of nights previously. It's busy tonight – a mixture of tourists and locals, winter sports blasting on the TV, ski gear stacked against the wall on the way in.

They make their way to a booth, order beers and chicken wings, and Alex tells Agatha some of the funnier stories from his job. He can tell she's amazed and appalled in equal measure at the snake oil he has to sell and he's not even telling her the half of it. He tempers it, in fact, with anecdotes about some of his nicer contracts for charitable and NGO outfits. He doesn't tell her that this is a negligible percentage of his work and more often than not, he's chasing lobbies that leave him needing Zopiclone to get to sleep some nights.

She surmises it, though.

'You're not happy,' she says.

'I'm very well paid to be unhappy,' he says.

'I can understand now why Vicky's lifestyle irritated you so much. You hate your job, but you keep turning up.'

'And it's easy to be free when somebody else is picking up the tab. I loved Vicky, but she never grew up. Our parents indulged her. With me, it was different. Whatever I gave them, it never seemed enough. I earned enough to pay off their mortgage. That's what my job did for them.'

'Did they ask you to pay off the mortgage?' Agatha says.

'What do you mean?' he asks.

'Did it salve your conscience about your job, thinking you were putting the money you earned to good use?'

Alex doesn't reply immediately. He's bristling.

'Sorry,' Agatha says. 'I shouldn't have said that. It's easy to be analytical about other people's lives, isn't it? I'm rarely so insightful about myself. Trust me.'

Her self-deprecation forces Alex to reflect on what she's said, rather than react to it.

'You're right,' he says. 'My parents didn't ask for their mortgage to be paid off. I wanted to make a point. I've been trying to make a point for the last sixteen years.'

'What happened sixteen years ago?'

Alex almost smiles. It's reflexive, something he used to do when he was embarrassed or nervous, not a sign of mirth; it's something he's had to work on. Smiling when somebody is having a pop at you is never a good idea. Keeping his face blank is the best way he knows not to show how he's feeling.

'This is starting to feel like a confessional,' he says.

'I've shown you mine, you show me yours,' Agatha says.

Alex half smiles.

'I was a bit of a tearaway as a teenager,' he says. 'Don't know why. Maybe because Dad was so busy and I wanted his attention, or something equally pathetic and clichéd.'

Alex pauses.

'Our area was poor enough,' he says. 'And I was . . . it sounds stupid, but I was too smart. And clever enough to hide it. I acted all Billy Big Balls, skipping school, being a smart mouth, so people wouldn't figure out I was actually a nerd. I had anger issues. Sometimes . . . I still do.'

'So, you've got in a few scrapes,' Agatha says, in a tone that tells Alex she's familiar with the tale.

'Some worse than others,' Alex says. He feels his chest constrict. The very memory of it makes him sweat.

'I got in a fight with a lad one night,' he says. 'It was over nothing. I can't even remember the details. We fought and I punched him so hard, when he hit the ground, he was knocked out. They thought he'd have brain damage.'

Agatha's expression is one of calm understanding but Alex still suspects she's judging him.

Everybody did at the time.

'He was okay in the end. The cops . . . well, I was close to getting in real trouble, but my dad and the other lad's dad — it just happened they were in the union together and between them, they sorted it. My headmaster stepped in as well, told everyone what a little closeted genius I was. My dad is all about class and how those on the lower rungs don't count, but he had plenty of pull in our village. Nobody wanted a sixteen-year-old's life ruined. But . . . it meant I had all that expectation on me, then. I'd been given a second chance. And boy, did my dad like to remind me of it.'

'And you went and worked for the money men,' Agatha says.

Alex snorts.

'My bosses, they knew a good thing when they saw it. What my parents saw as a problem, TM&S saw as killer instinct. Everybody knew I was good at pushing people's buttons. My dad expected I'd use that for good.'

'That was a lot of pressure to put on you,' Agatha says.

Alex shrugs.

'I thought paying their mortgage would prove something. But my dad was just annoyed by it, like I'd hurt his pride and rubbed it in with blood money, too. My mum wasn't bothered as much, because she wanted Dad to retire anyway. But she's always saying *wouldn't you be happier if you did this, or that?* And she's right. I don't want to do my job. I fucking hate it, truth be told. I just don't know what else to do.'

'Could you leave? Do you have enough money to do that?'

Alex lifts his beer and takes a sip.

'I could,' he says. 'But to do what? I'm not sure what would mark me as more of a failure in my dad's eyes – me working hard at something he thinks is a waste, or me not working at all.'

'Isn't there a middle ground?'

'If there is, I don't seem to be able to find it.'

'Then maybe the answer is to stop caring what he thinks.'

Alex feels a lump in his throat.

'But I can't,' he says. 'Isn't it normal to want your father to love you?'

'What makes you think he doesn't?' Agatha says.

Alex feels emotions tumbling through him. He stares at the table.

He's just beginning to get his composure back when he senses the atmosphere in the bar change.

He looks up and sees that Agatha is watching the room, concern on her face.

People are staring with hostility at the front door to the bar.

Miika has just come in.

Miika is still standing near the front door. He looks rooted to the spot.

Agatha spots the bar owner, Elliot, the same man who's run this place for the last thirty years, get up from his stool down the end of the counter near their booth. He tugs anxiously at his beard, his eyes darting left and right. She can see he's gauging the temperature of his customers and she knows he's about to tell Miika to leave, despite the fact Miika supplies the bar with its reindeer meat. This is, to Agatha's knowledge, the first time Miika has come in through the front door of the bar and not round the back, at least since Kaya went missing.

Before Elliot can say anything and before one of the other customers is brave enough to venture forth with their own two cents' worth, Agatha stands up and calls out.

'Miika. Come join us.'

Miika drags his eyes away from the bar, looks at Agatha with surprise, then walks over to join her and Alex in their booth.

Agatha glances cautiously at Alex. He shrugs. She's not sure if he still suspects Miika, but, after an afternoon of confiding in each other and what they learned about Hilda this morning, she knows he's willing to trust her judgement.

'What will you have?' Alex asks Miika.

'I . . . just a coffee.'

Alex slips out to the bar and Miika sits in his vacated seat.

'Thank you,' he tells Agatha.

'Don't mention it. Miika, there's something I need to tell you—'

She's interrupted by a new voice.

'There's something *I* need to tell him, too.'

Agatha hadn't seen Lassi approach – she didn't know he was in the bar, though she should have guessed. Tonight is poker night, the weekly game.

She feels his breath on her shoulder, where he's leaned in. He's close enough that he's making it look like he wants to speak in confidence, but loud enough to ensure the whole bar is listening.

Elliot has drawn closer, too.

'You have a nerve coming in here, Miika Virtanen. We all remember young Kaya working behind that bar. Isn't that right, Elliot?'

Elliot nods obediently.

'And now with what's happened to that other girl . . .'

Miika hangs his head.

Agatha turns on her seat until she's facing Lassi. She casts Elliot an admonishing glance until he lowers his eyes. He's always been too keen to impress people in this town but she knows he's a weak man.

'I bet you remember Kaya working behind that bar,' she says to Lassi, her voice low. 'I bet you kept a close eye on her.'

Lassi's eyes darken. He's trimmed that stupid beard of his, Agatha sees, and reapplied the hair colour that keeps him from turning full grey. Hell, she hates this bloody man.

'What are you implying?' he snarls.

'You know exactly what I'm implying.'

Alex has come back from the bar now and is standing behind Lassi. The older man senses him and moves sideways so Alex is not in his blind spot.

'I most certainly don't,' Lassi says. 'And I can't imagine for one second that you are going to throw insults at me while that man sits at your table. We all know what he is. And we've been talking about those other girls, too. Hilda and that Mary one. Not to mention Vicky.'

Agatha sees Alex bristle. She senses he could be about to punch Lassi, so she runs interference.

'As you're so interested in everyone and everything that goes on around here, Lassi, perhaps you'd like to know what I was just about to tell Miika,' Agatha says.

Agatha swivels to face Miika before Lassi can say anything.

'I've just come back from meeting with a Swedish police officer. We've made a breakthrough. Hilda Paikkala was living in Sweden as recently as last year. I don't have any update on Kaya's case, but I thought, given Hilda disappeared in similar circumstances, that might be information you'd find useful.'

Agatha barely gives herself a moment to catch Miika's stunned reaction before she turns and faces Lassi again. She knows every last set of ears in the bar is tuned in and absorbing what she's just said and she also knows that they're all thinking the same thing: if Miika isn't responsible for Hilda's disappearance . . .

It's a small chink in the case the town has built against him but it might be the chink that brings the whole house down.

Alex pushes past Lassi and sits beside Miika.

Lassi narrows his eyes at Miika and then Agatha.

'Just because he didn't do something to Hilda, doesn't mean he didn't do something to his wife.'

He meets Alex's eye.

'Or your sister.'

Before Alex can get back out of his seat, Lassi turns on his heel. Agatha grabs Alex's arm.

'Don't,' she says. 'You're still an outsider here, Alex. He owns half the town and employs most of the people drinking in here.'

She knows, from what he's just told her, that Alex has worked very hard to learn to keep his temper in check.

She won't let him sacrifice all that hard work for a nasty little shit like Lassi Niemenen.

Alex nods, unhappily, and she feels a surge of affection and sympathy for him.

'Sorry about breaking the news to you that way,' she says to Miika, then falls silent as Elliot arrives at the table. He puts Miika's coffee down but doesn't make eye contact, even though Miika holds his head up.

They wait for Elliot to leave before speaking again.

'No, I'm sorry,' Miika says. 'I appreciate you telling me, but I shouldn't have come in here. It's too disruptive. You calling up . . . it jogged all those memories again. I wanted to see . . .' Miika trails off and looks over at the bar counter, where all the customers are now pretending to be otherwise engaged.

'Twenty-one years is a long time,' he says. 'Kaya is not living somewhere like that Hilda one. It would be nice; it would put a lot of demons to rest. But Kaya is dead. I know it.'

Agatha notices a quick glance between Miika and Alex. They've already discussed this, she realises. Perhaps when she was searching Miika's house and left the two of them talking. And she'd most likely have already heard about it, if she hadn't been in such a rush to get down the mountain once she'd heard about Luca phoning the station.

'Who do you think killed her?' Agatha says.

Miika stares into his coffee, not looking at either of them.

'I think Kaya was having an affair,' he says. 'I don't know who it was. I never found out. She disappeared before I could confront her.'

Which of the men in this town could Kaya have been seeing, Agatha wonders? Who could have been with her and stayed quiet after?

It was what she'd suspected about Hilda after speaking to Anna in the café, that there'd been a man she hadn't wanted anyone to know about. In Hilda's case, she'd been right. Hilda was with a drug-dealing trucker.

A married man wouldn't want it coming out that he'd been seeing Kaya.

And Lassi Niemenen is married.

Koppe

1998

All the way home from her lover's house, Kaya wonders if that's all her life was ever meant to be. Married unhappily to Miika, fucking around town to find glimpses of joy wherever and whenever she could.

She's under no illusion now that anybody is coming to rescue her. She'll always be left to go home to Miika. Nobody is going to break up her marriage for her. And the irony! She hadn't wanted her marriage for so long. To have it go back to being so bad when it felt like it could be good again . . .

Perhaps she'd have gone along with that existence. But the baby has changed things.

The baby has made her want a better, safer future.

When Kaya arrives home, the house is empty. Miika is out in the enclosure, seeing to his animals.

Kaya goes inside. She paces the sitting room.

What should she do? Should she ask Miika straight out what he thinks?

It takes her a few minutes to notice.

Her drawing, the one she'd done of the baby fox. It's not on the dresser. Just as she starts to look for it, she feels something sharp pierce through her slipper.

She sees the blood at the same time as she sees the glass.

The picture frame that Miika had placed the picture in is on the floor, smashed.

It's been thrown there.

He threw her picture because he couldn't throw her.

How long is that restraint going to last?

Kaya starts to tremble.

There'll be no talking.

She has to get out of the house.

She needs to plan her escape.

Koppe

2019

Agatha lets Janic leave early for the evening. She tells him it's because of his good work on the Hilda Paikkala case; really, she wants him out from underfoot. He's only ten years younger than her but sometimes it feels like a lifetime.

Once he's gone, she and Jonas sit together in the back office and Jonas makes coffee.

'I think I'm tipsy,' she tells Jonas. 'I had two beers in Elliot's.'

He shrugs.

'If people only knew how much of a chatterbox you are in private, Jonas,' Agatha says.

Jonas smiles into his coffee.

'I want you to look into something for me,' Agatha says.

Jonas waits.

'Discreetly. Can you check if there's been any rezoning on the mountain or anywhere around the lake?'

'Rezoning for what?'

Jonas is interested now.

'Mining for precious metals,' Agatha says.

'Is this to do with those scouts Janic was on about? You know he was probably just skiving?'

Agatha smiles tightly.

'Why not ask the councillors outright?' Jonas asks.

Agatha shrugs.

'I have a feeling it might not be common knowledge.'

Jonas says nothing, but she can see he's intrigued.

'Plus, if I'm right and Lassi Niemenen is involved, the other councillors will just do what he says,' Agatha continues. 'Actually, how difficult do you think it would be to get a warrant to look at his bank accounts?'

'Very difficult,' Jonas says. 'Unless you suspected he was involved in financial fraud on the council.'

Agatha raises her eyebrows.

It's always a possibility, she thinks.

She fills him in on the Hilda discovery and what happened in the bar.

'So, the town might owe Miika an apology,' she concludes.

'Maybe. Or maybe it's just Hilda he didn't kill.'

Agatha frowns.

'You don't agree with Patric, then? That he should be left in peace?'

'Patric can't see beyond his own guilt.'

Agatha sits forward. She's guessed at what happened between Patric and Miika but Patric has never given her the details. Possibly for fear Agatha would have to act if she knew the whole truth.

Agatha has always seen Patric as more than a mentor. She hero-worships him, she knows that. But not blindly. Policing has changed over the years. Agatha is aware that she is probably far more by the book than Patric ever was.

'Tell me what happened,' she asks Jonas. 'When Patric brought him in. What did Miika say? Did he mention this Kaya-and-lover theory of his?'

'Yes, he mentioned that,' Jonas says. 'But Patric didn't believe him.'

There's a few moments of silence.

Then Jonas speaks.

'Patric was absolutely convinced Miika murdered Kaya and hid her body. He thought the lover thing was an attempt by Miika to divert attention from himself. I wasn't sure. I reckon Kaya could easily have found somebody to keep her warm at night. She deserved a little happiness. And she was a good-looking girl. Harry used to be obsessed with her. They worked together, in the bar, you know that? Before Harry got the job in the Lodge. I always thought she might have been seeing him.'

'Was he interviewed at the time?'

'Sure. He said they were just friends. He'd got married young, too. Said he felt sorry for Kaya. Said it in a way that you knew his marriage would also end up on the rocks, and so it did. But he claimed he hadn't seen her after the last shift they worked together. There was no evidence to the contrary.'

'So, Patric was fixed on Miika?' Agatha says.

'Yup. And frustrated that he couldn't break him. That last interview . . . he was tired. I went to get us coffees—' Jonas holds up his mug, ironically. 'When I came back, Miika looked like he'd gone ten rounds with a bear. And Miika is no lightweight. Patric . . . he wanted to kill Miika. He was convinced he could get the truth out of him. And Miika, he just sat there, blood pouring from his face. He was smiling.'

Agatha sits forward. She's barely breathed in the last few seconds.

'Smiling?' she says.

'Yeah. Like he knew he'd won. Because he'd provoked Patric to do something out of character and it still resulted in nothing. Patric wasn't the same after. And we never found Kaya or arrested anyone, so maybe Patric was right to beat him. Because maybe Miika did do it.'

They drink coffee in silence for a few moments.

'I think she might have been with Lassi,' Agatha says.

Jonas frowns.

'Do you think he's capable of killing a woman?' she asks.

Jonas considers this.

'I think Lassi is capable of a lot of things,' he says, eventually. 'I've seen him use people and toss 'em aside. Look at what he puts his wife through. It was her money that helped him launch his empire. And eventually he moved her out of town, away from her friends and neighbours, and put her in that big house, so she'd have nobody while he was down here playing king. He's got wickedness in him. But murder? I don't know.'

Agatha chews on this. She sits back, puts her feet on the desk and rocks the chair back on two legs while she drinks her coffee.

She knows her hatred of Lassi is irrational and it's irrational because it's personal. She might be targeting him because of that, but she needs somebody objective to tell her if that's the case.

'He slept with my sister when she was pissed drunk,' Agatha says.

Jonas doesn't say anything. He just puts his coffee cup down and listens.

'I came in and found him, getting out of her bed, his little thing shrivelled up and a big smile on his face. She was incoherent. He claimed she was aware of what they were doing. He looks at me sometimes and . . . well, you know Luca and I look alike. For all I know, he could be the father of one of the kids. He gave her money afterwards. Why would he give her money? She never accused him of anything, but I wonder. He's an evil little bastard.'

Jonas nods, sympathetically.

'I'm going to ask you this once,' Agatha says. 'And I want you to be absolutely honest with me. Do you think, if Patric realised that Lassi was involved, that he could have chosen to look the other way? I mean, after he beat up Miika, if Miika said something that made Patric realise he was wrong, that somebody else had taken Kaya . . .'

Agatha trails off. She can hardly believe she's even considering it. She thinks of all the times Patric has helped her, has stood up for her, has put himself out for her. She's known him her entire life. But she also knows that, in towns like this, sometimes things work a certain way.

Not any more. Not on her watch.

But years ago, when a small group of men were all pulling in one direction, all trying to keep Koppe safe from mining and build a viable life for its residents . . .

Could Patric have been afraid to rock the boat?

And yet . . .

Patric might have been a flawed officer, flawed enough to beat a confession out of a man, but Agatha can't bring herself to believe he'd ignore a murder.

But she must ask the question. Because if Patric is capable of crossing one line, maybe he's capable of crossing others.

Jonas shakes his head.

'Agatha, how could he *let* somebody get away with murder when there wasn't even a body? There was nothing connecting Kaya to Lassi. Whatever her husband said about a lover, whatever anybody might have suspected, not one person in town could confirm that Kaya was having an affair. You know Lassi. He's not exactly discreet. You don't think if he was screwing Kaya Virtanen, he'd have told somebody?'

Agatha realises he's right. Lassi probably would have taken pleasure in the town knowing he'd landed a twenty-two-year-old. But then, he'd never told anybody about Luca, either. Lassi was a good bit older than Kaya, even then. Would he have been clever enough to have realised some *conquests* could be misinterpreted?

Agatha knows she's going around in circles.

But there's something just not right about the whole thing. She feels it in her bones.

Alex hears him before he sees him.

Charlie bloody Mills, in Koppe, in the bar.

'Alex!'

Charlie bawls so loudly when Alex enters that every person in the place turns around.

Alex lets Charlie descend on him and grab him in a bear hug so tight that Alex is practically levitating.

'Charlie,' he gasps. 'What the hell are you doing here?'

'It's nearly Christmas, mate. Your sister just died and your mum's in hospital and forgive me the presumption, but I reckon I'm pretty much your best friend in the world.'

He is pissed as a fart, Alex realises. He wonders how long Charlie has been in the bar and who he's met.

Charlie brings their foreheads together. Alex is deeply uncomfortable with this intense proximity but Charlie is holding firm.

'I brought you a rake of gear over and a hug from your mum and I've promised I'm going to bring her back a present from you for Christmas. By the way, we're top and tails tonight. I don't want any Eton-type carry-on, just so you know.'

'Hold on,' Alex says, 'I'll be home for Christmas.'

'Come on,' Charlie replies. 'You think they're going to release Vicky's body this side of the year's end? Unless you're planning on going home and coming back – and I tell you, your folks don't expect that—'

'Wait, have you been up to Leeds?' Alex asks, still trying to catch up.

'Too right, I have. You think I'm going to leave my best pal's parents at the mercy of some provincial backwater hospital? That was quite a battle your dad put up on moving your mum. Wedded to the NHS, he is. Must have been a nightmare growing up with him. He's all "Labour this, Labour that", isn't he? Where you came from . . .'

'Did you get my mother into a private hospital?'

Alex's head is spinning. He can't put any of these pieces together. Charlie standing in front of him in Koppe; Charlie visiting his parents in Leeds (God knows what his father made of him); Charlie getting his parents to agree to a hospital transfer.

'Plus,' Charlie says, throwing his arm out and indicating the huge spruce at the end of the bar and the snow falling softly outside the large windows, 'like I said, it's nearly bloody Christmas and you're currently residing in Santa Claus' pad. Of course, I was going to come over. Just overnight up here, mind. I'm on a plane back to

Helsinki in the morning. I'm going to spend the weekend there and hit some nightclubs. And do a bit of business. I don't mind saying –' Charlie lowers his voice – 'that's a bit more my style than staying up here and freezing my balls off.'

'You have to slow down, Charlie,' Alex says. 'You took time off work to come here?'

'Sort of. I've tied everything up. Nice little end-of-year bonus. Your Cassidy contract's all signed off. You owe me for that, by the way. Anyway, enough of this work bollocks. Look at where we are, mate. I just met the lovely Beatrice – you should tap that, by the way. Good friend of your sister, she was. I can't believe you haven't used the grief card yet. She showed me your cabin and I've stuck some gear in there. What are you wearing, by the way? I've bought you Canada Goose, the whole kit and caboodle. The most expensive gloves—'

'Mittens are better,' Alex says, reflexively, because he really feels like he's in dream-mode.

Charlie stares at him.

'What did you just say? Mittens? Bugger, the cold really has gone to your brain. Let's get you a hot toddy. Then see if we can get some hot teddies for our bed.'

'Charlie,' Alex says.

His friend falls quiet. His face grows sombre.

'I know, Alex boy,' he says. 'I know. Your goddamn guts must be churning every minute of every day. I just wanted to check you were okay. Figured you'd do the same for me. We'll have a few drinks tonight and I'll be gone again tomorrow and you can get the head back down and find the cunt.'

Alex isn't sure he would have done the same for Charlie. Sorted out his parents and bought supplies and flown to the middle of nowhere without even a room booked? The guilt of how better a friend Charlie is to him hits Alex like a hammer.

'Thank you,' Alex says.

Charlie beams.

Beatrice approaches them. Alex can see Niamh, Nicolas and Florian at the bar, being served by Harry. They're out of uniform, off for the night. Niamh is wearing a tight black number, entirely inappropriate for the weather and garnering a lot of attention.

'I'll get in the drinks,' Charlie says. 'Remember, sharing is caring.'

He winks overtly, leaving Alex cringing. Beatrice waits until he leaves, then turns to Alex.

'I think you might want to talk to me,' she says.

'Why's that?'

'You've been talking *about* me.'

'Who told you that?'

'I have just been given the third degree by Miss Popular.'

Alex can only assume she's referring to Niamh and he can tell by a glance in her direction, and from Niamh's embarrassed expression, that he's right. He should have been more careful in what he said to her last night. She obviously left his cabin this morning full of suspicion about Beatrice and made it her business to confront the woman.

'You should know,' Beatrice says. 'I might not have been Vicky's best friend. But we never fought. And I wasn't *jealous* of her. She didn't have anything I wanted.'

The last sentence is uttered with such viciousness that Alex is taken aback.

He stares at her. He's unable to reconcile this version of Beatrice with the one who greeted him with gushing condolences when they first met. Beatrice is cool now, her defensiveness bordering on aggression. But she's also immature and petty.

He glances over and can see Nicolas observing the exchange, eyebrows raised.

You've got this one right, Nicolas old boy, Alex thinks.

'If you want to know who had a problem with your sister, you should be looking at the guys here, not the women,' Beatrice says.

'What's that supposed to mean?' Alex asks.

Beatrice shrugs.

'Unrequited love. It can get quite frustrating. Is it even love, then? Or is it obsession?'

Alex stares at Beatrice, then over at the tour guides at the bar, being served by Harry.

Beatrice is half smiling now. Alex bites the inside of his cheek, hard. He doesn't like this head-fucking. And he's damn sure Vicky wouldn't have liked it, either, all these half suggestions and accusations.

Beatrice is actually not that hard to figure out, he realises. She just wants to play a bigger part in Vicky's story. This little drama is important to her.

But he doesn't think that this woman is capable of killing somebody.

Beatrice's talent is shit-stirring.

'So, do you have something to say to me?' Beatrice says.

Alex nods.

'Yes,' Alex says. 'You've nothing to worry about, Beatrice; I haven't given you a moment's thought. In fact, you don't matter at all.'

With that, he walks away.

As he approaches the bar, he's momentarily distracted from eye-fucking the male tour guides by the scene playing out to his left. Charlie and Niamh.

Charlie has his arm around Niamh's waist in a very affectionate manner. And on closer inspection, Niamh appears to be a little the worse for wear.

Alex knows it's none of his business – and he also knows a psychiatrist would point out that somewhere in the recesses of Alex's brain, he's substituting Niamh for Vicky – but . . . he feels he should intervene.

He approaches the pair.

'Charlie, they do a superb cocktail in here, something with vodka in it. Could you get me one?'

Charlie frowns. He thinks he's on to a good thing with Niamh, Alex reckons, but now he's trying to figure out if he's gone and trodden on his mate's patch. It wouldn't matter if they were in London. All's fair in love and women, over there. But over here, grieving for his sister, Alex is allowed to have first pick of the cherries.

'Okay, old boy,' Charlie says, but leans in and whispers something to Niamh before he goes. Because Charlie is not good at losing, even to a friend he considers a brother.

Niamh giggles and Alex grimaces.

'Your friend is a lot of fun,' she says to Alex.

'He's also flying home tomorrow and, I'm not going to lie to you, Niamh, he is quite the ladies' man,' Alex says. 'Or would like to be.'

Niamh shrugs. He can see, at this proximity, that she is indeed very drunk.

'I thought you were into Harry,' Alex says.

Niamh looks over to the bar, where Charlie is being served by Harry.

'Yeah,' she says. 'But, s'all rules, rules, fucking rules with him. I didn't think he was serious but he means it. He doesn't want to be in a relationship in work. Talk about shutting the stable door . . .'

Her eyes soften and cloud with something; an expression reminding him of a wounded animal. And he realises then, as Charlie banters with Harry and Harry glances over, exactly what's going on.

'Don't do this,' Alex says quietly. 'You're not going to make Harry jealous by going off with Charlie.'

'It's just a laugh,' Niamh says, in a tone that says this is anything but fun.

'Charlie's not going to care about you,' Alex says.

'Well, you're not interested.'

She slurs this, leaning her body towards him, her eyes wider now. A question.

To which his answer is no.

'Harry's not worth it,' Alex says.

Niamh sways a little. She looks at him, angry now.

'I get to decide that,' she says.

She glances at Harry again, with a longing in her eyes, and Alex feels an overwhelming pity for her. She's a young woman, suffering a very recent trauma, in love with a guy who has no time for her.

Alex, who's never been in love, still knows what people in love are capable of.

He wonders again how blind she might be to Harry's flaws.

Blind enough to cover up for him?

★

297

Alex waits up for Charlie to come into the cabin. They'd separated in the bar; Charlie left with Niamh. Alex had tried to talk Charlie out of it, but he was too drunk to pay any heed, and a young, attractive woman was taking him home.

Niamh's eyes never left Harry's face the whole time she was walking out of the bar.

Harry didn't look at her once. Alex knew this, because he was watching Harry.

Alex knows Charlie and Niamh are adults. It's not his job to chaperone. But he can't help feeling guilty because he knows Niamh's actions are irrational and she'll regret them in the morning.

When Charlie comes in, a huge smile on his face, Alex sighs.

'I love it here,' Charlie groans, collapsing on to the bed like a starfish. 'I might stay.'

Later, when Charlie is fast asleep in Alex's bed, Alex rings his father.

'Hey,' he says. 'Charlie is here.'

'He said he was flying over today. How is he?'

'He told you he was fly— Are you buddies now?'

'He's a good lad.'

'Did he get Mum transferred to a private hospital?'

'It's just for her aftercare.'

Alex takes a deep breath. It's entirely hypocritical of him to be annoyed by this. He's the very one who wanted his parents to have private healthcare.

'He's a character,' his father says. 'A real Cockney.'

And now Alex knows how it played out. Charlie rocked up, gave it a bit of this and a bit of that, and won Ed around before Ed even knew what was happening.

'She's okay?' Alex asks.

'Right as rain. Sleeping at the moment. You should have seen the lunch they gave her. Enough to feed a whole family. Do you have any news?'

Alex sighs.

'Still nothing,' he says, abject failure in all three syllables.

'It's not nothing,' his father says.

Alex is staring out the window, looking at the mound of snow that's grown even bigger outside his cabin. He's not sure he's heard his father right.

'Sorry?'

He listens to his father's deep breathing for a few moments.

'When Vicky was born, I don't know if you remember this, but I took you out for the day,' Ed says. 'Some of the fathers, they were staying in hospitals for the birth around then, but I had my own father's attitude ingrained in me. Anyway, your mother wanted her mum with her. Somebody of use. Not me, passing out at the sight of . . . stuff. Anyhow, we dropped them in and you and I drove out to the Dales.'

'I remember,' Alex says. 'I didn't want Mum to go into the hospital. I thought she was sick.'

'You cried in the car until you saw where we were going, then you cheered up.'

Alex closes his eyes. He used to love the Dales. These days, he rarely thinks of them. Does he even notice the parks in London? When was the last time he sat on grass or walked anywhere he felt he could actually breathe?

'I brought you on a hike,' Ed says. 'A long one, and even though you were only six, you kept up. It was like you knew already you weren't the youngest of the house, that you had to grow up. And then we got lost.'

'We got *lost*?' Alex is aware he's parroting his father, but he just can't fathom a scenario where his dad could get lost in the Dales. His father has moss and flint in his blood.

'Yep. I got us lost. A mist came in, I couldn't get my bearings. I was worried the hospital would be trying to get hold of us, and there I was in the middle of the bloody hills, no sense of which way was home. You took my hand and you said, "Don't worry, Daddy. I have a packet of jellies in my pocket".'

Alex laughs. His father does too.

'The point is, Alex, even then, you were unflappable. You were only six and I'd never been so proud of you. It doesn't matter what happened when you were a kid. I want you to know that. I've been in plenty of fights in my time. You just had bad luck. The worst luck. I've always been proud of you. The way you picked yourself up and made a life for yourself. I might not be a fan of the job you took, but I always knew that you'd make a good man.'

His dad hangs up. It's abrupt and yet, totally predictable. Alex guesses Ed could just about cope with getting the words out – he couldn't cope with hearing his son's response.

Alex sits very still, listens to his heart thumping in his chest, unable to swallow for the lump in his throat. His father, in all his memory, has never spoken to him like that.

The way Ed had looked at him, when he'd picked him up at the police station that time. Alex had been sixteen and he'd almost killed a boy with a single punch. Alex had thought he'd never recover from that look of disappointment.

He wonders now, in this place so far away, if his father's expression was a projection of something he'd felt within himself. Had Ed been dismayed that he'd spent so much time fighting for other people, he'd taken his eye off the ball with his own son?

Alex allows the tears to fall. He can do that here, on his own, in a cabin in the frozen north. He can let himself feel something for all the years they've missed, if they'd only had this conversation earlier.

If only it hadn't taken Vicky's death for it to happen.

Alex is startled from his thoughts by a particularly large snore from Charlie. He's just about to make up a bed on the chair again when his phone rings for the second time. He stares at the number, unable to immediately identify the country code, which is something that normally only happens when it's a work call. But all his work contacts have been redirected to the office.

He's not able to talk with a stranger. The call with his dad has emotionally drained him. He just wants to sleep. But he answers, out of habit.

'Alex Evans,' he says.

'Alex?' An American accent. 'This is Bryce Adams. I hope it's okay to call you like this. The guy in the police station in Koppe, he gave me your number.'

Alex's pulse quickens.

'Right,' he says. 'Eh, that's fine. I'm glad you called.'

'I had to get in touch,' Bryce says. 'I have something important to tell you.'

Alex is at the window now, his forehead resting against the cold glass. He straightens up, every inch of him alert.

'I've spoken to the police and my friends have too, and listen, I want you to know that I went to your sister's cabin the night they say she disappeared, but I wasn't with her or anything. I know that sounds kinda unbelievable. She was a pretty girl, lots of fun. But, truth is, I don't think she was into me. And I've never forced myself on a girl. Never will. I told the police this. Vicky wasn't interested. She made it clear. I guess . . . I think she was kinda using me.'

'Excuse me?'

Bryce laughs uncomfortably.

'I know, right?' he says. 'I don't get that a lot as a jock. Hey, I don't mean to be offensive. I'm not angry at her. I mean, I wasn't. Look, girls' brains. They're different to ours, right. I got the impression, though, maybe there was some guy there she wanted to make a point to, or something?'

Alex says nothing but he thinks back to what happened in the bar tonight, Niamh leaving with Charlie to make Harry jealous. Had Vicky done the same with Bryce – but not to make someone jealous . . . to make a point to somebody that she *wasn't* interested?

'I left her safe and well,' Bryce says. 'She didn't seem scared or anything. She did say she was thinking of moving on. I asked her why, she said it was just time.'

Alex exhales.

'Is that all you wanted to tell me?'

He's disappointed there isn't more.

'I also wanted to tell you that Vicky was really cool,' Bryce says. 'I have a few photographs we took in the cabin that night. Even after I realised I wasn't going to be, well, you know. Selfies, funny pics. I haven't posted them on Instagram but I thought you might like them. I know when you lose someone, every single memory of them is super important.'

Alex takes a deep breath.

'Sure,' he says. 'I mean, yes. I'd like them.'

They exchange email addresses. Alex gets the sense Bryce feels some kind of moral responsibility towards him. They're not going to be friends. But Alex knows that Bryce will be the sort to message every Christmas just to check in, and he'll always tell the story of the fun girl he met in Koppe and how she was there one minute and gone the next.

The email arrives moments after they've hung up. Alex opens the folder of photos.

His sister is laughing in every single one. There's not a hint of distress or fear or any knowledge of what's to come on her face. Her eyes are twinkling; those dark brown eyes he's known all his life but never really appreciated.

In these laughing, smiling photographs, Victoria Elizabeth Evans, twenty-six years of age, is happy.

Alex lies back in the chair, his phone open on one of the pictures, and stares at the captured moment until the pain becomes unbearable.

It's late, but Martti doesn't express any surprise when Agatha turns up on his doorstep.

'What can I help you with, Chief?' he asks. 'How's Elon doing, by the way? I asked him to call back in but have seen no sign of him.'

'He's back out on the ice, fishing,' Agatha says. 'I don't think you have to worry. Whiskey is the only treatment he needs, Martti. And as for why I'm here, I'm after old medical files.'

It's almost midnight but Martti barely blinks.

'Anybody in particular?' he asks.

Agatha follows him through the house. It's similar to her own, and just like hers is the house that comes with the position of chief, this house is the one that comes with the position of doctor.

'The files all went digital in 2015,' Martti says. 'I'd have done it as soon as I arrived but it took a while to organise the system. You know how it is. My secretary wanted to do it the way she'd done it for her last boss. They'd a good set-up, though, even if it was just paper. There are records going back to 1965. The old doc kept them and we moved them into the basement here.'

'Kaya Virtanen and Mary Rosenberg,' Agatha says. 'And while I'm here, do you have a file on Vicky Evans?'

'Only post-mortem. She never came in to see me. Fit, healthy girl, by the looks of it.' Martti frowns. 'Kaya, Mary – those are the women who went missing . . .'

'You know about Kaya, too?' Agatha asks. Martti had only moved to Koppe in 2012. But of course he must have heard of Kaya. He'll have heard of Miika. Ergo, he'll have heard about his wife.

'We used to come up here for skiing,' Martti says. 'I heard about it at the time. And then there was Mary. And Hilda.'

'It looks like Hilda has been found,' Agatha says, tightly.

'Well, that's something. Where was she?'

'She was in Sweden. Ran off with a drug-dealing haulier. Love's young dream.'

Martti's eyes widen.

'Some people have all the fun,' he says.

The doctor leads Agatha down into his well-lit basement.

'I'm sure the chief at the time would have looked at these records,' Martti says.

'They're mentioned in their missing persons' files. I just want to check them myself.'

'What are you looking for?'

'I know Kaya Virtanen suffered some domestic abuse. Somebody got me wondering about Mary Rosenberg's fiancé. She came over here every winter and the doctor saw her a couple of times for her back. But I wonder if he noted anything else. Old breaks in her bones, things like that.'

'Things that would indicate she was abused, too,' Martti says, his eyes narrowing behind his glasses. 'And you're thinking maybe she just ran off, like Hilda. That she escaped a bad relationship. Kaya, too?'

'I don't know,' Agatha says.

She doesn't tell him there's very little detail in the police files about Kaya and Mary's medical records, but that she was able to read between the lines of what's there relating to Kaya. A broken nose. A black eye. Other little things that all lead to the same conclusion. She doesn't doubt Miika caused those injuries. She also knows that domestic violence runs rife up here and that many of the same men casting judgement on Miika have probably lashed out at their wives at some point in the past.

As promised by Martti, the old doc's system is a good one and they find the relevant files after only a few short minutes. They bring them upstairs and Agatha sits at the kitchen table and starts to read.

'I'll make the coffee,' Martti says.

There are no surprises in the first few pages of Kaya's medical file. The last Koppe doctor had treated her from childhood. Aged twelve, Kaya had broken her leg when skating. Aside from that, she'd been sent down to Rovaniemi to have her appendix removed. Then there are the few mentions of what Agatha knows are injuries consistent with domestic violence.

It's on the last page that Agatha reads something that catches her breath.

She reads it twice and lets it sink in.

That might explain a lot, Agatha thinks.

She barely notices Martti putting the coffee down beside her.

She's already scanning Mary Rosenberg's details. This file is light. It records a few ski-related injuries, but there's nothing that says beaten woman.

It doesn't matter, Agatha thinks. If the husband was psychologically controlling her, it wouldn't show up on these pages. She might still have wanted to get away from him.

And then, Agatha sees something identical to what she spotted in Kaya's file.

She covers her mouth.

Martti, sitting beside her, senses something is amiss.

'Am I reading this right?' she asks him.

He pushes his glasses up his nose and looks at both the pages, then at Agatha, shocked.

'Yes,' he says.

Agatha drives home. Her head is full of questions and theories but it is so late now she knows they'll have to wait until morning. She's tired and not thinking straight. As she turns on to the main street, a group of young men spill off the pavement, bantering drunkenly with each other. Agatha swerves in the snow and beeps her horn loudly at them.

'We can't see where the path ends and the road starts,' one of them shouts in English, laughing.

Agatha doesn't smile in return. Tonight, she's not the friendly town chief, on hand for the tourists. She's something else altogether.

She parks up and rests her head on the steering wheel for a few moments.

How had she missed this? Why hadn't she checked the medical files before?

Because there was nothing in the missing persons' files that made her think she had to check the medical records.

But, it couldn't be a coincidence, could it? Two missing women with the same entry in their files? Why hadn't that set alarm bells ringing?

A bang on the driver's window makes her jump and yelp at the same time.

Patric is staring in at her.

She gets out of the car.

'God, Patric, you scared the life out of me.'

'*You* scared the life out of me,' he says, his voice muffled by his scarf. 'Where have you been?'

She almost laughs – he's speaking to her like she's a teenager who has broken curfew.

'Doing my job,' she says. 'Why are you here this late?'

'I came to check,' he says.

'Check what?'

'Where are the children?'

'Oh!' Agatha realises. She places her hand on her forehead. 'The kids aren't here. They've gone up to Becki's.'

She understands now why Patric is so concerned. She forgot to tell him the kids wouldn't be in the house and he must have been worried when he called by and saw the place in darkness. Agatha hasn't spoken to him today; she hasn't been able to tell him there's been no further contact from Luca. Yet.

'Hell, Agatha. I wish you'd told me. I've been going out of my mind here. Why weren't you answering your phone?'

Agatha takes her phone out. It's completely dead.

'Battery,' she says.

Patric rolls his eyes.

'As long as you're safe,' he says. 'And I'm happy to know the kids are up with Becki and Henni.'

Patric is about to walk away, but Agatha grabs his arm.

'I'm glad you're here,' she says. 'I was going to call in to you in the morning. Patric, I need to talk to you about Kaya Virtanen and Mary Rosenberg.'

Patric frowns.

'What about them?'

Inside, they sit at Agatha's kitchen table and she quickly fills Patric in on the Hilda developments. Initially, his face registers surprise, but soon he's nodding, like Agatha has just confirmed something for him.

'Now it makes sense,' Patric says. 'Do you remember? No, wait, you weren't there for that interview. Jonas was with me. One of her oldest friends said Hilda could be silly about men. We thought the friend might have been a bit unkind – the owner of the café where she worked and his daughter just said that Hilda had a flirtatious nature. But her friend implied it went a bit further than that, that Hilda was the sort to drop everything for a man. That led me to wonder whether she might have been stupid enough to get into a car with a stranger who chatted her up. But, if she was actually seeing some criminal character and she ran off to be with him – yes, it adds up. Foolish, foolish woman.'

Patric shakes his head, then bangs his hand on the table.

'All those resources! All that time wasted.'

'I know,' Agatha says. 'Not to mention the rumours and speculation.'

Patric nods, distressed.

'There's more,' Agatha says. 'There was something in Kaya and Mary's medical files. Something that wasn't in the police reports.'

He frowns.

'What?'

'Both of them were pregnant.'

She can tell by Patric's face he's genuinely shocked.

'They were *both* pregnant?'

'How did you miss it?' Agatha asks. 'They both went for blood tests, both tests came back with high levels of HCG. The files didn't actually say *pregnant* but the blood tests and the HCG levels implied it.'

'I never saw the medical files,' Patric says, blankly.

Agatha frowns now, confused.

'I don't understand.'

'They weren't murder cases, Agatha. They were missing persons. The doctor told me what was in their files – what he thought was relevant, anyway. There was no legal requirement for him to hand over their records and he cited patient confidentiality. He told us that Kaya had some domestic abuse injuries. Christ, most of the town had seen it with their own eyes. Everybody knew Miika was fond of a drink and of using his fists. But Mary was perfectly healthy. We checked, just to make sure she wasn't lying somewhere in a diabetic coma or something. But the doctor said nothing about them being pregnant. That would certainly have given me pause for thought.'

Patric gets up and starts to pace.

'Why wouldn't he think it relevant?' Agatha asks.

'I don't know! It's not like we can ask him, the man is dead seven years.'

'Could he have been hiding it for a reason? How well did he know Kaya? Mary, even?'

'He'd have known Kaya as well as the rest of us,' Patric says. 'I don't know how well he knew Mary.'

'It has to mean something, doesn't it? The fact both of them had pregnancy tests and went missing? What if . . . ?'

Agatha trails off.

'Say it,' Patric says, halting his pacing.

Agatha is still hesitant. She knows she's blowing Patric's cases wide open and yet, she can't forget what she's learned.

She can't pretend he did a good enough job.

'I had a notion they were both fleeing abusive partners,' Agatha says. 'But what if they were pregnant by the same man? I asked Martti; he says he doubts the pregnancy confirmation blood samples were retained, so we can't check DNA. But if each of them had told the father and he'd, well, if he'd killed them . . . Or if the doctor had told the father? He'd have known they were pregnant, and if he wanted to help the father cover it up, that would explain why he never told you what was in the files.'

'But surely Miika would have been the father of Kaya's baby?' Patric says. 'And Mary could have been pregnant when she came over . . .'

'Miika told you he thought Kaya had a lover.'

Patric slumps into a chair.

'Yes,' he says. 'But there's no proof. Agatha, those women were years apart. It can hardly be the case that the same person who slept with Kaya then slept with Mary. Who in this town—'

'Lassi Niemenen,' Agatha says.

Patric opens his mouth, then closes it. He says nothing for a few moments, but then he shakes his head.

'No, Agatha,' he says. 'I can't believe that. I'm glad you found out about Hilda but I think you're barking up the wrong tree here. We don't have a serial killer in Koppe. We couldn't. Do you really think I would have missed that—'

'But Lassi also knew Vicky!' Agatha protests. 'It's starting to fall into place, Patric. Just because Hilda is safe doesn't mean we don't have a predator on our hands—'

'Or maybe I was just wrong about Miika Virtanen!' Patric shouts. 'Maybe he killed his wife, and Mary Rosenberg just had a goddamn accident on the ice!'

'Why are you so keen to defend Lassi?' Agatha shouts back.

'Why are you so eager to see him hung out to dry?'

Agatha's heart is racing. She and Patric have never fought before. She knows he's angry because he's defensive, and that she's just as angry because she needs to solve Vicky's case but, still, it's unsettling to be having this argument with her mentor.

'Lassi would have told everybody if he'd been with Kaya,' Patric says, calmer now. He, too, must be unsettled by their fight.

'Then somebody else,' Agatha says, because Patric has just made the same point Jonas did and Agatha can't help but consider the veracity of the argument. 'Somebody else in the town could have been with Kaya and Mary.'

'There was nobody in town Kaya could have been having an affair with,' Patric said. 'She was only ever down here for work in the bar with Harry and . . .'

Patric stops. Like he's just thought of something.

He and Agatha look at each other.

'Harry and Elliot,' Agatha says.

Elliot, who was part of the group of men who helped build the town and put it on the map. Lassi, Elliot, the old doctor. The town's most important men.

'Harry and his wife divorced a few years back,' Agatha says.

Patric nods.

'I remember,' Patric says. 'My Léah was dying and I couldn't believe anybody would let a marriage go so easily. So willingly.'

'She divorced him, didn't she?' Agatha asks. 'Why?'

Patric shrugs. Then he shakes his head.

'And Elliot is barely ever home. He sleeps in the bar. His wife practically lives her own life.'

Patric frowns in concentration.

'Agatha,' Patric says. 'It still just sounds like you're chasing shadows. Lassi, now Elliot. Or Harry. And don't they all have alibis?'

'Alibis can be faked.'

Patric is about to reply when he freezes.

Agatha has heard it, too. A noise outside, on the back porch.

Patric jumps up.

'What is it?' she says.

Then she remembers how she found him, waiting outside her house. Rattled, even for Patric.

'Patric – why were you really here tonight? Was it just that you were worried because my house was empty?'

He looks at her.

'I thought I saw somebody,' he says, his face colouring. 'Agatha, it was probably nothing.'

There's a knock on the back door.

Agatha starts to tremble.

'Don't open it,' Patric says.

'You said it was probably nothing. Did you see her, Patric? Did you see my sister?'

Patric doesn't answer.

He so badly wants to protect her, Agatha realises. And she's filled with fear.

She crosses the kitchen floor before he can stop her.

There's always been an invisible pull between them. A cord that draws the twins together.

She opens the door.

All of the missing women leave Agatha's thoughts.

There's an actual ghost on the doorstep.

Luca is standing in front of her.

Koppe

1998

The blood test has come back from the doctor's. Not that Kaya needed to see it. She wishes she hadn't even taken it. The way the old man looked at her when she came in. Like he knew it wasn't her husband's, because Miika wasn't there. Like the doctor was in on her dirty little secret.

She wishes she didn't exist. If she didn't exist, the baby wouldn't. That's how Kaya feels right now.

She's lying in bed. The mark on her cheek is red raw. Miika hadn't said anything to her. She'd just asked him if his dinner was okay and he slapped her across the face. He hadn't even been drinking.

She knows the slap was not because he was unhappy with his dinner. They both know what the slap was for.

Kaya's worried it's only the beginning.

She remembers the first time he really lost it. He punched her so hard in the face, her nose broke and she was knocked out for hours.

If he punched her like that in the stomach, what damage would that do?

How long will it be before looking at her growing belly tips him over the edge?

Kaya has checked her savings. She has money hidden around the house in places she knows Miika will never look – in the pantry, in among her now useless time-of-the-month pads, in the cabinet where she keeps the polish and cloths she uses to wipe down his mother's damned ornaments. Those stupid ornaments. They'd inherited them with the house, a house Kaya didn't even want to live in.

She has enough to get down to Helsinki and spend a couple of nights in a hotel. If she could find somewhere quickly, and cheaply, she could manage, but if her search goes on . . . how long before her money runs out?

She can't bring herself to go to her parents. They've never liked Miika, she knows they'll be happy. But they'll start asking questions about the baby. And Kaya knows she can't pretend to her mother that the child is Miika's. Which would mean admitting what she'd done.

Her parents might not approve of her choice of husband but what Kaya has done will disgust them.

Kaya can hear him moving around downstairs. He's coming up.

She curls into a ball, as tight as possible, trying to make herself small, trying to protect the child in her stomach.

The bedroom door opens.

She hears him come in, hears his breathing.

Her heart is galloping. She should have gone. She should have left by now.

It's too late.

'Sorry,' Miika says.

Kaya is so shocked, she doesn't move.

'It won't happen again.'

He leaves.

Kaya lies there, her heart slowing.

What was that?

Koppe

2019

Agatha stares at the mirror image in front of her.

The last time she'd seen Luca, her sister had been in a hospital bed. She'd looked like death warmed up, and even though they are identical twins, it sure didn't look it that night, the night after she almost killed her own children.

Now, Luca looks more like her old self, more like the sister Agatha remembers. The one who could lure you in. Who could cause so much damage.

She looks back at Agatha, uncertainly. The fact the door hasn't been slammed in her face is probably giving her hope, but Agatha still doesn't invite her in.

'What are you doing here?' Agatha says.

'Your call,' Luca answers.

'*My* call? I didn't ask you to come here. I told you to stay away.'

'I *was* staying away.'

'No!' Agatha shouts. 'Don't you lie to me.'

'I'm not lying.'

Luca is shivering. Agatha scans her face, her pupils; she's looking

317

for the signs. Her sister could be just cold but it's more likely she's faking it for sympathy.

'If your lips are moving, you're lying,' Agatha spits.

'But I'm not. I haven't been near Koppe since that last time—'

'Olavi is not a liar!'

'I haven't been here,' Luca protests. 'I'm living in Helsinki. Agatha, I swear, I have not been near the children. I wouldn't—'

Agatha slams the door.

She won't listen to it.

She stands against the door, holding it closed with her body. Every part of her is trembling.

Luca has done this before. Sworn blind. Sworn on her life, on Agatha's life, on the kids' lives. Been convincing with it, too.

Patric faces Agatha, his expression as horrified as hers.

Agatha is waiting for Luca to start banging on the door. To break the glass, maybe. She's done that before, too, when her snake lies haven't worked.

But all Agatha hears is a little, desperate laugh and it chills her to the bone.

That's followed by the crunch of footsteps on the snow.

Agatha sinks to the floor, her head in her hands.

Her phone, charging in the corner, rings; Agatha jumps.

It's starting, she thinks. The harassment.

'It's only Jonas,' Patric says, looking at the screen.

Agatha sobs, then, while Patric hugs her, telling her it will all be okay.

'It won't be okay,' Agatha says. 'She's here now, Patric. And she won't leave until she causes chaos. You know what she's like. She'll act normal, everything will be fine, and then she'll start doing things. Little things – I'll question if she even meant them. I'll question if I'm being too hard on her. Then she'll slip up. She'll call me a selfish bitch. Show me what she really thinks. It will get worse. And it has to get extreme before she'll stop. I knew she'd come back. I knew her promise meant nothing. She can't even do it for the kids.'

'I won't let her hurt them,' Patric says. 'I promise.'

Agatha is filled with despair. It's never-ending. She will never be rid of her sister.

Agatha wakes the next morning to an unsettled feeling in her stomach, before she remembers what happened the night before.

Luca is back.

The foggy feeling in her head takes a while to recede. Patric had made her take a sleeping tablet to send her off. Otherwise, she wouldn't have slept a wink.

Agatha checks in with Becki again, then stands in the shower, barely even aware of the water.

The kids are safe. Luca doesn't know where they are. Not yet, anyhow. If she's determined to find them, it won't take her long to figure it out. The detection genes run strong in the Koskinen family.

What if Agatha just left? Put the kids in the car, emptied her savings and drove to Sweden? They could start again, couldn't they? In a new town where nobody knows them; where they know nobody.

Where they've no friends, no support network, nobody looking out for them.

Agatha groans. Why should they have to run? Why should their lives be uprooted?

Not to mention, Agatha has a job to do. She has a duty to the people of Koppe. To the women who've died. To her cases. To Alex, even.

Agatha was always the sister who did the right thing. And she'll do it now. If it kills her.

Agatha winces. She's so stressed, she's massaged knots into her hair with the shampoo. Her scalp aches.

She rinses her hair and then clears her head of all thoughts of Luca. For now, at least.

It's this grim determination that gets her dressed and into her car, even if she does look left and right on the street before running out to the vehicle.

Agatha drives to the local council building to discover that the only staff present at this hour of the morning is the cleaning crew.

She didn't return Jonas' call last night. But this morning she listened to the message he left and it only served to validate the suspicion that's been niggling at her.

She recognises the young man mopping the floor of the corridor. Elliot's nephew.

'Hi,' she says. 'Lassi Niemenen's office?'

'Down the hall,' he says. 'But it'll be locked.'

'Right. I need to check something. To do with council work.'

There's a stand-off. The young man knows she's the chief of police. But she's not the boss in this building.

'I can get a warrant.' She sighs. 'But what I need to check has nothing to do with a crime. It's just to do with the town. I need to look at planning laws and I think the information I need is in Lassi Niemenen's office.'

The young man absorbs this and she can see him calculating what response will cause him the least trouble.

'Will you just be in and out?' he says, and she knows she has him.

Five minutes later, she's sitting in Lassi's office.

She phones Jonas from the landline.

'I recognise that number,' he says, when he picks up.

'I'm in Lassi's office,' she says. 'I got your message.'

'It might be nothing,' he says. 'How did you get in there?'

'Flashed my boobs.'

She can practically hear Jonas' blushes.

Agatha touches Lassi's computer. His private screen is pass-word-protected, but she can log in as a guest. Agatha curses. It was too much to hope for that she could just access his desktop. If he'd left it unlocked she could have faked seeing something by accident. But if she cracks his password, she's already made anything she finds unusable.

She's not entirely out of options. Luckily for her, the town's council business records are accessible to all local bureaucrats, including police officials. The database includes the minutes of monthly council meetings, the annexes to those meetings, as well as basic town operations, like planning applications.

'Tell me what you have,' Agatha says. 'This Canadian mining firm?'

'Confirmed a few years back that there's a large deposit of precious metals, particularly cobalt and nickel, in the Koppe region. Their application for a mining licence was rejected in 2016. Unanimously, by all the councillors.'

'And yet, now they're back,' Agatha says.

'It certainly looks that way. But I can't find any indication that land has been rezoned for mining, anywhere. So I don't know why they're sniffing around, just that Janic was right. There's a small group of them up in the hotel at the moment and word on the grapevine is that more are coming. There's blood in the water. Somebody has told them they have a chance.'

'Okay, I'll let you know if I discover anything,' Agatha says.

She hangs up.

Over the years, Agatha has learned to speed-read quite well, but even she's not that good. So she types in 'planning', then 'mining', then 'licences', and tries to get through the most recent applications as quickly as possible.

Nothing jumps out at her.

Agatha sighs and sits back.

She types in 'nickel'.

Nothing.

So she tries typing 'tourism development zones'. She knows the councillors weren't all entirely happy about the hotel being built on the side of the mountain, especially as it threatened some of the existing tourism businesses, like Lassi's Lodge. But she also knows that their biggest fear was that mining would come to the town. So, back when the hotel was built, the entire mountain was zoned solely for tourism.

She finds what she's looking for, buried among the details.

It's in the annexe to the June meeting.

Lassi Niemenen submitted an application to 'reconsider the zoning of the north side of the mountain for tourism purposes'.

Agatha reads his memo. Three times.

She can see how it might have been misunderstood or flown under the radar.

To somebody not doubting Lassi's intentions, it would read as he wanted it to be read. *Zoning for tourism purposes*.

But the mountain *is* already zoned for tourism.

What Lassi wants is the mountain's current zoning *reconsidered*.

For other purposes.

'Fuck,' she mouths, to nobody.

Lassi is selling out Koppe.

She grabs her phone and texts Jonas. They have a friendly judge in Rovaniemi. Jonas was right – a warrant for Lassi's bank accounts will be easier to land if there's a hint of impropriety at council level. Agatha knows the Lappish authorities are hypersensitive to corruption in local politics, following the allocation of suspect mining licences in the past. All Jonas has to do is tell the judge he thinks the councillors are meeting with mining companies.

Text message sent, Agatha sits back. She looks around Lassi's desk. Opens a few drawers. Nothing jumps out at her.

She goes to the filing cabinet. In the first drawer, it's all innocuous council business.

And then, in the second drawer, not even hidden, is a brochure from the Canadian mining company, the CRP Group. Inside the first page, there's a Post-it.

Looking forward to future endeavours.

Agatha takes the brochure.

Outside, Elliot's nephew is waiting anxiously.

'It's okay,' Agatha tells him. 'I just wanted to access the central database. I'm allowed to do that.'

'Then why did you need Lassi's office? You can do that from anywhere?'

That took you a while, Agatha thinks.

But, he's still not the sharpest tool in the box.

'Oh, I thought Lassi had left something on his desk for me.'

The young man's face relaxes.

'As a matter of interest,' Agatha says, 'you know that woman who went missing? Vicky Evans?'

'The girl in the lake?'

'Yeah. You ever see her in here? Visiting Lassi?'

'No.'

He shakes his head. He's eager for Agatha to go.

Agatha smiles.

She's a few feet down the corridor when he calls after her.

'My uncle Elliot did, though. I heard him talking about it in the bar after she went missing. She'd come in looking for Lassi but he was in a meeting. Elliot saw her outside his office. He came out and they had an argument. Elliot said Lassi was going to fire her ass . . .'

Agatha turns around, trying not to show anything on her face.

'When was this?'

'Just after she went missing . . .'

'Not when Elliot mentioned it. When did she come into the council office?'

'Ages before she died. Like, a few months anyway. June, maybe.'

'I see.'

Agatha hesitates. She can't figure out why he was reluctant to let her into Lassi's office but is happy to impart such important information.

'She was nice,' he says, looking down at the floor. 'I met her in the bar once or twice. She seemed like a nice woman.'

'Thank you,' Agatha says. 'She was.'

They stare at each other and the kid nods slightly in acknow-ledgement.

Vicky and Lassi.

Agatha is joining the dots.

The bar is not open yet and there's no answer from Elliot's house. A neighbour tells Agatha she thinks Elliot's gone on a snowmobile trip and will be away for the day.

So Agatha drives on. She wants to question Elliot about Kaya but she can do it another time. She doesn't know if he was involved back then – by covering up for Lassi or maybe even being responsible for what happened. But, right now, her focus is on Vicky. That's where all the evidence leads.

Lassi lives in a huge house outside town. It's ostentatious and – with the exception of a nod to local timber in its roof – not in keeping with the area. Too much glass, for a start. Nobody puts glass windows that large in a house in Lapland. They bleed heat.

But Lassi would rather be living in LA, so that's the house he's built.

Agatha waits impatiently at the electric gates. She's there so long she has time to consider the many benefits of large gates when it comes to people turning up at your front door that you'd rather not see.

They open eventually and she drives up the spruce-lined road. She remembers all this area as forest, back when Lassi lived in town, before he'd fulfilled all his entrepreneurial dreams.

He'd taken his wife's inheritance and, to be fair, while some men might have squandered it, Lassi made it multiply. Some of it was even for the good of the town. That's always been the problem with Lassi. If he was bad through and through, the townspeople would have turned against him. But he isn't, which means he can get away with a lot. How much, Agatha isn't sure.

Lassi opens the door. He has no porch, another ridiculous absence in a Lapland house. He doesn't invite her in, but Agatha catches a glimpse of his wife in the background, scurrying up the marble staircase in the centre of the reception hall, before he steps out into the cold. He'd rather freeze than allow her across his threshold.

'Ah. The little chief.'

Agatha stares at Lassi.

'Have you come to apologise for how you spoke to me yesterday?'

'I've come to ask you about your relationship with Vicky Evans. And while we're at it, Kaya Virtanen and Mary Rosenberg.'

Lassi tugs at his goatee beard.

'Two missing women and a dead one. I'd say this is a conversation we can have with a lawyer present.'

'Innocent people rarely need lawyers when they're talking to the police,' Agatha says.

'No, Agatha. Lawyers are always necessary. It's only poor people who don't use lawyers. Rich people always do. But seeing as you so blatantly doubt my innocence, let me tell you this for free: I had no relationship with any of the women you've mentioned, bar being an employer to one.'

'You've never had kids,' Agatha says. She knows she's in a tight spot, that she has a tiny window to provoke some slip from him before he does get a lawyer.

'Never wanted any,' Lassi says. 'My business is my baby.'

He examines her, knowing there has to be some relevance in her statement.

'It's strange none of the women you've slept with over the years got pregnant,' Agatha says, a thin smile on her lips. 'Come now, Lassi, we all know you've had some . . . let's call them, "extramarital adventures". Were you very careful? Or is there a problem with, you know?'

She glances down at his groin. When she looks up at him, his face is still placid but his eyes have darkened.

'If I had had affairs and if I'd fathered any children, it would still be of no consequence to you,' he says. 'Unless, of course, I decided to stake a claim to one of the kids. If the mother was, let's say, unstable. Then everybody would know who I'd fathered. Wouldn't that be interesting? Who knows, little Agatha, who I'm related to in town?'

Agatha feels the chill in the pit of her stomach.

They glare at each other for another few moments.

Agatha swallows and brings her focus back to the reason she's here.

'Kaya Virtanen was suspected of having an affair,' Agatha says.

'It wasn't with me. Not that any of us could blame her for cheating on that oik. And I wouldn't have said no, that's for sure. Why don't you ask Miika who she was with?'

'Miika doesn't know.'

Lassi snorts.

'He kept that girl on a short leash. Of course he knew.'

'What would you do, Lassi, if one of the women you were seeing expected you to leave your wife? You've never even considered it, have you? You run around on her, but you're loyal to her, in some twisted way. Would it make you feel violent towards one of your women, if they forced you to choose?'

Lassi shakes his head, like he's disappointed in Agatha.

'I'm not the only man in this town to have the odd, as you put it, "extramarital liaison",' Lassi says. 'There's no such thing as a pure soul. But I had nothing to do with any of your cases.'

Agatha tugs at her bottom lip with her teeth.

'A witness saw you arguing with Vicky Evans in the council offices last summer.'

Lassi smiles. Agatha's not looking at his mouth, though. She's looking at his eyes. She can see the calculations running behind them.

'I have no recollection of that,' he says. 'Which witness?'

Agatha smiles back.

'Can you tell me what was said between the two of you?'

'I'm afraid not, as I can't recall. Maybe you should ask your witness what he heard. Oh . . . did they just *see* an argument? Then perhaps they misunderstood. Perhaps we were just exchanging the time of day.'

'In the council offices? My witness says you were in a meeting beforehand and Vicky was waiting outside.'

Lassi is bristling now.

'Well, I'll have to try to remember for you. Now, as I said, if you want to speak to me again, please do it officially and through my lawyer.'

Lassi goes to step back inside. His hand is on the door when Agatha speaks again.

'I suspect I will have to talk to your lawyer, soon enough,' she says.

'Oh, yes?'

From inside her coat, Agatha pulls out the mining company brochure.

'What made you decide to sell out, Lassi? You've always been anti-mining. You led the campaign against it. Is the Lodge in that much trouble? Are you broke?'

Lassi doesn't say anything. He doesn't need to. Agatha can see it written all over his face.

'How do you think you'll get this past the rest of the council?' Agatha asks. 'They might trust you, but even they're not stupid enough to miss the mountain being sold out from under the town.'

'The town doesn't own that part of the mountain,' Lassi says.

Agatha frowns.

And then she gets it.

'When they built the hotel,' she says, 'you bought the rest of the land so nothing more could be built. Why not just build another hotel? Why mining?'

Lassi is silent.

Agatha shakes her head. She doesn't know if he's just greedy or if he's desperate because he realises he can't compete with the hotel.

'What I don't understand is how Vicky Evans put this together,' she says. 'Was it as simple as her overhearing you in your office? Why was she even there that day? Why was she looking for you? And why did she decide to blackmail you? Because that's what happened, isn't it? She saw those Canadian officials in with you and she put two and two together. There's no point in lying. Jonas has already issued a warrant for your bank accounts and we know regular payments were made to hers. I assumed it was her wages; it won't be hard to prove it wasn't.'

Lassi's face contorts into a snarl.

'There was nothing between me and that girl and you won't be able to prove anything,' he says.

He steps back inside and slams the door in her face. Agatha turns and walks slowly back towards her car.

Alone, she thinks about what just happened.

And she's also forced to revisit what he implied in their conversation and his reference to who he might have fathered in town.

She swallows back the bile in her throat.

He's hiding more. She's absolutely positive. Every time he tells her he knows nothing, it's like an alarm going off in Agatha's brain.

Agatha reaches her car and looks up at the house. Lassi's wife is in one of the upstairs windows, looking down at her, dolefully.

You've made your bed, Agatha thinks, cruelly.

She drives away from Lassi's house, through the electric gates that close like magic behind her. She phones Alex. It goes to voicemail and she leaves a message.

'Alex, I have something. Call me back.'

In one regard, Lassi might be right, Agatha thinks. Miika might have known who Kaya was having an affair with.

And Agatha needs him to tell her.

Her head is so full, she doesn't notice the car that pulls out behind her as she drives through town.

It follows her, all the way out the other side, as she heads towards the lake.

Alex wakes with a crick in his neck from sleeping awkwardly on the chair. The draught from the wide open cabin door is blowing bitterly cold air in his face.

Charlie's there, taking a large tray from Niamh, who can barely make eye contact with either of them.

'Would you like to, er, come in for breakfast?' Charlie asks.

Alex wants to die at how awkward the whole scenario is. He can't understand why Niamh didn't ask Beatrice or somebody else to drop the tray over. But having met Cecelia in the kitchen a few days earlier, he takes a leap and guesses the tray was in Niamh's hands and she was ushered on her way before she could protest. That, or Niamh is batshit crazy.

'No, thanks,' she says, blushing. 'I have to, em . . .'

She trails off.

'Right-o!' Charlie says. He tries to give her a tip but she won't take it.

When she's fled and Charlie's closed the door, Alex stares at his friend like he has ten heads.

'Are you some sort of fucking moron?' Alex asks. 'A tip?'

Charlie shrugs.

He places the tray on the table. It's filled with pastries and coffee and orange juice.

'It's not a full English but it'll see off the hangover,' Charlie says. 'Bugger me, I don't know how on earth you're going to drag yourself back to London. It's a bloody smorgasbord of women. The lads who work over here must have blue balls half the time. Thank fuck for the ice baths.'

'I don't have a hangover,' Alex says, calmly. He'd drunk a lot less last night than his friend, who has to be on a plane in a couple of hours.

'Quick bite, shower and then I'm out of your hair,' Charlie says. 'I flew into Ivalo, so it should only take me thirty minutes to get there. Unless you need me to stay?'

Alex shakes his head. He sits up straight and hears his phone fall to the ground. He must have slept with it in his hand most of the night.

'That wasn't on,' he says.

'What?'

'Niamh. Last night. The woman has been through a lot the last few days.'

'She came on to me, mate,' Charlie says. Then his face grows more serious. 'You're not very angry, are you, mate? I didn't force it, you know. I wouldn't do that.'

Alex says nothing. He looks at Charlie, sees the earnest expression on his friend's face.

'It's fine,' he says, his voice tight.

'Anyway, that's not important. Talk to me. Theories on Vicky. What do the police have?'

Alex sighs.

'They looked at an American tourist for a while. Interviewed everybody here. There are some dodgy characters about town. But, the answer is, they have nothing. I spoke to the Yank who Vicky was last seen with while you were snoring in my bed last night. He sent me over the last pictures taken of her.'

'The Bryce Adams guy?' Charlie says.

Alex nods.

'What's your plan then? Leave them to it? There's always the PI route, you know.'

'I'm not the police, Charlie,' Alex says. 'And the woman in charge, Agatha, she's actually decent. She knows what she's doing.'

'Got a whole murder squad, has she? A big case board? This doesn't look like the sort of place that has a CSI lab.'

Charlie says all this through a mouthful of Danish pastry.

'Yeah,' Alex says. 'I thought that at the start, too.'

He reaches down and fumbles for his phone on the rug, buried in the pile of blankets.

'People don't just get accidentally murdered,' Charlie says, with his usual tact. 'Did she piss off somebody here? Steal someone's fella? Knock a guy back?'

'Vicky wasn't the sort who'd *steal someone*,' Alex says, dismissively. 'I think it was something more serious than that. She left me a message. Of sorts. Something that I think has struck a chord with Agatha.'

He's found his phone and checks the screen. A missed call and voice message from Agatha. He'll call over to the station once he gets Charlie on his way.

'Well, your sister was the sort to get a few hearts racing, Alex,' Charlie continues. 'And these small towns. You know what they're like. Claustrophobia hits. Men get frustrated. Women get bitter. People cover up for each other. Scratch any small town, find a viper's nest. I'd best hop in that shower and get a wriggle on. The dance clubs of the frozen north wait for no man. Listen, before I do, I have to tell you that I haven't been entirely honest with you.'

'About what?'

'I didn't just come over to kit you out and do a bit of clubbing. One of the partners in TM&S is au fait with a couple of North American companies that want some lobbyists in situ here. You know this place is built on money, right? Mining.'

Alex looks at Charlie sharply.

Mining.

He's heard it referenced over and over. Tourism, or mining. The only things Koppe can offer. But it's only now he realises the link.

Vicky's email.

Precious metals.

Alex puts his head in his hands.

'I've been a fucking idiot,' he says.

'Mate,' Charlie says anxiously. 'I would have come anyway! It was just, I couldn't not take the chance to kill two birds with one stone.'

'Nothing to do with you,' Alex says.

He shakes his head.

What the *hell* had Vicky discovered?

'Who are you meeting?' he asks Charlie, looking up at his friend. 'Who does TM&S want to do business with? And is it mining here in Koppe? Or somewhere else?'

'The whole of Lapland, but pretty sure this little town gets a mention,' Charlie says. 'I'm meeting a Finnish lobbying group in Helsinki to see if we can get in on the action. Form some pan-international push, or some other such nonsense. You know TM&S will end up taking over, eventually.'

Alex is barely listening. He has to ring Agatha and tell her what he's realised, if she hasn't got there already. He opens his phone; the photo he was looking at last night is still there but is no longer zoomed in on Vicky's face. Now he can see the whole photograph: Bryce beside Vicky, the glass of wine Vicky is holding, the window behind them.

Alex squints at the photograph.

'Are you all right?' Charlie asks. 'You look like you've seen a ghost.'

Alex looks at Vicky's arm, extended in front of the window.

He has seen a ghost.

Of sorts.

A ghost that's just given him a message.

Koppe

1998

The one thing Kaya knows now is that she can depend on nobody but herself.

The second thing she knows is she needs money.

She thinks her plan will work. She's called her baby's father, told him exactly what she needs and why. It's a lie, of course, but he seems to have bought it.

She's sitting in her car outside the small garage on the outskirts of town when he arrives in his vehicle. He checks there's nobody around before getting out and jumping into her car.

He looks at the mark on her face, shakes his head. Then he takes an envelope from his pocket.

'It's the right thing to do,' he says, handing her the money. 'You've contacted the clinic?'

'Mm-hm,' Kaya says.

'Looks like he wasn't giving you any choice, anyway,' he says. 'Knowing Miika, he'd have beaten that thing out of you. It's not right, Kaya. You should leave him. When all this is done.'

She says nothing. Let him think she's gone for an abortion. Let him think she needs the money to stay down in Helsinki for a while. Let him think whatever the hell he wants. When she doesn't come back, he'll probably figure it out. He'll probably realise she's living somewhere with his child, but what will he be able to do about it? She'll be gone, out of his life. She has no intention of ever coming back.

'Kaya, listen . . .' he hesitates. 'I owe you an apology for what I said to you last time I saw you. I was . . . vicious. Lashing out. There are things—' He stops and looks out the window. 'There are things about my marriage you don't understand. I should never have started this thing with you. You and I know it was mutual but people, they might say I forced you. So, I wanted to scare you and I'm sorry. I can only imagine how frightened you've been. I'm a weak, terrible man.'

Kaya swallows. It's too late for his platitudes. She knows he's only saying this now because he thinks she's doing what he wants and he's feeling magnanimous. Maybe he thinks when the baby's gone, and after she's left Miika, he can pick up where he left off. He can have her again.

She should say thank you and goodbye and drive home. She plans to pack the rest of her things tonight and leave when Miika assumes she's going into work.

There's the sound of a van coming down the road and both she and her former lover sink low in their seats. The van slows, like it's about to pull into the garage, but then the driver has a change of mind and is off again.

Kaya should leave . . . but instead, she turns and faces this excuse for a man, who thinks he has her backed into a corner.

'Yes, I guess people would say things about you,' she says. 'Your reputation is so important, isn't it.'

'Kaya—'

'Of course, we know it was mutual. But yes, I can imagine some people might think you'd taken advantage. With you being such a powerful man and all. They might ask, when did you first look at me? Was it when I was still in my school uniform? When did you first kiss me? I could protest and say I was all grown up. A whole twenty-one years of age. That I wanted it. But would they believe me? Victims tend to say things like that, don't they?'

He grabs her throat and pushes her up against the window on her side.

'You wouldn't. You wouldn't say something like that. That's evil.'

She can feel his spittle on her face. His eyes are bulging in anger, the veins popping in his temple.

Kaya smiles, even though her throat hurts and she's finding it hard to breathe.

Let him kill her. Let him kill the woman who's carrying his baby, and the child, too.

Let him live with the guilt.

The thought crosses his mind, she can tell.

Just as she's gasping, he blinks, realises what he's doing and releases her.

He looks at her throat, then at his hand, as if seeing it for the first time.

The air in the car bristles between them.

'I'm sorry,' he says.

'You'd better go,' Kaya whispers, her voice hoarse. 'In case some-body sees you. Go home to your wife.'

He can't look at her.

He turns and gets out of the car.

Kaya grips the envelope of money. Then she smiles, places it in the glove compartment and drives home.

To hell with these men. They think they can use her. Well, now she's using them.

Koppe

2019

Once Alex has seen Charlie off, he heads to reception. Nicolas is there, filling in paperwork for a departing guest.

'Nicolas,' Alex says. 'The night Vicky went missing, did you see her in that bar when she was with the Americans? Or when she came back here?'

Nicolas frowns.

'No, Alex,' he says. 'I wasn't here that night, remember?'

Alex looks at Nicolas, quizzically.

'I was up at the hotel?' Nicolas says.

Alex nods.

'That's right, you said.'

'What do you need?'

'It doesn't matter,' Alex says, hurriedly. 'I just wanted to know if you remembered seeing her. Do you know where Harry is?'

'He's about to bring a group to the waterfall for ice-climbing,' Nicolas says. 'He'll be at the bus outside, getting them onboard. If you rush—'

Alex is already gone. He finds Harry out back, ticking off names on a sheet as tourists step onto the bus.

'Fancy some ice-climbing?' Harry asks him.

Alex shakes his head.

'Can I talk to you for a minute?'

Harry nods and hands the sheet to another guide. He follows Alex a few feet away from the bus. Alex has his hands in his pockets to keep them warm; his right fist is clasped around his phone. He's looked at the photo again and again and he knows what he saw and what it means.

'You said you were very fond of my sister,' Alex says.

Harry nods.

'How fond?'

'What?'

'Friendly-fond, or, in-love-with?'

Harry shuffles uncomfortably.

'Alex, I told you, I didn't have anything to do with Vicky—'

'Just fucking tell me,' Alex shouts.

Harry looks at him, startled, then over at the tourists to see if they heard. They're all on the bus, and the doors have been closed to keep the heat in. Nobody is paying the two men any heed.

Alex waits, glaring at Harry. He just wants people around here to start telling him the truth. Not their version of it. The actual truth.

'I was . . . I suppose I was a little in love with Vicky,' Harry says. 'But nothing ever came of it. I swear it.'

'Did you use Niamh, that night? To get at Vicky?'

'Of course not. Niamh wanted to sleep with me.'

'Did you make Vicky feel uncomfortable? Were you the reason she wanted to leave?'

'I didn't make her uncomfortable! I was in love with her . . . from afar. I know how that sounds. I would never have made advances towards her and I wouldn't have put her in a difficult position. She was . . . she was too good for me. She was too good for everybody at the Lodge.'

The engine on the bus roars to life and the other guide pokes his head out the door to call Harry's name.

Alex's jaw clenches.

'Sounds like you put her on a pedestal,' he says. 'And there she was, bringing guys back to her cabin . . .'

Harry's face darkens.

'Sure,' he says. 'Vicky made her point to me. Not explicitly but . . . she was with other guys. Enough for me to get it. If I'm guilty of anything it's . . . I guess, being jealous and doing stupid things because of it. Like screwing other women. But I didn't kill Vicky. I wouldn't have laid a finger on her.'

The other guide calls Harry again.

Alex takes a deep breath.

'Go, do your job,' he says.

Harry hesitates, but then he turns and walks back to the bus.

Alex takes his phone out then, checks the photo again and sees the lie.

He listens to Agatha's voice message before calling her, a frown on his face.

When he dials her number, it rings out.

Agatha pulls up at Miika's farm and immediately notices that his snowmobile is gone.

It's taken her a while to get here, coming by car. She'd swung by Becki's on the way, where she found the kids helping to make trays of cinnamon bakes. Well, Olavi and Onni were helping. Emilia was on the couch in the lounge, keeping an eye on the American teenager who was playing some horrific war game on the Xbox. Agatha knew what Emilia was doing, even though the teenager was at pains to act bored.

Agatha doesn't mind Emilia being interested in guys who aren't going to be hanging around. There will be a few more safe years, Agatha reckons, then she's going to have to watch Emilia like a fox. Whatever happens, Agatha will keep that girl safe from the types of guys Agatha knows are out there.

If she'd taken the snowmobile, she probably would have met Miika going into town.

Her phone rings – it's Alex again. She knocks it off. She just wants to have this one conversation with Miika, to ask about Kaya's lover again, and then she'll tell Alex what she suspects. That Vicky was blackmailing Lassi and that Lassi, who had most likely killed before, killed again.

It's almost three hours now since Agatha woke and she hasn't even had coffee. She gets out of the car, walks to Miika's front door and knocks. No answer. She tries the handle. It opens straight away.

She's not in the habit of letting herself into people's houses to make hot drinks but she doubts Miika will mind.

This is what Agatha tells herself as she rifles through the cabinet beside the kitchen table while the kettle builds up to a boil.

She picks up the picture of Kaya. Agatha has a vague memory of seeing her down in town the odd time. She'd always thought Kaya was so grown-up and glamorous, the way all young girls look at older girls, imagining their lives are so much freer and better.

Agatha puts the picture down. She opens a drawer.

She's not really looking for anything.

She can't help it. She's just . . . curious.

She pulls the top drawer open; there's nothing in it of any importance – a handful of old bills, scissors and measuring tape, some pins. The drawer underneath is the same. But when she tries to close it, it catches against something in the bottom drawer.

Agatha has to shake both drawers and eventually, with brute force, manages to push the middle drawer in by pulling the bottom one out.

Something catches her eye just as something else catches her ear. Agatha stands bolt upright, her pulse racing. The last thing she needs is Miika walking in here and seeing her rooting through his kitchen drawers.

She hears the crunch of footsteps on the snow outside and desperately tries to shove the bottom drawer closed but it's stuck again and Agatha starts to panic. Maybe if she just stands in front of it, it won't be noticeable? He'd have to look down to see it sticking out. She can talk a lot, keep him distracted.

Agatha is considering her options when the door opens and Luca walks in, dark hair loose on her large white puffer jacket, eyes glistening.

Agatha's jaw drops.

Frying pan, fire, is what she thinks.

'What are you doing here?' she gasps, fearfully.

'I've been following you,' Luca says, with a light laugh, as if it's obvious.

The blood drains from Agatha's face.

She went to Becki's before she came here.

She went to Becki's . . . she led Luca right to them.

Agatha has to get to the kids. She moves towards the door but Luca blocks her way.

'Oh, for God's sake, I followed you to Becki's,' Luca says. 'I saw the kids through the window. I didn't go near them. I left as soon as you did and followed you up here. Listen to me. I only want to talk to you. If I'd wanted to see the kids, I'd have waited until you left. If I'd wanted to see them, Agatha, I'd have seen them.'

Agatha doesn't know what to do. Should she rush her sister to get past her? Should she humour her?

Her instincts are telling her to go, and yet, if Luca was right behind her when Agatha arrived at Miika's cabin, then what she's saying must be true. Which is not what Agatha would have expected.

Still, just because she left the kids alone this time, doesn't mean she will the next time, especially now she knows where they are.

Luca laughs again.

'Your face,' she says.

'Stop!' Agatha shouts. 'Just fucking stop. Tell me what you want. I'm not doing this again, Luca. Tell me why you're here and then I want you to go away and never, ever come here again.'

'Or what?'

Agatha's heart stops.

That was always something Luca used to say. *Or what*. She always wanted to know how far you'd go. How far you could be pushed. Luca treated everybody around her as though they were all unwitting subjects in some anthropological experiment she was running.

Agatha studies her sister, trying to predict how this is going to go, but as she does, Luca's face changes.

The fire in it dies and Luca just looks tired.

'Oh, for fuck's sake,' she says. 'Look, I know you're not going to believe me but I'm going to tell you anyway. I'm not nuts any more. Like, I never was, but, yeah, I know. I did some nutty shit.'

To hell with this, Agatha thinks.

She runs at Luca, tries to push past, but Luca is stronger than she looks. She's able to withstand Agatha's tackle.

'Listen to me!' she shouts. 'I'm on medication, Agatha. Proper shit. The doctors, they reckon I have bipolar disorder. They're right, Agatha.'

Agatha steps back and stares at Luca.

Luca had never conceded there was anything wrong with her. Any time she'd agreed to talk to anybody or accept medication, it had always been under protest.

'Are you kidding me?' Agatha says. 'You've come here to tell me this now? After all this time? I know you're bipolar, Luca. I've known it all our goddamn lives. I just didn't know what it was called.'

Luca holds out her hands and laughs. But then her expression grows serious.

'I haven't had a drop of alcohol or touched a non-medicinal drug in two years. You can't, with the shit I'm on. And I've stuck to it. Have to, with the courts and stuff. But, I . . . Agatha, I've no interest in disrupting the kids' lives. I know they're safer with you.'

'So, why are you here?'

'Your message! It made me panic. You sounded upset. And then when I rang back, Emilia was in the police station. I didn't know why she was there – I thought something had happened. I don't have your mobile number, I can't email you, so I had to come up and see you were okay.'

Luca says all this, barely stopping for breath.

It almost sounds convincing, too.

'Olavi saw you last week and don't you dare tell me he didn't,' Agatha says. 'He saw you outside his school.'

'Oh my fucking Christ!' Luca exclaims. 'I would never call him a liar, Agatha, but I was nowhere near his school! How could I have been? I haven't been in Koppe in years. What was I wearing? Did he say I spoke to him?'

Agatha tries to process all this.

Why didn't Luca talk to Olavi? She never had that sort of self-control before. She never just watched the kids . . . she always approached them. Grabbed them in overly tight hugs. Showered them with unwanted affection, like everything was normal and she wasn't someone whose mood could flip in a blink of an eye, like she wasn't the woman that filled their nightmares.

Luca starts to laugh again and the sound of it is jarring.

'My God,' Luca says. 'Isn't it obvious? He saw *you,* Agatha. We're fucking twins!'

Agatha blinks.

No, surely not. Could she have been so stupid? She casts her mind back.

Agatha had passed the school that day. She hadn't called over to say hello; she'd been too busy.

Olavi would have expected Agatha to say hello. If he'd seen her, and she'd been staring over but not waving or calling out . . . is it possible, for a moment, he thought it was his mother?

Had Agatha caused Luca to come here because of a child's mistake?

While all this is going through Agatha's head, Luca continues talking.

'I know what I did to those kids, Agatha. I know I messed up. They're better off with you—'

Luca stops. Agatha looks at her. Really looks at her. She hears it now. Her sister's voice sounds different.

It sounds . . . honest.

'I know how frightened they are of me,' Luca says, quieter, her head hanging. 'I remember their . . . I remember them crying in the car that time. You know I never meant to hurt them like that, Ags. Not physically. I made a promise. I've kept it. I'm only human, but the one fucking good thing I've done is give those kids a chance with you and I deserve some credit for it.'

Tears spring from Luca's eyes. Even though Agatha can see they're half for the kids, half for Luca herself, she's still surprised to realise that they are, in fact, genuine.

Agatha wants to reach out to her; it's completely natural. At the same time, she knows she won't. That bond was torn. It can never be fixed. She can never care for Luca as a sister again; not now Agatha has to put the children first.

Agatha moves towards the far side of the room. Her shin hits the open drawer. She looks down and her eyes land on something.

She stares at it in the silence.

Now she knows what she's looking at, what it is that caught her attention.

Agatha bends down and takes out the small book.

She runs her fingers across the leather binding.

'Agatha, what the fuck are you doing up here, anyway? Didn't we use to dare each other to come here as kids? Doesn't Miika the wife-killer still live here?'

Agatha doesn't respond. She opens the book and flicks through drawing after drawing.

'She took it with her,' Agatha says. 'It's in the file. She always had it with her.'

The house had been searched after Kaya disappeared. She knows it was searched. She remembers everybody in town talking about it; she's seen it in the case records.

As Agatha's fingers flick through the pages, one drawing catches her eye and she turns back.

It's a sketch of a man, lying on his side. A man in bed. Naked.

Agatha's hand flies to her mouth.

'Agatha? What is it?'

'We're not safe here,' Agatha says.

'What? Agatha, what's going on?'

Agatha is about to answer when she hears something outside. A snowmobile.

Her car is out front and she presumes Luca parked beside it. If she walks out now, she'll have to act completely naturally. Can she do that? Can Luca?

He's far cleverer than she gave him credit for. He's clearly able to read people. And manipulate them.

Agatha can't risk it. She can't convincingly pretend she hasn't found that book of drawings.

Perhaps they could slip out the back and when he comes into the house, they could race around the front, get into Agatha's car and take off.

She looks straight at Luca.

'You know the way you're allegedly not nuts any more?'

Luca frowns.

'I need you to do something fucking nuts.'

Koppe

1998

Kaya expects Miika to be out with the reindeer when she returns from exercising the dogs that morning, and he is. Feeding his beloved beasts, spreading lichen around the enclosure, checking their fur. She'll miss those animals when she's gone. But they don't mean anything to her any more. Let them keep Miika company. Her stupid husband and his stupid deer. He'll probably kill the dogs. He won't bother with them, if Kaya isn't there to feed and run them.

She waves at Miika, but he ignores her. She isn't surprised.

She just needs to act natural for the next couple of hours. She only wants a few things from the house. Some clothes to keep her going, her sketchbook. Everything else she can leave. When she 'goes' to work tonight, she'll seize her chance.

She has enough money to last a couple of months in Helsinki. She can get a job as soon as she arrives and work until the baby is born. Then, when the time comes, she will have plenty of savings, along with the help she'll get from the state, to manage on her own for a while. As soon as she's able, she'll find childcare and return to work, then it's just a matter of building a life. Other women do it, all the time. Kaya has already shown that she can survive the worst situations. This one, without any men, will be a piece of cake.

Maybe, eventually, she'll even move beyond Finland. She's always wondered what it would be like to live near the Mediterranean.

Kaya smiles and lets herself into the house.

She busies herself making some food in the kitchen. Miika's favourite dinner. She doesn't want to give him any inkling she's leaving him this very day.

She hopes he chokes on the dinner.

How quickly she went from being happy and thinking they might have a future together to not caring if he lives or dies. When he slapped her, he slapped the hope out of her. She knew how things would be. Even after he apologised, she knew the bigger she got, the worse it would get. His love for her is conditional. It doesn't extend to raising another man's child. He'd force her to choose, or do the choosing for her. And now Kaya is done with men making choices on her behalf.

To hell with Miika.

She slips upstairs every few minutes to put an item in the bag she has stashed under the bed.

A couple of hours before she should be leaving for work, she rings her parents' home. There's no answer.

Kaya starts to feel upset.

She just wants to hear her mother's voice. It's going to be a few days before she calls again and she fears that when she goes, people might worry she's had an accident.

She doesn't like the idea of her mother and father worrying about her and it will take Kaya time to find the courage to ring them from Helsinki and tell them why she's there.

Miika comes in and sees her on the phone when she's dialling a second time.

'Just ringing Mom,' Kaya says.

He grunts and goes to the kitchen.

The phone rings out again and Kaya replaces the receiver, a lump in her throat.

Maybe she'll try to phone them from a garage when she's on the road. If not, she'll just have to suck it up for a day or two. Perhaps her mother will guess what's happened. Perhaps she's been waiting for Kaya to run.

She slips upstairs, goes into the bathroom and flushes the toilet, then goes back into the bedroom and opens her wardrobe.

Her outfit for work is already laid out on the bed. Kaya only wants her drawing book now. She's stashed it in the back of the wardrobe, behind her shoes. Miika has never been interested in looking in the book but, still, it's become like a diary to her and she didn't want to take the chance of him picking it up absent-mindedly. These days, she either has it with her or it's well hidden.

Kaya reaches for the book but all her fingers find is empty space.

'I saw you, you know.'

She hadn't heard him come up.

Kaya's head whips around. She gets off her knees and faces her husband.

He's holding her book in his hand.

'When I passed the garage earlier. I saw his car and yours parked outside; the two of you trying to hide in the front seats like teenagers. Is that where you fucked him? In your car? He wouldn't even shell out for one of those hotel rooms they keep building, no?'

'Miika—'

'I suppose he couldn't have you in his house. With his wife there. Unless you waited for her to be out visiting her sick mother. Cancer, isn't it? Did you have sex in their bed while his wife was visiting her dying mother, Kaya?'

He flicks open the drawing book while Kaya stands there, trembling, shame running through her.

To have it thrown at her like that, like she's some thoughtless . . . slut.

Kaya is mortified. She suddenly feels very, very small.

He's in the doorway. If she runs for it, he'll block her way.

'Did you fuck him in my bed, Kaya? These could be our sheets.'

Miika turns the book around to show her the page on which Kaya had drawn her lover.

'Did you really think I'd rear his child with you? Or that I'd let you run off and make a fool of me? Where do you think you're going, anyway, with your bag? And the car that I paid for? Whore! You filthy, lying whore!'

Kaya's cheeks are on fire. Something rushes through her; the strength of the emotion takes away all the embarrassment and apology and humility.

She suddenly stares at Miika and sees him for what he is.

'How fucking dare you?' she says. 'You, of all people. You brought me up here. You think I wanted this life? To be a little wife to a fucking reindeer farmer in the middle of nowhere? To make you dinners and clean your house and lie on my back while you grunted over me for two fucking minutes once a week, with the smell of alcohol on your breath? To be your punching bag because your life hasn't worked out how you wanted it? What the hell else were you ever going to do, Miika? You were always going to end up here. Taking over your father's farm, drinking and beating up some woman. I wasn't. I settled for you. That's all it was. Taking what I thought was the best of a bad bunch. You were a disappointment. I was going to do something better. And I still am. Now, get the fuck out of my way.'

Miika is staring at her, completely stunned at her outburst. Kaya is practically standing on her tippy toes, she's so full of rage. If he tries to hit her now, she'll hit him back. And she won't just hit him. She'll kill him. She won't stop until he's dead.

But to Kaya's absolute surprise, Miika doesn't hit her.

He gets out of her way.

Koppe

2019

The police station is empty. Alex shakes the locked door, upon which a notice has been pinned. *Back in thirty minutes.*

He's leaving the porch when he sees Patric.

Patric frowns at Alex's obvious frustration.

'There's an ice hockey match on the lake,' Patric says. 'Jonas and Janic are down there.'

'I can't get hold of Agatha,' Alex says. 'I need her. Urgently.'

'Have you tried her mobile?'

'Of course I've tried her bloody mobile,' Alex says. 'I've been trying it and trying it. She must have it on silent or something.'

Now, Patric looks very concerned.

He's about to say something, when a car pulls up beside them. It's Lassi.

He rolls down the window and stares out at Patric and Alex.

'You need to rein in that goddamn trainee of yours,' Lassi says.

'Excuse me?' Patric replies.

'You heard me. What I do with my business is *my* business, you hear me? She's been down at the council offices, breaking into my office, snooping about.'

'What have you been up to in the council?' Patric asks.

'That's not the—' Lassi stops abruptly. 'Tell her to stay the hell out of my way. I've done nothing illegal.'

Lassi glares at Alex.

'And I'd nothing to do with your bitch of a sister's death, either.'

Lassi speeds off before Alex can lean in and grab him through the open window.

Patric stops Alex from running after the car.

'Leave him,' he says. 'Agatha has obviously unearthed something and he's pissed about it. She'll deal with him.'

'But where is she?' Alex asks. 'And why do you look so worried?'

Patric has started walking but he turns and answers Alex.

'Her sister turned up last night,' he says.

'Luca?' Alex asks. He knows what this means and he's instantly worried for Agatha, too.

'Yes, Luca.'

Patric pulls out his phone, takes off his mitten with his teeth and dials a number.

He speaks in Finnish but Alex can hear him addressing somebody called Becki.

When Patric hangs up, his face is pale.

'Are the kids okay?' Alex asks.

'The kids are fine,' Patric says, but he still looks distressed.

'Where is she?' Alex says.

'She's gone up to Miika's. On her own.'

Patric resumes walking in the direction of his car, parked across the street.

Alex doesn't even ask – he falls into step beside him.

★

Agatha and Luca make their way out the back of Miika's house and move fast around the edge of it.

Agatha hasn't told Luca what's happening but her sister seems to sense the danger they're both in; she's following Agatha's every move, as wordlessly and silently as possible.

They stand at the side of the house, breathing in the cold air, flakes from the light snowfall landing on their faces.

Agatha hears the screen door on the porch close and it's then that she and Luca rush around the front of the house towards her car. They both jump in: Agatha reaches for the ignition.

And finds there is no key.

'He's taken the key,' she whispers, far calmer than she feels.

In her head, she's screaming.

Why the hell would he take the key?

Because he doesn't plan to let us leave, Agatha.

'My car,' Luca hisses. 'I have my keys.'

As evidence, she produces them from the pocket of her puffer jacket.

The two women jump out of Agatha's car and into Luca's.

Agatha has a passing thought – this heap of junk? – but dismisses it.

Until Luca turns the key and the car won't start.

'Jesus Christ, how did you even follow me up here?' Agatha asks.

'It just takes a few goes . . .'

Luca is about to turn the key again when Agatha grabs her wrist.

'No,' Agatha says. 'If you keep trying to start it, he'll hear, and if we can't get it going . . .'

'What do you want to do? We could surprise him, knock him out. I'll be a distraction – you could creep up, pull your gun. You have a gun, don't you . . . ?'

Agatha tunes her sister out; she thinks fast.

She has the drawing book in her pocket. How long before he realises it's gone? Not long after he can't find them in the house, she imagines. That's why he let her search the house alone that time. Because he knew it was in the drawer beside him, while he sat at the table. That book means everything and he'll know that Agatha will understand that.

'We hide,' Agatha says.

They get out of the car.

With one quick look at the house, Agatha grabs Luca's hand and they run towards the sheds.

'The forest,' Luca urges.

Agatha doesn't answer, she just keeps pulling her sister. She doesn't want to be in a gun battle where she can't sight her opponent. She also knows that she only has her service revolver and no idea what sort of weapons he owns.

She needs to be able to see him. If they're behind cover in a shed, she can keep an eye on him when he enters and, before he can spot her, she can train her weapon on him. Plus, in the shed, she can phone for help. She can feel her phone buzzing on silent in her pocket; her battery and reception are fine. She can call for back-up.

They just need to wait it out until she can either contain him or get help to track him if he runs.

The women enter the nearest shed. It's filled with equipment hanging from the ceiling. Some of the more modern culling machinery; several ancient, rusted scythes and axes.

'Fuck me,' Luca says, staring around, eyes wide.

Agatha silently agrees.

They've inadvertently chosen the slaughter shed.

'Over here,' Agatha says, pointing to a corner filled with shadows.

It will give her a good vantage point for the door and she knows there's no other way into this shed.

The metallic smell of blood is strong in her nostrils as they take up position.

Luca knocks over an old pair of snowshoes; the large tennis racket-type soles clatter on to the ground. Both women wince, but Agatha knows the sound is louder for them; that nobody outside would have heard it like that.

'Agatha,' Luca says.

'Shh,' Agatha hisses.

'No, I have to—'

'Luca, can you shut the fuck up and just let me do my job? You shouldn't even be here.'

'But I am and I want you to say that you believe me. I didn't come to see Olavi. I haven't been in Koppe. I've missed you, you know. We're still sisters. My therapist says I can't keep carrying guilt for the things I did but I do have to accept that I did them. I am sorry I hurt you—'

'Christ, I believe you!' Agatha snaps. 'Now, be quiet.'

Luca looks like she's about to resume her pleading, but one look from Agatha and she nods obediently. And suddenly Agatha does believe her sister, even that she's on medication, because the old Luca wouldn't have followed Agatha into the shed. She'd have waited for Miika to come out of the house and charged at him. Old Luca would have run at Miika to see what he would do.

Agatha returns her gaze to the door. She takes out her phone, cutting off a call from Alex in the process. Why does he keep calling her? And now Patric. Agatha cuts him off, too.

She dials Janic: it rings out. She tries Jonas next. The same thing.

'Fuck,' Agatha whispers, quickly typing a text to her deputy.

She draws her gun. They can't stay hiding in here. What if he doesn't come in?

She's quietly panicking, trying to figure out what to do next, when the shed door opens.

Agatha turns off her phone so he won't hear the buzzing of anybody returning her call.

A man's frame blocks out the light, but from his silhouette Agatha can see he's carrying a rifle.

Koppe

1998

Kaya is lying curled up on her side.

She doesn't think Miika meant it to go this far.

When he stepped out of her way in the bedroom, Kaya had been momentarily relieved. Invigorated, even.

But something about her stepping over the threshold of that door must have made him snap.

First, he grabbed her hair.

Kaya had tried to fight him, but he was far too strong, and all of the anger and resistance she felt started to ebb as her usual survival instinct kicked in. Hunker down, foetal ball, protect herself and the baby.

The slaps and punches in the bedroom; they were classic Miika. He wanted to pummel her, to take out all his rage on her face but, actually, he didn't hit her stomach, he refrained from doing that.

She thinks he might have left it there; with a bad beating. Then, maybe he would have kicked her out, or forced her to have an abortion, something like that.

But she didn't just take it. She'd had enough. When it looked like he was done, Kaya pushed herself up off the floor again and slapped him. Then she ran past him, trying to get to the stairs, putting every last ounce of energy she had into making it out of that house and to her car.

He caught her again before she reached the first step. They tussled on the landing; he roared something at her, she didn't even hear what it was he said.

Next thing, she was falling.

When she hit the bottom step, the damage was done. The pain in her stomach was so bad, she immediately knew what the wetness spreading between her legs was caused by.

That was only eclipsed by the pain in her head.

He's standing over her, looking down.

Call somebody, Kaya wants to say.

If he calls an ambulance, she might be saved.

He can't just leave her here.

She can't speak. Her mouth opens and she feels like she's gargling water. No, something thicker than water. It's her own blood.

'M—' She chokes.

Her eyelids feel heavy. She's tired. The agony is so bad, her body wants to shut down. To sleep off this beating, like all the others.

Her husband is still looking at her, his face a mixture of shock and resolution.

She's seen him look like that before.

At the animals, when they're dying.

Kaya's going to die. She'll die in this house she so badly wanted to get away from.

And Miika just stands and watches.

Koppe

2019

Agatha and Luca stay perfectly still while Miika stands in the door frame. He seems calm, in control, which leaves Agatha more terrified than she's ever felt. He knows she has that drawing book. He knows she's figured out that if Kaya didn't take the book like he said, then there's only one reason he would have lied.

In the dark, she feels Luca's fingers brush hers and then take her left hand in a grip.

The last fifteen years of pain and strife between the sisters is momentarily suspended. Agatha is grateful for Luca's hand.

Agatha is about to announce herself, to tell Miika she has her gun trained on him and he needs to drop the rifle, but something stops her. She can't be sure that, as soon as he hears her voice, Miika won't know where it's coming from and take aim.

She doesn't know how quick he is. She also doesn't know if she has it in her to put him down first. Agatha has never shot anybody.

She knows this man murdered his wife and that he's capable of murdering her.

Agatha can't die. The kids need her.

Because if Luca is getting help and Agatha dies, she fears the kids could end up back with Luca. And Luca never stays in control for long. That's just the sad, tragic truth.

These are the thoughts rushing through Agatha's mind as she weighs the risks of revealing herself to Miika.

She has to do something, but before she can decide, Miika leaves the shed.

Agatha and Luca look at each other in the semi-darkness, their eyes adjusting once more.

Do they stay where they are?

Do they make a run for it?

Agatha listens hard.

A few minutes pass.

Then she hears the snowmobile start up outside.

He's leaving.

Oh, thank God.

Miika's trying to escape. Or, he thinks they've fled into the forest.

Agatha waits until she can no longer hear the buzz of the snowmobile.

Then, still holding hands, the sisters make their way to the door.

Luca lets out a little gasp at something and slips. Agatha tightens her grip before Luca can crash to the floor. When she's steady, both women look down at the thick, viscous liquid that almost brought Luca down. It's just a dark patch, but Agatha knows it's blood.

She follows Luca's gaze and her chest tightens.

Something is staring at them from one of the butchering tables; glassy, wide-open eyes.

Agatha's heart stops for a moment, until she realises it's the head of a reindeer.

At the shed door, Agatha peeps out. The snowmobile is gone. Luca's and Agatha's cars are where they left them. They can try Luca's car until they get it started.

They step outside on to the snow and start to run to the car.

Halfway, it catches Agatha's eye.

There, in the trees, is Miika's snowmobile.

Abandoned.

She can feel him before she sees him.

Agatha turns around.

Miika is standing behind them, his rifle trained on Agatha. He's stepped out from behind the shed.

She still has her gun in her hand.

She raises it.

Patric is driving too fast. The road is empty and there's plenty of daylight but they're still at risk of crashing. Imagine if that's what took him out, Alex muses. After all this. Before he's even had a chance to tell anybody what he's figured out.

'Slow down,' Alex says.

'Agatha's in danger,' Patric says.

'What do you mean?' Alex says. 'She has nothing to fear from Miika, surely?'

'I don't . . .' Patric hesitates, then shakes his head. 'Luca is on her tail. She turned up last night and she's nowhere in town. Somebody saw her car this morning, heading out of town.'

'Luca? Would she hurt her? I know what she did to the kids, but it was an accident, wasn't it?'

'Accident,' Patrick scoffs. 'Did she tell you about the time Luca stole the snowmobile and brought it out on to the lake?'

Alex nods as they go into a particularly hairy turn. His heart is in his mouth.

'Agatha followed her out on the lake and tried to stop her,' Patric says. 'Luca took it all as a big joke, figured they could race like they used to when they were little girls. When Agatha wouldn't play ball, Luca drove her snowmobile into Agatha's. You've seen the power in those things. A crash like that, they were lucky the machines didn't explode. If Agatha hadn't been thrown clear, the thing could have sliced her leg off. As it was, she just had concussion. And Luca didn't even show remorse. There's something wrong with that girl. Always has been. It just wasn't noticed because the parents were useless, and then when they died, everybody let her get away with stuff because she was a poor little orphan.'

'People can change,' Alex says.

'Not Luca. She always has to push it. She swore she'd stay away and here she is, back again. She thinks she's Teflon, that girl. I'll kill her before I let her harm Agatha and those kids.'

Alex falls silent. He feels sick, from the insane driving and the story.

'Why do you need her, anyway?' Patric asks.

Patric looks across to him and at that moment, the car swerves violently.

'Christ,' Alex cries and tries to press the imaginary brake pedal on his side of the car, but Patric manages to straighten the vehicle; he works the gearstick and takes his foot off the accelerator rather than using the brakes.

When they're on a steady course again, Alex answers Patric's question.

'I think I know who killed my sister,' he says.

★

'I don't want to shoot you, Miika,' Agatha says.

Luca's hand is holding hers so tight, it's going to leave bruises. Agatha remembers that feeling. When their father died and their mother was wailing at the funeral, Luca had gripped Agatha's hand. Sympathy, support, mortification at their mother's antics. When she was in labour with Emilia, the same grip. When Luca had signed the adoption papers to hand over the children, she'd grabbed Agatha's hand, but that time, Agatha had shaken it off.

This time, Agatha squeezes back, then releases. She needs both hands for what's about to happen.

She eases off the safety catch on the gun she still has aimed at Miika's head. She's ready.

'You went in my house,' he says. 'You took something that belongs to me. You got a warrant for going in there?'

'No,' Agatha says. 'I don't. Which means anything I took can't be used as evidence. So, all you need is a good lawyer.'

Miika studies her. He knows the game is up, he's not even considering trying to lie.

'It's been weighing on my mind all these years,' he says. 'I kept thinking, people will find out. Then, nobody did. I never meant to kill her, you know. I could have. When I found out what she'd done. And I certainly gave her a beating. But, in the end, she just tripped down the damn stairs. It wasn't even intentional. She was gone, just like that. I might have given her a chance, given us a chance, if she'd chosen me. But I saw her with him. She was taking me for a fool. Planning her getaway with him, the two of them in her car, going over all their little deceptions. When I saw that, I just wanted to hurt her. But I didn't murder her. Not intentionally, anyway.'

Agatha doesn't know if he's telling the truth. She doesn't care. Kaya died. Instead of reporting her death, he reported her missing. Hid her body. And let her parents suffer that, for all these years.

'I know what you're thinking,' he says. 'I should have reported it, told you lot it was an accident. But I'd hit her, you see? So nobody would believe it.'

Agatha opens her mouth but Luca gets there before her.

'I understand,' she says. 'Nobody ever believes me when I say I didn't do something. Because, usually, I've done a whole lot of shit before that.'

Miika stares at Luca.

'Sometimes I think, fuck it,' she continues. 'If they think the worst, I'll do the worst. They already think I'm worth nothing, anyway.'

Agatha wishes Luca would shut up. And at the same time, she can see that her sister's words are resonating with Miika.

'We used to tell ghost stories about you, as kids,' Luca says. 'Miika, the wife-killer. And we all reckoned you were a serial killer. I was kinda glad the town had this villain. Took the heat off the shit I was doing.'

Luca snorts. Agatha winces. As usual, her sister has gone too far. Miika's face fills with anger.

'I didn't touch those other women,' he says. 'That bit, that's what nearly made me talk. But then I thought, if I admit now that Kaya is dead, who'll believe me when I say I'm not responsible for the others?'

'Nobody is saying you are,' Agatha says, her tone measured. She glares at Luca, hoping she realises how badly Agatha needs her to stop talking. Luca shrugs. It's her *I'm only trying to help* look.

'But you withheld evidence,' Agatha continues, directing her attention back to Miika. 'So there will be a charge of some sort. If you cooperate, it will be taken into account. Where is Kaya's body?'

Miika says nothing.

'I'm asking because, if there's a body, a post-mortem will help to confirm how she died,' Agatha says. 'Even now, after all this time.'

Miika's eyes dart to the side, down the mountain. The lake, Agatha thinks. Her heart sinks. They'll never recover Kaya's body. Vicky Evans was an anomaly. They dived whole sections of the lake at the time of Kaya's disappearance. And Mary's. It's far too large a volume of water to dredge or ever fully cover. The lake only gives up what it wants, when it wants.

'Yep,' Miika says. 'No body. I'll never be able to prove the truth.'

Agatha is about to say something when she hears the sound of an approaching car engine.

'You called for back-up,' Miika says, angrily. 'You think you need a gang of you to bring me in?'

'She didn't!' Luca says. 'She's on your side.'

'Nobody's on my side.'

'Miika,' Agatha says. 'You have a weapon pointed at me. It doesn't look good. You need to put that down.'

'I only brought this because I didn't know what you'd do,' he says.

'Miika, we can sort this . . .' Agatha trails off. The car has come into view. She quickly looks away from Miika to see whose vehicle it is. It's Patric's.

She turns back to Miika. His face is twisted with fury.

The car rolls to a stop and now Agatha sees that Patric and Alex are in the front seats, their mouths hanging open at the scene they've stumbled across.

She's about to shout at them to stay in the car when she sees that Miika is no longer pointing his rifle at her. He's aiming now at the car windscreen.

Without even thinking, Agatha cries out.

Miika turns, momentarily distracted.

So his rifle is pointed at her when it goes off.

In that instant, Agatha hears Luca's howl of outrage.

There's a split second, between Agatha hearing the rifle's shot and Luca's scream, when she knows she's going to die.

Even in that moment, the mother in her worries for the kids, but the police chief in her knows at least Alex Evans' parents won't have to endure a second death. Patric will have his revolver. He'll shoot Miika before Miika has time to fire again.

Agatha doesn't die.

Luca, her twin, the sister who shared a womb with her, pushes Agatha out of the way as the bullet is fired. Luca, who always thought she could do anything and get away with it.

The bullet hits Luca in the back and she falls to the ground.

Agatha is dimly aware, as she drops to her knees beside her sister, of Miika letting the weapon fall from his hands in shock, of a car door opening, of another gun being fired.

When she looks up, Miika too is lying on the snow, blood seeping from his body.

Patric is holding his gun aloft; his hands are shaking. He takes off his hat, wipes the sweat from his forehead with it.

Alex, stunned, looks from Agatha to Luca, to Miika and back to Agatha.

He rushes over as Agatha holds her dying sister in her arms.

Agatha pulls down the zip on Luca's jacket. The bullet hit Luca in the centre of her back and passed through. She and Alex both place their hands on Luca's chest as the blood pulses out. It's not enough. Luca's eyes are already closed. There's too much blood. It spills over Agatha's and Alex's hands like water, making their fingers slide and intertwine as they try in vain to keep Luca's life inside her.

She's gone, even if her body doesn't quite know it yet.

Patric runs across to Miika. Agatha can see Miika is trying to say something.

Patric still has the gun and is standing a foot away. Now, it's aimed at Miika's head.

Agatha, her heart wrenching and in shock, still knows what she has to do.

Her sister is gone.

Now, she has work to do.

'Hold her,' she implores of Alex — her voice sounds like it's coming from somebody else.

'You stay with her, I'll . . .' Alex says, helplessly.

'Please, just hold her,' Agatha repeats.

Alex takes Luca's head in his arms and cradles her as Agatha stands. The front of her coat is covered in Luca's blood. Her hands are slippy on her weapon. But still she walks towards Patric.

'Put your gun down,' she says.

Patric doesn't even look at her.

'I've got this, Agatha. Take care of your sister.'

'Luca is dead,' Agatha says, her voice cold. 'Put the gun down.'

Miika is trying to draw breath. She looks at him quickly; she can see he's dying. The rifle is far from his hand, he's no threat.

He's mouthing something to Agatha.

She thinks it's *sorry*.

He didn't mean to kill Luca.

He closes his eyes. He's gone, Agatha realises. The man who could answer everybody's questions is gone.

Patric looks at Agatha.

'It's okay—' he starts to say, then he realises her gun is pointed at him.

'I know,' Agatha says. 'I know, Patric. I saw Kaya's drawings. She drew her lover.'

Patric's features go blank, then they rearrange in fear, in pain.

'It was you,' Agatha says. 'You were having the affair with Kaya. Miika knew. He saw the drawing of you and he killed her. You *must* have known he'd done it. You had to have known.'

Patric lowers his gun.

'I didn't,' he says. 'She was meant to leave. I thought she'd left.'

Agatha wants to grab at the life raft. She wants to believe that of all the things Patric did wrong, covering up for murder wasn't one of them. But she can tell, just looking at him, that he's lying.

That, in his heart, he knew what had happened. And he knows she knows.

'It was a stupid mistake,' he says, quietly. 'I know how weak that sounds. Kaya knew I wouldn't leave my wife. I couldn't, Agatha. My life would have been ruined. Kaya was so much younger. People would have said things. I begged her, I pleaded with her to see it from my side. I offered to give her as much help as I could. She was determined to do it her way. I wouldn't have just lost my wife; I'd have lost my job. I'd have lost my reputation, everything. And when she was gone, even when I thought something might have happened to her, I didn't know what good it would do for it all to come out. I couldn't help her, then. She wasn't here any more.'

'He blackmailed you,' Agatha says, the realisation sinking in. 'When he told you he knew you were sleeping with Kaya, you would have known then that he killed her. He gave you a choice. Tell, and he'd reveal everything about you. Or help him keep it quiet and both your secrets would be safe.'

Patric hangs his head.

Agatha brushes away the tears that are falling freely from her eyes.

'I always thought I could tell when people were lying. You taught me how, Patric. You said, they change their story, Agatha. Listen to the details. But you kept to your story, didn't you? You pretended you had nothing to do with Kaya. All these years . . .'

'I can't bear for you to know this,' Patric says, his voice desperate. 'You've been like a daughter to me, Agatha. I never wanted to disappoint you.'

'But you have!' Agatha cries. 'She was only twenty-two, Patric. How could you? How could you leave her family in the dark for all these years? You were the chief of police. You took an oath.'

Patric hangs his head.

'I have never forgiven myself,' he says. 'I made a terrible, terrible mistake. My wife . . . she couldn't conceive. Her mother was dying. It was a horrible time. She wouldn't let me touch her. I wasn't the first man to have an affair with a pretty young woman. But how much was I supposed to sacrifice? I know now what a selfish bastard I was. I didn't at the time. I wasn't much older than you are now. As the years went on, though, I realised, but I had to let it go. I couldn't give Kaya justice.'

'But you kept quiet, even when those other women disappeared. You never thought he might be responsible for them? Even if he wasn't, the whole town thought he was. People might have ignored Mary's real killer, because they assumed it was Miika. Vicky's, even. Alex and I have been on a wild goose chase thinking it was Miika and if it was, we'll never know now!'

'I knew he wasn't responsible for them,' Patric groans. 'For God's sake, Agatha, he killed his wife for having an affair. He wasn't some predator hunting women across the country. And you found Hilda, didn't you? She's safe.'

'Stop!' Agatha sobs. 'Don't even try to defend yourself. You were wrong. How could you do this to those women?' Then, softer: 'How could you do it to me? I . . . I loved you like a father.'

Patric nods. Agatha can see the defeat in his eyes.

'You were always going to be a much better cop than me,' he says. 'Didn't I tell you? You were my second chance. Please, remember the good things I did, too. Remember I loved you, and those kids. I'd have done anything for you.'

He smiles at her. That old, familiar Patric smile.

Agatha's face fills with confusion.

Then Patric puts his gun in his mouth and fires.

Agatha falls to her knees in shock.

Within seconds, Alex has his arms around her.

They sit there, three bodies on the ground around them, the white snow dyed red as far as their eyes can see.

Alex and Agatha are sitting in the back of one of the police cars.

Agatha is staring straight ahead. Alex is still holding her hand but he's not sure she can even feel it. She looks like she's in some sort of awake-coma, so Alex is shocked when she turns to him and speaks.

'Why did you come looking for me?' she says, like it's just dawned on her.

Alex swallows. Is now the best time for this?

He shakes his head.

'Nothing,' he says.

'It couldn't have been nothing. You tracked me up here.'

Agatha is still covered in her sister's blood. Patric's, too. She'd tried, pointlessly, to resuscitate him. Whether to save him or kill him again, Alex isn't sure.

Alex is covered in their blood, too.

He wants to tell her why he was looking for her. But he can't see beyond that blood.

Then, another inner voice.

He came to Lapland to find out who killed his sister, not to help solve who killed some woman twenty years ago.

'Just take a few minutes,' he says. 'We can talk when we're back down in the station.'

He doesn't even know if Agatha will still be in charge of Vicky's investigation. Maybe the quiet one, Jonas, will take over.

Alex swallows. *I'm sorry, Vicky,* he says in his head. *I'm sorry. Just give me a few more hours. One more day.*

This is control, he thinks. I've done it. I can hold myself together. Even in the absolute worst of scenarios, I will not lose it. I won't make this about me.

Agatha stares out the window. Alex follows her gaze.

They're putting one of the bodies into the back of an ambulance.

It's Luca.

Alex never even spoke to her. This woman who played such a huge role in Agatha's life.

'She was my sister,' Agatha says.

'I know,' Alex says.

'I hated her. But I loved her. I understand now. I thought we'd get a chance at redemption. One day.'

Alex swallows.

Agatha turns to him. He looks away. He can't meet her eye.

'Alex,' she says. 'Tell me. What is it? Just say.'

'I think I know who killed Vicky,' he whispers.

Agatha tenses.

'Who?' she says.

'Agatha, what you just went through—'

'I am the chief of police, Alex. And I want to arrest the person who murdered Vicky. Tell me what you know.'

Alex takes out his phone and pulls up the photograph. Then he begins to speak.

Agatha has showered and changed. She still doesn't feel normal but she feels a little less abnormal.

The kids don't know yet. Agatha rang Becki, in case she heard something on the grapevine. When Agatha finishes this interview, she'll go up there and she'll break it to them that Luca is dead.

Agatha doesn't think they'll be surprised. Luca was never going to be a person who aged. But nobody could have predicted her dying like this. The fact that she gave her life for Agatha's – that means something. It means something very, very important.

And Agatha isn't sure if that makes it harder or easier.

Would she have felt better if Luca had died with Agatha hating her, instead of forgiving her? Agatha doesn't know. She does know that, if Luca had lived, they most likely would have gone through more drama and chaos. Luca didn't have it in her to stay on the straight and narrow. No matter what she said.

Agatha wants to believe it's better this way. For all of them.

She can't think about Patric. Not yet.

For now, Agatha needs to put it all out of her mind and think only of Alex.

And getting justice for Vicky.

Niamh Doyle sits in front of Agatha in the interview room.

Agatha had wondered if Niamh had lied to give Harry an alibi. Alex has told her he'd wondered that too. She'd seen, even in the initial interviews, how much Niamh thought of Harry and how little Harry thought of Niamh.

But, what Alex has discovered . . .

Agatha already knows Niamh is going to break. She's not a criminal mastermind. She's just somebody who got extremely lucky in one sense: she didn't appear to have a motive and she allegedly had an alibi. But in every other sense, she's been unlucky and it's because she's not a natural killer. She acted on instinct; there was no planning.

If there'd been planning, Vicky's body would never have surfaced from the lake.

And if she'd been less stupid afterwards, if she hadn't inserted herself in the investigation by reporting Vicky missing – something she'd obviously thought was a clever way to rule herself out – if she'd stayed away from Vicky's things, if she'd stayed away from Alex . . .

Agatha points at the bracelet in the evidence bag on the table between them.

'You told Alex Evans that Vicky gave you this bracelet for your birthday,' Agatha says. 'This bracelet, that we found on your person this evening.'

'Yes,' Niamh says, nodding.

She hasn't asked for a lawyer yet. She still thinks she can get out of this. Yet another stupid move. Lassi was right. Rich people know how important it is to have a lawyer. When you're innocent, but also when you're guilty.

Especially when you're guilty.

'When was your birthday?' Agatha asks.

'Last June.'

Agatha nods at Jonas, who nods back.

He takes the blown-up photograph from the file.

'This is a photograph provided to us by Bryce Adams,' Agatha says. 'It was taken the last night Vicky was seen alive, in her room. You see what she's wearing on her arm in that photograph?'

Niamh looks at the picture. She flinches.

The bracelet is clear as day on Vicky's arm. It's not conclusive, but Agatha reacted the same way to it as Alex did.

'We have statements from other people in the Lodge who saw Vicky wearing that bracelet over the weeks before she died. Alex was under the impression she didn't like it and never wore it. He was wrong. And if you'd spent more time with Vicky in those last few weeks, you might have realised that she'd taken to wearing it regularly.'

Niamh stares down at the table.

'I have a signed statement from Harry Lavrov saying you spent the night with him, the night Vicky is alleged to have gone missing,' Agatha says. 'But his statement also says that you left early that morning. Harry has confirmed you were due to take tourists on an ice-climbing expedition.'

Niamh says nothing.

'Vicky was scheduled to clear ice-skating tracks that morning so she was also due out early,' Agatha continues. 'Furthermore, Harry has clarified for me that the night you spent together was initiated by you. He claims he was very drunk, that he got inebriated after he saw Vicky take Bryce back to her cabin. He says he wasn't interested in you but you had blatantly been interested in him for quite some time. He also says – I'll just read you his words here . . .'

Agatha takes Harry's statement from the file.

'*Niamh would have known I had feelings for Vicky Evans but she never mentioned it. After I'd taken some alcohol, I asked Niamh if she thought Vicky would ever consider me or if she was too good for me. Niamh seemed hurt by this. I regret this conversation.*'

Agatha looks up at Niamh.

'He goes on to say that after sleeping with you, he also told you he regretted it. You know what I think happened, Niamh?'

Niamh is still silent but Agatha can see she's trembling.

'I think you went looking for Vicky that morning. I think you were still upset at Harry's rejection. Maybe you knew it wasn't rational to be upset with Vicky. You were friends; perhaps you even knew she wasn't interested in Harry. But you were feeling hurt and dejected and you couldn't take it out on him. So you took it out on her. You fought with her. I don't know if you meant to hit her with the ice pick. And I doubt you meant her to go into the lake.'

Niamh says nothing, but now she's crying and Agatha knows her theory is correct.

'The problem is what you did after that,' Agatha says. 'You left her there. You got rid of her belongings. I will prove all this, you do understand? We have the bracelet, we have Harry's statement, and right now police officers are combing your cabin. What else will they find there? Are you absolutely positive they won't find traces of Vicky's blood on anything you were wearing? You know, even the hottest washes don't get rid of all DNA evidence, Niamh. I'm just saying, when I do prove it all, what's going to make it look bad for you is how you covered it up. That amount of scheming – it's going to seriously undermine any chance you have of pleading manslaughter. Unless you cooperate. If you cooperate there's a sliver of hope for you. The prosecutor might just see what I see. A young woman who made a terrible mistake and thought hiding it was the only option. A young woman whose heart was broken – and we all know what that feels like, right?'

Agatha's heart is broken right now. But she has to keep going.

She doesn't know if she can prove what Niamh did.

She needs Niamh to confess.

And she's going to prod her until she does.

She can see Niamh absorbing all this. Her eyes keep travelling down to the photo and the bracelet on Vicky's arm.

She looks up at Agatha.

Ultimately, Niamh is twenty-four years old and Agatha can see that her instinct is right. Niamh is not evil. She's terrified.

'It wasn't my idea,' she says, her voice barely a whisper.

'I'm sorry?' Agatha says, sitting forward.

'It was an accident. We fought, like you said, and I hit her. I was so angry at Vicky. She could have had anybody and I wanted Harry. When I told her what he'd said to me, she said she was sorry. But, it was the way she said it. I knew then – the whole time she'd known he was in love with her and she'd let me chase after him like a bloody eejit. I was so angry at her. We were best friends. That's what I thought. I

379

was never jealous of her; we never fought. I didn't even get angry at her when I found out what she was doing with . . . well, it doesn't matter. She was Vicky. I loved her. But all that time, she *pitied* me. I lashed out. It should have been my hand. I only intended to hit her with my hand. But I had the ice axe. There was so much blood. Even though she was alive – I knew what I'd done. I knew I'd killed her.'

A shocked silence follows the admission.

Agatha waits, then releases the breath she's been holding.

'Go back,' she says. 'What do you mean, you didn't get angry with her when you *knew what she was doing with* – you broke off there. What were you going to say?'

'Nothing.'

Agatha stares at Niamh.

'Did you know Vicky was blackmailing Lassi Niemenen?'

Niamh looks up, shocked.

'I . . .'

'There's no point in not telling me the truth,' Agatha says. 'We already suspect that's what was going on and we're in the process of compiling evidence.'

Niamh blinks.

'He tried to sleep with her and she knocked him back. He was going to fire her. But then, something changed. I didn't know what. I just know she stormed out of here one day and said she was going to have it out with him in his council office, that she was going to humiliate him in front of his fellow councillors. Then, suddenly, she was strutting around all happy. She didn't tell me what he'd said when she confronted him. I knew then that she had something on him, but I didn't know what.'

Agatha nods. It's further proof of what she's already suspected.

'That morning, the morning you killed her,' Agatha says. 'Let's go back there. What happened afterwards? Why did you clean out her room?'

'I wasn't going to. But I was panicking and *he* saw it and he told me what to do. He said if I got rid of her stuff and I reported her missing, then nobody would know and nobody would think it was me.'

'Who did?' Agatha says. 'Who's he?'

'Lassi, obviously,' Niamh says, blankly. As though Agatha should have known they'd never stopped talking about him. 'He saw me, out on the lake. He was out for an early ski and he caught me coming back and said he'd seen the whole thing – me hitting Vicky and her going in the lake. He said Vicky was a bitch and . . . he said he'd help me if I helped him. He . . . he made me have sex with him. To keep my secret, I had to sleep with him.'

Niamh's face looks like she's just tasted curdled milk.

Agatha's stomach churns, too. She knew it. She knew Lassi Niemenen was hiding more. That he'd been involved, somehow.

'I loved Harry,' Niamh whispers. 'And I loved Vicky, too. I didn't mean to kill her. I only took the bracelet because I always loved it on her. It was to remind me we'd been friends. It . . . it smelled of her perfume.'

'What did you do when the ice broke?' Agatha asks. 'Did you try to help her?'

Niamh is staring at the table.

'I didn't even see her go into the water,' she says. 'I was walking away. And then I heard a splash and turned around and she was gone. There was nothing I could do.'

Koppe

1 November 2019

Vicky still thinks Niamh is going to come back and help.

You could have had anybody. That's what Niamh said before she hit Vicky. *You were my friend.*

When Vicky stumbled away, she'd no idea where she was going. Her head hurt so bad, she just kept moving. She barely realised Niamh had hit her. But whatever had been in Niamh's hand, it had done something bad. Something very bad.

And then she heard the ice crack.

She called out to Niamh, but then she was underwater.

As the snow starts to fall and Vicky's hands slip on the ice, she can see Niamh.

Her friend is standing a few metres away, watching Vicky. She looks down at her feet and Vicky knows she's trying to decide if the ice is thick enough to slide across on her belly and offer Vicky her hand. Please try, Vicky thinks. I'd try. I'd help you. I didn't mean it. I should have told you I knew Harry loved me. But I didn't even want him. I did everything to show him I wasn't interested. I only stayed here to get enough money from that asshole Lassi so I could move on. I would never have hurt you. That's not me.

She thinks all this, but she can't say it.

As she watches, Niamh starts to walk away. She pauses only for a moment, to lean down and pick up something from the snow.

Its diamonds glint in the light. Vicky's bracelet. The one Alex bought for her. Alex. Her big brother. She misses Alex. She loves him, always has. She wishes she'd never let him down. That she could have lived up to what he saw in her. She wishes she could tell him that.

Vicky is too shocked, too cold, to call out for more help.

If Niamh leaves her here, she'll die.

Niamh keeps walking. She doesn't look back.

Vicky's head fills with thoughts of Alex and her mum and dad. The people she might never see again.

She still doesn't really think this is it.

She will be saved. Somebody will come. She's too young to die.

When she slides beneath the water, her eyes are still open.

The cold is doing funny things to her head.

It's peaceful down here. She can't feel the pain any more.

The light grows duller and duller.

Vicky is tired. She might sleep. When she wakes, she'll be out on the ice again. She'll be skiing or skating or riding her snowmobile.

She won't be alone.

Even now, she thinks she can see someone coming to help her.

Like her, the woman is floating, hair swirling around her face, arms outstretched, reaching up for the surface.

Vicky holds her hand out to her, before her eyes close.

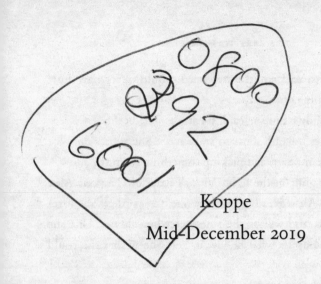

Koppe
Mid-December 2019

Christmas will be upon them soon.

Agatha is sitting in Becki's dining room. The table is heaving with food and drink that Henni is sending out from the kitchen and her friend keeps walking past with even more treats, touching Agatha's shoulder every time, just to reassure her.

Alex is on the floor, his legs crossed, playing Xbox with Olavi and Onni. Emilia is sitting at the table with the American boy, watching TikToks. Agatha's absolutely positive those two are going to kiss before this holiday is out. It will be a little vacation romance, something they'll both treasure. Agatha is glad of it. She's happy Emilia has something to distract her, if only momentarily.

They haven't reacted too badly to the news about Luca. They're still absorbing it but they're also being children. They rarely saw Luca and when they did, it wasn't a positive experience. Agatha is their mother and Luca was somebody who scared them. But she can tell that even they are re-evaluating Luca in the wake of how she died and, with that new perspective, the grief will hit them. Eventually.

They're more devastated right now at Patric's death.

Agatha hasn't told them the truth about Patric. Not yet. That, too, will probably come out.

But she can't say it aloud, not for a while. The betrayal she feels is excruciating.

It hurts more than her parents' deaths.

And yet she still feels protective of Patric. She doesn't want people to know what he did.

Jonas had put his hand on her shoulder when she'd shown him the drawing book.

'Patric tried, with you, to make up for what he'd done,' he'd said. And Agatha knows that's true but she also knows it doesn't make things right, as does Jonas. Patric's selfishness put a lot of what happened in motion. And, in the end, he was too selfish to even face the consequences of that.

She wanted to save him. To make him live so he could redeem himself.

And she misses him. She can't help it.

It's all too complicated, how she feels. Agatha isn't sure if she'll ever come to terms with it all.

Alex laughs at something, then gets up, shaking out his stiff knees, and comes to sit with Agatha.

He takes a bottle of beer and clinks it against hers.

He's flying home tomorrow.

Agatha doesn't know if she'll see him again. She kind of hopes she will but she can't see him wanting to come back here, even though he tells her he understands Lapland madness now.

Her phone buzzes and she picks it up. It's a text from Janic, who's working unasked-for overtime, confirming what she already suspects.

'Mary Rosenberg's ex-fiancé,' Agatha tells Alex. 'Apparently, in the last couple of years, another ex-girlfriend filed a report against him alleging he was controlling in their relationship and that he continued to stalk her afterwards. God love the poor woman he did marry.'

'So, you reckon Mary did plan her escape from him?' Alex asks. 'Once she realised she was pregnant?'

'I hope so,' Agatha says.

'Then maybe she's safe somewhere,' Alex says.

Agatha nods. She prays it's so.

Yesterday, Lassi was arrested. The warrant for his home turned up several of Vicky's belongings from her cabin. The rest he must have dumped in the lake, but they'll never know because he's admitted nothing. Agatha is certain he thought he'd got rid of all Vicky's belongings, if the look of shock on his face was anything to go by. She's also pretty sure his wife had a hand in ensuring those items remained in the house, if the look on hers was to be believed.

There's nothing like the revenge of a woman scorned – and Lassi's wife has endured a lot of scorn.

The warrant that allowed access to his bank accounts also threw up some interesting information.

The accounts showed a large deposit from the Canadian mining company – a down payment on Lassi's land, the rest to follow when he secured the rezoning permits.

And smaller amounts, withdrawn regularly and, Agatha imagines, handed over to Vicky Evans to buy her silence.

Alex knows the full truth about Vicky, now. It saddened him, Agatha could tell, but he didn't judge his sister. Vicky was about to lose her job because she wouldn't fuck the boss. Neither Alex nor Agatha can view her too harshly for deciding to bleed the man dry. He was only getting what he deserved.

Niamh is sitting in a custody cell awaiting her first court appearance. Her family are trying to have her extradited. Agatha isn't convinced she's told the whole truth. There's no doubt Lassi manipulated her but she's also painting herself as too much of a victim for Agatha's liking. She senses that beneath the tears and the outward show of remorse, Niamh really just feels sorry for herself and is still angry at Vicky for getting her into this situation.

The fact she kept the bracelet . . . Agatha is disturbed by it. Was it really in Vicky's cabin? Or did Niamh take it from Vicky's wrist that morning?

They may never know.

'What time is your flight tomorrow?' Agatha asks.

'Midday,' Alex says.

They watch the children.

'Are your parents okay? Now that they know what happened?' Alex shrugs.

'As okay as they can be. Mum is stronger than she thinks. My dad . . . I get the feeling whatever fire he had in him has burned out. It used to drive me nuts, how belligerent he could be. I wish he had it back, now.'

'It will get easier,' Agatha says. 'Not better, but easier.'

'It's just hard to get our heads around,' Alex says, 'the notion that she died in a stupid fight over something that wasn't even her fault. If it had been Lassi or Miika or even the Bryce guy, that would have made sense. But she'd no interest in Harry. Even he knew it.'

Alex turns and looks at Agatha.

'I didn't sleep with Niamh, you know,' he says. 'That morning you came over. She made a move, I said no. We got drunk and the next thing I knew, I woke up and she was still there, wearing one of my T-shirts. When I think back, there were a few things she did that were just a bit . . . unstable. I assigned a lot of it to grief but, now I know.'

Agatha says nothing. She's quietly pleased, but it doesn't matter.

'My dad told me that he loved me,' Alex says, his voice filled with surprise.

'Why wouldn't he?' Agatha says.

'I don't know. It just . . . it was nice. I'd like it to stay that way.'

'Just because you're going back to work in London, that doesn't mean—'

'I'm not,' Alex says.

'Not what?'

'I don't know if I'm going back to my firm. I can't keep doing it. It's killing me. They just can't pay me enough, any more. I'm pretty sure if I leave, I'm going to regret it in about six months but, fuck it, if you can't change your career after something like this, then when can you?'

Agatha smiles.

'Well, good for you,' she says. 'Do you know what you might do?'

'I don't know. Is it too late for me to become a professional ice skater?'

'It's never too late for anything,' Agatha says.

'That's what my pal Charlie said when I told him. But then he asked me to go in on a lap-dancing club with him in London and I'm buggered if I'm going to spend my days greasing up poles and making sure women are wearing the right thongs.'

Agatha smiles, but Alex falls quiet.

Agatha wishes she could say what's on her mind.

Things like, I like you. I enjoy your company. I feel like nobody will ever understand what we've both been through. My life has its complications but I don't think this is all there is for me. Not any more. Maybe it's not too late for me to meet somebody. Even if these are weird circumstances and quite possibly professionally inappropriate.

Instead, she takes another sip of beer. She's swallowing when Alex says:

'When do you guys celebrate Christmas over here?'

Agatha puts the beer down.

'Christmas Eve,' she says. 'That's when *Joulupukki* comes to the houses and gives the children gifts. We sing a few carols and we have a feast before visiting the graves of loved ones. Why? Are you thinking of adopting some of our traditions when you go home? You should buy some gnomes for your parents, you know. They've lots in the airport but you should get them in Koppe. Much cheaper.'

'Well,' he says, without looking at her. 'I sort of thought it might be nice to see Christmas here. It's taking me a few days to sort out Vicky's return. I'm not sure I want to bring her home this side of Christmas.'

'But, your parents?'

Agatha's holding her breath. She's afraid to look at him, to break the spell.

'Mum's still in hospital but they'll understand. They won't want Vicky left alone over here and it's a lot, to have to bury her a day or two before Christmas.'

'I understand,' Agatha says.

'Would you mind me hanging around?' Alex asks.

Agatha has to bite back the smile. It's far too wide for somebody who's trying to be blasé.

'I wouldn't mind at all,' she says. 'There's an ice hotel in Levi. I could bring you down; they do the most exquisite carvings in the ice. There's a banquet hall and then you sleep in the ice rooms on a frozen bed—'

'That sounds like my idea of hell,' Alex says. 'What do you people have against being warm?'

'Okay then. Just another snowmobile ride. Or skating. Or, have you done a cross-country ski yet? They're easier than the slopes.'

Alex looks at her. Agatha can feel herself blushing, but that's okay, because he's blushing too.

They're just two grown adults, blushing.

'I had better cut the labels off that expensive gear my mate Charlie bought me, so,' Alex says. 'My thermals are starting to take on a life of their own, I've got so much use out of them.'

He says this deadpan and it's not until he cracks a smile that Agatha starts to laugh. It's not that Alex has been particularly funny; it's that his smile is beautiful. Warm and friendly and joyful. And she just needs to laugh. And so does he, evidently, because he joins in. It's a release, from everything they've been through, and also, the strange awkwardness that's crept in between them.

Maybe it will come to nothing, all this, Agatha thinks. Maybe he'll go home in the new year, and that will be it.

But, until then, they can enjoy it. She can *let* herself enjoy it.

The kids look up, wondering why the two adults are laughing.

Becki passes again, equally bemused.

Agatha and Alex don't notice everyone is watching. They only see each other.

Acknowledgements

Thank you to the wonderful teams at Quercus and Hachette Ireland, as always, for their dedication and work on this and every book. Thanks to Stef and Nicola, in particular, for your loyalty and passion.

Martin, Isobel, Liam, Sophia and Dominic, you have my gratitude for letting me live with a computer attached to my fingers while I wrote this, including on holidays in that haunted house in Donegal. Martin, I know you can't wait to do an ice swim and I promise, I'll have a beer waiting for you after. Love you.

Thank you to all my early readers, including this time my amazing script editor Sonia, whose crazy brain sent me back into an already finished novel to add more layers; and to my brilliant television writing partner Dave, who, as well as being one of my biggest writing supports, is exceptional at finding plot holes for me to fix and is always right, damn him.

And a huge thank you to you, the reader, for finding my books, buying them and letting me share a little piece of my imagination with you.

This book is dedicated to the memory of one of my best friends, Tommy, who died during the Covid crisis. Tommy, if there are doors wherever you are, I'm sure you're knocking on them. You will be forever missed.

Author's Note

While the descriptions of Finnish Lapland in this book are drawn from very real and very beautiful places, Koppe is a fictional town.

Read on for an exclusive extract from

Jo Spain's gripping new thriller

DON'T
LOOK
BACK

Saint-Thérèse
21 September 2022
Present

All is not lost, the unconquerable will.

The words of the epic poem fill Luke's head as he walks on the soft white sand, grimacing as he reminds himself that, today, paradise is lost.

Normality beckons.

The beach is small by the island's standards. He has already covered one length of the cove and is now on the return leg. This is one of the private bays, set aside for a certain kind of tourist. Pristine, idyllic – perfection for a small fortune.

Through the hazy, late morning sun, he can see his and Rose's villa. There are tall palm trees to either side, a burst of blushed pink bougainvillea against its white wooden slats.

He walks close to the water's edge, letting the foam from the gently encroaching waves splash against his feet. In his left hand, he holds a bottle of island-brand beer by the neck. It's too early for alcohol but he's still on holiday. At least for the next few hours.

It's as relaxed as he's felt in . . . ever.

What he wouldn't give for one more day.

Luke thinks of his reaction when Rose sprung this surprise trip on him. She'd collected him from work in a taxi, with a suitcase, his passport and an uncertain smile on her face. Would he be enthused or annoyed?

He'd been taken aback.

He's up to his eyes in his job – the very reason they hadn't had a honeymoon in the first place. There's something about autumn and pensions. People of a certain age start to ask themselves existential questions about the seasons of their own lives.

Do they have enough put away to retire on?

Luke's company gets extremely busy in September.

But how could he complain? This trip is the first time Rose has taken charge, organised something, and when she told him of her plan, he wanted to encourage that in her, not respond negatively.

In any case, he wanted this holiday. He needed it. The sun and the beaches and the restaurants, the cocktails and lazy mornings and strolls hand in hand.

And she must have needed it too, even more so, because as soon as they hit midweek and the date for returning home loomed, he sensed a change in Rose.

He knows why she's being like this.

Rose moved to London for a new start. It was somewhere she could be anonymous. But he knows she still doesn't feel safe. Though she tries to hide it, and tells him regularly she's fine, he sees the signs.

That look in her eye when she thinks she's seen someone she recognises. The little flinch when a bang sounds or somebody accidentally brushes against her.

Maybe they could stay, Luke muses. Leave England behind.

Even though Saint-Thérèse was colonised by the French initially, the locals mainly speak English now.

Luke could get a job. He imagines the market for pension advisors on luxury Caribbean islands is already well served, but perhaps he could turn his hand to something more fun. Learn how to teach scuba-diving or to paint villas.

Rose is a teacher. Her skills are more transferable.

How would Rose react if he suggested it? She'd be sensible and say it wasn't viable. That it was running away – and she knew what that entailed even if he didn't.

Up ahead, he sees Rose emerge from inside the villa to stand on the deck. She's spent the morning sleeping, trying to recover from the killer headache that came on last night. Their last evening on the island, but Luke had been able to tell by her pale face and bloodshot eyes that Rose hadn't been up for anything but an early night.

He watches her now. The wind pulls at the red sarong-type dress she's wearing, and in the sunlight he can see the silhouette of her body, the curve of her hips, the swell of her chest. Her blonde curls lie long against her back as she tilts her face up to the sun.

He can't get enough of her body. The feel of her, the taste of her, the smell of her. No matter how many times they're together, every time he sees her, he wants her.

Long may it last.

He raises his bottle, takes a final sip of beer and turns away from the water to join his wife.

They're mostly packed. While Rose was in bed, Luke had sorted their suitcase.

They have time before they need to order the taxi to the airport.

He'll see how she feels. Perhaps, now rested, she'll be up for a last swim or a glass of wine on the deck.

As he approaches Rose, she switches her gaze from the horizon to him and he sees her face.

He knew she was off-kilter for the last couple of days, but this is new.

Rose looks desolate.

Luke jogs the few steps up to the villa's deck. He puts down the beer bottle and wraps his arms around her waist, concerned.

'Hey,' he says. 'What's wrong?'

'You have the suitcase ready,' she chokes.

Luke frowns.

'I'll get you whatever you need from it,' he says. 'We don't have to order the taxi for another couple of hours. Do you still have a headache? We could try a walk on the beach?'

Rose rests her head against his chest. Her whole body feels like a sigh.

'I know,' he says, softly. 'I don't want to go back either. But, I've been thinking.'

'Luke—'

'Hear me out. What if we went home for a while and planned another trip? A longer one, I mean. A proper adventure. A few months. Six months, even. We could go to Europe. Or Australia. You could take a sabbatical, couldn't you? We should do it before kids come along. Everybody says it's the one thing you don't regret. Why not?'

Luke stops talking. Rose has started to cry.

Something is very, very wrong.

'I'm sorry,' Rose mumbles through tears. 'I can't go back to London.'

Luke squeezes her tighter.

'Sweetheart,' he says. 'What is it? Tell me.'

'Luke.'

Rose pulls away and looks up at him again. She's stopped crying but the expression on her face . . .

It's not one Luke has seen before.

It's terrifying. She's terrified. As if she's too frightened to speak. And then she finds the words.

'I *can't* go back,' she says.

Luke suddenly feels very cold. His conscious brain is thinking, whatever it is, it's fine; we can go home and sort it out. Nothing could have happened that warrants this sort of fear.

But Rose is trembling and Luke knows whatever she's about to tell him is not going to be good.

'He's dead,' she says.

'Who? Who's dead, sweetheart?'

Rose sucks in a breath that sounds like a sob.

'*He* is. I killed him.'

Luke drops his hands from her waist. He stares at his wife, sure that he's misheard her.

'What?' he says. 'Did you say you killed somebody? Killed who? Rose, what are you talking about?'

'The day we left. Before I collected you from work. I killed somebody.'

Luke shakes his head. Rose may as well be speaking in tongues.

'I don't understand,' he says. 'You haven't *killed* anybody. What are you talking about?'

Rose grabs him now, placing both her hands on his arms;

Luke only realises how badly he's started trembling when she's holding him steady.

'Luke, listen to me. Listen to what I'm saying. I killed him. *Him*. He's in our apartment. I can't go back. Do you understand? There's a dead body in our apartment.'

Sometimes the truth is not all it seems.
Sometimes a confession is just the beginning . . .

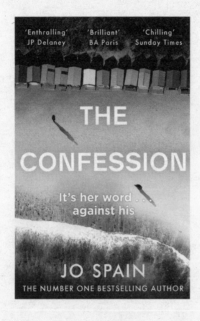

'Brilliantly dark'
Daily Mail

Out now in paperback, eBook and audio

Six neighbours. Six secrets.
Six reasons to want Olive Collins dead.

'Dark, funny, well-plotted, sinister. Superb'
Will Dean

Out now in paperback, eBook and audio

Their perfect life was built on the perfect lie

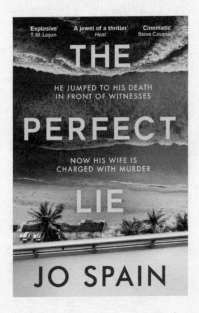

'This will have you absolutely gripped'
Prima

Out now in paperback, eBook and audio

QUERCUS

**One family. One night.
Ten years of lies . . .**

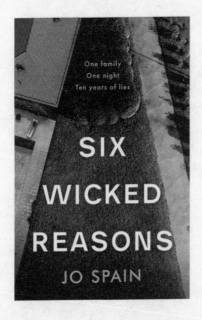

'Clever, pacey, compulsive'
Sunday Mirror

Out now in paperback, eBook and audio